The Man Who Loved Alien Landscapes

Albert Wendland

DOG STAR
BOOKS

Published by Dog Star Books
Bowie, MD

First Edition

Cover Image: Bradley Sharp
Book Design: Jennifer Barnes

Printed in the United States of America

ISBN: 978-1-935738-61-9

Library of Congress Control Number: 2014933191

www.DogStarBooks.org

for Carol

Acknowledgements

I want to thank the following people who have helped in a variety of ways to make this book possible: Michael Arnzen, Stephanie Bond, Lawrence Connolly, Bryan Dietrich, Nalo Hopkinson, Richard Hutchinson, Lee McClain, Renee Nelson, Cherie Shulter, my colleagues at Seton Hill University who expressed interest and shared congratulations, and all the wonderful faculty and students in the Writing Popular Fiction program whose skill, achievements, and warm camaraderie were a constant inspiration to me. A special thanks to Heidi Ruby Miller of Dog Star Books for showing interest in the text. And a very special appreciation to my wife, Carol, for her love, support, and long patience with all the time that goes into writing. My best to each of you.

Foreword

Yeah, Dr. Albert Wendland knows how to write.

I first met him when I was invited on-board as adjunct faculty for Seton Hill University's MFA program in genre fiction a few years ago. A professor at the university, he wasn't quite what I'd expected. No goatee or pipe, no elbow patches on his tweed jacket or golden retriever at his feet, no fire in the fireplace or absent-minded searches for lost pens, none of those usual endearing traits of your stereotypical professor of English. Instead, I found myself shaking the hand of a young, young and ruggedly handsome type with an infectious grin, dynamic manner, and the piercing eyes of a guy interested in everything—a Renaissance man with the insufferably bad manners to be accomplished, smart, and impossibly good looking.

Not, as I say, what I expected at all....

Al Wendland didn't start out to be a college prof. Turns out his first love was science fiction, his first books those by the immortals: Heinlein, Clarke, Anderson, and others. Determined to follow in their hallowed steps, he started by majoring in physics, intending to become an astronomer by day and an SF writer by night. Perhaps someone should have pointed out along the way that it's easier to observe the stars at night... but it didn't matter because then that Renaissance thing kicked in and he added English to his list of majors, which led to him teaching literature at Seton Hill University. A few years later, he co-founded that university's MFA program in genre fiction.

Wait—genre fiction? Romance novels and fantasy and westerns and crime drama and horror and... and—oh, merciful God!—science fiction?

I was stunned when I learned the program existed. There has long been an ivy-walled dichotomy, you see, between genre fiction and what academia is pleased to call serious literature...important literature...even—dare I say it?—legitimate prose. Writers of mere genre fiction...the tradesman's entrance is at the rear.

What the academics forget, however, is that writers have a hell of a time making a living with the 21st Century equivalent of Moby Dick. I'm not knocking the

5

classics by any means, but the people who write genre fiction are first and foremost entertainers, not academics, not "observers of the human condition," and, with a very few exceptions, generally are not professors of English literature. For their part, the public may read Hemingway or Stein or Faulkner for fun, sure...but then for sheer entertainment and the wonder of ideas there's Heinlein and Clarke and Anderson and...yes, Wendland.

You see, Al practices what he teaches. Not only does he know Hemingway and Faulkner and the human condition, but he can also tell a whopping good story. The man is an entertainer; he can write.

And here's the proof. You have before you The Man Who Loved Alien Landscapes, and it is genre fiction...a science fiction novel, in fact, and unabashedly so. Inside are alien worlds and titanic space habitats and a brilliant and paranoid hero, all skillfully blended together with long-vanished galactic secrets.

Science fiction...good science fiction, by a college professor of literature who loves good SF. Enjoy.

I promise that you will be entertained.

William H. Keith
January, 2014

Chapter One: The Finding

"Why are we stopping here?"

Mileen asked the question that no one asks after coming out of light-space, and the captain and co-pilot on the spaceship's bridge had no answer. With the Airafane Clip drive you knew your exit point. You set the coordinates before leaving time-space and you never arrived where you didn't intend. Though the drive was a product of alien engineering that few people understood, it always worked.

Until now.

The commander, Jayne Fowler, scowled at Mileen as she tried to find an answer in her instruments. "I have no idea. We're eighteen light-years from where we should be."

Lonni Elwood, the co-pilot, said, "Something's overridden the input parameters. The coordinates are set for *here* and not for where we were supposed to emerge." She stared at the figures on the screens. "But I punched in the numbers myself! They were locked!"

Jayne sounded suspicious. "If it wasn't you then what did the override?"

Lonni spread her hands and shook her head.

"Maybe *that*?" Mileen pointed to the viewport before them.

Not far off, serene against the stars that buffered the edge of a reflection nebula, drifted a peculiar spaceship.

It seemed too streamlined to be real, too sleek, too silver. It looked like someone's ideal of what a spacecraft *should* be, aerodynamic even here where wings and smoothness were not needed. The slim fuselage sported a classic spindle shape with a sharp pointed nose. Four fins on its lower-half swept out in exotic curves, concave on both top and bottom, with vernier rockets attached to the ends like models of the fuselage itself. At its base opened an archaic rocket-exhaust, making the ship look more like a circus ride or a hood-ornament on an expensive groundcar—a dream of what might have been if space travel had gone the way of fantasy. It glowed with luster in the nebula's light, tangible, real.

Jayne asked, "Any signs of life?"

Lonni's fingers trembled as she flipped switches and read the displays. "Nothing across the spectrum. Nothing in comm. No heat dumps or neutrino emission."

"A derelict," Mileen said, pensively.

No one else spoke.

"Wait, radar's picking up another." Lonni pointed to the right of the ship. "There, against the nebula. You can just see it."

They saw only a vague tangled shape, spottily illuminated by the stars and dust clouds. "Enhance the image," Jayne said. A separate window, brighter and magnifying, opened on the viewscreen.

This object was too difficult to label. Its fat towers, lumpy spikes, dark pits and curved arches formed an oblong jagged labyrinth that defied any single impression. It resembled, all at once, an explosion in freeze-frame, a fist of thorns dipped in mud, the end of a tree ripped from the ground with its roots exposed to hard weather, a complicated and bony clump of much abused driftwood. Unlike the gleaming spaceship, its surface was dull, grayish-brown, and it had a reptilian or skinlike texture, not as if wet but randomly glinting with bluish light from the nearby suns, giving a sense of wrinkles or scabs, stretch-marks, grooves.

The longer the three on the bridge stared at it, the more bizarre it became. To Mileen, it was downright sinister, a handful of chaotic protrusions macabre and threatening—like a fossilized weapon or half-melted fingers.

"Let's get everyone together," Jayne said, breaking into Mileen's thoughts with an enforced rationality. "There's protocol to follow."

Lonni spoke into the intercom for all crew and passengers to meet on the bridge.

That meant six people. Their ship was an Airafane type-2 spacer with a bridge, six cabins, a mess or meeting room, a sizable storage compartment (now loaded with trade cargo) and an aft engine space. It had been rented from Banner Transport back on Annulus and paid for by Montgomery Imports, the company behind this small venture. The ship was returning from a business trip to the planet Ventroni.

The pilot and co-pilot (Jayne and Lonni) and the steward, Omar Mirik, made up the crew. Mirik was an unnecessary addition but in hitching a ride from Ventroni he had negotiated for a berth by offering free service. The three passengers were Mileen, her fiancée Henry Ciat, and his business partner, Rashmi Verlock, who with Henry had been scouting new products and suppliers. Mileen's presence on the ship was, like Omar's, unnecessary, but she was a semi-professional landscape artist and she had wanted to e-paint the famous Spiral Palms on Ventroni. Henry at first had been eager about her coming but lately tension had grown between them.

Mileen walked reluctantly to her cabin. She had left Henry sleeping and she knew if she didn't wake him he well might miss the pilot's message. They argued earlier about arrangements for their impending marriage and afterward he had fallen asleep—his standard "out"—which was why she had wandered up to the bridge. She couldn't relate to the others on board and Jayne she found especially irritating, but Lonni sometimes was easy to talk to.

Mileen opened the door and shook Henry awake. He muttered unhappily, his face, handsome even in sleep, turning away from her.

She shook him again. "We've emerged from light-space where we shouldn't have, and beside us are two strange derelicts."

His head swung back. He opened his eyes. "The drive stopped working?"

"We're eighteen light-years short of Annulus. No one knows why. And the derelicts look strange. One's too perfect and the other's too ugly."

Henry lay still for only a moment, then he jumped from the bed and hurried out, the sudden exit typical of him.

Mileen followed. She too was distracted by the discovery and resolving their earlier argument could wait.

They gathered on the bridge. Omar, the rough but well-built steward, eyed Mileen as if debating whether to flirt with her. Rashmi, Henry's business associate, looked curious enough not to have his normal poker-face. Lonni sat withdrawn and mouselike. Henry fidgeted in his chair with a restrained intensity that made the others look sluggish.

Jayne, back in hard commander mode, told the five of them, "All right, this is the situation. No Airafane Clip drive has ever malfunctioned. And we wouldn't know how to repair it if one did. Since it's impossible to tamper with, and since Lonni assures us the coordinates she entered were correct, it must be a fault of the interface programs."

Lonni looked down, avoided anyone's accusing stare.

"And the figures themselves are set for here, where we ended up. So I'm confident that once we change them for Annulus and start the drive engine, we'll arrive where we should. We're not stranded."

Henry asked, "The duration of the jump didn't change, did it?"

Jayne shook her head. "It never varies."

But, thought Mileen, no jump ever ended where it shouldn't have either.

"What about the derelicts?" Rashmi said. "Could they have an effect?"

"Possibly. But if that changed the transfer settings, it's never happened before." Her tone was emphatic. "I don't think the ships are the cause. How could they be?"

Glances drifted toward Lonni again but she still didn't face them.

"Now, the derelicts…" Jayne indicated the viewport where the two objects appeared. Other magnification portals displayed images in different parts of the E-M spectrum.

Everyone stared blankly at them.

Omar asked Jayne, "No life indicators, you said?"

"Nothing we can see. The ships appear dead, if that second one *is* a ship. Have any of you seen anything like it?"

Mileen, with her alien artwork, and Henry and Rashmi, both employed by a company that specialized in off-world curios, had experience with extraterrestrial findings. But they shook their heads.

"That first ship could be someone's 'yacht,'" Omar said. "If you had enough money you could build a hull like that around a type-2 engine, with a single gravity-plate sitting inside the exhaust tube. The rocket appearance could be just for show. But I don't know about the other thing. It looks like it's pulled inside-out, the 'holes' part of the outer surface. Maybe there's no interior."

Jayne reminded them, "The law requires we explore each object, enough to ascertain there's no life on board. Then there's the chance of—"

"Salvage!" Omar finished, with obvious glee.

But Henry raised his hand. "This mission was financed by Montgomery Imports. All profits would go there. Of course, there'd be bonuses for everyone, and we can't assume—"

Jayne broke in, "We'll follow the rules, but let's first see what we have. We're forgetting there might be victims on board."

Silence again.

"Lonni, you're in charge. Omar and I will float over to the first ship, then report back. If any of you passengers want to come you're welcome, but only *one* of you."

"I'll go," Rashmi said, before Henry could.

Jayne looked relieved, as if Rashmi would have been her first choice. "All right. Let's suit up."

As Rashmi backed into the environment suit, laced up its connections and clamped seals, Henry spoke rapidly and quietly with him, a conversation they stopped when others drew near.

Mileen frowned as she watched the two of them. Though she told herself both Henry and his partner were just doing their job, exploiting all chances for profit, she felt uneasy. When Henry spoke with Rashmi he became secretive, his liveliness freighted with schemes for money. This made her feel abandoned, angry.

As Jayne, Omar, and Rashmi cycled through the airlock and emerged from the accelero-gravity field that the Airafane g-plate provided for the craft, Henry hurried back to his cabin to check any data on the legalities of salvage. Mileen followed.

She watched his focused intensity as he searched the ship's archives through his uplinked cellpad. When Henry didn't have a clear goal he sometimes indulged in emotionalism—doubt, jealousy, a defensive temper. But when he knew what he wanted he was like an engine revving for a race. If Mileen had said now, "Let's settle our earlier argument," he wouldn't know what she was talking about.

It was the perfect time for her to interject, "After we get back to Annulus you should look up Mykol Ranglen."

He stiffened. "We don't need him."

"But he can help you in matters like this."

"He'd help *you*—not me."

"That's not true," Mileen said. "You know that."

He glanced at her starkly, then continued his search. "I don't want to rely on him."

She knew Mykol would help either of them. For all his paranoid isolation he recognized people's needs and responded to them. But Henry saw Ranglen in only one way—as Mileen's ex-lover. Thus her defending him could become a trap.

She also knew what Henry secretly recognized: Ranglen understood her more than Henry ever could.

He turned to her with a look that seemed suddenly fragile. "You know how Rashmi and I want to break from Anne and start our own business. These derelicts could be our chance."

"I thought you said everything would go to her and Montgomery Imports."

"There are all kinds of loop-holes. Everything depends on how we handle this."

"We haven't discovered anything yet."

"But we can profit from just the find itself," he said. "The discovery is ours. It could be big, for *both* of us. You know I want you to be independent with your art… to have your own studio, start a museum."

Mileen knew. Supporting her work was his obsession. She believed him when he said his greatest interest was her.

"I know I've been busy on this trip," he continued, "that it didn't turn out the way we wanted. I shouldn't have let Rashmi set up the schedule. But I'm glad you came. And this might be the way for us to go off on our own—away from Annulus."

Or away from Ranglen, Mileen wondered. Henry once said that Annulus was too much "Ranglen's world."

But she didn't want to dampen his energy. As always, their deeper disputes could wait. "Grab your stuff and let's go."

He smiled, all frank and innocent good looks, clutched his cellpad and pulled her close as they squeezed through the door and raced to the bridge. There the comm-links would bring the reports of the explorers.

Lonni maneuvered the ship closer to the silver craft so that the passage across in free-fall would be brief. Henry sat in Jayne's chair and Mileen stood behind Lonni's. In this control area, raised one step above the deck proper and dark with only instrument glows, they huddled together to hear the transmissions. The spacesuits on board were not equipped with visual feedback so they relied on audio.

They watched the spacewalkers glide across on weak chemical-thruster bursts, slowly if not gracefully. The vast starfields loomed behind them.

Though Jayne and Rashmi stayed mostly quiet during the crossing, Omar maintained an eager commentary. *"From what I can see, the hull of this ship is the smoothest I've encountered. But I can tell places where there are covers and latches. I can see an airlock door. Everything else is hidden. The people who built this wanted very clean lines."*

Jayne said, *"It doesn't look alien."*

"I agree," Omar said. *"I can't see any writing yet but there's nothing surprising about the construction."*

The suited figures, like bulky snowmen, neared the ship. Then they swung around and glided feet-first toward it. Their powered grip-boots planted them onto the hull, held firm.

"All right," Omar said. *"We're beside the airlock. I can see the controls, and they're simple hand-cranks, made to be understood. I'd swear this ship is human even if it's not a standard make."*

Lonni asked, "How's everyone doing?"

"Fine so far," said Jayne.

Omar added, *"I'm getting excited."*

Rashmi stated flatly, *"I'm good."*

From the bridge they could see someone, probably Omar, bend down to turn the recessed crank. As it spun, the door panel moved slowly aside into the hull. The vacuum allowed no sound to be heard, but breathing and the interior rustling of the spacesuits came through the comm.

Omar said, *"The airlock hatch is sliding open. It's dark inside. But our lights show that everything seems standard. Nothing surprising yet."*

"Good," said Lonni. "You're doing well keeping us informed."

Mileen noticed how Lonni demonstrated more command and self-assurance when Jayne was absent.

"I aim to please," Omar said.

Lonni smiled.

"Okay. Wish us luck. We're going in."

One at a time, the spacesuited figures moved awkwardly into the hatch, like animals too misshapen for such an elegant tower, or thieves too clumsy to be dangerous. They disappeared inside.

To Mileen the ship now looked breached, the opening like a bite in its silver skin. The image struck her. The artist in her squirmed for release.

"It's a bit cramped," Omar continued, his communication more scratched now with interference, like a wind of sand blowing against the speaker. *"But still, everything looks standard. The controls indicate there's no atmospheric pressure on the other side of the inner hatch....Hey!"*

The three on the bridge jerked forward.

"Guess what," Omar said, annoyingly playful. *"The words beside the door are in Common English. I told you! The fixtures are a little old-fashioned, maybe forty years or so— hard to tell with everything now so standardized, but certainly terrestrial. Everybody's cool."*

That final line only suggested the real tension they must be feeling. Those on the bridge listened closely, their eyes narrowed, as though that could make them hear better.

"We're...we're inside." Omar's voice became higher-pitched and a little winded. *"Very dark in here. Our lights make the shadows jump around too much. All the power's off, of course. Even the emergency batteries must be drained."*

More shuffles, loud breathing.

"We're inside a hallway," he continued, *"where the airlock led. It's cluttered... functional, not as nice as the outside....Now we're approaching what must be...must be the control room. I—dammit!"*

Again the three on the bridge lurched.

"Sorry about that. I just bumped into a panel. Really, sorry. Scared everyone here too. We..." A long pause. *"Wait...oh, shit...."*

Silence, as if everyone stopped moving. Then soft rustlings and drawn-out gasps. *"There're people here, Lonni. There's...oh, no!"*

13

And now the pause was very long. Nobody on the bridge moved.

Lonni finally said, "Omar?"

No answer.

"Jayne? Rashmi? Someone say something!"

Then Omar spoke, with a tense formality that seemed forced, and very unlike his normal banter. *"There are people here, Lonni. They're sitting in the acceleration couches. Three of them, and they're all human. A man, a woman, and a boy—the last is a child. A fourth couch is empty. They're all dead....And they didn't die naturally. They've got...little puncture wounds in them."*

The three on the bridge said nothing. Mileen tilted back a little, as if threatened by Omar's words.

They could hear much creaking and shuffling through the comm, grunts, indecipherable expressions.

Then a burst from Rashmi: *"Here! Look at this."*

More motion. Followed by silence.

But Lonni didn't wait this time. "Jayne, what's going on?"

No one spoke.

"Answer me!"

Still no sound for a long period.

Then Rashmi said—Rashmi, not Omar—and with a dry calm, *"We're coming back now."*

Lonni looked stunned. "You just got there."

Jayne said, in her firm commander's voice that allowed no questions in response, *"We're returning, Lonni. We'll explain when we get there."*

Abruptly Mileen bent over Lonni and yelled into the comm, "Is there a lifeboat missing?"

No answer.

Lonni and Henry stared at Mileen.

She added, with more emphasis, "You said there were four acceleration couches, so was a lifeboat on board and is it still there?"

Jayne finally responded but with a tint of bitterness, as if her authority and procedure had been questioned. *"All right. I'll check. The rest of you get going."*

The three in the control room stared back at the ship and saw a spacesuited figure emerge from the airlock. They couldn't tell who it was. It leapt from the craft on its maneuvering thrusters and came in faster than it should. Then another figure followed and also leapt across.

Lonni, showing puzzlement, looked at Henry and Mileen. Jayne had allowed the team to break up—they all knew she normally wouldn't permit that.

As the two figures drifted in close, Jayne's voice finally reached them. *"Yes, the ship had a berth for a small lifeboat, an RLV. But it's gone. I'm coming across now."* Mileen knew that RLV meant "rescue light-space vehicle," one capable of faster-than-light speed.

Jayne emerged from the ship and flung herself away from it.

The three on the bridge stayed where they were—the airlock of the small type-2 craft was just a few meters away—while the spacewalkers cycled through pressurization and the gravity field. Lonni fidgeted and resumed her earlier nervousness, apparently ready to give command back to Jayne. Mileen and Henry exchanged glances of thoughtful concern. Henry had a look of appeal in his eyes, like an abandoned child needing reassurance. Mileen gazed back at him dutifully.

But when he turned toward the sounds from the airlock she stared at the second ship instead—the tangled one, the "exploded" one. Its mystery called to her, as if speaking in a strange and ancient voice that touched fears and longings in her. She felt a sudden wave of vertigo.

And she thought, Where are you now, Mykol Ranglen? I need you now.

She grabbed Henry's shoulder. He covered her hand and smiled uneasily into her face, stained-glass colors from the instrument panel glowing on their skin.

The airlock finished its cycling and the three explorers crawled through the hatch with their helmets off. Drained and pale, they plopped down in the extra couches behind the raised control deck. Odd expressions ran across their faces, canceled each other, left a blank.

"We need some cold water," Jayne said. Their hair looked sweaty. Lonni poured it for the three of them.

Henry and Mileen waited.

Jayne spoke first, in a neutral tone that seemed forced, "The three people—human—had been killed. They had puncture wounds in their chests that looked too small for bullets. We didn't want to touch the bodies so we don't know the cause for sure. Maybe little darts."

No one added to that description.

"We'll have to find how long ago this happened. Omar, that's your job."

They had no doctor but the steward was responsible for information-searches through the ship's archive. "Right," he said, with little enthusiasm. He slouched in his chair without looking at the rest of them.

The three in spacesuits drank their water quietly. Jayne sat unmoving for a length of time remarkable for her. Omar seemed light-years away. Rashmi looked either bombed out or tightly restrained—studious, in a vault.

Mileen put these reactions down to the horror of finding long-dead victims in space. But she wasn't sure. The three in their suits were an enigma to her and apparently also to Lonni and Henry. Lonni seemed baffled as she stared at Jayne, not getting back what she expected. And Henry looked at his business partner Rashmi but received no sign or response from him.

"Mileen was right," Jayne finally said, only repeating what they already knew. "A lifeboat was missing."

Mileen replied, "It had to be a child."

They all looked at her. Omar asked why.

"They sound like a family. A father, mother, and an older kid. If attacked, they would've put the youngest in the lifeboat. That's why one couch was empty."

No one disputed her, but no one seemed eager to agree with her either. Jayne said, "Why didn't more of them leave in it?"

"Either they couldn't fit or else their staying was some kind of delaying tactic, against whatever killed them."

The three considered this but said nothing. Again the uncomfortable silence stretched.

Then, in a shrunken and trembling voice, Lonni asked, speaking for the three who had been left behind, "Just what aren't you telling us?"

Henry bent forward to hear better. Mileen didn't move.

Rashmi, Omar, and Jayne looked at each other.

Then—unbelievably—a smile grew on Omar's face, shocking the three on the raised bridge. He almost laughed. "Well, boys and girls..."

He leaned forward, glanced theatrically at each of them. "And all of us here on this stupid little ship in the middle of big goddamned nowhere..." His mouth broke into an oily grin. "Each of us here together today, each of us fine and precious darlings, we are all—*all*—about to become very...very...*very*...RICH!"

Chapter Two: Cops

Two weeks later, Mykol Ranglen's solitary life and mild temper could not prevent his involvement with a murder.

Ranglen was "in transit," as he liked to call it. He had returned to Annulus (the "High Ring Above New Worlds") after exploring a planet from which he'd get an article, several poems, and maybe even the setting for a novel. But in order to work on them, he first moved into an unimpressive hotel room. The feel of displacement in such rooms—of release from time, of living "in hiding" or "drop-out mode"—allowed him to focus on the task at hand. He often said he didn't mind his alienation as long as he could use it to his advantage.

But then late at night two police detectives knocked at his door. A big male, a small female, and their two sour, irritating moods.

"Are you Mykol Ranglen?" the female asked.

"It's pronounced 'Michael.'" She had moved the accent and called him "Mih-KOL." He wondered if the mispronunciation was intentional.

They opened the classic black billfolds and waved their Annulus Security badges. The woman said, "We're police investigators, homicide. Hussein Hathaway, Pia Folinari. May we come in?"

Ranglen shrugged and stepped aside. Since he was a sometime novelist, he liked the name "Pia Folinari." He wondered if he could use it.

The man entered first, cutting across the woman's path and making her glare at him. He had a big face, no chance of a neck, a block of jaw that even his short beard couldn't soften, olive skin, short black hair, and he wore a black shirt with gray sports-jacket—to hide his shoulder holster, of course—and casual dress-shoes that could double as fast trackware in a chase. He bulked a head over Ranglen and his chest made an imposing wall. Mykol felt intimidated already.

The man lumbered past, surveyed the room and looked insulted by its bareness.

The woman, about half her partner's size, faced Ranglen and said, "You're the writer? A consultant for alien-import companies?"

"Yes, I've done that work."

He studied her and felt she looked fragile for a cop. Her pale skin and slight frame, greenish dirty-blond hair hanging in shags just below her ears, made Ranglen feel she should model clothes for elves instead. Yet her gray eyes probed him unashamedly, in a raw deep-six search for guilt that was more threatening than the man's bulk. She didn't care what he thought of her, nor her off-the-rack screw-you outfit of black jeans, tight-breasted fuchsia-and-purple top with flimsy brown leather jacket. And she dared you to ignore the gun-butt in *her* armpit, all exposed for you to see.

While Hathaway walked about the room, Folinari—God, how he loved that name—pulled out her cellpad and kept Ranglen's focus on her and the questions. "Do you know a Henry Ciat?" she said.

He nodded. Mileen's fiancée.

Folinari waited, stared back at him, tapped her cellpad. "*How* do you know him?"

"He's a business associate. As you said, I do consulting on extraterrestrial products. He worked for the same company I did."

"Montgomery Imports?"

He nodded again.

Though Hathaway still "wandered aimlessly," Ranglen assumed he listened with attention.

She checked through several uploaded notes. "When was the last time you saw him?"

"He came to me a week ago, with some questions about geological conditions on an alien planet and how they would affect an industry that was to be built there."

"What world, and what industry, please?" She looked down at the screen of her cellpad and seemed only half interested in the answers. Ranglen felt he was taking a lie-detector test, that the questions were just calibration for already established facts.

"I'm sorry, but I'm sworn to secrecy with all the business companies I work for."

Folinari gave a light sneer. "We can subpoena this information."

"Then you'll have to. Until a court orders me, I can't break those agreements."

Her eyes narrowed. She muttered, "All right. We'll deal with that later. How close were you to this Henry Ciat?"

He repeated, not close at all.

"If that's true, then it'll be easier for me to tell you this. Henry Ciat is dead."

Ranglen had no trouble showing surprise—for he *was* surprised. And regretful, though perhaps not for the reasons that the investigators sought. Ever since the detectives arrived, Ranglen had wondered what Henry might have done. But he hadn't expected him to be dead, or…Wait—these cops were homicide. "How did he die?"

She started to say something but Hathaway stepped in front of her again, as if in a planned switching of roles that she had forgotten. Folinari looked annoyed, but she turned away and walked about the room, stabbing glances into its corners.

Hathaway said, "He was murdered."

Ranglen said nothing. Then, finally, only, "How?"

"I'm not at liberty to share those details. His body was found earlier today at Hatch Banner's landing field."

Ranglen didn't nod or change his expression.

"Mr. Ranglen, we're hoping you might clear up some details about this case."

"I can't see how. Our relationship was mostly professional."

"Yes. But there *is* a peculiar twist."

Ranglen stared back and waited.

"We of course searched the body. And we found one of your business card-links on him. Written on the back of it, in hand-writing that matched Mr. Ciat's other documents, was the phrase, 'Mykol knows'…with an exclamation point." Hathaway paused for effect, his gaze steady on Ranglen.

Folinari stopped wandering and watched him too.

The room became ominously still.

"So, Mr. Ranglen, what we want to know is…why would Mr. Ciat write that?"

Folinari added, with more accusation, "Or, given that note, what exactly it was that Mr. Ciat believed *you* knew?"

Ranglen glanced at Folinari, then back to Hathaway. "I said before, he was just a business acquaintance. He came to me with questions about the geology of an alien planet. That was all. The card could have been in his pocket for weeks—months even."

Both detectives waited. They were good at waiting.

Ranglen summoned the strength to out-wait them.

Hathaway said, "Yes, that card might have been there for a while, though it looked new. But the problem is that…those words could be the last words he wrote before meeting his killer—or even what he wrote *after* he met the killer. In either case, they're very important. For if they were his last words…and they refer to you…then that makes *you* very important."

Ranglen looked appropriately unsettled.

Folinari added, with unprofessional zeal, "Will you talk to us now, Mr. Writer? Mr. *Big* Writer?"

The gloves are off now, Ranglen thought. "Are you trying to implicate me in this? Should I have a lawyer here?"

Hathaway dropped his stare—Folinari did not—and tried to reassure him. "I don't believe that's necessary."

"Then what are you accusing me of?"

"We're accusing you of nothing. We want only information."

"I've told you all I can. The business side I can't talk about. And he was just an acquaintance."

Folinari broke in, "Mr. Ranglen, where were you late this afternoon?"

"Do you mean where was I when the murder might have occurred?"

"I mean, where were you late this afternoon?"

Ranglen lacked an equally good comeback. "I was here, working. But I made several inquiries that I'm sure can be corroborated. I checked for the schedule of some upcoming lectures I have to give at University Hill."

Hathaway said, "Yes, we've already confirmed that. I wish you'd understand that we're not accusing you."

This information jangled his nerves—they already tested his alibi.

Folinari took a different approach, more personal and prodding. "You've been in this hotel for three weeks, ever since you returned from that newly opened planet you visited—that's right, we know about your trip. You have at least two homes we can find, both of them comfortable. Yet you never seem to stay in them long. Why are you living now in a hotel?"

Ranglen's irritation grew. They were infringing on his private life. "Where, and how I live, is my business."

Folinari ambled about. "Well, your cellpad is open here, and I can see you were writing an article."

Dammit, she had scrolled through the file while Hathaway occupied him. "That document is private and you have no permission to read it."

But Ranglen knew that Annulus Security had broad powers.

"You do a lot of writing, don't you?" she said. "Novels, essays, even poetry. Do you have another file for the poems? I've checked your stuff and it's interesting... though I've read better."

Now she was goading him! He told himself she probably hadn't read a poem in her life until now. "I have nothing that would interest you."

"Everything about you interests us, Mr. Ranglen. You haven't had a formal 'job' in years. Is consulting and publishing that lucrative?"

"I don't have expensive tastes."

She laughed. "Yes, this hotel isn't exclusive. But your 'homes' are nice. And you're quite the interstellar traveler. It's hard to tell but you seem to overstep many travel restrictions and customs requirements. That's not easy, you know. Just how many people have given you clearance?"

God, they *had* checked. He wondered at the number of business cases they must have reviewed. Ranglen believed in taking full advantage of his freedoms—of which, granted, he had more than most people. "It's part of my work," he insisted. "Each company provides clearance, and I have a number of academic associations."

"Yes, we've made a list of all your contacts. It's a long list." Her off-hand tone made the words menacing.

But she changed the subject by leafing through a set of painting reproductions lying on his desk. He had been making comparisons between nineteenth-century art from Earth and embellished photographs of the world he had visited—you'd swear the British Romantics had been there. She scowled. "Why are there no people in these pictures?"

"Actually, each one *does* have a person."

She looked at him and awaited explanation.

"The observer," he said. "You could say there's more 'person' than 'picture' in each of them."

She tilted her head and half nodded. Ranglen, if not so damned annoyed, might have been complimented.

Hathaway grunted.

Folinari ignored him. "Look, off the record, what's your angle? I'm just curious. The writing, these pictures—what are you after?"

Ranglen pondered. Maybe she was trying to avoid the cliché of single-minded just-get-the-crook cop, or maybe she worked a variation of good-cop/bad-cop—or dumb-cop/dumber-cop. Whatever it was, he answered truthfully. "It's an interest of mine, how people react when they see an alien landscape. All sorts of preconceptions and assumptions arise, and yet, for once, they're facing something new, different...other."

She stared back at him. "And you write about it?"

"I write about many things. But about that, yes."

Hathaway loudly cleared his throat, as if he were jealous of his partner chit-chatting with the suspect.

She didn't meet his eyes. A creepy tension filled the room.

She said to Ranglen, "You must encounter many alien artifacts, valuable finds."

"That's why so many companies want me as a consultant."

21

"Have you ever been tempted to keep those artifacts and sell them on your own? Collectors would pay."

"No. Never."

"Mmm," she said, as she leafed back through the pages on his desk. Had she really expected him to admit to anything?

Hussein reminded Folinari, "We're not here for artifact theft."

And Ranglen felt a touch of sympathy. Their awkwardness masked the difficulties that all police faced now. With the Airafane Clip drive, "leaving town" was simple: just incorporate a light-space engine into a ground car. Of course, stellar freedom still required time, privilege, and money—technology changed a lot faster than dogged human social structures—but suspected criminals could now travel light-years without being tracked. This made the police, plus many governments used to regulation, less sure of themselves, and thus less polite to their public.

But he felt something more was going on, something particular to just these two.

"Only a few more questions," Folinari said. "How did you meet Henry Ciat?"

"Through Anne Montgomery."

"The head of Montgomery Imports, correct?"

"Yes." They knew that.

"And how did you meet *her*?"

At a college party where she was so drunk she made a spectacular pass at him. "In college," he said.

Folinari maybe knew of the incident for a smirk appeared briefly on her face. "And Hatch Banner at Banner spaceport, where the body was found—you've known him too. For how long?"

"Since my teens." Hatch was quite illegal then and did whatever he wanted, but Ranglen wouldn't go into that.

"Do you realize, Mr. Ranglen, you're at the center of all the people involved in this case?"

"That's coincidence. Most transport to Annulus comes through Hatch's spaceport. And both I and Henry worked for Anne. The connections are predictable."

She disregarded his comments and looked down at her cellpad. "Do you know of the last business venture that Henry Ciat was involved with for Montgomery?"

"No."

"A short business trip to Ventroni?"

"I'm sorry, no."

22

She stared at him now. "But you said you talked to him a week ago. That would have been right after he returned."

"He didn't discuss it."

"You said he asked you questions. So wouldn't they have been connected with the trip?"

"The questions were vague. That's standard in consulting. The people only tell you as much as they need to. And I can't repeat what he said for the legal reasons I mentioned before. But I will say this—all he spoke of did not involve Ventroni."

Her gaze hardened. He felt she was giving him a radiation search.

Hathaway grumbled. "We're almost done here for now, Mr. Ranglen."

Folinari wasn't near done. She shot her X-rays at him too, but she fell short of disagreeing with a partner in public. "All right. But know something, Ranglen. We'll be talking to you again."

"I'll be glad to help you further."

"You've hardly helped at all."

Hathaway added, "We'll expect you to stick around. Don't leave Annulus."

"I understand." He wondered if they noticed he did not agree to follow that order.

Folinari said, with a false cheeriness, "In that time you can finish your article, even write a few poems."

"I'll be sure to do that." He added, taunting, "What kind would you like?"

"Don't all of you poets write *love* poems?" Her tone was venomous.

Ranglen seized the opportunity. "Well, Ms Folinari," and he took his time reciting,

"On love I would write
If only this were true:
There be only one reader,
And that reader only you."

This was so ludicrous that everything went still.

Then she gave a loud mocking laugh, while Hathaway seemed offended. 'That's enough! We need to go now."

Folinari glared at both of them and moved toward the door.

But she stopped, remembered something. "Oh yes, one more question. Almost forgot."

Ranglen knew there was nothing careless or "last minute" about the question at all—which he was meant to realize. The little addition of "almost forgot" proved that.

And it was exactly what Ranglen feared.

"Henry Ciat was engaged to be married to a Mileen Oltrepi. We tried to contact her but we were unable to. You know her, don't you?"

Yes, he knew her.

"In fact, you brought them together, right?"

Where the hell had they gotten that? "She attended my lectures. She wanted to do field work for an interstellar company, more for her art than any business interests, so I introduced her to Henry. They needed the assistance and she could travel with them, see the things she wanted to e-paint."

"And after that, they stayed together, right? Even became engaged."

Ranglen nodded.

Folinari's stare remained knife-like, but Hathaway spoke the main point, "You and Oltrepi, you were once involved with each other, correct?"

You want a motive, don't you? "We were close."

"It *was* a romance, though."

He hesitated only briefly. "Yes."

"You didn't think they should get married, did you?"

"Who have you been talking to?"

"Please just answer the question, Mr. Ranglen."

He said, but in a tone that seemed pried from him, "I wasn't sure it was in their best interests."

"And you told her that?"

"Only because she asked me. It was not my business, nor my agenda if that's what you mean. Otherwise I'd have said nothing."

Folinari chimed in, "You were just the helpful experienced advisor."

He looked at her with what he hoped was a derisive glance. "What do *you* think?" She just laughed.

Hathaway said, "You wouldn't know where she is, would you?"

"I have no idea."

But here he lied.

And they obviously knew it. The room took on a death-like quiet.

After a while, though, Hathaway relented. "If you hear from her, please contact us."

"I haven't talked to her in months. I doubt if she'd call me."

Folinari teased. "Oh, *I* don't know. It's an old scenario. The lover dead, the woman returns to an old flame, a helpful and *advising* old flame—who writes poetry yet!" She gazed briefly but piercingly at Hathaway. "Hell, *I'd* call."

Hathaway, Ranglen thought to himself, looked like the universe right before the Big Bang.

But the cop said only, through clenched teeth, "Let's go."

Pia's fit and smartly-wrapped body glided smoothly toward the door. Hathaway followed it, watching it.

Ranglen concluded that whatever once passed between the two had been either very foul, or very romantic, and then ruthlessly suppressed. He wanted to say, if only in a meager attempt to help, they should just break the rules and run off together. All their restraint didn't give them an edge. It only made their interrogating sloppy.

They maintained a careful distance between them as they walked down the hall.

Ranglen watched without moving.

But immediately after he closed the door, his resistance faded—his whole body shook.

My God, he thought. How much did they know?

Was Mileen dead or just in hiding? She was smart enough to realize she'd be in danger even without Henry murdered.

And Henry...just how the hell did he get himself killed? Why did he have to drag in Mileen? And Ranglen too!

Damn it! Damn it!—Henry really *did* find a Clip.

Not caring if he was watched, by his two star-crossed fascist police or anyone else, Ranglen grabbed his cellpad and hurried from the hotel room.

Chapter Three: Annulus and Henry

Ranglen stepped from the transport shuttle and saw the arc of Annulus in the sky. An old wonder—and an old anger—filled him then. Annulus was *his* world. But it had been taken away.

Shaped like the outer edge of a shallow dish, the ring-shaped surface of the habitat rose 15 degrees from its inner rim, whose diameter was 260 kilometers with the outer rim at 380, producing an area on the upper surface almost that of Wyoming back on Earth. It was composed of a circle of accelero-gravity plates that interlocked and produced attraction fields. An alien blueprint—discovered by Ranglen—said to find a newly created asteroid, to follow instructions and let the resulting nanotechnology transform the moon into this ring of plates with a sculpted surface.

The annular structure then flew off through the developing stellar system—the blueprint stipulated it should be constructed beside a new star still with its accretion disk. The ring gathered material from that disk and made soil, rock, water, even air on its upper surface, forming lakes, mountains, rivers, plains. Plants grew from terrestrial templates embedded in the blueprint (suggesting the aliens once visited Earth). Then humans in spaceships brought more plants, animals, development, towns.

They named the place Annulus. No alien proviso covered the title.

The ring sat 45 degrees above the plane of the new stellar system, at a sufficient distance to avoid titanic radiation or debris. The filmy, globulous, and much too active young star sat in its apron of extended haze, the disk a rollicking and wicked brew of dust, pebbles, rocks, and asteroids that jostled each other in their long build-up to planetary creation. The surging flares from the cranky new sun and jets of plasma from both of its poles had no effect on the tiny habitat, for such blasts were screened by a hyperbolic energy field that emerged from above the ring along its axis.

The wide umbrella-like shield, selectively transparent to the E-M spectrum, swept down beyond the ring's outer edge. It partially opaqued and provided an eight-hour shadowed darkness that slid around the annular ring, a "night" for each terrestrial-length "day," the scheduling determined by those trifling humans again, an intrusion allowed by the independent but generous blueprint.

As he left the shuttle station, Ranglen could see the star's accretion disk behind the arch, like a child's gauzy blanket of lace, dull yet sparkling, a miniature galaxy of sooty glow now in detail because the central proto-sun was darkened. Five hours were left of so-called night, and the light from the ring-arc shone like that of a poetic moon, a flattened bow of spectral color with a narrowed center.

Ranglen knew the red outer rim was exposed desert and the yellow ring beneath it praire grass. The gravity plates allowed water to flow toward the center of the ring, so rivers ran into blue lakes and dark-green forests encircling the inner rim. In those lower sections, mists laced the trees and melted into the central cavity, which lay black except for a flattened bowl in the center, slightly below the ring proper and connected to it by transport tubes. The soft rim of watery fog, where the gravity faded and wisps floated in gossamer sheets, resembled a fringe of blue aurora.

From Ranglen's viewpoint, the name "Annulus" was incorrect. It should have been "Rainbow" or "The Bridge." But if you looked from a ship that flew above the ring, the habitat resembled an opal circle of concentric colors with a round gray spot in the center. And if you were an astronomical historian, you'd be reminded of the old color-saturated photographs of the Ring Nebula taken from Earth, before they found the cloud's shape was really a doughnut surrounding a football.

And the whole structure wouldn't exist if it weren't for Ranglen.

He imagined himself in moments of grandeur saying to all humans everywhere—as he tossed over the keys and reminded them to lock up when they were done—"Here! It's yours! Do with it what you will!" And he'd add, to universal applause and laughter, "It's one small gift from a man, but one giant leap for humanity!"

He crossed a field of moon-colored flowers. He reached the shore of gliding rocks where the gravity thinned and the water bannered out in membrane flags. Rocks shifted and turned there, bergs of sea stacks like couples in a waltz. But Ranglen was too worried to admire the scenery. He followed a path along the "shore," walked around a cliff till protected from view. He continued between rock walls till he found a slab as wide as a mattress.

He sat on the rock and faced away from the central opening. Though he couldn't see it, a satellite hovered in the black sky above, between the outer edge of the ring and the rim of the sun's accretion disk.

All wireless messages on Annulus, through both surface and satellite relays, were monitored by Security. But the Federals of Earth owned this particular satellite even though it hovered in Annulus space. With the right technology—it required complicated protocols—the satellite could be used to receive and send, in a narrow beam, a signal to other spots on or off the ring. Though the message wasn't secure, only the Federal government of Earth and *not* Annulus Security could tap it. Ranglen couldn't avoid the signal being accessed by Earth, but he had to prevent anyone learning the signal's destination. Through intricate programs on his cellpad, the beam would be routed through false leads that should make identifying the goal almost impossible.

Almost.

He also knew the signal's source could be traced, the guarded spot where he now sat. The Bureau of Intelligence from Homeworld, the colony planet that had financed the building of Annulus, knew of it already, plus the Federal Investigators from Earth, but the Bureau didn't know that *Earth* knew, and Annulus Security didn't know of it at all. Ranglen's permission to use this spot, encircled by a security blanket to thwart surveillance, was one of the perks he got in return for giving up any claim to Annulus. (He had wanted the habitat to become a kind of national park, but politics, money, "development," and hierarchy had the last say.)

Ranglen was certain that Annulus Security—represented by that moose Hussein and his miniature Mata Hari—as yet knew nothing. This still was just a simple murder to them. If they were aware what *really* was going on, the whole police department would come and arrest him—confine him, interrogate him, maybe torture and kill him. And then the inevitable leaks would bring in the Federal Investigators from Earth, the Bureau of Intelligence from Homeworld, the multisystem corporations, the adventurers, the insane.

With Mileen caught in the middle of them.

Tension shook his fingertips as he opened his cellpad, locked in the target and tapped keys to enter the codes. The link would take several minutes to complete and then to unscramble at the destination.

While the programs ran, Ranglen's thoughts went back one week to when Henry had come and talked with him.

Poor Henry, murdered and gone.

He had called and asked for a private conferral at Ranglen's hotel, all very mysterious. Ranglen half-expected Henry to gloat over winning Mileen. But that was unfair. Henry loved her and their relationship was likely more solid than any Ranglen could have supplied her.

Ranglen also knew that no one ever possessed Mileen.

The man came to the hotel room looking tense and preoccupied. His eyes wandered as if he felt guilt and couldn't face Ranglen directly. He was too eager to get to the point, too excited to stand still. Such energy had encouraged Ranglen to recommend him to Mileen (as a useful colleague, not as a lover). He could be the worldly, if simple, balance to her intense perceptual art. But Henry's confidence seemed pushed to a limit. He didn't smile, didn't laugh at himself as much as before. And he said, with barely disguised desperation, "Mileen and I need your help."

Ranglen noted how mentioning Mileen enforced his attention.

"This might set her up forever, free her for her art. Studios, publicity, travel, everything."

"What do you want from me, Henry?"

He looked pained, as if Ranglen's bluntness were an affront. "Just information. You're a business consultant, right?"

Ranglen nodded. But he didn't ask—if this were to help Mileen—why she wasn't here instead of him.

"You have to keep this private," Henry insisted.

Ranglen agreed.

Henry still hesitated, not wanting to share his secret—which Mykol felt he knew already.

"If you discovered that a Clip was located on a planet, how would you find it?"

Ranglen guessed right. Henry sought the biggest and most dangerous treasure in the galaxy.

He added, "You realize now how much I'm trusting you."

Ranglen nodded. "But I have to be honest, Henry. A Clip isn't found. It finds you."

Henry's hand jerked out as if to disagree, then fell back. He made a wry face. "I think I've already learned that. But you don't just sit around and wait for it to appear. What's the trick?"

Ranglen didn't ask how Henry had discovered a planet where a Clip might exist. He knew better. Clips were too precious to discuss cavalierly.

"Clip" stood for "Carrier-Locked Integrated Program," a small but dense storage-information device written into a substance no thicker than paper and no wider than a fly. They had been planted on worlds with plate tectonics, left there by an ancient interstellar race called the Airafane, of which a few artifacts still existed. The devices were hidden in subduction zones, where continents slid under each other, inside octahedral crystals that resembled fluorite. These crystals were near indestructible because of an assumed stasis field that stopped functioning when the crystal reached the surface again, after being transported through the mantle by subterranean currents. They came up through the crust via mid-ocean ridges where continents spread apart.

Such Clips were incredibly valuable, since all those found (four known to date) contained blueprints for advanced technology that made their discoverers super-wealthy. The first Clip had been found on Earth in a "black smoker," a volcanic vent in the middle of the Atlantic amid sea-floor spreading. It contained the secret of light-space and FTL transportation, which of course changed the history of humanity, taking it out to the universe.

A second Clip found on a different planet provided accelero-gravity, and thus a means of sublight propulsion and artificial "gravity," anti- or otherwise.

A third Clip contained instructions on how to build Annulus. That Clip Ranglen had found—though not everyone knew this.

The fourth Clip contained military secrets, apparently, that the government of Earth had never divulged.

This last discovery indicated how the Clips were not just gifts from the past. They were part of a survival/revenge scheme planned millennia ago. Based on artifacts found on various worlds and records contained in at least two of the Clips (the fourth, as said, was never made public) indicated that the reason for the Airafane burying this information was to help any future race, like Earth's, protect itself and ward off another group of ancient aliens called the Moyocks, who once enslaved and then tried to exterminate the Airafane. Artifacts of this race had also been found but as far as anyone knew, the Moyocks had died off as much as the Airafane.

The Airafane apparently had wanted to keep the Clips buried for such long times to ensure the Moyocks never found them.

Such knowledge brought an ominous tone to Earth's new presence in space. The galaxy was haunted by events from its past, and not in ways strictly ghostlike. Humans now entered an ancient battleground once bloodied by genocide.

"Henry," Ranglen said, "if you know of a planet where a Clip exists, you need to inform the authorities. Otherwise, you're in terrible danger. You could be killed."

Henry shook his head. "You're the only one on the outside who knows. And I trust you. If we can move fast enough, we can get the Clip, claim finders' rights and *then* negotiate to pass it on. That way we'll get most of the windfall. We'll give you a cut."

"I don't want a cut. How many people know about this? And is one of them Mileen?"

"Only a small number."

"Then that's too many. Report it! Now! For Mileen's sake if not for yours."

"It's too big of a chance. I know you were able to find one, Mykol. Mileen told me. How did you do it?"

He hadn't told Mileen the whole story but he did admit to her he had discovered the third Clip and been there at the start of Annulus, that he played a large part in creating it. It was a brag—he couldn't help it. And Ranglen agreed that such a find *was* too big, too beyond any realm of human experience. Each discovery rebuilt civilization overnight, caused a century of change in a year. You can't walk away from that.

But he said, "You came here asking for my advice. Here it is. Get to the governments as fast as you can. Go to all of them—Annulus, Homeworld, the Confederation, Earth. Be generous and humble. They won't trust you at first, but then they'll love you."

Henry, predictably, grew suspicious. "You're just saying that because you want Mileen protected."

"Of *course* I want her protected, but it's also the best thing to do."

"Think of what we'll get out of it, Mykol—what *she'll* get out of it."

Ranglen then realized that Henry was doing this all for *her*. A Clip would make the greatest wedding present in history. For once Henry wasn't thinking about business—he was being romantic.

"Henry, listen to me. Sure the first Clip made its discoverers rich. But the second Clip was fought over and people died. More would have been killed if the government hadn't stepped in and made it a law that any new-found Clip should go directly to the ruling officials—at that time the Confederation. But the FTL from the first Clip was so cheap it made everyone independent. Companies, adventurers, they all think that no one can catch them, that they can get away with whatever they want."

"Just the hint of finding a Clip brings in everyone. With the third one more people were killed—believe me, I saw it. And nobody knows what happened with the fourth. If you find anything, you'll have to contend with Annulus Security, which would bring in Homeworld's Bureau of Intelligence, and finally Earth's Federal Investigators, and they can be worse than gangsters. No one knows how many might be killed. Is that what you want? Dragging Milene into all that?"

Henry waved his arm in dismissal. "Just tell me how it's done, Mykol! What's the secret?"

Ranglen groaned. "Don't search for the Clip yourself. Instead, take what you know and go to the representative of the Bureau of Intelligence here on Annulus. Skip local Security. Tell them you have Clip information but you refuse to divulge it until an interstellar committee is formed with representatives from the Confederacy and the Federal Investigators from Earth. Say that you sent the same information to all the representatives—and make sure you do it before the negotiations. They won't question this set-up, for too many people will know of the Clip and a conspiracy will be avoided.

"Once they convene, with everyone present, tell them what you know. It'll be the only time you have any control, so you'll need to use it wisely. Then…get out. They'll begin to suspect—quickly—that you're holding something back. In time they'll arrest you and not let you leave. So don't wait. Go to another planet and stay there for a year. Take Mileen with you and keep close to each other. You'll eventually get a nice reward—not all at once, but you and she will be set for the rest of your lives."

"But we'll get more if we negotiate with the Clip in hand, or keep it and form our own company."

"You won't get as much *death!* Governments will kill you as easily as corporations."

"But if we keep the information—"

"You don't understand! All they need is the planet's location. Only the *Clips* are important. The people who find them are expendable."

"Mykol, please, just tell me how to find it. Let us make our own decisions."

Ranglen spread his hands in defeat. Henry exhibited the classic stubbornness of the shallow-minded who, once reaching an original idea, cling to it to prove, more to themselves, just how insightful they can be. But Henry wasn't shallow. He was a shrewd entrepreneur sadly clouded by dreams of treasure—or dreams of love.

"There's no secret, Henry, no magic formula. All of the finds were accidents. It's as if the Clip makes the decision to become noticeable, that it's lost in some quantum probability-wave that collapses when the right finder appears. The clue for the explorer might be magnetic resonance, as with the first one, or mass anomalies, like the second, or a sudden intuition on the part of the finder, the third—*me*. That's another reason why you shouldn't pursue this. You could search that world for a hundred years but then the next person could find it in a second. You can't plan this. You could spend your life wandering in pursuit of it. Do you want that for Mileen?"

Henry curled his fingers into claws. "Mykol, I *have* to do this! Can't you understand?"

Ranglen tried to remain calm. Henry's anger indicated the man wouldn't budge. "Look, all I can say is what you already know. Clips are found in areas where continents stretch apart, in mid-ocean ridges or rift valleys. I can recommend surveillance satellites with programs that can review the data. Follow the lines of continental separation. Then wait for a clue, an anomaly, anything suspicious. And investigate it.

Maybe you'll be lucky. Or maybe you'll spend the rest of your life chasing a dream. I don't have your answers."

Henry seemed too focused on his destiny to accuse Ranglen of mocking him. "That's all you can tell me?"

"Go with your instincts. What more can I say? I believe the Clips are more responsible for being found than we are in finding them. If you feel any attraction to a part of the landscape, then go there. That's how I found mine. I saw a slight rise with a stone cap that looked protective, and that's where I found it, the crystal sticking out in plain view."

Henry said nothing, appeared wistful. Ranglen believed he fantasized on how he someday would find the Clip, pulling the imitation fluorite crystal from a rock—and then handing it to Mileen. Ranglen hoped she'd discard it with distaste.

The conversation seemed at an end.

To get his attention, Ranglen asked, "How are you and Mileen getting along?"

Henry looked surly. "Fine, thank you. I know you thought we wouldn't make it."

"I had my doubts, but I did encourage her to marry you."

"Yeah, I heard. Opposites make good marriages, you said—the businessman and the artist, logic and compassion. She told me that."

Ranglen nodded. But he also wondered how much "logic" Henry had left.

"I hated you for analyzing us," Henry said. "But you turned out to be right. It works between us. I don't understand her, but…"

"You just 'love' her."

Henry looked embarrassed. Ranglen knew he normally would never talk of these matters. "What we do makes little sense to each other. My work, her art. But…we respect it. It's not easy, but…"

"It sounds fine."

"We just got back from a trip together—a business trip, but I took her along. It was supposed to be a special time for us. My partner set up so many meetings I hardly saw her." He paused, then looked at Ranglen with fervent eyes. "Can you see now why I *have* to do this?"

Ranglen didn't agree but he kept quiet. He took a chance and asked, "Did you find the Clip's location during that trip?"

Henry avoided Ranglen's stare. The lack of an answer seemed confirmation. And, moving on, Henry said quickly, "Why don't you come with us?"

"What? To find the Clip?"

"You know what to do more than we do. You can help us."

Ranglen was touched. This showed that Henry still had common sense, in terms of both finding Clips and his past jealousy over Ranglen and Mileen. But Ranglen said, "I can't."

Henry stared at him.

"It's *your* adventure, Henry. You'd hate me if I came. And I wouldn't let you keep the Clip anyway. I'd turn it over. If you were anyone else I'd send in the information right now, without your permission. It's only because of you I'm not doing that."

"You mean only because of *Mileen*."

Ranglen sighed. "Look, I feel you deserve your chance. I won't stand in your way. I won't tell anyone why you were here. If asked, I'll say you just wanted to know about some industry on a new planet. I wish both of you the best."

Henry grew quiet again, either brooding or contemplating. "All right, but know that asking you to join us was *my* idea, not Mileen's. She only thinks I came here for information."

Again Ranglen appreciated being told.

"Well, I'll go then." Henry wasn't happy but he seemed resolved to being on his own. He said no more and left the room.

That was a week ago.

Now Henry was murdered. And Mileen missing.

Ranglen stared out to the scraps of blue mist. He felt guilt. Should he have gone with Henry? But it would have been a disaster. He'd never allow them to keep the Clip. Should he have emphasized the dangers more? But you couldn't convince people of them. They had to be experienced.

Or did Ranglen's *lies* kill Henry?

He tapped keys on his cellpad. His call would have negotiated channels by now and should be as secure as he could make it.

It was a call to his "safehouse." Years ago he had said to Mileen, before she left with Henry, "If you're in trouble, you can go there." He had been quite generous in telling her its location and entrance protocols. When she left with Henry, part of him regretted giving them to her, but he felt she would never compromise this one way in which she could hurt him.

He worked his cellpad, waited for the lock-in. It finally came.

He sent off a simple identifier code to which she could respond with the code he had given her. Several minutes would elapse between each written message. He could only send text—the tight long-distance prevented audio.

He waited.

A beep finally came. His code had returned.

Unacknowledged, it said.

So, she wasn't there. Even if she were occupied she would have entered an automatic return message.

He sent an inquiry for diagnostics on his security system. Again he waited.

The data returned and indicated his locks had not been disturbed. No unauthorized entrances had been made, no codes broken.

He checked the status for other systems—power, life-support, area surveillance.

All functioned well, all were undisturbed.

Ranglen shut down communication except for an automatic alarm that would sound if his signal was acknowledged.

He considered whether he should go to the police, tell them of all Henry had said, put the case in the big hands of Hussein Hathaway and the sharp of mind Pia Folinari. They'd be good soldiers to have on his side—for all their affectation and bluster he respected them.

But he knew that the slightest hint of Clips would remove them from the case. No one would care about a murder then. All the authorities would want Mileen only for the information she held. She might be imprisoned, even drugged or tortured. And if other ears were listening—as they apparently were, given Henry's fate—she could wind up dead.

He *should* report it. It was the law, the law as read to him when he found the Clip. All the freedoms he owned now were a result of his obeying what was said then. And given the forces of Annulus, Homeworld, Earth, and the Confederacy, willful individualism could get dangerous.

But he made his choice a week ago when Henry came to him and he kept quiet, reported nothing, gave Henry—and Mileen—their chance.

No, he'd have to do this alone. If he went to the government not knowing the world where the Clip existed, he'd only start a landslide of pursuit. And Mileen would be caught in the middle of it.

But if he could locate the Clip, have it in hand and *then* give it over—

And if he could just find Mileen, know she were safe....

Long ago, after seeing her staring intensely at a landscape and telling him in detail how she would e-paint it, not to copy it but to put into it the powerful yearning they felt for each other then, he had written to her,

When we touch, words fail,
We consume in desire.
Was it you, or I then,
Who was born in fire?

And now he decided—

I will find you, Mileen, if only for you to feel such longing again. I don't care if once more we drown in each other, lose ourselves *in* ourselves as we so often did in the past. Henry abandoned you. But I will not.

He stood up and hurried back to the station.

He had much to do.

Chapter Four: Anne

After sleeping three hours and gobbling a breakfast at a nearby restaurant, Ranglen arrived at Anne Montgomery's office before it opened. She herself let him in.

Her office overlooked clouds and a valley. The building caught the vapors that drifted from the inner to outer rim of Annulus. The room's wall could be left transparent or opened for the mists to trail into the room. Ranglen claimed she wanted to *be* a cloud, equally serene, freed of all things two-dimensional, flat. "You should have been a bird," he once told her.

"I should have been an angel," she replied.

He didn't know how to read that comment.

Anne's exotic black hair, like a cloud, sat full and coiled on her shoulders. She wore a conservative black business suit that showed off her "darker" attributes, the raven eyes, the near-sepia skin and obsidian jewelry. Her look was professional and sultry all at once, though it didn't seem a come-on, as if saying, If you find me attractive that's your problem, I have a profitable company to run, maybe later, but not now.

Ranglen *had* "seen her later," but his relationship with her was never ideal. They were intimate without being close. Ranglen found her too in control of her business while too at sea with her emotions. They always separated, with both feeling lucky nothing more had occurred.

She sat on a chair facing Ranglen, crossing her legs and showing off her functional but elegant black boots, while behind her, on the walls, hung tasteful racks of alien figurines, carvings, fossils, pottery, gemstones, bottles, fabrics, crystals, weapons, and other things he couldn't identify. The assortment had grown since the last time he was here. "You've become a collector?"

"They're fakes, Mykol. Are you implying something?"

He couldn't read that comment either, so he went to work. "You heard about Henry?"

"Hatch told me. I was warned to expect the police today."

"That's why I came early. Don't tell them I talked to you."

"Are they suspicious of you?"

"I had an alibi but they don't trust me. They think I know where Mileen is."

"And obviously you don't, because you'd be with *her* then and not with me."

He said, drily, "I'm worried about her, Anne. Did they ask where she was?"

"Yes, but I don't know. I haven't seen her in months, since after she and Henry got serious. You think she's in danger?"

"I believe we'd know by now if something happened to her. Henry wasn't hidden, so why hide her?"

Anne looked thoughtful but said nothing.

Ranglen persisted. "I need to know what *you* know, Anne. Henry worked for you. What was he doing when all this happened?"

"Henry doesn't work for me anymore. He quit, with his partner, Rashmi Verlock, after they returned from a trip to Ventroni. We opened a new branch there. They met with clients, reviewed the items offered for sale and brought back samples."

"How soon after their return did they quit?"

"A week. I wasn't surprised. They wanted to start an import business on their own. I felt they'd be good at it. They saved capital and even asked me for investment suggestions."

"Their quitting didn't bother you?"

"Of *course* it bothered me. They were good workers. Henry had charm. Everyone wanted to deal with him. But I knew they wouldn't be with me forever."

Ranglen glanced out the window to the bridge-arc of Annulus. It ran across the sky in full-colored splendor, a handle of flowstone for Anne's personal basket of clouds. He felt she surrounded herself with grandeur to compensate for her suspicious mind—or maybe to imitate Mileen's aesthetics. "Why did they quit now?"

"They said they found something on Ventroni they could market, that it wouldn't conflict with my investments—they were emphatic about that."

"They didn't tell you what it was?"

"No. I wouldn't have told them in a similar situation."

"But if it was something your company wasn't a part of, why couldn't they describe it to you? Wouldn't that convince you it wasn't related?" Ranglen assumed they'd say nothing to Anne but he wanted to learn how she reacted to them.

She laughed. "You're naïve—you always were about business. It's an unwritten rule, 'No questions.' It's how we maintain respect for each other. You believe what people tell you and let them keep to themselves."

"But surely you wondered."

"The point is not to think anything, to honor them."

"Come on, Anne!"

"Come on, yourself! It doesn't work that way. I congratulated them, and it wasn't my business to figure them out. That attitude protects us."

First roadblock of the day, Ranglen thought. And it didn't surprise him it happened with Anne. He took a different approach. "Which day did they tell you they were quitting?"

She checked her cellpad. The day after Henry had come to Ranglen's hotel.

He asked about the companies they visited on Ventroni, whether he could have a list of them, their products, the kinds of things Henry would have returned with.

She scowled. "Those are trade secrets too, but I guess you won't give them away."

Ranglen was often her consultant and he never divulged anything she held in confidence.

She sent him the list through her cellpad. "There was a lot of small stuff too, samples, unimportant. These are the ones who made agreements."

Ranglen scanned the names of the companies. "Eye Serv, a long-range surveillance group. InQuestonics, writes programs for communication machines. Arms-Watch, sells hand-guns. 'Put a pistol in your pocket.' (God, that's terrible!) C.C. Deech, makes small machines for construction companies." He looked up at Anne, showed his disappointment. "But all this is tech. Weren't there any specialty items, alien stuff? Isn't that your niche?" He pointed at the shelves behind her.

She said stiffly, "Such items might be illegal."

"I'm serious, Anne."

"I am too. You know I import only in bulk. All of it is genuine but none of it's museum material. Specialty shops want it, but it's not unique enough to be contraband." She added, "No one's ever questioned me about this before."

Ranglen groaned. "I know you're legal, Anne. But what about the people who work for you? Like Henry?"

"It might occur. It's easy enough. But not in *my* cargoes. The stuff is dumped on the outer rim if it's done at all. I do my importing through Hatch and his place is tight. If Henry did anything, I never caught him. And I doubt if he did because it wasn't easy for him to lie—one of the reasons why people liked working with him."

"What about his partner, this Rashmi Verlock?"

"He was different. No one put anything past him. But again, it's not smart. It could ruin their chance to start a company. I don't think he would."

Ranglen disagreed but kept to himself. He saw things from the perspective of Clips. "Tell me more about him."

"He wasn't like Henry. You could read Henry's moods but not Rashmi's—his face never changed. I don't know whether he was calculating or just not talkative. It's not a good quality in business. People came away feeling he held something back."

"He was the planner of the two?"

"I assumed. Henry had style and Rashmi had brains. I'd trust my investments with Rashmi, just not all of them."

Ranglen waited a moment before asking, "Did you wonder if they held some items back from you on this last trip, something undeclared?"

She smiled wryly. "Yes, I wondered. But if they did, they got them past me. I checked the inventory, not to find what they brought but to make sure they didn't cheat me. Nothing was missing."

Ranglen tapped his fingers on his knee. "I assume they could have spoken with contacts on Ventroni who weren't on the schedule."

"Of course. They were representatives from a successful company visiting start-up groups. I'm certain they heard a hundred schemes. And…well…there's something you should know about Ventroni."

Clouds moved up against the window and drained the light, made the mood sinister. Ranglen—suspicious—felt it too much a coincidence.

She said, "The government is corrupt on Ventroni. Illegal exports could easily change hands. That's why it's impossible to track down who they met. I didn't want to get involved with the place, but it had profits."

He waited a moment. "So, what are you saying?"

"I'm saying that if they *did* do something illegal, the chances are better on Ventroni than elsewhere. Some of the company-heads there are gangsters—at least *I* think so. Nothing's certain, and murdering someone would be extreme for them, especially here on Annulus."

It wouldn't help business, Ranglen thought. But he'd never say that to Anne. "Did you refer to any of this when they came to you and quit?"

"I hinted at it. 'You guys didn't make any deals on Ventroni that could get you into trouble?' I wasn't trying to discover anything, just showing my concern. But they acted normal. No changing-of-the-subject. I think they even thought I was being 'motherly,' which annoyed the hell out of me. I just wanted to make sure they weren't being jerks. But they were confident enough that I trusted them. In fact, I remember feeling their scheme might be more profitable than what I assumed."

Ranglen wondered. He had not received the same impression of assurance from Henry.

Anne continued. "There's something else. I don't know if it's related or not. But I had a security breach recently. In fact, two of them."

Ranglen was surprised. Anne's organization was known to be tight.

"About a week before Henry and Rashmi left for Ventroni, our security programs signaled a break-in to information-storage. It was quick, but successful enough to grab something. The tracks were covered and we still can't decide which information was copied, but we think it had to do with inventory.

"The second breach occurred after Henry and Rashmi left for Ventroni, while they would have been there. This one was more penetrating, and we're sure it had to do with personnel. Records of everyone in the company were tapped. Only a little could have been gleaned from any one file, and we don't know how many files were probed. But still, it made me nervous. I changed all our shields after that."

Ranglen felt more than nervous. "Am I in those files?"

"I *knew* you'd ask that. Yes, but if it's any consolation, so was I. And I had more in there than you did—like my own personal journals."

It wasn't consoling. "Nothing could be tracked? Where the breach came from?"

"Not where it originated, but we know the information left in a focused beam and not through wires. It rode our own broadcasts and was shot off into space. We ran programs to get the direction but we had no luck. I can trace the progress if you like, send you the reports."

"Yes, please." This knowledge bothered him.

As she worked her cellpad she said casually, "Are you hiding something, Mykol?"

"Excuse me?"

She looked at him sardonically. "You're too obvious. You're holding something back."

"Anne, please."

"You're also predictable."

"I—" He went quiet, refused to say anything.

She frowned. "I see nothing has changed between us." She examined her screen again and returned to the subject. "The information's scattered in various files. I'll get one of my techs to do a quick summary, then send it to you scrambled, by wire."

Ranglen nodded, appreciating her security consciousness.

Outside, the clouds moved away and the sky opened. The ragged edge of a small billow drifted lazily into the room. Anne must have opened the window from her cellpad but he had noticed no difference in the air currents or temperature. He found this disturbing.

He said, "If Ventroni was so corrupt, why did you want to go there, and why send Henry and not someone else?"

"The potential gains were bigger than the risks. All the companies I dealt with were legit. And don't feel I pampered Henry. He was like an overgrown kid at times, but he and Rashmi made a good team. The best I had. Besides, I let Mileen go with them. I knew she'd keep him happy."

Ranglen sharpened his attention. "She was part of the trip?"

"Henry asked if she could go—she wanted to do her art there—and I said fine. He was eager to show off, and it was at his expense."

Ranglen was shocked. "You let him pay her way?"

"Hey, I run a business."

"But you were close to Mileen."

"Only in college. We didn't maintain anything afterward. And then...of course... there was you."

He and Anne had stopped seeing each other the same time he became involved with Mileen.

He said, with an emphasis he wanted to be serious, "Be careful what you say to the police about her. They'll jump at any feelings you show."

"I have nothing against her. She just struck me as too 'successful.'"

"She never said bad things about you."

"She didn't have to. She had all the trophies."

Ranglen glared back at her.

"You want to know what really bothered me about Mileen?"

He nodded, reluctantly.

"She only went to Henry because she couldn't have you. She never should have gone off with him."

"We agreed to the break-up. It wasn't just me."

"And that wasn't enough reason for her to grab Henry."

"'Grab' Henry? You're exaggerating. She needed more than what I could give her and Henry was willing. He did love her."

"That's why what she did was wrong."

"So you're saying she caused all this?"

Her eyes lanced at him. But then she relented. "I'm sorry. I didn't mean that. I just liked both of them more than what you think."

Ranglen tried to look sympathetic.

"Hearing about Henry was a shock," she said. "It brought back everything I felt for him, for all three of you. I *knew* you would come here today—asking your questions and trying to save her again. Don't you get tired of it? She can fend for herself. She never needed to seek out people—they came to her. That always annoyed me."

A wisp of cloud glided across the room, looked sad. Ranglen wondered if it was a projection that responded to Anne's voice-inflections—or maybe it hid a surveillance device.

He asked, "Do you know why anyone would want to kill Henry?"

"I wondered about the tie to Ventroni. But otherwise I have no idea."

He was ready to leave now. "Okay. A suggestion: don't lie to the police. But don't offer information they don't want either. And don't be specific about what we covered."

"Have I ever compromised your freedoms before?

"No." He didn't elaborate.

"How do I make you understand, Mykol? You and Mileen were my idols. Both of you such fine artists—full of abandon, throw life to the wind. I never could live that way, though I wanted to."

"You should be grateful."

"And you should be more free with yourself. You come in here wanting information but you give nothing in return."

Ranglen's expression remained guarded. He stood up. "I have to go."

"Oh for God's sake—you *always* do this! In your books you talk about having no boundaries, about being open to the 'other.' But you're the most shut-in person I know."

He didn't understand where all this was going.

"I remember you at a party once," she said. "You kept to yourself, standing on a balcony and overlooking the crowd. I walked up to you and said that you must feel so isolated. You just smiled. 'I don't mind being alone,' you said, 'as long as I have a good view.' I thought you were joking. Later I understood…that's how you live."

He looked away—then realized he was doing exactly what she said.

She shook her head. "Never mind, forget it. Go running off into space again, then come back and hide in your cheap hotels."

He really didn't like this.

"All right, I'll shut up. But if you encounter in your travels anything I can market, will you tell me about it?"

"Don't I always? And how did you know I was about to travel?"

"You evade questions and get secretive, like some damned spy. And then you 'go underground' as you once called it."

Ranglen hated to be predictable.

"I hope you find Mileen," she added.

"Thanks for the time, Anne."

"Sure. Whatever."

Another question hit him. "I assume you used Hatch to outfit the Ventroni flight. How do you arrange that?"

"I have an open account with him. Any reps I send out call his office and make the arrangements. The transport's then billed to me."

"Would Hatch have sent the bills for this trip by now?"

"I'd need to check. He's always late. Why do you want to know?"

"The police will want to see them." But the real reason was that Ranglen wondered if Henry or Rashmi had taken private excursions of their own.

"You want me to send the information to you?"

He thought a moment. "No." He'd get that from Hatch, and he didn't want to tell her that Hatch was his next destination. She probably guessed—but if he said it aloud, then if questioned by the police she'd have to tell them.

"By the way," Anne said, "speaking of Hatch, you might ask him about his own contacts on Ventroni. I swear he's smuggling. You can tell by the questions he asks me. But he never sends anything my way."

Ranglen shook his head. "I doubt it. Smuggling would be a step backward for him."

"But I still wish he *would* let me know about his markets."

Ranglen nodded, told her to be careful.

Anne's cellpad chimed. She took the message and looked at Ranglen. "Two police detectives are here to see me. Hussein Hathaway and Pia Folinari."

Ranglen stayed calm. "The man's a bull and the woman's a shark. Do you have a back door?"

"Can you walk on clouds?"

He smiled wryly.

As he stepped through the door of her office, Hathaway and Folinari approached. The man looked the same but Pia now wore black leather slacks with matching jacket and a loud white-and-red top, with a lot of neck and midriff showing. Her gray eyes still glittered like hailstones.

He said a cheery hello to them.

Hathaway narrowed his eyes.

Folinari beamed. "Well, Mr. Ranglen. Fancy meeting you here."

"Fancy. Yeah."

"Advising old friends?"

"I was checking on a business deal. I have to work, you know."

"I guess it must be hard to live on just writing, especially poetry. No one buys poetry, right? I read a lot of yours after leaving you last night."

"It kept you awake?"

"Sure. It's romantic."

"That's the only kind that sells." What the hell was she getting at? True confessions through labored flirtation? "Do you need me for anything?"

"Not now, Mr. 'Man Who Loved Alien Landscapes.'" She referred to the title of his last collection. "Maybe the *truth* but…not now."

She glided past him.

Hathaway growled. "Don't make any sudden departures, Mr. Ranglen. We still want to talk with you."

He nodded, muttering, "I wouldn't dare."

But then Hathaway bore down on him like a mountain, shocking him. "You don't get it, do you? I *know* what you did last night, after we left. You communicated with an unauthorized satellite in Annulus space, one not recognized by Annulus Security. That's not just illegal. It could be *treason*. I could throw you in jail and slap you with 'high crimes against the state,' bury you for years as a political prisoner. Do you want that? Huh?"

Ranglen tried to look stoic but a hot fear poured through him.

The detective added, with smooth vehemence, "You're not the king of Annulus, Mr. Ranglen, in hiding or not—and you're not the king's joker either."

Ranglen took this as a coded message, that Hathaway knew he was the founder of Annulus but that even this distinction could not protect him.

Yet for unauthorized use of foreign communication he should be arrested, not intimidated. And Hathaway had spoken only *after* he lost his composure. Maybe he alone knew about the satellite.

Ranglen glanced at Folinari. She looked furious. She must be hearing this for the first time.

He gambled, said to Hathaway, "Then…arrest me."

Hussein's features barely moved. "When I'm ready."

Ranglen knew not to let himself smile.

Hathaway marched into Anne's office. Folinari followed him like a heat-seeking missile. Anne raised an eyebrow at Ranglen, but then looked worried as she closed the door.

Ranglen trembled, worse than he had after the questioning at the hotel. His well-crafted secrecy, his privacy, his freedom to go wherever he pleased—were they lost now?

And were he and Mileen in even more danger than he'd thought?

He hurried down the corridor and entered the elevator, wanting to get down out of the clouds.

Chapter Five: Hatch

In another life, Ranglen wanted to be Hatch Banner.

The gray dish at the center of Annulus hung slightly below the ring-plane and was attached to it by six spokes. These spokes held transport tubes, and they followed the 15-degree slope of the ring's surface from the inner rim to the outer edge of the dish. The shield, 20 kilometers wide, slanted inward at the same rate but then curved into a basin at the center. An open and complicated latticework filled that basin, holding a maze of storage facilities, workshops, hangars, warehouses, repair docks, gantries, cranes.

On top of these structures sat the black vanes of gravity-plates. Here the pseudo attraction, weaker than on the ring itself, reversed direction and made "downward" point up toward the center of Annulus.

The opposite side of the dish, the curved portion that faced outward or "down" from the ring (or "up" if you stood there) was more impressive. From it arose a vast array of multi-shaped needles—spaceships!—bristling up as if the shield were a huge pin-cushion.

Here lay the main Annulus spaceport. And at this spaceport, Hatch Banner was king.

Ranglen knew Hatch since before the third Clip was discovered. Indeed, Hatch participated in the construction of Annulus, recognizing that the structure hanging here at the bottom of the ring would make an excellent spaceport—he assumed that was why it was part of the Airafane blueprint. Though Hatch ran his business, he was not an entrepreneur like Anne but more a glorified mechanic, a foreman rather than CEO. He never passed a chance to work directly on his beloved spaceships, to get his hands dirty, to cut and splice and hack and weld and move components from frame to frame.

Ranglen thought him a body-shop maestro, the best friend a spaceship—or, in this case, an escapist paranoid—could ever have. Though he could be difficult socially (his opinions got in the way of his reason), his technical skills were always stellar.

Ranglen emerged from the transport tube and rode up past the holding frames of dissected ships brought down from above, gleaming in the banks of hard illumination.

Workers didn't need spacesuits here since the dish sat in its own lens of air, maintained by Airafane suppression fields, and the lighter gravity allowed everyone to move in long-distance jumps like hordes of insects.

He stepped from a lift-frame into a cavernous interior. He found Hatch arguing with mechanics over an exposed Type 6 hull. When Hatch saw him he yelled louder to bring the argument to a close. Then he marched up to Ranglen. "Let's walk. I expected you sooner."

Quick bluster was common with Hatch.

He stood taller than Ranglen and looked gaunt, walked with a fast but wayward gait that was hard to follow. His grizzled face showed wear and age, the jet skin wounded from exploding machinery, as were his hands. He didn't believe in body restoration. He once had been handsome and quite sought after for his rollicking generosity and adventure. His eyes had a vintage "wicked gleam" that slipped at you sideways and held volumes of irony. Those eyes were pale now, damaged too, and looked misplaced in his cracked skin, like bluish milk pools in black canyonlands. His graying hair formed a permanent wave that swung on his forehead like a flag. He wore, always, slack-fitting and filthy overalls, with a ragged bandanna around his neck that, people swore, was sometimes washed but never changed.

He said, not looking at Ranglen, "You hear about Henry?"

"Yeah. Sad."

Neither of them added comments. The reserve seemed part of this machinists' world.

"He was found nearby?"

"Near one of the empty spaceship docks. A security guard discovered him. I didn't get here till they cleared away the body."

"Do you know what killed him?"

"Puncture wounds. Made from tiny darts, not knives or bullets. Five wounds in his chest, like a pentagon. But the darts weren't left there. The security guard told me." Hatch's speech seemed more clipped than usual.

"What did the police ask you?"

"About his relatives and friends. I gave them names, occupations, nothing more. I said that Mileen was his fiancé, Anne his boss, Rashmi Verlock his business partner, and you...well, I said his 'friend.' They wanted to reach Mileen. And they were especially interested in you."

Because of the card-link, Ranglen assumed, but he asked why.

"They just perked up when I mentioned your name."

"So you described him and me as 'friends'?"

Hatch looked reproachful. "Don't get nervous! I just said you brought him and Mileen together."

Hatch had disagreed loudly when, in the past, Ranglen and Mileen ended their love affair. Ranglen felt it might wreck his friendship with Hatch. So he was suspicious now of what Hatch told the police. "Which officers questioned you?"

"A big guy named Hathaway and a small woman with twice the attitude—she had a funny name."

"Pia?"

"That's it. They come to see you too?"

"In the middle of the night. They weren't polite."

"They suspect you?"

"Yes, but I've got alibis. They—"

"They're interested because of you and Mileen."

"What did you tell them about us?"

Hatch shrugged. "They asked if you two had been together. They spoke as if they already knew."

Ranglen winced. The two officers probably knew nothing. They were just good interrogators who could make it *seem* they knew, and thus learn whatever they wanted. No wonder they came to him in the middle of the night.

Hatch added, without much apology, "What do you expect? It was probably obvious you didn't like Henry."

"I never disliked him."

"Yeah, right."

"Goddammit, Hatch—now they suspect me."

"So? Any truth to it?" Hatch didn't look at him, which proved he was serious.

"Why the hell do you say that?"

Hatch strode on. "Mileen's in danger. And I can't help thinking *you* put her there."

This angered Ranglen, but he wasn't surprised. Hatch and Mileen shared a common experience that bonded them when they first met.

In the century of accelerated space exploration that followed the discovery of the first Clip many families and marriages had been abandoned, resulting in—just one of the social problems then—vagrant children. Both Mileen and Hatch had no idea of their family connections. They had grown up, though at different times, in government-supported "children's homes" or "rehabilitation centers," since foster care had become difficult in the vast movements of population. While attending college through government loans Mileen met the older Anne, and through her Ranglen and eventually Hatch.

The similar pasts of Hatch and Mileen made for a strong attachment between them. He had been footloose and in-and-out of trouble most of his life (after running away from the government home), and Mileen became a necessary palliative in his later days. In her he saw his intense youth and tried to help her, and in him she found a flexible mentor.

Ranglen protested, "How is it *my* fault?"

"She loved you, Mykol. She never would have gone with Henry if you two had stuck together."

"Dammit, I've argued this already today. Going with him was *her* choice."

"She once came to me, shouting, right before the break-up, wanting to know why you were so secretive, why you went off by yourself so much. She worshiped you, Mykol, but to you she was only a distraction, not good enough for your high pursuits."

"That's *nonsense!*"

"She'd be safe now if she had stayed with you."

Ranglen went silent. This same thought haunted him also. He said, eventually, "If you're so concerned, then why aren't you out there looking for her yourself?"

"I don't know where to start. And I don't have the same freedom that you have."

"Look, we—"

Hatch said emphatically, "I don't care if she was a disturbance to you, Mykol, that she messed up your precious lifestyle. I know she's difficult. But she was *alive* when she was with you. And she lost herself when she went with Henry. She wasn't the same person. She shouldn't have left you—and you shouldn't have *let* her leave you—for some stupid salesman who could never understand her, who worshipped her but could never *know* her."

Hatch stormed forward and left Ranglen behind.

Ranglen managed his anger and raced to catch up. He said to Hatch, "Okay, I get it now. You're scared for her. You don't want to learn what you might find."

Hatch looked bleak. He slowed his forward pace a little. "Of course I'm scared. You are too."

"Then talk to me. I don't want to fight you. Tell me what you know."

Hatch waited before answering. "You have to promise me you'll find her, Mykol—that you'll do it before she gets herself killed."

"That's why I'm here."

Hatch still marched on but not as impulsively.

Technicians surrounded them. Fierce blue-white welding flames gushed plumes of yellow sparks, metal banged, tools pounded, drills whined and presses thumped.

At last Hatch said, "So...what do you need?"

Ranglen threw his questions at him. "Did the police ask you how you knew Henry?"

"I said he was a friend of a friend. That's how I mentioned you. That he sometimes used my spaceships for business trips. That's when I gave them Anne's name."

"Did Henry ever rent a spaceship himself?"

"The police asked the same question. He never rented alone. It was always through Anne."

"Then what was Henry doing here when he got killed?"

Hatch made a sinister grin. "You think just like the police, don't you? They asked that too. I said I didn't know. And I *don't* know. I refused to speculate. They weren't happy about it. I thought that little Pia would bite my ear off."

"Did they ask about the last time he—through Anne—used one of your ships?"

"It was a trip to Ventroni. They asked a lot about that. But I didn't say much. They wanted to know about the cargo. I referred them to Anne. They asked more about the passengers than the crew."

"The police are talking to Anne now, and they'll probably have more questions about the trip."

"I'll give them what they ask for and not a drop more."

Ranglen smiled. "So...you're implying there's something about this trip that the police *should* know, but you're not telling them until they ask you directly?"

Hatch didn't answer.

Ranglen waited. But he grew impatient. "Come on, Hatch! What didn't you tell them?"

Hatch still hesitated. But he finally said, "The ship made a stop on the way back to Annulus."

At that moment, as Ranglen grew excited, they walked through portals onto the surface of the spaceport itself.

From that surface, with its openings and lifts and ramps and cranes, in a slightly curved splendid bouquet, sprouted the great interstellar ships, the harvest crop of this spaceport's activity. Huge liners like beached whales swarming with blisters, arrow-sharp speedsters all fuselage and wings, exotic craft resembling flowers, trees, saucers, wedges, or globes. Some looked like factories standing on end, some like radiant nighttime cities squeezed into dynamic shapes, some painted in black-and-white checkers or covered with party-stripes of color, some surging with militant imperialism that came from missile tubes and beam projectors, and some like dreams, glass-blown goblets, boomerangs, hawks, sharks and manta-rays, candelabra, cathedrals, multi-faceted gems. You could find anything your heart imagined.

This is why Ranglen wanted to be Hatch. The stars were not commercialized here, not bought and sold as they were with Anne. Outer space and its exotic transport were tangible here, vibrant, brought to life, in a grunge-and-tumble power flow like a river in flood—crude, heavy, blunt, a rush.

"Hey! You coming?"

Ranglen followed, returned to the subject. "So the ship stopped while coming from Ventroni. How do you know? Did the crew tell you?"

"They told me nothing. They said the flight was normal. But I had suspicions when I saw them. I wasn't here when the ship came in so I didn't see Henry, Mileen, or Rashmi. But the crew acted weird. They answered my questions without giving answers. And they didn't seem to care if I was suspicious or not."

"What did you do?"

"I checked the ship's data. You know you can't read Airafane technology. But you *can* read the human-made instruments. Like the rate of consumables used on board. The data suggested more time had been spent on the return trip than the outward one. I'm sure of it—they stopped somewhere."

"In the Ventroni system or near Annulus?"

He looked at Ranglen. "You're better than the police—they should have asked that but they didn't. Based on the interface between the Clip drive and the programming that controls it, you can tell that the drive was activated twice. Once on leaving Ventroni, once more in deep space. *Two* FTL jumps occurred."

"But that's—"

"I know. It either had to be planned, so the engine would know where to enter time-space, or a glitch in the interface program occurred and ordered the ship out at the wrong spot. But that's never happened. Airafane components override errors. I checked the human programs on the ship. They worked fine."

Ranglen had to control his eagerness, and he didn't want to be sidetracked with premature conclusions. "No one on board said anything?"

"Not surprising. Since the technology can't be checked, the people don't have to be honest about where they went. They sign destination and activity logs, but there's nothing to compare them against. If I can't tell where they stopped, why bother with the truth?"

Ranglen pondered. He knew Hatch's capabilities—if anyone could figure where they stopped, it'd be him. And he was certain Hatch still held something back. Even in a matter as serious as this, Hatch made you work to get it.

Ranglen said, "Who made up the crew?"

"A commander, co-pilot, and a steward."

"For just three passengers? Where's your profit?"

"Two are required for all passenger trips with light-space jumps no matter how many people are on board. It's the law. Usually I'd demand more clients but Anne's willing to pay. The steward was extra. He was on Ventroni and needed to return to Annulus. He offered his services by hitching a ride. Happens often."

A transporter-lift crossed the open path before them, forcing them through a labyrinth of conduits and cables. "Tell me about them."

"The commander was Jayne Fowler. An old trooper who's been around for years, worked with me even before I came to Annulus. A little dated now and not easily approached, but dependable. She could have been as good a mechanic as I am but she wasn't interested. I'd give her any piloting job as long as the passengers don't require her to socialize. Henry and Rashmi had been with her before. They knew what she was like and they were glad to get her. Business people are happy when the crew leaves them alone."

They picked up the pace after rounding the lift. "Lonni Elwood was the co-pilot. She's new with us. She came from a different piloting group after her job with them didn't work out. Don't know why. She was unclear and I didn't ask—I don't care what they've done as long as they can perform now. She had experience but I felt she would never make captain. Not enough presence for command, or not enough energy. Maybe that was her problem with the other group. She was okay with me, though."

"The steward?"

"Omar Mirik. I didn't like him. He had a big mouth, and he got in trouble with some passengers a while ago. He talked back to them and they complained. I almost fired him but he apologized and he's been fine since, more control of his temper. In fact, he's become one of my best stewards."

"Can I talk to any of the crew?"

"No, because of a coincidence that probably is *no* coincidence. The police should kick themselves for not asking about it. A week after the ship returned from Ventroni, all three of them quit."

Ranglen chuckled.

"Yeah," Hatch added. "Peculiar, isn't it? The three of them together made an appointment to see me. Jayne was professional. She politely asked for a release from her contract though she didn't say why. Omar said less but he looked excited, nervous, smug, all at the same time. 'I've got a secret' was written all over him. I think he wanted to rub my nose in it. Lonni...well, she was the strange one. She didn't say a word, didn't care. She didn't even look at me, and not because she was embarrassed but because, I assumed, she was exhausted—or else drunk. She looked terrible. Old, broken."

Ranglen made a show of pondering. "Odd for all of them to quit at the same time."

"Not really. It happens a lot with spaceship crews. They don't have exciting lives, especially if they're transporting business reps from market to market. They dream of making the big money, a quick kill in any market—salvage, alien finds, a Clip. Get-rich schemes develop, and suddenly the crew starts a business on no more than a hunch. Most of them fail, but the legend of the one that does make it big sustains the dream. It hurts to watch them. It's all these damned Clips, you know, what they've done to us."

Ranglen groaned. He had heard Hatch's stand on Clips before.

"You know how I feel, Mykol. We don't get these things for free. We're being manipulated."

Ranglen's paranoia didn't extend to ancient alien conspiracies. "The Airafane are dead. Anything that happens to us is *our* responsibility."

"We've gone to the stars in just over a century. That can't be good."

"You're complaining? You *love* spaceships."

"It's not by our doing."

"So what's your point?"

"Look around you—nobody wears a spacesuit here. The air is kept in by a restraining field that *we don't understand.* It just came with the Annulus blueprint. We use all this stuff but we're not masters of it. It's changing us before we even decide to change."

Ranglen attempted a scornful look. But he sometimes agreed. A Clip that explained, for example, how to generate the force fields that came with Annulus was yet to be found. So the race was on, the *human* race, to invent them before such help was needed. Some politicians, historians, and people like Hatch, believed that winning this race was crucial for human pride and integrity. Yet most people were too busy enjoying Clip products to care—forging ahead, exploiting, building, leaving whole worlds of the past behind.

"No one bothers to invent anything new. They just fill in the blanks, waiting for what the next Clip will bring. I tell you, we're losing creativity, going extinct—we're being 'set up.'"

Ranglen waved his hand in disgust.

"People have died!" Hatch insisted.

"Yeah, like Henry."

That brought them back to reality. They walked on in respectful silence.

Ranglen said, to move them away from conspiracy theories, "How's my ship?"

"Primed and ready. I guessed you were coming, so I took the liberty of preparing it."

Ranglen was only half grateful. As with Anne, he didn't like to be predictable.

"I know what you're thinking. But you should be happy. I entered information into the navigation files, under the usual codes. You can access it."

Ranglen sighed in relief. Hatch must have performed his magic on the craft that returned from Ventroni, deducing where it had stopped. Ranglen didn't ask what was in the data—he knew Hatch would say nothing. The man was more paranoid about surveillance than even Ranglen.

A ship ahead of them descended for a landing, a bulbous thing with squat fins that extended into legs. It touched down, bounced on its shock absorbers and came to rest. Ranglen and Hatch slowed their pace as they approached it. They absently watched the ground crew perform the lock-down.

"Do you know where the three crewmembers are now?"

"I tried to reach each of them after Henry's death, just to warn them about the police, but every connection said they had moved."

"Can I track them, find them?"

"I don't know about Jayne. At one time she and I were close but not anymore. For Omar I have no idea. But a worker here told me he'd heard that Lonni had gone 'under the ring.'"

Ranglen hadn't thought of that. It was a clever place to hide.

"I'll give you one or two contacts there," Hatch said. "Mention my name." He transferred the information from cellpad to cellpad, through a physical link to avoid interception.

They had almost completed a large circle back to the hangar. Hatch slowed as he approached the entrance, said firmly to Ranglen, "You find her, Mykol. Before *they* do—the police, Homeworld, Earth, the Confederation, whoever killed Henry."

"That's my intention."

"I know you've got your 'methods' and secrets. But I'm worried."

Both of them slowed their walk even more, reluctant to re-enter the machine-shop. Hatch turned to Ranglen and said, "There's something else. On that trip to Ventroni, Mileen wasn't registered on the original passenger list. Henry didn't want Anne to know she was covered on company money. He said Anne would squawk. She's touchy about Mileen. And Henry never wanted to offend Anne. So he took her in secret."

Ranglen pondered. Anne said she knew Mileen had been on board, that she even forced Henry to pay for her. "Why do you say that?"

"When the police check the flight records they'll see that Mileen wasn't listed as a passenger, which might make them more suspicious of her."

Hatch always covered for Mileen. No surprise there, and maybe Henry had spoken with Anne *after* he talked with Hatch.

Ranglen stared at the huge craft they had watched land. Gantries and ramps now nestled around it, its portals opening to unload cargo.

He asked, casually, "Did Mileen ever come here for her ship?"

"The one you bought for her? No, it's still here."

"Did she come here at all in the last two weeks?"

"With Henry, you mean?"

"With him or alone, maybe just to talk?"

"No. I wish she had. It's been a while since I've spoken with her."

He still gazed at the spacecraft where workers and cranes now lifted out baggage, crates, container units.

"Speaking of Ventroni," Hatch said, "that ship you're looking at just came from there."

"What? The big one?"

"Arrives here twice a week. Cargo carrier."

It reminded Ranglen of what Anne had said to him to tell Hatch. "Anne thinks you have contacts on Ventroni, that you're a smuggler again."

Hatch's laugh was darkly sinister. "She's out of her mind. And she should watch her own back."

"She wasn't serious."

"The hell she wasn't. She'll say anything to get a line of product."

Hatch's tone surprised Ranglen. Hatch wasn't usually so critical of Anne.

In the portals of the spaceship, workers uncovered a flashy ground transport vehicle, a GTV or "groundcar." They drove it down the ramp and left it not far from Hatch and Ranglen. It was big and plush and obviously expensive, white and beige and dark-dark red with two extensions at either end, the longer ones in front holding a driver's tapered dome. The car looked aggressive.

"Nice," Hatch said.

A man from the ship walked toward it with a dock official who apparently finalized its transfer. Documents were copied and signed with cellpads. The man, who sported spiked blond hair and data-feed glasses that hid his eyes, looked angry. He hurled the hard-copy at the official and then marched with big strides to the car. He slid into the driver's dome, roared the engine, flung

The Man Who Loved Alien Landscapes

the vehicle into the access lane inside the hangar and bullied his way through the traffic of cargo carriers.

Referring to the man's stormy exit, Ranglen said to Hatch, "He doesn't like your spaceport."

Hatch looked stunned as he stared after the car, his mouth hanging open and his pale eyes intense with thought.

Ranglen asked, "Did you know that guy?"

Hatch glanced curtly at Ranglen. "No…Thought I did. But it wasn't him." He walked into the hangar with quick deliberation.

Ranglen said after him, "You sure about that?"

"Don't worry about it, Mykol."

"I worry easily." He had to speak louder since Hatch was gaining distance. Such a sign-off was common with Hatch but this was more abrupt than usual. "Is there something important here I should know about?"

Hatch barely turned his head. "Nothing! And aren't you supposed to be out there finding the great love of your life?"

"You mean of *your* life."

Hatch stopped, half turned and took a step back. Ranglen expected rage on his face, but the expression more resembled fear.

"Just find her," Hatch stated, flatly. "You owe her that. And you owe *me* that."

"Who was that guy from the ship?"

Hatch walked away, said over his shoulder, "Be careful, Mykol."

"Dammit! What the hell was that all about?"

Ranglen lost him in the crowd of mechanics.

He glanced to see where the car had gone but it had already vanished and soon would be rushing up a transport tube. Ranglen wished he had taken a closer look at the driver. He wanted to interrogate the dock official but she, too, was gone.

Suspicion flowed through him. The coincidental ship from Ventroni, the man with the car and Hatch's reaction to him, Hatch's resulting bad mood—which had simmered inside him for the entire talk. What did it mean?

Lonni Elwood might have the answers. She had *been* there.

He hurried back through the levels of spaceport—the activity, the workers, the ships pulsing with brute power. Hatch's world.

Ranglen no longer wanted to be part of it.

56

Chapter Six: Lonni

Ranglen, like most visitors "under the ring," came with trepidation and irrational fear, a sense of "there but for the grace of God go I"—or, more accurately, for the grace of money, privilege, and power.

A framework of the so-called gravity plates ran beneath the surface of Annulus. Shaped like vanes or wide blinds, they formed a huge arcing wave, like a horde of crows with interlocked wings. These generated the gravity that kept everything on the upward surface from floating away.

Two schools of thought tried to explain them. One said that Einstein's well-known equivalence between gravity and acceleration was incorrect and the plates took advantage of the difference, hence the name accelero-gravity. Another group said that the devices manipulated the underlying Higgs field and thus controlled mass, repulsion, and attraction. Both theories made accurate predictions, but the equations for one were incompatible with those of the other—and also with most known physical laws. So each theory struck Ranglen as weak.

The plates always worked, though, and more reliably than human explanations.

The lattice that held them ran outward from the ring for a kilometer or so into the central cavity, rising 15-degrees from the slope of the surface like flying buttresses that flew nowhere, and preventing the field from breaking off too suddenly. There the brew of lake water, standing boulders, tumbling icebergs, bannered out in pinwheel grace and formed a lace-edge fantasy, the liquid apron that Ranglen had watched earlier that morning. And within these supports (not as thick with surveillance and maintenance as those under the ring-surface itself), in the Gothic grid-work that ran along the lattice shelf, in these less-patrolled angles between struts and frames, dwelled the vagrants of Annulus.

Given explosive interstellar expansion, it was no surprise that the people who couldn't keep up with the change—the side-lined, the poor—would find themselves landing in out-of-the-way places, abandoned by humanity's new adventure that moved too fast to carry everyone. Hatch and Mileen were two examples.

Though these two had weathered the experience well, many others became discarded debris. On Annulus, in order to escape notice, they chose to live "under the ring," or at least in this fringe shadowy border where, literally, they hung on an edge.

Ranglen didn't know if the phenomenon angered him or made him proud. Though the chaotic dispersion caused by Clips weakened the devotion to ethnic, racial, or national traditions, boundaries of class did not fade as easily. Ranglen admired the courage or endurance of the disadvantaged who chose, or were forced, to live now where they did, outside of "universal" expansion. They gave up all chance for government support, while others simply had no choice. Thus, though he hated that so many people were still shut out, he loved that some of them preferred it that way, had declared, "No!"

And he hoped they were an aesthetic crowd for, if it were any consolation, an aurora-like drift hung above them that easily could be called sublime.

Wearing grip-sleeves on his shoes, he maneuvered the struts in the strange counter-gravity of this place, where plates scattered throughout the grid sometimes even faced each other and balanced g-forces. The lattice was bound together as much by Airafane restraining fields (which also held the air) as by Airafane composite clamps.

He approached—at the end of his labyrinthine journey—a nondescript and faded hut that looked desperate. Various informants had led him here. The trail hadn't been easy. He had to use all of Hatch's leads plus various bribes—the culture of this underworld was most private.

His hunt narrowed to one support on one sub-frame of one buttress that loomed above him, and then to this flimsy abode with wrapping-fabric walls and open flaps drifting about the entrance. He assumed he never would have found the place except that Lonni was new to the setting and, alas, did not cover her tracks well.

Ranglen grew anxious. If Lonni didn't have the answers he needed he didn't know where to go next.

She emerged from the hut, also using grip-sleeves, a gaunt figure with stark features in worn spacer's overalls and high-ankled working boots. When she saw him, she first looked curious. But then—as if realizing he were an outsider—fear heightened the cragginess of her face and she quickly backed inside to escape.

"I'm not here to hurt you!"

He moved toward the opening, the flap of which she hadn't pulled shut. He peered in with care.

In the dim light of a single battery-powered lamp she stood guarded behind an Annulus buttress, around which the hut had been built and whose angle provided the best cover. One large greenish eye gleamed at him from a face almost hidden in shadow, the rest of her body sheltered by the strut—with only a gun in her hand exposed, a large and scary-looking weapon that seemed made to threaten. It was aimed at him.

He was impressed with her defensive position. He backed off, realizing she might fend for herself better than he expected. He wondered if he'd get anything out of her at all—or if he'd get shot.

Her face emerged from the shadows. She looked less intimidating than her gun—her features shrunken, her lips pale, her ropy locks of chopped hair colorless and thin. Her green eyes, the most striking thing about her, leapt side to side in frenzy. Only the weapon gave her an edge. And Ranglen had no doubt she *would* use it.

She said rapidly in a high-pitched voice, "Who are you and what do you want?"

"I'm a friend of Hatch Banner. He told me you might be here. He wouldn't have said anything if he didn't feel you were safe with me."

The eyes, so large in that sunken face, weighed and debated. "A friend of mine was murdered. I'm protecting myself."

"I knew Henry too."

"Henry's *dead*. That doesn't make me feel safe with you."

Good point, Ranglen conceded. "I know you stopped on the trip back from Ventroni. Henry came to see me afterward. He might have told you."

Her eyes narrowed. "You're Mykol Ranglen?"

"Yes. And I don't care about the Clip. I'm here only because I want to find Mileen. She's my friend, and she's missing."

"That's *crap!* Everyone says they don't care about the Clip."

"I once found a Clip. I got everything I wanted."

Her mouth froze open briefly—maybe from awe. "Are you serious?"

"The third Clip, the one that built Annulus. Not many people know I found it. Mileen did. Didn't she tell you?"

Lonni lifted the gun toward him. "Of *course* she didn't! That was *stupid!*"

Ranglen realized his mistake. With Clips, you either kept the secret forever or you told everyone. He said rapidly, "I just wanted to show you she was my friend."

"She said you were, and that you could be trusted. But that doesn't explain why you're here."

"I need information. Mileen's missing and I'm trying to find her."

"She's probably dead. They're *all* probably dead. It was smart of Mileen to leave so quick but even she might have been too late. She was first to disappear, you know."

"I didn't know. Why—"

"I left right after she did. They all looked ready to kill each other. I came here."

Ranglen probed, warily. "You say Mileen disappeared?"

"She left all of us. I think she left Henry first."

"They argued?"

"I don't know. It was after we quit our jobs, which she thought was crazy. Maybe she and Henry did fight. Suddenly she was gone. They all behaved badly then. They scared me. I came here and when I heard about Henry I *stayed* here. I even went deeper."

He didn't ask her how she learned Henry was killed. He watched her instead, fascinated and haunted by her. Everything had been taken away from her, leaving only the gun, the hut, and the buttress for defense. But her contempt and terror still sustained her. She was filled with resistance and yet ready to burst.

"Lonni, listen to me. I need your help. I need to know what happened out there."

"It's better you don't know. Everyone on board the ship was dead. Do you want the same thing?"

"*Who* was dead? *What* ship?"

"For God's sake, didn't Henry tell you anything? Maybe he lied to you. He kept to himself, you know. Just like Rashmi. All Henry wanted was Mileen, and she could be a bitch. She tried to be nice but it wasn't easy. You never knew with her, with any of them."

"Why do you say that? Why—" Ranglen stopped himself and tried to stay calm. "What happened on that trip from Ventroni?"

While the gun moved in tight little circles, she seemed to come to a hard decision. She straightened, but wedged herself further into her protective corner. "If I talk to you I want my privacy."

"No one knows I'm here except Hatch."

"I can move from this hut the minute you leave, find another spot. You'll never see me again."

"I understand. I can get you what you need—food, money."

"I want *nothing* from you. I want to be left alone. I don't have to talk about any of this but I know Henry vouched for you. I trusted him. Maybe this will stop them from getting killed."

"I promise. I—" He sighed, then tried to cover the sound of it. "Just begin at the beginning."

She took a deep breath, licked her lips, stood motionless for several moments.

And then the words flowed out. "They *blamed* me! But I had nothing to do with it! Someone overrode the Clip drive. It wasn't an accident! I'm good at what I do. Someone went in and changed the settings. It wasn't me but they all felt I did it. I could tell what they were thinking."

"Lonni, please—"

"*Dammit*, I'll tell you if you just wait a minute! I've been thinking about all this too long. I don't understand it. I don't *know* what happened!"

He reminded himself to keep his questions neutral, more as comments than interrogation. "You said you stopped somewhere on the way back."

"It dropped us where the figures had been set—but not set by *me*! Someone on board had to know about the derelicts. That drive didn't fail. It was over-ridden."

"So the Clip drive stopped working."

"Yes, it stopped!—that's what I just said. A couple of light-years from Annulus. Don't ask me for the coordinates. I knew once but I dumped them. I got a neuron-swipe. 'Complex numerical alignments deleted.' Just in case anyone came searching—like you! It played hell with my sense for numbers. I couldn't pilot a ship now if I tried. I get lost if I take a walk. But I'm not going back to my job anyway."

Ranglen was appalled. A neuron-swipe was supposedly a removal of selected memories but more a cauterizing of the brain. "Lonni, you—"

"I don't care! I can find other work here. 'Under the ring.' We're exploited here but we don't give a damn. We hate your big rainbow paradise."

Ranglen admired this rebellion in her, this go-to-hell dead-end strength. But he still needed answers. "So...you found something out in space."

"We found two ships. One was perfect, the other crazy. On the first, on the pretty one, we found dead bodies. People had been murdered with holes cut in them, a little group of wounds in each chest. A man, a woman, and a small boy. We saw no weapons, just the corpses. They dragged me on board. 'You gotta come, Lonni. We need you, girl.' That's what Omar said, but Jayne tried to be nice to me too. She's another bitch. They wanted me to read the computers, get the coordinates of a star system they found—one that had the octahedral symbol. Clips, you know. Everyone knows that symbol means Clips."

Ranglen felt brief guilt and despair—he was the one who discovered the significance of the symbol.

"Frozen blood must have floated in the control room after the murders. I pictured strands and beads of it, in arcs. Pieces like black confetti still hung there. I bumped into it and knocked it about. It drove me crazy. But I read their goddamned information for them. I got what they needed. Don't ask me about it now. It's gone, dumped. Give me a number over ten and I won't remember it. Selective dyslexia—it's better than getting drunk! I can't even tell you how old I am. The things we do to ourselves, you know? You're all going to be like me someday."

She waved the gun carelessly—Ranglen tensed.

"They didn't do anything to hurt me, you see. They were polite. They felt they'd be rich so they didn't mind babying me. Even Omar—that bastard claimed I was his sweetheart. I think he once wanted to rape me but he put that behind him. I was his darling now. And Rashmi—he didn't know how to be nice but he wanted to be. He was a joke. But he would have been better on board that ship with the blood and all. More his style. And old Jayne, crazy Jayne, even when she blamed me she apologized—and she never did *that* before. Henry was the nicest. But they all changed. It was scary to watch. They turned inside out, like the big ship itself. Even Mileen went crazy. She yelled at them, 'The lifeboat, dammit! Doesn't anyone care?' She wouldn't let them forget it. All the time, 'The lifeboat! The lifeboat!' She really got on their nerves."

"Wait a minute—a lifeboat? An RLV?"

"One was missing from the first ship. Mileen thought a child had escaped. The people dead were a man and a woman—parents maybe—and the boy, but one more couch in the control room was empty. She believed the lifeboat must have taken a child. And she wanted us to search for it. But nobody cared. They only wanted the coordinates of the star beneath the Clip symbol. After we got back Mileen even came to me and asked me to pilot a ship to where the lifeboat had landed, she—"

"Wait! This was after you returned to Annulus?"

"The time we all quit our jobs, right after Henry came to you. She begged me, even tried to bribe me. I said she could have my own spaceship if she wanted it—I wasn't going anywhere—but she just pleaded with me on and on. I threw her out. Then I got the neuron-swipe. No piloting now. No one'll ask me to pilot again."

Ranglen thought quickly, praying that Mileen *had* taken Lonni's ship since Hatch said she didn't use her own. "Did you see her again?"

"No. I came here. And I was glad. I got away from all of them. They wanted me close to them but I pretended to be crazy—the crazier the better. Mileen never found me. *You* found me, but you're not one of them and that's why you could do it. They didn't have any sense left."

"Did Mileen try to go to the lifeboat world?"

"How should I know? I told you I didn't see her again. She just wanted to use me—like the rest of them. 'Help me, Lonni.' I got so sick of that. I *hated* that!"

"How was Mileen when she came to you? Was she angry, in fear?"

"God!—it's always Mileen with you. You and Henry and even Omar. What the hell is it about her?"

"I don't want her hurt."

"Why do you worry? She can handle herself. She was a fool for coming to me but she wasn't frantic, not crazy like the others. She had her moments but she changed after Henry returned from seeing you. I could tell she started making plans. She knew what she was doing. It didn't surprise me when she left. Hell, her leaving encouraged me to leave too."

Ranglen asked, to distract her for a moment away from Mileen, "What about these ships you found?"

"The first one was streamlined, perfect. All silver and polished, sharp as an arrow. But the second—God, it was horrible. Mileen didn't want to get near it. They *forced* me to. It was like a big piece of driftwood with slabs sticking out, all worn and broken. But up close you could see it was made of nothing but spikes. Long brown tubes with metal points, all different sizes and packed beside each other. The whole object was covered with them, or maybe *made* of them. The biggest were like narrow tree-trunks, others like flagpoles, posts, spears. All were dirty with rings around them, white crusts or black grime, tar or something.

"They looked used, as if ripped from the ground, like they were part of some construction project. Omar even saw equations in the object. He thought it was a 'higher-dimensional analog of a mathematical theorem that had gotten out of hand.' Maybe he was joking just to drive me crazy. Omar was the one who forced me to go to it. Henry didn't. Henry was sweet. Of course Henry was the one who got killed. It's all your fault, you know."

Ranglen, shocked, stared back at her.

"Yes, it's your fault! Henry kept us together when we flew home and during the week after we got here, when we agreed to lay low before we all quit. He kept talking about you, praising you. 'Mykol will have all the answers.' He had to say that because the idiots were fighting among themselves, screaming at each other since they didn't know how they could find anything that small on an entire planet. Henry always said, 'Mykol will know, I'll go to Mykol.' He showed us your card-link, wrote on the back of it, 'Mykol knows!' Silly things like that to try to keep them sane."

Ranglen said nothing.

"I didn't care about any of it. Already I was moving away from them, if just in my mind. Henry insisted they wait until he talked with you. They agreed with him.

Imagine—they agreed! Last time *that* happened! So Henry comes back after seeing you and—the poor baby—he doesn't have an answer. *You* didn't have an answer. Everything's vague and doesn't make sense. 'It will find us,' he kept saying. 'Mykol said so.' That wasn't what they wanted. They almost killed him then. I'm sure they killed him later, thinking he had gotten the answer from you and kept it to himself. I told them that someone should have gone with him to meet you but they wouldn't listen. They trusted Henry. He was like that. Sexy Henry. But they got him in the end!"

"Everything Henry said was true! There's no method to finding Clips!"

"And maybe *you* killed him once you got what *you* wanted."

"I don't care about the Clip. I told you that."

"No one would believe you. *I* don't believe you. No one believed anyone then."

"It's just like I said to him, the—"

"Oh forget it! It's all crap! And it doesn't matter now. The Clip's at fault if you want to think that way. Maybe they *are* sent to drive us mad—I've heard some people say they should be destroyed. I thought that was stupid but I understand now. I saw a control room filled with blood. I want to erase that memory, like I did the numbers, but it won't go away."

Ranglen fought for control. He could feel himself being absorbed into Lonni's frenzied terror. "Could you tell how long ago the people had been killed?"

"Omar thought twenty years or so. The instruments on the ship weren't ancient. We thought it was some wealthy yacht. Inside, it was more normal but customized. On the outside it looked like a fancy drawing, like what someone—with money—would have shown a builder what he wanted for his toy. Not like that other thing, the exploded mess. God, how I hated that thing."

"Was it alien?"

"How should I know? What's 'alien'? *We're* alien—look at how we act!"

Ranglen felt compelled to help her but he didn't know how. Her struggle seemed less a search for knowledge than a desperate means of saving herself. "What else about that object, anything?"

"It scared me. I really wanted to dump those memories. But that's gut-level stuff, not as abstract as a series of numbers. That's what gets to you in the end, the stuff you can't download at the end of the day—what you want to forget! The ships were too unreal, you see. Maybe they made up some big work of art and that's why Mileen reacted to them. I don't know. That was the problem, you felt you weren't meant to understand, that it was an intentional slap-in-your-face. 'I dare you to make sense of us!' And everyone else just laughed. They bought into the whole contradiction of it, the yin-and-yang, the 'theater,' the display. Mileen looked at them seriously but the rest just saw a big joke—and their money. Omar wanted to get out and walk on the spikes, leave a silly memorial as good luck. He wanted to fly our ship through the openings and dive into the holes. No one wanted to really *study* the ships. They didn't care. They were fools and idiots!"

"Lonni, Lonni—"

"They *toasted* each other with drinks stolen from the cargo, planned their ridiculous future. I never saw Jayne act the way she did. She made a pass at Rashmi, at Omar, at Henry, at all of them. But not Mileen—she hated Mileen. I had faith in Henry, but he too got sucked in. Omar became some evil clown. Rashmi—he didn't make any sense at all. He turned into a statue—he lost life instead of gaining it. And poor Mileen, all worked up one moment and then quiet as hell. Talk about contradictions. Sometimes she was as dead as a tomb—just like the ship!—and at other times she was on fire, yelling at everyone. Who the hell did she think she was? She didn't know any more than the rest of us. And I wanted out—as far as I could get!"

"You said you left everyone after Henry came to see me. So how did you hear that he died?"

"A friend who worked for Hatch told me. He was there when the body was discovered."

The friend had to be the person who told Hatch where Lonni had run to. "So you don't know then how they reacted to Henry's death."

"No, but I can imagine. Or maybe I *can't*. You won't believe how hysterical they became. I never would have expected Jayne to throw away her career. To retire, yes. But to get involved in this? That's not like her. And Rashmi—ha! I think he believes he has self-control. Hardly! He gives you nothing while he churns inside. Omar you could almost understand. He was just a prick. I couldn't tell if I hated him or Rashmi more. Or Jayne. Or Mileen. I only liked Henry. And he was killed!"

Ranglen let silence brood for a moment. "And then you came here."

"And then I came here. I *like* it here."

"But why, Lonni? Why live like this?"

"You tell me! You're the big writer, aren't you? That's what Mileen said. Whoever listens to people like me? All of you just want to plunge ahead and build more things like Annulus. But if this world's so great then why are people like us beneath it? Why do we have to hide here? That's bad planning, don't you think? Faulty engineering? Didn't anyone realize we'd clutter up the system? There are a lot of us here, you know. And we have lives. We're *people*, dammit! Or do you just want to forget that?"

"But you're not safe. If I can find you then anyone can."

"I don't care! None of us do."

"But you *do* care. You wouldn't be talking to me if you didn't. Let me get Hatch to find you a pilot, fly you to some other world."

"I've already flown away—to here. And I don't need to be reminded I can't pilot anymore."

"I can help you."

"I don't want your help! None of us do. I've joined a community—we're isolated here but we understand each other. You're not part of it. You think you're sympathetic but it's just pity—or bad taste. All of you don't like this blemish in your world. It's embarrassing, proof that people have run away while you play all your phony stupid games."

"Lonni, we—"

"You thought the Clips would change everything. But it's all show, just different people exchanging places. New names but old structures. New wealth throwing out the old. We'll still be here. We'll outlast all of you because you don't want us. Even if everything changed we'd still be discarded. What difference would it make?"

"But you can't—"

"Look, I'm tired! You got what you wanted. Leave me now. Like everyone does. You're just here to use me anyway and throw me back. It's best that you go."

"Wait, I—"

"There's nothing more I can tell you. It's enough. Just leave me alone."

"Mileen—she—"

"The *hell* with Mileen! *Damn* Mileen! Damn all of you."

"I still need to know—"

"You've learned enough. Really, it's time." She waved her big pistol at him.

Ranglen stared at the front of its barrel. Then at her—in a weird poised face-off match. He asked, as if the answer were casual, "Where did you get that gun?"

She surprised him by replying. "It was part of the cargo on board the ship. An Arms-Watch special. We all took one—and sometimes we were close to using them on each other. One probably killed Henry."

"Didn't anyone notice the guns were missing when you got back?"

She smiled bleakly. "No one said a word."

"What does it shoot?"

"High impact precision darts. Little splinters. Very nasty."

Ranglen felt ill. "One at a time, or in a continuous stream?"

"One at a time. Rather interesting, eh? I heard that Henry had five wounds. But who the hell would shoot him *five separate times*? And who would be sick enough to make them in a circle just like those in the corpses on the ship? Do you have the answer to that? Do you see now why I came here? And do you understand why I want you to *leave*? Now! This minute!"

Yes, he understood. But he didn't see how coming here made her more safe. And knowing how Henry had been shot haunted him now as much as it did her. He had hoped the death was accidental, or self-defense, but now he knew it was obviously intended.

He said, with a sincerity he hoped was evident, "Lonni, please, let me help you."

"I know I'm in danger. I know better than you do. And I also know you can't protect me."

"I think it's worse than you believe."

"You don't know what I'm living through. How can they hurt me any worse than this?"

"You're *alive*. You could lose that."

"Yeah, well…"

"I beg you, let me—"

She extended her gun-arm until the pistol's barrel loomed close to him. "I'm serious. It's time for you to go. Just…get out."

But there was so much more to learn from her. She had described Mileen in ways that shocked him. He felt this might be his only chance. She'd probably move on, go more underground. "What you tell me could save lives."

"You just want the Clip."

"I told you—"

"Oh, I'm *sorry*! I forgot! You already have one! But then what you *really* want is just to know more about your darling Mileen."

He couldn't disagree.

"Look. What do you want from me? What can I give you that you don't have already? What have *you* ever suffered? What do you write about? Mileen liked you but I don't know why, and I never understood what she was after. What do people like you live for? What do you believe in?"

She stopped for a moment, and because she left an opening, he gave her his answer. "I believe in you."

She just glared at him, with no snappy return. But she said, "You're crazy. And you still better leave. I don't want to be anyone's reason for existing."

"You're a survivor, Lonni. I couldn't do what you've done."

"I'm desperate. I wouldn't do it otherwise. And I wouldn't wish this on anybody."

"Still, we—"

"I want you to go!"

"Lonni, please…"

"Get out! Now! Leave! This moment!"

He moved reluctantly toward the open flaps. "Just…be careful. And if you ever want out of here, or away from Annulus, just let me know. I'll see you make it safely." He thought of giving her his card-link—but after what happened with Henry he didn't.

"Don't expect to hear from me," she said.

"And don't allow people to approach you as easily as I did."

"I'll manage." She waved the dart-gun. "I'll keep this close."

She still didn't move from where she stood, obviously knowing she was guarded there and not willing to give up the advantage. He admired her for that.

With regret, he left.

As he maneuvered away from the hut, he saw that the cantilevers around him were spotted with little habitats like Lonni's. Not many, but enough. A few faces peeked out, then disappeared when he looked more closely. The refugees of the great diaspora, the ones fallen behind and making a community here—in the light of a faux underwater grotto. They had only themselves.

Did the blueprint for Annulus include them too? Were the Airafane wise enough—or callous enough—to see that even their incredible gifts would not get around to everyone? Ranglen doubted it. Annulus was a surface world, literally, all laid out for everyone to see, and down here people built the true human addition—what humans always do best, make a sub-sub-basement, an underground.

Which, Ranglen remembered, Anne had said was his own favorite environment.

He hurried away, upward, toward light.

But he caught a glimpse of what he believed was the spike-haired man he and Hatch saw at the spaceport. The man poked his head around a stanchion and watched him. He didn't have his dark datafeed glasses now.

He disappeared the instant Ranglen noticed him.

Ranglen side-stepped in pursuit. He hurried onto a connecting catwalk—not very quickly or comfortably because of his grip sleeves and the light gravity. Vistas of latticework rushed by, infinity shots down tunnels of supports.

He reached the spot where the man had stood. It was empty.

Then he heard—felt—a whisk of air beneath his chin.

A dart stabbed the buttress beside him.

It had missed his neck by only centimeters, then dissolved in a little cloud of mist.

The unstated message was clear: I could have killed you. Just wanted you to know. He glanced around, saw nothing.

Ranglen believed the man *allowed* himself to be seen, that he wanted Ranglen to know the threat behind the near miss of the dart. It must be the same weapon that Lonni had.

The kind that surely killed Henry.

Ranglen felt sick. Maybe Lonni was right. Maybe he was in more danger than even *he* believed.

Chapter Seven: Balrak

Ranglen's hotel stood near a crossroads of the rapid transit lines that laced Annulus. Someday the area might grow into a town but now it was little more than several motels, general stores, restaurants, and support services for travelers, whether tourists in self-contained shuttle cars or the drivers of heavy transport. Most drivers avoided automatic guidance systems to maintain a "frontier" mood, but the roads contained power-grids so true independent steering was not allowed. Ranglen enjoyed the feeling of adventure such road-stops provided, a sense of on-the-go.

As he passed through the lobby of his hotel, an elderly woman sitting on a couch stood up and approached him. "Mr. Ranglen," she said in a firm voice, "could I speak with you?"

She wore a vest with many pockets and loops for tools, stiff leggings, thick boots. It looked like efficient working-wear, and it obviously had seen much use. The clothes contributed to her worn but dependable appearance, like that of a knowledgeable trouble-shooter, and she moved with an authority that long ago she stopped bothering to hide. Her graying hair was managed if not attractive, and she had a weathered woody face that added to the impression of her strength.

"I imagine so. Who are you?" But he already guessed.

"I'm Jayne Fowler. I and a friend would like to talk with you."

"Rashmi Verlock?"

She nodded, showed no surprise he guessed correctly. Ranglen remembered such an attitude from others who chased Clips. Surprise never seemed to strike them again. "He's waiting in the restaurant next door. There's no room or privacy here to talk."

Ranglen kept his sarcasm to himself. He wanted to tell her the two of them were foolish for being here so obviously in view, but he was too tired after his long day.

He followed her through the door. Nearby, further along the shuttle lines, stood a "Square Meal," part of a modular chain throughout Annulus. The swooping rainbow bridge in the sky provided backdrop.

Inside, the woman led him to an isolated booth where a darker man sat. Rashmi Verlock seemed made of stares and overcooked nerves. His face leaned forward till his eyelids covered the tops of his irises, which made him seem distrustful. The day-old black stubble on his chin matched the two-week bristle on his scalp. He must have shaved his head after returning from the derelicts—Ranglen could not imagine why. He wore a short-sleeved white shirt and white pants, which didn't make sense either. He stood out too much, and Ranglen assumed that the last thing Rashmi wanted was to be noticed. Maybe he felt light clothes were less obvious under infrared surveillance.

Ranglen frowned at his own intolerance. He was becoming too cranky, and Lonni had left him with feelings of remorse, confusion, fear, especially after the final dart-shooting. But so much emotion had degenerated into sarcasm. And he wanted to be alone—to review what he had learned, to plan his escape routes. And as he hadn't eaten since breakfast, he intended to order a full meal no matter what these two wanted to talk about.

"Mr. Ranglen," Jayne said, as if she and Rashmi had agreed she should do the talking—while Rashmi probed him with his deep-from-under stare. "We want to interest you in a business deal."

"The last person who talked to me about that is dead."

His crude comment didn't unsettle them. Jayne said blankly, "We need your help."

"You need *more* than my help. And I'm not feeling very generous today."

Rashmi squeezed his lips tighter.

Before Jayne could say anything more, the waiter came. Ranglen ordered: gene-tailored white turkey with vegetable dressing, shaved yellow cucumber-corn, grain potatoes in white apple skins, burnt-rice biscuits with olive butter, a Cronenburg salad with deviled sprouts, and a big pitcher of iced tea. The waiter smiled in appreciation.

Jayne and Rashmi looked appalled.

"I'm hungry," Ranglen said.

The waiter stared at the other two and waited. They ordered only water, apparently all that their stomachs could handle. The waiter left.

Ranglen said to them, "Look, I'm sorry if I'm impolite, but someone shot at me today. The police don't like me. I'm missing some friends. And all I can tell you, you already know."

Ignoring everything Ranglen just said, Rashmi's words came out narrow and hissing. "There *has* to be a way. How can something so small be found on a whole planet?"

Ranglen was impressed that Rashmi had come right to the point. "It's not found. It finds you."

Rashmi looked both disgusted and angry. Ranglen knew how he felt.

Jayne insisted, "They've been found in the past."

"But there's no consistency. Those finds were half accidents."

"So we should look for 'accidents'? Just sit around and wait?" Jayne, at least, maintained a dry humor.

Ranglen went through it all again, plate tectonics, surveillance satellites. He wondered if he should just distribute brochures. He was annoyed he had nothing new to add, and he was growing sick of treasure-hunters. Lonni, in her drastic hideaway, struck him as more noble than either of these two.

And their disappointment showed a dangerous mania, especially painful to see in Jayne, who seemed an unlikely bearer of it (Rashmi appeared more at home). They didn't want to believe that most of the decision-making, however vague and fraught with probability, came from the Clips. No one ever did. Even Ranglen was tired of the notion. Why should ancient relics be in charge?

Jayne and Rashmi looked about the restaurant as if to make sure they weren't being watched. A little late, Ranglen thought. If the police were near they were recording every word.

And where the hell *were* the police? Why weren't they popping out of the walls right now? Didn't this table have everything they wanted?

Rashmi said finally, in a voice so sad and wistful it was comic, "So…we look for mid-ocean ridges."

Ranglen tried to stay expressionless. The line without its context sounded absurd.

Jayne leaned forward. "Look, we're in no position to bargain. Henry assured us you'd be fair to deal with so we're being frank. We want you to come with us. We'll grant you a third of all we make."

As usual, Ranglen hated predictability, in other people as well as himself. And this invitation was pure cliché.

But this time, he seriously considered accepting. Finding the Clip was becoming more crucial the longer he couldn't find Mileen, and they would have the coordinates for where the world should be found. The problem was that, if he did go with them, he'd give the Clip straight to the authorities, to keep the police busy and thus steered away from Mileen and himself.

Jayne and Rashmi wouldn't approve.

And, if he went, he'd also be compromising his own freedom. The two would quickly grow suspicious of him and never let him out of their sight, making sure he remained the guide. They didn't need to give him the coordinates anyway—they could take him to the world "blindfolded" where they'd just order him to unearth the Clip.

The waiter brought the drinks. The tea wasn't sweetened. Ranglen complained and the waiter left to bring more.

To see how they'd respond, he said, "You'd give me a third of all you make? What about the others? You weren't the only ones to find the coordinates."

Their expressions went blank, as if the plan they followed was so established it could never be challenged. Jayne said, "The others have gone their ways. Rashmi and I are working together." Rashmi didn't grunt or blink.

"All right," Ranglen said. "This is my final word. I'm sorry, but *no*. I wish you both luck. I'll do nothing to hinder you. But you're in terrible danger—and you've put *me* in danger. I'm probably being watched, and you also because of Henry. When the police learn what this is about—and I'm sure they're close to it by now—you might have a thousand people following you."

Desperation heightened Jayne's voice. "We're out of our league. We know that."

"I urge you to report what you know to the authorities. I told Henry how to do that."

Jayne looked abandoned. Rashmi held in his breath so tightly that Ranglen tried not to laugh, or sympathize. Where was Jayne's rationality now, or Rashmi's business sense? They had trashed not only their vocations but their selves.

The waiter brought Ranglen's meal, then glanced hopefully at the other two customers. They looked more glum than before. He slunk away.

Ranglen dug in.

Rashmi muttered to Jayne, "So...I guess we *are* on our own now."

Ranglen offered helpfully, "You want some of my turkey?"

Their expressions didn't change.

They stood up to leave—ignoring the water they had been served.

But Ranglen gestured for them to sit again. "Wait a minute. Maybe you do have something I want."

They paused, sat down.

"I'm trying to find Mileen. Do you know where she is?"

Disappointment lined their faces. This time they were the ones terse and practical. "You know what we know," Jayne said. "We have nothing more."

"Did she want to find the lifeboat because of a possible survivor?"

They showed no surprise at his question, but Jayne withdrew her hands across the table and her eyes locked on him more tightly.

She knows something, Ranglen thought.

Rashmi broke in, "How did you learn what Mileen wanted?"

"That's not part of the bargain."

Rashmi jumped at that. "So there's a 'bargain' between us? Will you come with us then?" His business-sense now came forth, if too late and a little thin.

"I said no. But I told you everything about finding Clips. You at least could tell me what you know about Mileen."

Rashmi simmered with anger, which told Ranglen he had nothing to trade.

But Jayne...she seemed too pensive and careful, as if trying to make a decision but fighting it.

Ranglen asked, "Something you're not telling me?"

"I don't have to talk about it."

Ranglen waited.

Maybe kindness, or a belief in fair trade-offs, made her say, "Look for her on the planet where the lifeboat went."

Ranglen sneered. "That's *obvious*. I've thought of that already."

Jayne shrugged. "You asked. I answered. Take it or leave it."

"You're hiding something."

Jayne stood up again.

"Wait!" And Ranglen said directly to Rashmi, "Do you know why your boss, Anne Montgomery, had a security breach? Before—and during—your trip to Ventroni?"

Rashmi resumed his stoniness, said nothing.

Ranglen tried again, "Do you know why she might have lied about Mileen being with you on that trip?"

Still no change. Yet Jayne looked thoughtful.

"And who has spikey blond hair?"

Jayne and Rashmi glanced at each other as if pondering whether they should answer him. They didn't.

"Okay," Ranglen said. "That's it. Let me eat now. Goodbye...good luck!"

Not hesitating this time, Jayne marched toward the door. Rashmi followed as if leashed to her.

Ranglen soon regretted his tone. He felt that Jayne probably knew nothing. Lonni said Jayne had been lax in not looking for the RLV, so maybe she just felt some latent guilt over Mileen insisting they find it.

Still, he should have controlled his impatience. He felt he shut her down.

He finished his meal, not enjoying it, and paid his check.

As he hurried out the door he saw a huge limo parked nearby. He recognized it as the one he and Hatch had seen unloaded at the spaceport—beige and white and dark red, with extensions that made it look hostile. He glanced at the car's tinted windows but couldn't see who sat inside.

Someone stepped in front of him, a man with spiked honey-colored hair—the one he had seen back at the spaceport and the one who presumably had shot at him near Lonni's. The man was slim but looked powerful, with stern deep-set eyes. He wore a sleeveless black t-shirt, obviously to show off his tattooed muscles, and gray work pants with many pockets that bulged, perhaps with weapons. He was handsome in a stark unfinished way, but the face was dirty and unshaven, and the hair—even *his* hair—looked unkempt.

He said, with a casual hardness, "A person I represent wants to talk with you."

Ranglen couldn't help saying, "I'm just so popular today."

The man's surliness didn't change.

"Let me guess," Ranglen said. "You're Omar Mirik."

Unlike Jayne and Rashmi, Omar was taken aback, which surprised Ranglen. He also looked overworked, his eyes heavy, his hands shaking, in a state where he *could* be surprised. He admitted nothing, which Ranglen took as yes.

"And the man I'm to meet is in that limo over there?"

Omar nodded with a jerk of his head. His lack of politeness seemed natural to him.

"I didn't say yes," Ranglen said.

"A friend of yours was killed. You want the same?"

The words threatened but—weirdly—the voice did not. There was more going on here than Ranglen understood, a contradiction between the man and his manner. If this *was* the same person who had shot at him, then his mood had changed.

"Lead on," Ranglen said.

As he approached the plush vehicle, its wealth and gloss stirred apprehension. Ranglen realized he now had encountered all of the crew and passengers on the trip to Ventroni—except Mileen. And he didn't believe she was in the limo. So, who was?

Omar lifted the door and Ranglen entered, followed by Omar who slid in beside him onto sleek and luxurious upholstery that had that delicious new-vehicle smell.

A man sat across from him in subdued light.

His hair stood out first, a thin cap of distinguished white-gray. Then his face, chiseled, roughly etched by what must be a brutal history, an age with a toll not in years but in intensity. The eyes shone a disconcerting pale brown, almost golden, like dark glass. He looked freshly shaved, not a trace of the gray-white hair on his overly bronzed skin. His immaculate outfit was costly but not showy—a full-sleeved white silk shirt, a dark red vest-like wrap, beige pants with no trace of wrinkle. He looked like his car, with a similar hint of monkish aggression. The power and affluence of the clothes, the vehicle, and his self-assured look spoke volumes. Omar Mirik was out-classed.

"Mr. Ranglen," the man said, his voice deep, vast, oceanic. "My name is Reese Balrak. I'm a businessman from Ventroni. I'm sure you've never heard of me."

Ranglen knew he didn't need to acknowledge but he shook his head.

"I've been informed by Mr. Mirik here of the possible location of a Clip. Obviously, I want to find this object. I ask for your help. I know you've discovered a Clip in the past. I know that others already have asked for your service. I believe you've refused them. I'm certain I can be more generous than they." He glanced briefly toward Omar and nodded.

Mirik opened the door, exited. He closed it behind him and walked to the front of the car—a kilometer away. He entered the driver's dome, or the control room (Ranglen barely heard it opening, the insulation was that good). The car moved forward with a purr. Under its own power and direction, it left the small town behind and glided along a non-automated road—such roads on Annulus were usually reserved for official vehicles. That Balrak could use one demonstrated his influence.

Ranglen said, "So, you're from Ventroni?"

"Yes, though I have interests here on Annulus and on other worlds as well."

"Someone told me your planet is riddled with gangsters." Ranglen's defense against mounting nervousness was to get snide. He knew it wasn't smart, but as he learned with Jayne and Rashmi, the long day had made him rash. He frightened himself with the cracks he made.

Balrak spoke with calm precision. "Whoever said that is welcome to an opinion. I'd agree that Ventroni harbors a great share of 'entrepreneurs extreme.'"

Ranglen admired the phrase. "I'm sorry. As I've told others today, I just can't help you. It's nothing personal. You're all welcome to your efforts. It's just...out of the question."

Balrak's smile was almost charming. "Mirik told me you would refuse. You apparently feel no one has control over finding the Clips. I'm certain you're wrong."

"I'm certain I'm right. And you don't have much faith in my expertise if you deny what I say."

"I think that, instead of being unable to help, you're only being *selectively* helpful."

"Maybe I'm being selectively careful."

"Then you're not being careful enough. You're in grave danger, Mr. Ranglen, which I'm sure you know. From other people, but also from myself."

It was getting harder for Ranglen to cover his tension. "Let's go with you first. Why don't you tell me why?"

Balrak smiled again. "Look around you. Look at this car. I represent great wealth and influence. Obviously Mirik will do exactly what I tell him, including acts of physical—and fatal—violence."

Ranglen said, to show he wasn't totally in the dark, "So he came to you with the story about the Clip. He wanted you—and he—to get to it before anyone else could."

"That's not quite true but it doesn't matter. He knew I had the resources to reach it before others."

"I'm sure. But then why am I in danger? Are you threatening me?" This struck even Ranglen as a foolish question but he couldn't help being obtuse.

For the first time, Balrak seemed to enjoy the conversation. Till then, it was polite but predictable dealing. "Would you like a demonstration?"

"Look, I—"

Balrak grabbed Ranglen's left wrist and twisted it, hyperflexed it, pulled the arm and rotated the shoulder—forced Ranglen down. Balrak's knee then shoved into his back against the spine, thrust him lower till his ribs pressed into the carpet. The move trapped Ranglen's right arm so he couldn't respond with a palm-shove to the chin. Balrak pressed harder—Ranglen lost his breath, his stomach threatening to heave.

All this happened in a second.

"Do I make my point?" Balrak said.

Choking, Ranglen nodded.

Balrak let go of him and sat back down. Ranglen reseated himself and tried to settle his upset stomach. He regretted the size of his recent meal.

"You won't be sick, Mr. Ranglen. But you might want to be."

Ranglen leaned back slowly, gently. "You're enhanced?"

"To a certain extent, but more I've just kept in shape. I could do that three times before you could react, break both of your wrists. Kill you, cripple you, give you wounds that would cause great pain but not leave any marks. I can do anything I want with you. I hope you see that and I don't have to prove it. Mirik's not needed to persuade you physically. I'm better."

Ranglen felt the pain diminish, but he still feared nausea. That alone gave all the advantage to Balrak. He glanced at the doors to see if they were locked.

"They're not locked," Balrak said. "But you're not going anywhere at the moment. Shall we continue?"

Ranglen forced himself to breathe steadily.

Trees and fields passed by behind the darkened windows. Ranglen felt in another world—Balrak's world. "Okay. I grant that you can hurt me." He swallowed a bad taste in his mouth.

"I said you won't be sick."

"I'm not convinced."

Balrak looked briefly out the window but then faced his captive. "While you regain your composure, let me tell you several things.

"I'm a man of a specific faith. Faith hasn't survived the Clips very well. All the old religions of Earth have undergone difficult transitions, and they have not re-defined themselves quickly enough to maintain relevance in today's world. Of course, they'll manage to do so in time. Religions always adapt to survive. They claim they have eternal answers and yet they change as society changes. But my own personal faith has never been shaken. It doesn't alter, and it's something I cherish because it sustains me. It is tied to no doctrine or set of laws. It's not a product of history or culture. It is strictly mine. And it works, always—far better than anything else we know."

Ranglen gave no reaction.

"I won't go into detail, for you wouldn't understand. But let's just say I believe in something larger than you or me, larger than humanity—and larger than any mythological creator that early civilizations always seem to need. I am committed to this belief. It brings me a purpose. And I am not kind to people who stand in the way of my progress. I am...absolutist...in matters of will.

"Forgive me if I'm bragging but I'm trying to help you, to provide you with support for a decision you soon will need to make. I myself am not violent but I can create violence, through actions of my own or those of others. I can orchestrate it and make it quite memorable. I often need subterfuge so I can do what I want. For example, I can kill and never get caught. I *have* killed. And yet I still maintain a free and ample lifestyle. For all my powers, I am very private. I seldom talk. I give orders but I seldom elaborate. I've never described these characteristics to anyone. I hope you realize how privileged you are in hearing this."

Ranglen felt a little over-privileged but he duly nodded—which he shouldn't have done, for he felt the motion deep in his stomach.

"You're lying, Mr. Ranglen. You've never met anyone like me before. You don't know how to respond to statements like mine. You joke at them and try to distance yourself. You play the fool to maintain a barrier. I know all about your defense mechanisms. And you, in turn...you know all about privilege, don't you?"

Ranglen's pulse quickened. "What do you mean?"

"Ah? No attempt to joke this time? You do know what I'm getting at, don't you?" Balrak's smugness seemed a permanent part of him.

"I assume I'll be enlightened."

Balrak grinned. "I expect such lines from you. You never let people know how much you really *are* privileged, do you? You like to keep your secrets to yourself. Too much to yourself, I have to add."

A dark fear swelled inside Ranglen. Physical pain was threatening enough but Balrak now aimed for something deeper, personalized for Ranglen alone.

"And, by the way, that police investigator—the tall one, Hathaway—he knows things that would surprise you. You should watch out for him."

This brought Ranglen's fear to a higher level. "Just what are you getting at?"

Balrak straightened his vest. It had been slightly tilted in the scuffle before. "I, along with a small group of people, know that you found the third Clip, that ultimately you are responsible for the creation of Annulus. This has given you certain freedoms, and quite a lot of money, more than what most people have here."

Ranglen muttered, "I'm a light spender."

"Yes, I know. I've studied you extensively. I've read *everything* you've written, and everything written about you. I've had people watch you, research you and analyze you. I've studied their reports and I've ordered up more. And all this quite recently."

Ranglen waited.

"Let me tell you what I've learned. You prefer freedom more than anything else. You don't want to be tied down by possessions, by any heap of material 'things.' You buy big houses and then you don't live in them. You follow a life of escape routes and getaways. You like people to think you're paranoid. You *yourself* like to think you're paranoid. But in truth, you're not, or at least not that much. You just feel that you, that everyone, should simply live *as if* paranoid…vigilant, guarded. You indulge in quirks of dramatic fantasy. You prefer your shadows, hide-outs, undergrounds, exits, and you cherish secrets like an addiction. It's almost obsessive, but maybe it's more just a neurotic tick that never stops ticking, driving you, consuming you."

Ranglen didn't dare make a comment.

"And you're always on the go. You never stay in one place long enough to share of yourself. You favor a quaint self-imposed exile. What was it you once said? 'I don't mind being alone, as long as I have a good view.' Yes, I've had people talk to your friends, take notes on you. You're an anachronism, Mr. Ranglen, a Romantic poet in an age that doesn't believe in romanticism or your special blend of gothic isolation. It doesn't matter if it's valid or not. You simply like that role. You choose your aloneness. You *want* to hide. And the funny thing is…*I understand.*

"I know what it's like to be different. No one believes as I believe. No one supports my cause as no one supports yours. I bet you feel that people read your books for all the wrong reasons. I can relate to that. Under other circumstances we'd have so much to share and talk about."

Ranglen couldn't help mocking him. "You're a Romantic poet too?"

Balrak smiled with near warmth. "Actually, to maintain that imagery, you might say I'm more the Satanic hero...Byron with teeth. While you, you're from one of those period landscape paintings, the slug on a mountainside poised under an avalanche. You're the victim facing annihilation."

The almost-friendly tone of these lines chilled Ranglen. "So, what *is* your cause?"

"Let's call it triumphant individualism. You understand that, don't you? You and I both have our secrets, and maybe yours are even bigger than mine."

Ranglen waited, dreading.

"You see...only I—and a very few others, mostly in the Federal Investigators of Earth—know your *real* secret."

The threat of nausea stirred in him again.

"You didn't find just the third Clip," Balrak said. "You found the *fourth*."

Ranglen tried to keep a straight expression. How the hell did Balrak learn this?

"I must say you look terrible, Mr. Ranglen. Will you be sick after all? Have I made a mistake? I can get you something for your stomach, or a mild sedative."

"I'll manage."

"I wouldn't want you to leave with any permanent harm."

"Have to cover your tracks, eh?"

"No, not really. I can do whatever I want. There's really no one out there who can stop me. But, to avoid any complications, I did hurt you in a way so no marks were left—as I think you know."

"Very thoughtful of you."

"Let's get back to the point. You've performed an incredible task, something no one else in history has succeeded in doing."

Ranglen kept still.

"You're the only person who has found *two* Clips. *In a row*. That makes you rather special. Rather *fantastically* special, I might add."

Ranglen wanted a smart comeback but he didn't have any.

"So, given those reasons, I'm here to offer you a job. I want you to work for me. *Me*, exclusively."

"I was just lucky in finding those Clips."

"That's ridiculous! You've got a *method*, and I want it."

"It was coincidence."

"I don't believe you, and even if that were true, it still would make your resume very impressive."

"I don't want to find another Clip."

"I can understand. What more could you hope to get with it? You don't care about fame. You've got money. You don't appear to seek universal happiness—as I understand it, anyway. But, clearly, there's something...or, should I say, some*one*...that you do want."

His pulse beat even faster.

"I'll be honest with you, Mr. Ranglen. I don't know where Mileen Oltrepi is. I wish I did know, for I'd find her, hold a knife to her throat and threaten you with slicing her...just to have control of you. If I ever do find her that's probably what I'll do. But I don't think I'll have to."

And then, at that very unfortunate moment, Ranglen's cellpad made a soft buzz.

Ranglen was furious—he hadn't silenced it but set it to vibrate, which made a noise just loud enough to be heard.

He knew what the message was. He had programmed the machine that morning to respond to only one call.

A return message from Mileen.

"You intend to answer that?" Balrak said.

"You'd let me?"

"Mr. Ranglen, I'm not imposing restrictions on you. I intend for you to come to me and work for me willingly. Soon I'll drop you off at a transport station and you can return to your hotel. I'm not kidnapping you."

"I'm shocked."

The buzz persisted.

"Will you please answer that?"

Ranglen pulled out his cellpad slowly. His hand shook.

The buzz stopped. He checked the display and felt slightly better. "No audio or text," he said. "It's just an acknowledgement." With no caller identified.

"Who is it from?"

Ranglen's mind raced. "The police."

"Let me see."

If Ranglen hesitated he'd reveal too much. He handed over the cellpad.

Balrak checked the display. "It says here your call went out at 2:49 this morning. That was right after the police came to see you."

He was beyond being surprised at what Balrak knew.

"What did you say in the call?"

"I reported a connection to a possible suspect in Henry's murder."

"And the police are just responding now?"

"I told them to leave an acknowledgment if they found anything."

Balrak scrolled through the menus. "The message you sent to them isn't here. Nor is the present caller identified."

"They were scrambled and automatically deleted."

"Why?"

"The *Clips*, for God's sake! You know how people act!"

Balrak didn't say anything. But he scanned further through different files. "The call you just got—all that it says here is 'message received.'"

"Like I told you, it was just an acknowledgment." Ranglen felt immensely grateful that Mileen hadn't been talkative.

"Why wouldn't the police say what they found?"

"I was supposed to follow up myself. Come into the station."

"That seems silly. Why would they bother?"

Ranglen shrugged.

Balrak searched. "The destination of your call isn't given either. Nor is the source of the incoming message."

"Those were also scrambled. It's a good security program. If you want a copy, I'll send it to you."

"Why do you need to cover your tracks so well?"

"Paranoia's good for you. It keeps you on your toes."

A hint of a smile. "Yes, that's the tone I heard you would use."

From *who*, goddammit?

"What suspect did you tell the police about?"

"Some gangster on Ventroni."

Balrak's smile got wider.

He handed back the cellpad.

"Speaking of messages," he said, "I will expect a call from you in a day or two, depending on how long it takes you to recover from our talk. You then will offer me your help."

"'Recover'?"

"You'll understand. Someone like me can be a disturbance in such a sedate life as yours. There's just you and your 'exploration' as you call it, that 'haunted blend of nostalgia and longing that drives one to alien worlds.' You said that in your writing, remember? I admired the line. I empathize. I've often felt that way myself. I know how insubstantial such a feeling can make you seem, 'like some ancient mariner from a deep past when landscapes were still sacred.' I liked that line too. You're elegant, Mr. Ranglen. Maybe the passion is a bit too existential, maybe it's too fraught with defensive sarcasm, but I know that feeling—how it keeps one alive, builds the desire that remains pure. Yes, I'm familiar with all you say. I know much more about you than what you think."

Ranglen said nothing.

"And I believe we've reached your drop-off point."

He didn't like Balrak's use of "drop-off," or "recover," yet he couldn't see any stereotypical threats outside—no cliffs, rapids, wrecking crews, artillery. Just a transport station in an open field, and a small station at that.

Omar stopped the car, grimly walked back and flung open the door for Ranglen.

Balrak said, "I hope to hear from you soon. I'm sure we can work together."

Ranglen's mind was in too much turmoil to come up with a reply. Mirik didn't look at him as he stepped from the car, but stared at Balrak instead, with what appeared to be anger.

The driver-enforcer-steward-snitch slammed the door and tramped back to the driver's dome, reminding Ranglen of how he had acted at Hatch's spaceport. Then he gunned the engine and sped the car away. It had no wheels and thus flew on its own gravity plate. Very expensive.

A convulsion swept through Ranglen. The sudden release of tension caused a burst in his stomach. He threw up his dinner.

When his insides settled he looked around. The station was isolated. Nothing stood by it but the track for the shuttle and automated vehicles, the flat surface of the utility road which Balrak had used so blithely, and a lot of yellow grass that swung up and away in a graceful curve, to join the flattened rainbow in the sky. He saw just one person sitting at the station.

His stomach still bothered him, as well as his self-esteem and confidence, but he felt more in control now. Encouraging his "recovery" was the realization—he could allow himself now to feel it—that Mileen was alive, and that he knew where she was. The acknowledgement he received was also an admission of location, which Ranglen knew the message intended, and it was nearer than any world where the lifeboat from the derelict could have landed. He had been terrified in the car that she might say something—be reassuring, explain her absence.

Thankfully, she had not.

But he was shocked that Balrak hadn't kept him. The biggest power he had over Ranglen—Mileen—he had given up, admitted he didn't know where she was.

He looked around him, scanning for threats as he walked up the ramp to the station's platform. He didn't cross to the opposite side, avoiding the other person, apparently a woman in a long coat and hood.

A fear lurched in him—maybe this was Mileen. Based on what he saw of Balrak, he was sure the man could pull such a trick.

Black hair curled out around the edge of the hood. He breathed more easily. Mileen's hair was red.

He walked closer. The person didn't acknowledge him, didn't look up.

Ranglen noticed a dark pool on the cement in front of her, the bench stained with it too.

Carefully, Ranglen moved nearer. He leaned down so he could see the face beneath the hood.

The woman was Anne.

A hole sat in the middle of her forehead. Blood caked her black hair.

Ranglen, in a daze, cautiously pulled aside the coat. Holes poked the black dress she had worn that morning—a small circle of puncture wounds, covered with blood.

In her lap under the coat sat an open metal case with instruments inside, plastic casings with wires, large cylinders, the illuminated screen of a cheap clock. The case was tied to her waist with a chain.

The alarm on the clock suddenly wailed.

Ranglen jumped—the noise screamed in all that stillness. Then the alarm stopped, as surprising as when it started.

Ranglen looked into the case again.

The numbers on the clock had changed to a 10, and then the seconds clicked down. 9. 8.

By 7 he realized what he was seeing.

6 passed before he could move.

At 5 he ran.

He reached the edge of the platform when a blast of hot air slammed him in his back, flung him outward on a roaring gust. The air glowed around him and he felt terrible heat. In an instant he knew that Balrak had cheated—the explosion was set at 3, not zero.

He was in a billow of fire—and about to hit the ground.

Chapter Eight: Pia and Hussein

Ranglen awoke in a hospital bed. He pushed through shrouds of semi-delirium and found the face of Pia Folinari.

"Good morning," she said to him, all peaches and cream.

Her face suddenly looked so appealing. He muttered, "Am I alive?"

"Yes, of course, but you were bruised, burned, and unconscious for a while. It helped that you were running when the explosion occurred. They can tell that, you know, what you were doing. But no one cares about forensics anymore."

Ranglen groaned at her cynicism. He tried to move but most of his body was too numb, or hurt.

"You relax," she said. "I'll come back later."

Before he let himself fall back asleep, which he dearly wanted to do, he said, "Am I under arrest or something?"

She sounded disappointed. "No, we hardly suspected you. Besides, we're off the case. I think they felt we were too petty for this. 'Leave him alone,' they said. You must have some very powerful friends."

"Not a one. But why are you here?"

She looked awkward—he didn't think she could ever appear that way. "I'm on my own. I wanted to make sure you pulled through."

He felt charmed but cautious too. He also had to ask, before the drugged vagueness took over, "Anne...she's...?"

Pia hesitated for just a moment. "Yes. I'm sorry. But she was dead before the blast hit."

"She had puncture wounds. Henry did too, right?"

"Yes. Go to sleep."

"I know who did it."

"So do we, but nobody cares. Just sleep."

And he did.

Much later—at least he believed it was much later—Ranglen awoke but Pia wasn't there.

Damn, he thought. He'd almost looked forward to seeing her as he climbed the rungs to consciousness, though he didn't feel as needy as before.

Nurses came in, made a fuss, watched over him, and then came the doctors who discussed his injuries. They called his experience barotrauma, reaction to a quick change in air pressure—an explosion, in other words.

Though his eardrums were intact, a scalp-laceration from the fall had to be clamped shut, as well as other cuts on his arms. Abrasions and bruises covered his body, especially his hands. He had fallen with arms thrust out to protect himself so his fingers and palms suffered the worst. His knees too, and his elbows. He complained of neck pain but they found no spinal injuries.

His clothes had protected him from most of the burns, but the hair on the back of his head had been charred, the nape of his neck and the backs of his ears badly singed—they all shone red and blistered with first- and second-degree burns. The doctors had applied skin restoration for any damage to the dermis, but these areas were small and the surface wounds could heal on their own.

He experienced some numbness in his left hand and a strange echo in his hearing, so they wanted to keep him under observation till tomorrow. But for being "in fire," he realized his injuries were quite minor.

Ranglen intended to leave early and not wait, as the doctors ordered. Balrak would probably send Omar to check on him. And other people would show up too—all injuries went into a central databank that surely was monitored. Ranglen sighed. His name alone would raise an alarm.

He had to get out of there.

He was still sore, weak from all the medical apps. Pain stabbed him if he moved the wrong way, but he listened carefully to all the instructions about treating his wounds and taking prescriptions.

He tried not to think of Anne.

Pia came to see him. He remembered with an embarrassed smile how he found her attractive when he woke up—the result of trauma, he told himself, victim in distress desperate for attention. Though he was happy she was off the case now, her authority and attitude still scared him.

Big sidekick Hathaway didn't come with her. And she was "dressed up"—in wide green pants and dress heels, a tight and tiny green top beneath a pert little white jacket. Sheer elegance for her, and her greenish-yellow hair even looked styled. She wore big earrings.

He couldn't help teasing her. "You look 'fetching,' like you're going to a fund-raiser."

"Maybe I am."

"Undercover?"

"You never know." She didn't elaborate.

She complimented him for sitting up. "Interesting head-wound. You look like a pirate. How soon are you getting out?"

"Tomorrow....Where's your partner?"

"He doesn't know I stopped here."

Ranglen grinned. "What's between you two anyway?"

She looked sour. "We had a relationship once, but then we were partnered. I said 'no more,' that we had to stop. He wanted more. It's been tense ever since."

"He's crazy about you."

"Partners aren't allowed to be romantically attached. I respect that rule. We're good cops. If we get involved again we'd have to find different partners. I don't want to lose him—as a partner."

Poor Hussein, praised and damned in the same breath. "You looked mighty angry at him when I saw you at Anne's." He wanted to know what Hussein had said about the satellite call.

"He knew information I didn't. You bet I was pissed. And he never told me where he got it either. He didn't act on it, so I figured it was a tip that wasn't in the works yet, that he just wanted to show off, to goad you."

"He succeeded."

"I was furious. But then they took us off the case."

"When?"

"Late yesterday. We were told to back off, that the case was bigger than they thought and other people would handle it. Made me angry. I was having fun questioning you."

"Yeah, you enjoyed reading my poems too."

"They're not my standard reading."

He took from that the best he could.

She said, "I have a question. What's so important about this case that we're called off it? And why do you have access to an Earth-run satellite? What's so special about *you*?"

This visit was professional after all. He shrugged, said nothing.

"Not going to tell me?"

He shrugged again. But he was growing tired of so much deception. He even trusted her—to a certain extent. But his habit of concealment was too ingrained. "Let's just say that certain people are interested in certain acts of mine."

"*That* really helps. You annoy me, Ranglen."

He made a faux gesture of being hurt. She ignored it.

He asked, "If you're off the case, where are the people who're supposed to be on it?"

"No one came to see you today?"

He shook his head.

"Odd." She pondered. "It was odd yesterday too. We were questioning people and we had a tail on you, but we kept getting called back to the station, slowing our work. They knew you talked to Banner, then they lost you and didn't find you again till you entered the limo with Balrak. That's why they got to you right after the explosion."

So they knew about Balrak but not Lonni. He didn't ask about Jayne and Rashmi. "A little coincidental, don't you think, that they knew about Balrak?"

"No. They were watching him since he came here, just to keep tabs on what he might be doing. But it wasn't the closest surveillance."

"Who is he?"

"A big wheel on Ventroni. He's involved in illegal imports and exports—all the standard drugs and contraband. But he also traffics in people, providing labor to opening colonies. Some high-ups think he's even beneficial, finding outlets for the deprived and homeless. Others say he's just a marketer in lives. That's my opinion."

"Slavery?"

"More like indentured servitude or bonded labor. But he has a ruthless hold on the market, and most others that he gets involved in. He usually keeps to himself, stays behind the scenes. That he came to Annulus to deal with you personally was a big shock. Everyone buzzed. But because he *was* involved, they pushed the investigation higher. Homeworld wanted to be part of it too. Hussein and I, after being jerked around, were dismissed. Weird, since Ventroni is not part of Annulus *or* Homeworld jurisdiction. And Ventroni security is touchy about intruders."

"Corruption?"

"You didn't hear that from me."

Ranglen thought of Henry, and Anne. "Why puncture wounds?"

"It's a new weapon from Arms-Watch that shoots darts, little fletchettes. In fact, the ship that Henry was on had a sample cargo. We got from Banner—who, by the way, was hard to get *anything* from—that five guns were missing when the flight from Ventroni landed."

Lonni's pistol must have been one of them. And Omar Mirik's.

Pia misread his pensive expression. "You didn't know Montgomery worked in weapons? Nothing fancy. No terrorist stuff. The fletchettes are designed to dissolve in the body after the puncture. But they can be traced through chemical residues, so they might not sell. Bad investment for Anne....In more ways than one."

Ranglen stared into the space before him.

"Balrak can't be touched," she added. "No one from Annulus has the authority to arrest him."

"He killed Henry too?"

"I assume. The autopsy was inconclusive. They never tested for the darts and by the time they learned about them it was too late. But it's not my concern, not anymore. And...Ranglen—you're still not answering me. What's the big deal? Why would Balrak even come here?"

For Pia to ask the same question twice must be a terrible come-down for her, almost like begging. He took a deep breath. "You'll hate me for saying this, but it's better you don't know."

She frowned. "I expected that. I have a good idea what's going on, though."

"You're probably right. If you are, then you realize you should be glad you're off the case."

"It doesn't make me happy."

Ranglen gave a lopsided smile. "Does *anything* make you happy, Pia?"

She scowled. "Back off, Ranglen. You want me to interrogate you again? Throw you into jail?"

"No, I like you better when you're not a cop."

"Don't kid yourself. I'm *always* a cop."

Ranglen grew quiet.

"And now you're thinking about Anne again."

He nodded, impressed that she knew.

"You're wondering, why her?"

That wasn't correct but he answered anyway, "Balrak wanted me to know he meant business."

"Why did he have to be so emphatic?"

"Maybe it's his style."

"It's not—and that's the point. Normally he operates quietly. He doesn't like to show himself as the man in charge."

"He was away from his own world. New place, new behavior."

"Here he should have been *more* out of sight."

Pia was good, and because of that Ranglen didn't want her probing further. He tried to look preoccupied, that he was losing interest.

"Shutting me out, eh?"

He smiled thinly.

"Clips can be so bitchy, can't they?"

Okay, she had said it. He'd grant her the point and then maybe the two of them could move on. He still almost trusted her. So he acknowledged her statement by not denying it.

She grunted, unsatisfied. "I'll stop asking. And, by the way, be careful when you leave here later."

He avoided looking at her.

"Oh, stop it! I know you'll sneak out as soon as you can. And—a suggestion—you might want to go when the visitors are leaving. There's a lot of activity then. Just be aware they'll notice sooner that you're gone."

He didn't react, and she said nothing more.

He watched her for a spell, appreciating her hard, direct self. "Why are you here, Pia?"

"Don't read too much into it, Ranglen. I get bored. And I don't want to attend this silly dress-up function."

They both were quiet.

"All right," she said. "Time to go, since I don't want to be here when you do something illegal, like leaving the hospital before you're discharged. So take care. I still might read your poetry, but it's making less sense to me now."

He raised his arm and finger to make her wait. "Hey, seriously, I'm glad you came."

"Yeah, yeah."

"You're more than your job, Pia."

"Not when I'm on it."

"You said you weren't working."

"Maybe I lied." She became grave and added, "Look, I have to warn you. You made a mistake now. You asked me about Henry and Anne, but you didn't ask about Mileen. She's been your big concern all along. So…if I *were* on the case, I'd suspect now that you've learned where she is. And, believe me…I'd interrogate the hell out of you and get every bit of information I need."

He kept his face blank.

"So, be careful. If anyone else talks with you, don't make that mistake twice."

He said, before she reached the door, "Thanks for the warning....Say hi to big HH for me."

"Not a chance. He hates your guts."

"Big jealous type, eh?"

"I wouldn't tell *him* that."

She didn't wave as she left, and she didn't look back.

Ranglen felt almost disappointed.

But then he thought only of leaving. He finished eating and placed the tray outside the door so the clean-up crew wouldn't come in. The staff used eating time to catch up on records-keeping so he knew he wouldn't be examined for a while—they usually checked on him every two hours. He didn't wait for the end of the visiting period as Pia had suggested.

He gathered his clothes, stuffed them under his gown and strolled to a restroom down the hallway. It was close to the stairs. He changed inside one of its stalls, hard to do with his bandaged hands but he was learning how to use them. He dumped his hospital gown into the waste dispenser and tried to remove the identifier wristband but couldn't, so he hid it up his sleeve.

Then he walked down the stairwell, passed the reception desk but didn't step through the door. He moved to a separate entrance where supplies were delivered and security would be less. He strolled through the portals untouched.

Much too easy. Had to be something wrong.

"Going somewhere, Mr. Ranglen?"

Sitting by the entrance was big burly brute Hussein.

Ranglen moaned, turned to face him.

Hathaway pulled out his cellpad and entered a code. "You don't have to worry. I just cleared your unauthorized exit from the hospital. They won't search for you."

Ranglen mumbled, "Ah, such power." He was afraid that Pia had maybe set him up. But he didn't see her—and he still wanted to trust her.

"Power cuts both ways," the detective said. "In having it, it sometimes has power over you."

"That's so profound."

"I'm sure you can relate. You don't look too healthy so you better sit. You've got an ugly head-wound."

"Makes me look like a pirate." He was tired already from just that little walk, weaker than he expected, and both his forehead and neck hurt. He blamed it all on running into Hathaway.

He sat gingerly on the hard bench.

"You also look like you changed in a closet. I don't think you would have gotten far, and your wristband has a tracer that would raise an alarm before you left the premises. I'll remove it for you."

"You're too kind."

"Don't mention it."

With a special tool, Hussein removed Ranglen's wristband and tossed it in a receptacle. His style away from Pia seemed more casual and humane, but also more tough. Since Hussein wasn't acting the way Ranglen expected him to, Ranglen remained on close guard.

The cop spoke first, "I think we have some things to discuss."

"You talk like Balrak." Slow, methodical and a little wordy.

"Well, I don't work for him, if that's what you mean. In fact, I work for the same people you do."

This wasn't what Ranglen wanted to hear. He took a long and deep breath.

"I don't feel there's much difference between us," Hussein continued. "But I'm sure you're listed more generously as 'consultant,' or 'paid expert.' I'm just 'informant.' Yet, when you come down to it, aren't we both just spies?"

Ranglen stared at the pavement, said nothing.

"And spies accidentally running into each other—that's rather dicey. No one knows anyone who's really what they are."

Yeah, too wordy. Or maybe he's been reading my poetry, Ranglen thought. He felt nostalgia for the Hathaway who had come to his hotel room, a person more predictable and easier to play. "Could be," was all he said.

"Do we understand each other?"

"Not yet, but I'm curious. You're saying they enlisted you?"

Hathaway sat back and folded his arms. "A number of years ago I got into trouble on Earth. Annulus had just been built, and Homeworld had broken from the Confederacy. So all of us here on the 'High Ring Above New Worlds'—in our own new Security force—were pretty cocky. I visited Earth as a guard for some diplomats but, after hours, I did something I will regret for the rest of my life....I killed someone, and not while on the job. I was provoked and I only meant to hurt him, but, you know...And it's true that you never forget it."

He went on, "I was arrested by the Federal Investigators and, in their own devious little way, they cut me a deal. Earth didn't trust Annulus or Homeworld and they wanted someone 'on the inside,' not to be a steady source of information but just to be available, to be ready if needed. So they dropped the charges and I was able to keep my job.

"And they never bothered me, not for all the years that followed. Not until the day that Pia and I came to *your* room. And then the word's delivered, not even scrambled. They pull me in and say, 'Get Ranglen. We've got a message for him.' So…here I am."

Ranglen felt saddened and tired of it all. A heavy painkiller back in the hospital would be nice at the moment.

Hussein asked, "How did they get to *you?*"

Ranglen's narrowed lips let out breath. "I found the third Clip. That's all they needed."

"You're kidding. Wouldn't that have given *you* all the power?"

"Not when they want the Clips so badly. I got plenty in return. Remember how you and Pia wondered why I was so free to come and go? I have no restrictions on travel. Annulus allowed me that out of gratitude but it wouldn't have meant much if Earth hadn't agreed."

"So you held out on giving them the Clip?"

"It was more complicated but that's a quick way of putting it. I made sure others got it too, including Homeworld. Earth wasn't grateful. After the dust settled, the Federal Investigators wouldn't free me till I agreed to work for them exclusively."

Actually it was a lot more complicated than that.

And it wasn't the third Clip. It was the fourth.

Hathaway looked a little too smug. "So you're on their payroll too."

"No, they don't give me anything, and I'm not attached to any contact. I'm just supposed to let them know when I have a lead on new Clips."

"I guess you didn't do that this time."

Ranglen smiled humorlessly. "I guess you're right."

Hathaway gave an ugly grin. "No wonder they're pissed."

"Was that the message you were supposed to give me?"

"Not in those words."

"Are you pulling me in, turning me over to them?"

"They want to speak to you with 'undivided attention.'"

"To chastise me or take away my rights?"

"I assume they want to shake their sabers at you, or their bombs. Rant a little, bully you, and then order you, 'Do your job!' They'll add some bizarre anti-blessing."

"It seems stupid."

"That's what they do."

"And you're the heavy?"

"I'm supposed to deliver you and then stick around, so...yes, maybe I am."

"I guess you'd be good at that."

"I guess you'd be right."

Ranglen didn't smile. "My recent injuries wouldn't excuse me, eh?"

"You know, I never liked your sarcasm."

"Okay, sorry. But they're not taking me back to Earth, are they?"

"I doubt it. They seem to want you free. Yet they also want your obedience. They intend to wear you down, break you, and then say, 'All right, you can go now. Just bring us what we want.'"

Ranglen grew angry. "They don't *know* what they want."

"They want Clips."

"They want Clips for them*selves*. And they won't get that from me."

"They said you'd be stubborn."

"They all get the Clip if I find it—Annulus, Homeworld, the Confederation—not just Earth. That's *my* side of the bargain."

"You think they'll allow that?"

"They need the Clip first before they can exploit it. They don't have it yet."

"They're aware of that."

"Then why all this nonsense? Why are you even here? If they want me to find it, why get in my way?"

"They want you to find it for *them*."

"And I won't do that! I don't care what they say. They can nail me to Annulus for the rest of my life but they know I need freedom to find new Clips. That's why they gave it to me—and why they were furious when they had to. They want to be in charge of everything—people, history. But Clips take that away from them. The Clips *are* subversive."

"Look, I'm not disagreeing, but—"

"Then why are you doing this?"

"It's my job. I'm a cop."

"But you don't have to be *their* cop."

"I don't have as many privileges or freedoms as you do."

"If you stop me now then everyone loses."

Hussein stared at Ranglen, deliberating. "You're that sure you can find the Clip?"

"I have a better chance than anyone. I'm good, Hussein. I'll show you—hell, I'll *give* it to you."

Hussein shook his head. "There must be dozens of other people searching by now."

"There'll be hundreds soon. Earth is scared. Why do you think you and Pia were yanked off the case? They wanted me free even if they *are* pulling me in."

"Wait a minute—the Investigators don't influence Annulus or Homeworld."

"The hell they don't! What about my satellite message? Earth gave you that information, right? Annulus didn't know about it, and yet the satellite sits in Annulus space."

"They still don't rule us."

"Don't be naïve. Clips create turning points in history. Do you think they'll let treaties or partnerships stop them?"

Hussein had no comeback. He said, as if to sidetrack Ranglen, "Then how does Balrak fit in? Why was Montgomery killed, and Ciat?"

"*I don't know!* And your holding me here won't help me find out."

Hussein waved his hand. "Ranglen, you don't care who was killed, or even whether you find the Clip. You just want to get to your precious Mileen and keep her alive."

"Of course I do. But I can *make* her safe by finding their damned Clip for them. They just have to let me. *You* have to let me."

"I'm not free either."

"You're more free than you think. That's what the Clips do—keep us a step ahead of authority. They bring surprises that complicate power. The FTL drive *was* a liberator. We're not ruled—as long as a Clip is out there to be found."

Hussein suddenly looked unsure. He turned away in confusion.

"Just let me go," Ranglen persisted. "What can they do to you that they haven't done already? And—" He paused here, tried to hide his desperation. "Did you ever think that maybe you're *supposed* to release me?"

"What the hell do you mean?"

"Think! Bringing me in just delays me but they know it's best I keep going. They need to make their show of control. It's in their nature, just like you said. So they call you to pull me in. You're compromised so you do your job. You'd never question them but they know you hate them for giving in to them. And they know I'm right and that I might convince you—that's why they're scared."

"Wait, you're saying I'm *supposed* to let you go, that they *planned* this?"

"I think they planned for both possibilities. If you bring me in, they remind me who's in charge, which strokes their ego but time is lost. Yet they also feel you might let me go, and then they can rest even better—they've stepped on me through you and I'm reminded to bring the Clip to them, but they've lost no time. It's schizophrenic but they have to be crazy since no one's really in charge now. They know it but ignore it. They need to feel more content than right."

Hussein looked helpless. "That's stupid!"

"Of course it is! But they don't rule by logic. With magic popping up out of the ground, control is a self-deluding fantasy. They're no better than the rest of us—we're equal! It's such great irony. It's what the Clips insist on, what *I* insist on. I won't do it, Hussein. I won't give the Clip to just one group. And—I guarantee you—I *will* find it."

Hussein looked away, hiding his confusion.

"I won't lie to you," Ranglen continued. "They'll be rough with you. It'll be all you said they'd do to me. But since you'll know why they're doing it, *you* can be the smug untouchable. You'll know what you did was really correct. They'll be aware of that too though they won't admit it. And in the end they'll respect you for it. They'll never say that, but after you leave they'll be happier with you."

Hussein shook his head. "If I let you go, why should I even go back to them?"

"You're a loyal cop. You do your job."

"And what would I say?"

"They're expecting you to lie, to come with a cover story. 'He got away from me.' 'I couldn't find him.' 'The bastard's good.' Say anything! It doesn't matter. They'll yell, but then they'll let you go just like they would've done with me. And then they'll commend you."

Hussein stared into empty distance, his face bleak. "This is nuts."

"Then ignore everything I said and think of this: who would you rather find the Clip? Them, or me? If I hadn't done what I did with the third Clip, there would be no Annulus, no independent Homeworld. They probably would have kept the secret in a vault—which is what I think they did with the fourth Clip. You like Annulus, don't you? It's a good environment, a good place to live. So...you decide. We're the future, Hussein. I believe that. And the choice to create it is still ours."

Hussein clenched his fists. "For God's sake, why didn't you just call them after you first talked to Ciat? That's what angered them the most, you know."

"If I had, they would have taken over and ruined everything, sent in an army."

"They want to do that now—a fleet, battleships!"

"And they will if I don't get moving and find that Clip."

"You should have gone with Ciat."

"He asked me to. But he deserved his chance."

"So you let him go alone and he got himself killed. They said you're not a team player."

"They're out for themselves and not some damned team."

"They think you're out for *yourself*."

"Dammit, Hussein! Do you believe that?"

"Yes....No."

"Then why are we sitting here? Let me go! Maybe, in whatever Clip we find, there'll be something to help *our* side."

Hussein looked tormented. Ranglen let him struggle and concentrate.

Then he finally said, "You've got to leave Annulus immediately. They know they can't track you once you're gone. And if you leave, they'll think you're on the trail of the Clip. They don't like that you're looking for Mileen."

"I have my priorities. But I can still get the Clip for them."

"Dammit! Dammit!..." He suddenly looked defeated. "All right....Get out of here."

Ranglen couldn't help smiling. "Thanks, Hussein."

"*Don't* thank me. Just hope they'll believe me."

"Belief has nothing to do with it. They'll know what happened the minute you walk in." Ranglen stood up—his muscles had stiffened from all the tension and his back throbbed. He almost staggered.

"Look at you!—you can hardly walk. What the hell am I doing?"

"I'm fine, believe me." He hurt like hell. "One quick question. What happened to Balrak?"

"He left for Ventroni, or at least we think so. Balrak's why the Investigators are nervous. Look, you've got to get out of here—fast."

"Jayne, Rashmi...what of them?"

"We lost them when the station kept pulling us in. We heard later they met with you, but—last I know—we weren't sure where they went. They haven't turned up dead though."

"Your surveillance stinks."

"They don't want us involved!"

"And...Mileen. Have you heard anything?" He wouldn't make the mistake that he did with Pia.

"Still nothing. But again—I'm off the case."

"Look, I know where Lonni Elwood is hiding. She knows nothing. She had a memory swipe. But can someone watch over her? She's terrified, and she can be found if I was able to do it. I don't want her getting killed."

"I'll check on her myself. But the Investigators will want to know why once I do it."

"Be honest with them. They'll like that you're giving them information. They'll leave her alone for as long as I'm out there, but they won't protect her." He told him where she was.

"Okay. Get out of here."

"I'm sorry for all this. They'll treat you like crap."

"Go! Go!"

He staggered away. Hathaway looked scornful.

A wild and perverse part of Ranglen almost yelled back, "Say hi to Pia for me." But he restrained himself.

He headed straight to Hatch Banner's for his ship, not stopping at the hotel. He had left instructions there on what to do with his belongings if he didn't return, right after Hathaway and Pia came to interrogate him.

He boarded a transport tube that rode down to the spaceport, awaking suspicious stares from passengers for his disheveled, bandaged, and limping appearance. He smiled broadly in return—they didn't know how to take such an expression so they turned away. But the authorities could stop him if they wanted to. Security and clearance gates stood at both ends.

He breezed through. No one chased him yet. Though he believed everything he told Hussein—and he was immensely grateful for the man's sacrifice—he still knew that, at a whim, the Federal Investigators or Annulus Security could drop a cage on him.

And he ran into a wall when he asked for his ship.

Everyone said go to Banner's office, but Hatch usually left station-wide orders to let Ranglen pass through. Something was wrong.

He hobbled to Banner's desk. A weasel-like and grumpy youth now worked behind it. His dirty overalls, sour demeanor, and neglected babyish hair yelled that he hated this desk-job. He snarled when Ranglen hurried in. "What do *you* want?"

"Where's Hatch?"

"How should I know? We're backed up on twenty deliveries, parts are missing, inventory's a mess, and the 'high king' decides on a vacation."

"Hatch never takes a vacation."

"He said that's where he was going and he didn't leave a link for us. He's out of his mind."

"Look, my name is Mykol Ranglen. I—"

"Never heard of you."

"I have my own private account with Hatch. He keeps a spaceship always ready for me."

"Ridiculous! We don't do that for anyone. And that bandage on your head is bleeding."

Ranglen longed to strangle the kid. "Okay, forget it. I keep the keys for the hangar with me so I'll just go there on my own. Let your workers know I'm coming and give me an exit window."

"No way! If I don't have clearance from Annulus Central, you don't go anywhere."

"Look, I'm telling you—"

The kid jumped from his chair. "And I'm telling *you!* I don't cater to his goddamned friends! He plays favorites—it's no way to run a business! If you walk toward that hangar, I'll—"

Ranglen grabbed a wrench and slammed it against a metal cabinet, hurting his hand but wanting to make noise. "You give me a launch window *now* or I'll tear this place apart!" He felt dizzy.

"You bastard! I'm calling the port guards, Security—" The kid raced to the alarm switch on the wall (one sat on his desk but he apparently didn't know it).

Ranglen tripped him and the kid hit the floor. He threatened him with his wrench. The kid whined, scurried away behind a stack of crates that then fell on him.

Ranglen stumbled out of the office and hurried toward the hangar where his ship was kept, hoping that Hatch hadn't moved it. He entered his keys and the standard clearance codes. He realized now he should have done this first and not tried to find Hatch, but he needed that exit window.

The kid ran out of his office, shouting, "*Stop that bastard! He's stealing a ship!*"

Workers turned toward Ranglen and alarms sounded.

Ranglen threw up the bay door of the hangar and jumped toward his craft. Thankfully the entrance-ramp was lowered and the main hatch open, the way Hatch usually left it.

A mechanic rushed into the hangar behind him, carrying a cutting torch with a needle-sharp flame. More people followed.

Ranglen threw his wrench at them, then leaped into his ship and hurried to the bridge. He raised the ramp while the workers tried to pull it down. They failed. The lock closed.

He punched in coordinates with his bandaged hands and powered the gravity plate, gunned the thrusters.

Something banged against the hull. He glanced at the screens and saw workers throwing tools at him—probably his wrench. The weasel-faced kid ran in screaming, waving his arms and shouting orders.

But the ship moved. People scurried out of its way. Ranglen flew it through the hangar's opening as the bay-doors quickly closed behind him.

A vast latticework of lights and gantries rose above him. The jets and accelero-gravity drive propelled the ship upward—but in what direction? He had no launch vector, no cleared path. Taking off like this was suicidal.

But the higher he went the more openings appeared. Frameworks and beacons passed below as he saw an area of open space and he hurtled into it. The comm links screamed warnings and orders. He shut them off.

The ship rocked as it passed through security nets, scans, probes, mass deflectors. Velocity slowed. Soon he'd be stopped, captured, taken back.

He flipped the handle that worked the one instrument Hatch had added just for him—Hatch said it was illegal but Ranglen supplied enough money and Hatch installed it.

The pummeling, jamming, and scanning stopped—the device was an exclusive military scrambler.

Ranglen hit more buttons. He moved faster. He brought up a rear image on his screens and saw bursts of light—manually operated defense munitions. The people at the port overrode their automatics to counter Ranglen's foiling of them. He wasn't free yet.

The ship thumped and shook—a grazing hit. But he could see the spaceport resolve into a circle as he gained distance. If he could just keep moving for a few seconds more. And the big ring-chandelier of Annulus with its gray-black underside emerged from behind the spaceport's shield. He thought of Lonni.

Another boom. The ship staggered.

Ranglen couldn't wait. Though he was too near other transports and satellites for a plunge into light-space—he might drag in other objects or be held back himself—he had no other choice. Bigger ships would soon chase after him with more accurate guns.

He slapped the buttons for light-space.

The ship rocked, disorienting his senses. But the rough transition finished quickly.

Instruments indicated the ship had made safe passage out of time-space, but mass probably had been pulled in with it and torn apart. Whatever got destroyed he hoped was too small to carry passengers.

He tried to breathe more easily, tried to convince himself no lives had been lost. At least he felt safe, for now.

But recalling Lonni made him pull out his cellpad and check for messages. One had come from Hussein, sent soon after he talked with him. It read: "Sorry, Mykol. Elwood is missing. I found no trace of her at her hut."

Dismay swept through him. Too drained now to muster resistance, Ranglen gave in to his fears. Maybe she left the hut and hid herself, but he believed most likely she was dead.

He felt for her…for Anne, for Henry.

He checked if any calls had arrived from Mileen but he found nothing.

He eased back in the acceleration couch, too exhausted to do anything. Blood dampened his head-wound, which throbbed in pain. His ears and neck ached persistently. His hands beneath his bandages hurt.

He didn't care.

In seconds he was asleep.

Chapter Nine: Safehouse

Two days, three hours, 46 minutes and 7.85 seconds later.

The time spent in light-space never varied. Every jump, no matter how much distance in our universe was covered, underwent the same inboard time, while the transition for people left back in normal space was instantaneous. The proposed reason was that the Airafane Clip drive worked on the difference between our universe, now called time-space, where c—the speed of light—remained constant and time varied, and another universe called light-space where t was constant and c varied. The resulting physics got a little extreme, so some scientists claimed that light-space was not a co-existing universe but one *created* around any ship when a jump was made, that the duration of this universe was simply invariant, and that its size—or space—as determined by the input parameters of the jump, placed its cessation conveniently elsewhere in our universe.

Ranglen found all this unconvincing.

But he was quite happy for the two days spent in light-space. It gave him a chance to recuperate. He plugged himself into his expensive medi-clinic (ordered through Hatch) and allowed it to tend to his burns, wounds, and aches. He spent his time resting, with judicious exercise to get his strength back. By the time he re-entered time-space, he felt confident that he had recovered enough.

His FTL jump had taken him only to another part of Annulus' star system. He came out below the ecliptic and coasted up to the accretion disk. It grew brighter above him, a curved lid of glitter and haze, grooved with dust, loose rock, slight beginnings of planetary cores. Ranglen sought a particular asteroid. It was hard to find, the orbit always changing. The computer picked the most likely location and then spiraled out till contact was made.

When Ranglen first found the rock years ago, his scanners noticed an anomaly. By sight, the place was not unique—like any other asteroid it looked beaten by the universe, a symbol of random violence and fortitude. But the gravity at the surface was not as strong as it should be. The composition wasn't special, as his sensors indicated, so he decided that the object couldn't be solid.

It must have caves.

He soon discovered artificial tunnels lacing the asteroid, some quite large, but they lacked function. Most of the chambers had walls of stone but some were reinforced with trapezoidal frames made of a concrete-like material. The floors were smooth, artificial, some with wide stairways. The passages held no signs of life, no live-in habitats, no power, no water, no air, nothing. With one exception, no artifacts were found.

The one exception was the fourth Clip.

Ranglen assumed the place had been made by the Airafane but he had no proof. He wondered if the tunnels were built first and then the asteroid folded around them. Maybe the chamber-nest wandered into the stellar system from outside, an older object gathering a skin of new accretion. He analyzed the material of the floors and frames and found nothing extraordinary, neither proof nor disproof that it came from a different sun. In his wilder fantasies, he wondered if every new star had one of these objects orbiting it, some ancient guardian eventually buried in the core of a planet, maybe to survive after the world formed. But he saw no reason for it.

Ranglen eventually gave the Clip to the authorities but he lied about where he found it, and kept the knowledge of the asteroid to himself. Humanity had gotten Annulus but, selfishly, he felt this cavitied rock belonged to him. It spoke to his Romantic side.

He strung lights, sealed compartments and flooded them with air, brought power generators and environment control, laid gravity plates for easy walking. He installed automated hangar doors over the entranceway—found hidden in a gulley—to allow his ship access and then to hide it. All this took years since he did it on his own. He brought furniture, books, stoves, beds, computers, plants. He brought reproductions of his favorite paintings and several originals by Mileen. He even brought Mileen.

But she hated it.

She called it cold, haunted, lonely, dead. And after a while Ranglen agreed. No matter how he tried to make it livable, it always had the sense of a base camp or an abandoned archaeological site. He found himself eating and sleeping more on his ship, neglecting the lavish components he installed. The place felt closed-in, introspective, alone. He found no "Other," just reflections of himself. The mystery lost its flavor.

But it still had one big advantage. He—and Mileen—couldn't be found here. It was a perfect "safehouse."

The computer beeped. It found the asteroid.

Ranglen moved up to its pock-marked form. He drew his ship into a deep chasm under an overhang. He activated the door he had inserted, just big enough for a small ship like his to enter. He glided in on gentle thrusters and clamped down the anchor struts.

Another ship already sat there, a small one-person roustabout.

He donned his space helmet and cycled though the airlock, then padded across to the other ship and entered its hatch, which already gaped open. The airlock pressurized and he walked through the door, into full gravity.

Mileen sat in the pilot's chair, tall and elegant even when sitting—hair sienna, eyes dark-blue, mouth and face reluctant, wary.

"Hi," he said.

"Hello," she returned. She looked too motionless, too held in.

"How long have you been here?"

"Longer than I wanted to. I hate this place. Why couldn't I have met you somewhere else?"

"Because here you're safe. You know that."

"It's horrible." He once described the asteroid as a love nest. She didn't agree.

He walked gently toward her. "You probably stayed in your ship the whole time, never came out of it."

"Of course I stayed here. I'd never sleep in one of your caves. How can you stand being here alone?"

"It's never for long."

"I'm glad I didn't marry you. You probably would have had us living here."

He reached her now. He sat on the lone second chair in the cramped control room. "Is this Lonni's ship?"

"Yes. You talked to her?"

Ranglen nodded.

"She must have said I was crazy."

"Pretty much."

"Maybe that's my reason for not wanting to stay here."

"Mileen, you're just—"

"Don't say anything, Mykol. You don't know how I feel."

"I—"

"They murdered Henry!"

He reached for her but she pushed him away, said, "Something happened to all of us back there. Happened to *me*. I feel out of control now. Each of us got to the same point. What's doing this to us?"

"Maybe you've just been alone too long."

"Yeah—*here!* All you can do is *think* when you're here."

"I told you you're safe."

"I don't want to be this safe. I want to be alive again. I want what I was and I can't get back to it. Henry was killed. And he was the only one who had any sense."

Ranglen reached for her a second time but again she pushed him away, saying, "You don't understand. You don't know what it's doing to me."

"I've been there, remember?"

"No, you've never been where I am—not you, not locked-in, all-controlled you."

"Mileen…"

"*Dammit*, why won't you understand me? I don't *feel* anything! I'm scared I might have expected it—even wanted it."

He waited, dreading. "Wanted what?"

"Henry…dead."

Ranglen said nothing.

"Do you get it now?"

This time she didn't resist when he touched her.

"I hate this place."

"We won't stay long."

"Why am I like this?"

"We're alive. Let's enjoy it."

He tried to hold her but the chairs didn't allow much intimacy. They stopped talking and just sat together.

Then, eventually, he told her about Anne.

When they first met at one of Ranglen's lectures, an immediate fire started between them. Mileen, still in college, was mature beyond her years and she brought an intensity of perception and insight that awoke something dormant in Ranglen. They hungered for each other. Too much so. It nearly destroyed them.

Mileen's tallness and dark-red hair made her striking. Her sharp face and frank blue eyes probed and locked on the objects of her gaze, as if her attention could be ruthless. She resembled a trial-lawyer zeroing-in for a kill, forceful and snappish after holding herself back. She didn't look like an artist.

She sometimes dressed like a professional accountant but it couldn't hide her flame of curiosity. When focused on her painting, her concentration grew so severe that she seemed possessed, broken from the world. Such passion made her striking. People turned to look at her, not realizing the pull was more than visual. What got them was the intensity of her attention, of eyes that seemed to illuminate as well as watch, of her wide mouth that wanted to draw the essence from experience.

Ranglen, and later Henry, found her irresistible.

Their relationship at first began tentatively. To inspire her art she attended his lectures on the aesthetic reactions to alien worlds. Anne (who already graduated and was starting her business) recommended him as more inspiring than college-based teachers, and after Anne introduced them they quickly agreed to meet again. He was, in Anne's words, "mysterious, magical, and exciting," with his tousled dark hair and ice-blue eyes, fleshy lips, craggy face, and eternally slim build. The two shared no more than ideas at first but a deep sensuality soon took over.

The attraction ignited. They devoured each other.

They fed on their mutual disbelief in boundaries, which seemed to justify them sinking yet further. They didn't intellectualize any of their actions. But through their mutual creativity they tore down the walls between them. Her painting and his poetry became both extension and cause of their love-making. They lavished in their mental and physical contact, each part of one wanting each part of the other.

Brutally honest, they both knew their desire was a self-consumption and that their love would have to be transitory at best. It burned too bright. Mileen had a consciousness based less on reflection than gut instinct. To Ranglen, she was a tangle of contradictions, a sensory demon both lost and found. She knew what she wanted with a strict survivalist's skill—to be supported both materially and sexually so she could finish college and pursue her art, to have a fire burn just for her. From the beginning she knew that Ranglen was too preoccupied to provide all she needed. She could not inhabit and possess him fully.

But they didn't care. In some ways their knowing anything long-term could not work became an excuse to let the attraction grow stronger, to feed off each other more. They didn't bother about their mutual drowning.

Since Ranglen's own parents died young and she was an orphan who lived mostly on her own, they both viewed their surroundings as if they'd soon have to leave them, as if their claim on them was through suffrage only. So they observed everything with precision and passion. They drank in their worlds as deep and long as they drank in each other.

106

It made them too similar. Ranglen knew what such love could do to them, that it could destroy as well as ennoble them, use and discard them. He had been there before. But it was too strong for them to avoid. They had no restrictions. It was terrifying and wonderful. They fell deeper yet.

Her art grew better. It gained an eerie overwhelming passion. Her landscapes, Ranglen said, though realistic, looked possessed by a latent spirit of place, some hard patina of saturated longing. Realism made strange. She started a series of huge paintings of geological strata with names like "Navajo Sandstone, 190 Million Years." Rockbed products of ancient time. One reviewer on Homeworld said, "You'll never look at a roadcut in the same way again." But she wasn't interested in geology—she got all her data from Ranglen. It was just her means to make the obvious more impressive, make it sing and scream.

"Do you think my art is religious?" she once asked him.

"It has a rapture, but it's sensual, not mystic."

"I'm not religious at all. I believe only in us."

"Yet you don't paint people, only landscapes."

"Because of how they affect me. I want to throw them out at the viewers. All foreground and no background, a ton of detail."

"You don't want to label or own the landscape. You want a sensory understanding of it, to be a part of it. I know that well."

"'The Man Who Loved Alien Landscapes,' eh?"

"You don't want conquest, you want consummation."

"Mykol, we're too alike. It can't be good for us."

And it did have to end.

She felt she was losing herself in him—which in one sense she enjoyed, but she felt he was not as much lost in her. The relation was uneven, he more independent than she was. She accused him of being *able* to leave her, which haunted and disgusted her. They started to feel constrained by each other, which became an excuse for them to part. They felt their desire was bigger than both of them, and they backed away from it in desperate expediency, following an "out" that surprised both of them. They scared themselves, which shamed them into feeling they had to make a choice.

When his normal season of lectures ended it was silently agreed they both would move on. She had graduated college now and wanted to do professional field work. He had writing, consulting, and traveling.

Through Anne, Ranglen introduced her to Henry, with whom she could start an internship. Ranglen liked to think that the flame of their romance carried over into hers with Henry—that it never would have happened if their own entangling hadn't been so strong. It was a selfish thought but it helped the transition, especially since he felt that Henry wasn't good enough for her and that maybe they themselves had failed their relationship. He thought of her afterward with conflict, that their break-up might have been more convenient than right.

And so, now, when they met once again in Ranglen's little island in space, after encountering such terrible events and each of them wanting a quick escape, with resistance low from becoming fugitives, with embarrassment after the deaths of Henry and Anne but finding their need simply too great, they fell into the habit of loving again. They slid, without grace or decision, into their old sensory realm, their refined knowledge of each other's needs. They found they still carried such knowledge with them.

"Did you love Anne?"

"I don't know. I enjoyed being with her. I know I loved you."

"Did you love *me* or the landscapes I painted, what those places became in my eyes?"

"That's clever, but no, it was you."

"I remember you saying once I was like a planet."

"I said you were a world of sensation and wonder. I wanted to explore you, inhabit you, swim in you."

"Your fingertips slid over me when you said that."

"Then I shouldn't talk when I make love?"

"No, your words had the right effect. I always went where you wanted me to go. But I wondered, 'Does he love me or what I represent for him—a world he actually *can* touch?' You can't make love to an alien planet, but you can love me."

"Most men would say we should change the subject now."

"You don't have to. You're not like most men. You claimed I was the only alien landscape you loved."

"I said you were like all landscapes, that I looked into your face like staring into a pool of clear water. I wanted to dive into you, get lost in you."

She moved beneath the exploration of his hands. "You don't need to arouse me."

"It comes with the package."

They talked like that, as they stayed together for hours on her ship. They grew near, parted, then touched again, indulged in nostalgia and somber regrets. It helped them delay the inevitable.

But the inevitable came. "What happened on that trip from Ventroni?"

She covered the same details as Lonni, then said, "A strange feeling hit me when we saw the derelicts, like something lurking at the edge of my mind. I was scared. That's not like me. And everyone else—except Lonni—grew excited. They screamed, 'We're rich!' Omar pulled me into his room and tried to kiss me, promised me everything if I'd leave Henry.

"I knew then how serious it was. Lonni went crazy. She wanted out and kept trying to prove she wouldn't be a risk to them. Of course they didn't believe her. Omar hated Henry too, especially after I rejected him. The emotion went up in everyone. I'm sure Omar was the one who killed Henry."

"Another man might have ordered him to." He told her about Balrak.

She listened but said little in response, as if Balrak's not being with the original group made him too abstract to be a threat.

"Lonni said you wanted to follow the lifeboat," he said, "the RLV."

"I believed a child was on board."

"How did you know?"

"I *didn't* know. Yet at the same time I felt certain. I tried to persuade them to go to the planet where the lifeboat had gone. The coordinates were still there in the launch cradle. But no one cared. They just wanted the Clip. I got furious—*my* emotions went up too. Henry had to settle me down." She laughed, bleakly, her eyes distant with remembering. "Afterward, Omar made his pass at me. I guess he liked me angry."

"Back on Annulus, when did you leave Henry?"

"Three or four days before he got killed, not long after he talked with you. It was my decision. I didn't want him to feel conflicted. He needed to go treasure-hunting and I wouldn't stand in his way."

"But he was doing it for you."

"I don't believe that," she said. "And if so, then I was right to remove his 'motivation.' He reached his limit so I made the choice for him. I almost left him earlier because of all his needs, but instead I said 'yes' when he proposed. I wasn't very logical."

"But he truly loved you."

"You think I didn't know that?"

"You said…" He hesitated. "You said you 'expected' to hear he was dead."

Agony seeped into her face. "I felt a strange relief, which is terrible. All this was too big for him. He would have become lost in it, buried by it. When I left him, one part of me wished him luck, but another part said farewell and almost accepted that he was doomed. When I heard he had died I felt—horribly—he had gotten out early."

This should have appalled Ranglen but he knew the effects of Clips too well. "You just followed your survival instinct."

"I hated myself, but I felt free, that I had a better chance alone than with him."

"How did you hear about his death?"

"I left Lonni a way to reach me through the comm on her ship. When she heard about it she sent the information. I don't know how she learned it. She kept her ears more open than you think. She's tough. I liked her."

"So then you came here?"

"Not immediately," she said. "I took a light-space jump to have time to think. That was a mistake. It was *too* much time. But I set the emergence for near here. I came in on thrusters, not wanting more time in another universe. It took almost a day to find the place. I took the search programs you gave me, so I guess I meant to come here all along."

"Why did you use Lonni's ship? Why not your own?"

"Because of Hatch. I'd have to see him in order to get it, and he would have asked too many questions. Lonni's ship was out on the rim."

He paused before saying, "You asked Lonni for help in getting to the lifeboat world. Why didn't you come to me?"

"Because I didn't know if you were with me or not. We had been through too much, Mykol. It was all over. And the one thing I learned was not to assume anyone is certain. Besides, I thought of Henry. He wouldn't have wanted me to."

"You didn't trust me?"

"Of course I trusted you! But you always wanted to be free. Not owned, not owning. Look at this place. Look at your houses—they're half empty! You live in hotel rooms. Anyplace you stay you leave as soon as possible. You told me once you wanted to break free of history, to join the future, but you're more like some lover who sneaks out in the night."

"I never did that to you," he said quietly.

"It's the way you live. It's not how we finished but it's how you think."

"Then why did you agree to break up with me?"

"Because I wasn't sure I could rely on you. Henry I could. He'd never leave me."

"Except for the Clip."

"Not even then," she said. "I let him go because he needed to go. Sure, the Clip ruined everything. You could tell—his mind was possessed. He never had the

110

confidence you had, so when something like this came along he had nothing to stand on, or at least nothing he'd admit to. He always wanted to support me, but he didn't realize—or couldn't accept—that in most ways I supported him. Not materially but emotionally."

Ranglen sighed. "You weren't like this before, Mileen."

"How am I different?"

"You never spoke of other people this way. You've grown hard."

"I've grown *clear*. I see better now. I see *you* better," she said. "You used to talk about the Clip drive and how it almost liberated Earth, that war and oppression were left behind. But then all those things caught up with us again. People brought them. You're like that too, Mykol. You want to break ties and become anonymous. You don't want to be held or defined. So when a relationship gets complicated, you slip away."

"You do too."

"Maybe, I don't know. But you're *always* leaving. Anne felt the same way about you. You escape to other worlds but you bring yourself with you. We all do. There *are* no alien landscapes. It's the only theme in all my paintings."

He watched her closely.

"Don't look at me like that! The man I was about to marry was murdered—Anne's dead, Lonni's disappeared, and we're hiding here like outlaws. What do you expect from me?"

Ranglen exhaled a long breath.

"So," she added, "what do we do now?"

"You're part of this too. You tell me."

"I want to know if anyone survived the lifeboat. And then, there's the Clip. Everyone else is looking for it. I imagine we'll do that too."

"I *have* to find it," he said, "to make up for ignoring the Federal Investigators. Remember how I said I had to cut deals to get where I am? I'm supposed to report any new hints of Clip finds. I didn't do that."

"Why?"

He glanced at her. "I had other interests."

"You mean *me*? So now you're saying you did all this for me?"

"I felt you were in danger."

She laughed. "And you wonder about *my* motivations." She added, more seriously, "Look, I'm grateful. But I'm also angry and disappointed in everyone. I think we're monsters. We don't deserve to be out here."

"We're no different from anyone else. Look at the Moyocks and the Airafane. They hated each other."

"Look at *us*."

But Ranglen tired of self-immolation, especially when applied to an entire race. What else did they have except themselves? "Do you know the coordinates of the world where the lifeboat went?"

"No. I had difficulty reading them from the instruments on the derelict. That's why I wanted Lonni to take me there."

"What about the location of the Clip world?"

"Henry had those numbers but he decided it was better I didn't know them, that it would be safer for me. I guess he was right. He got murdered."

"Were they written down?"

"They all memorized them. I could have insisted on seeing them but I didn't want to. Then Omar and Rashmi smashed the control screen on the derelict so no one else could read them."

"Our first step then is to go to the derelict," Ranglen said. "We can get the location of the lifeboat world from it. There might be navigation files on the RLV."

"But I don't know where the derelicts are."

"Hatch read the figures from backup files on the ship you were in. He can access those—don't tell his customers. And he put the data in the files on my ship."

Mileen chuckled. "Good old Hatch. My kind of guy."

"But Hatch has also disappeared." He told her what the kid at the spaceport had said. "I think he went searching for the Clip."

"Not a chance. He hates Clips."

Ranglen didn't speculate. He was beyond trying to know people's intentions when they dealt with Clips. "He also left information on my ship about how to read deeper into the files on board the derelict. He wasn't sure if that would work but he said I could try. I accessed all this on the way here."

Mileen looked thoughtful. "After we get the information, we'll go to the lifeboat world first, right?"

"If we get the coordinates for the Clip planet, we shouldn't."

"Please—I have to."

He became almost angry. "That's exactly what Clips do to people. Suddenly no one 'chooses' anymore. It's all, 'I *have* to.'"

"But I mean it, Mykol," she said.

"Yeah, yeah. Let's not decide now. We might have to change plans when we get there."

"I think we should be on our way soon."

Ranglen agreed.

The idyll was over.

Before they left, he checked something in another part of the asteroid.

He pressurized a chamber deep inside the labyrinth and entered it with Mileen. Concealed in its stone wall was a safe. Ranglen worked the myriad locks and combinations. The door opened and he carefully looked inside. He then pulled out two halves of a crystal that resembled fluorite.

The octahedral mineral had cleaved along the boundary where the color changed from a glassy yellow to deep purple. Both colors ran in alternating light-and-dark bands through the two pyramidal shapes.

He held both halves and stared at them.

"So that's it, eh?" Mileen tried to sound unimpressed.

He had told her it was the one thing he found in the asteroid, lying on the floor in one of the hallways in the micro-gravity. It seemed to have been randomly discarded, leaving no indication of where it had been found. He said these two pieces of the so-called "carrier-lock," a container for a Clip, were all that was left, as if someone else had discovered the Clip and taken it away.

But he lied. Inside it he found the fourth Clip.

His keeping the container was still significant. When he turned in the third Clip the Investigators insisted he give them the crystal too. He did, and he never saw it again. They always kept everything related to Clips.

So Ranglen, with the fourth Clip, told the Investigators he had lost the container, which wasn't true. They weren't happy about that. And from that day on he wasn't trusted.

He kept it in his safe in the asteroid.

"Let me see it," Mileen said.

He placed it in her hand.

She touched the two halves with near reverence. "It's amazing that you can almost shave it, that it comes off in flakes."

"It behaves differently from actual fluorite."

"You could peel a slice off."

"Only now you could," he said, "not when it's buried in the mantle of a planet. The field it generates makes it impenetrable. No temperature can melt it."

"Can I take a piece of it?"

He smiled sadly. "You just can't help yourself, can you?"

"I'm sorry. But this is probably the closest I'll get."

He surrendered. "Go ahead."

With her fingernail she chipped off a sliver a few millimeters wide. Then she aligned the two halves till they snapped together. She held the resulting octahedron in her hand, rolling it in her palm. "Okay, I'm awed." She gave it back to him, and pocketed her small chip.

Ranglen said, "Anyone else but you, knowing it was here, would have broken in just to see it."

"I wouldn't enter any of these chambers alone."

Ranglen palmed the crystal. "Maybe I should take this with us."

She was surprised. "To the derelicts? Why?"

"As a good luck charm."

"What if it's found? Won't people say you were holding out on them, that you didn't report it?"

"After what I've done, that wouldn't be significant. And besides, it's just a piece of fluorite now, *near* fluorite. People who seek Clips often take a crystal of it as good luck."

She shrugged. "If you want."

He thought for a moment. "You're right. I'll leave it here. It's protected here."

He placed it back inside the safe.

Before leaving the asteroid he returned to the chamber, alone this time, and wandered into the adjoining hallways. He had pressurized several of them earlier. He prowled through the near zero-G, but he didn't stay long. He just wanted to experience the strangeness of the place again.

He remembered how he had dreamed of making all this into his "castle," that he'd fill it with gravity and subdued light, turn it into his own private labyrinth, his mystery cavern out in space. But it was all a fantasy. The place was too gloomy. Mileen knew he could never stay here.

That gloom was exactly what he wanted now.

When he opened the safe earlier, he had seen that the two halves of the carrier-lock sat in the exact place and position where he had put them the last time he was here.

But the single hair he had placed on top of them, held there by a slight adhesive, was now gone. He had arranged the strand so that the smallest disturbance would dislodge it, and that he would see this immediately when he came back to examine the pieces.

Someone had handled the crystals, and then returned them.

Mileen didn't know the combination to the safe. No one did. He even tested her fascination with the carrier-lock through his suggestion of taking it with them, but she hadn't shown interest.

He wandered a bit more. He came to no conclusion about what had happened.

Then he pulled from his pocket a small shard he himself once shaved from the crystal. It was bigger than the one Mileen took.

This he *would* bring with him on their trip.

It would be his secret.

He returned to Mileen, and, soon after, they left in his spacecraft.

Chapter 10: The Derelicts

Two ships locked in unlikely marriage—beauty and beast, needle and haystack, miniature hare and exploded tortoise.

Ranglen set aside his labored metaphors and plotted a course. He knew they'd spend time on the silver spaceship so he wanted the first flyby near the big piece of "driftwood"—he called it that, for lack of a better name.

A nearby cluster of young stars, fierce and blue-white, awoke emissions from a nebula parked nearby, whose energetic light cascaded through canyons of murk. The glows shone delicate and pale, but compensations made by the viewscreens brought out structure, milky dyes floating in ink: oxygen's fluorescent greens, hydrogen's excited reds, reflected dust's gossamer blue.

But Ranglen paid attention to the object before him.

The light from distant furnaces dripped and ran on the gothic spires and pig-like knobs. He struggled to describe this incredible mass. It was like several hands with fingers spread and then tangled together, a tight ball caught in the moment of trying to break apart, the fingers bent, fat or thin, broken, calloused, mangled, dead. An organic wreck.

"I hate being here," Mileen said.

"Not too many places you like anymore. Aren't you excited by this? Don't you want to paint it?"

"The first time I saw it I did. But it's given me something like writer's block."

To Ranglen this was no joke. "It's that bad?"

"When you're numb, you can't paint. This is worse. It gives me pain."

Ranglen kept quiet. He never had seen Mileen so put off by experience. It was different from what the Clips did to everyone else. He didn't like it.

As they nudged closer to the object and glided by, Ranglen switched on floodlights and swept the curved exterior/interior. They showed that the huge object wasn't fractal. Though the surface modeled a Kaluza-Klein geometry, like some big

116

tortured Calabi-Yau structure, the close-up view was different from wide-angle. The surface lay corrugated, an assortment of cables bunched together, lying side by side and running across the bone-like construction.

As Lonni had speculated, maybe the whole thing was composed of only these bundles of pipes—spears, cords, staffs. It looked like an electrician's nest of wires, a double handful then twisted apart.

These spikes, or whatever they were, seemed metallic but not very polished, glinting sullenly from the bluish stars but showing an overall brown tint, like dirty bronze, mottled with ochre, black, and dull red. They looked old, left out in bad weather too long, caked with grime and rusted by neglect.

In the entire structure no hatches could be seen, no antennae, no weapons, no propulsion system, no guidance controls, no sensor dishes. No "fore," no "aft"—no function, no sense. A host of negatives. Nothing but shape, enclosure, and density, like a pile of debris from a construction site that fell through a wormhole and came out warped.

Ranglen said, "Maybe it's a work of art."

"If it is, the judges rejected it and dumped it here," she said. "Can we move on now?"

Maybe she was jealous. Professional envy.

Ranglen could have stayed for hours, gliding his ship under the arches, dipping down through the hole-like tunnels, enjoying the majesty of big changing perspectives around him. But time was short. And he didn't feel the same tension that obviously coursed through Mileen—she squirmed in her chair, glanced at the object with difficulty.

They left the enigma behind, but its presence still loomed unseen.

Mileen walked to the small dining area. Ranglen's spaceship was relatively plush. It ran on a type-2 Airafane engine which was larger than needed for the size of the craft, and it was designed to be controlled by only one person but it could house two people comfortably and more under cramped conditions.

He decided Mileen was just trying to keep busy. On the way here, in the two-day light-space duration, they both had been quiet. Ranglen reviewed Hatch's downloads and she exercised and slept, worked on sketches with electronic embellishment but more as a means of keeping her talents sharp, in use. She was not inspired. The binge of sharing and intense love-making back in the asteroid was half in the past.

She returned to the control deck to watch the approach of the smaller derelict, not speaking, not indicating why she had left in the first place or what she had been doing. Then, "You won't ask me to go on board, will you?"

"No. I want you here at the controls."

"If you need me to come with you I will."

"It's all right."

"I don't want to go back there again."

"I understand. I'll need you by the instruments anyway." It wasn't necessary, but Ranglen assumed she wouldn't want to go and he had prepared this requirement.

"Let's not stay too long either."

"I don't intend to."

"Can I get you anything?"

He almost laughed. She never waited on him, so what brought on this solicitation now? "Will you relax?"

She didn't smile.

The pointed toy of the other ship drew closer. It was too ideal, like a polished model. Why would anyone construct it except for indulgence and whim? The swooping fins, the flawless symmetry, the rocket exhaust, the small tubes on the tips of the wings that imitated the fuselage, the hypodermic-needled nose, the feeling that the craft could only go forward.

It was a fantasy of sensuous curves—like the perfect folds of cloth in a Renaissance drawing. All flow and sharp points, a celebration of line. Mileen should appreciate it since it so clearly was designed for appearance. Ranglen wanted one. For all the varieties of ships at Hatch's spaceport, nothing resembled the beauty of this.

He asked, "You never found why your ship emerged early on the way from Ventroni?"

"No. And 'early' is subjective, right? The time that passed was still the same."

"Yet the exit location was not the one set."

"I never understood how that's established anyway. It's a location relative to what?"

"To the spot of departure," he said. "But, to be accurate, you can't define your exact point of arrival. 'Diffeomorphism invariance' still holds."

"Huh?"

"Instead of the event being defined in space-time, the event defines the space-time itself, determines the coordinate system for the location. That's why it works."

"Whatever you say." She acted unimpressed.

"You know where you'll emerge because the event defines the point of emergence—actually, the *matrix* and not the point."

"You're showing off, Mykol."

He grinned. She was right. He also was trying to keep their minds occupied.

"Nobody understands it," he said. "I'm just using the current jargon."

"Could you just pilot us in and get this job done? I know you love this stuff, but..."

He obligingly moved the ship closer. "I don't want to get too close. I could set up a permanent connection between airlocks but I'd rather not."

"I agree."

What they didn't say is that they both wanted to avoid "touching" the ship—they might feel contaminated. "Yeah, no one wants to get friendly with a haunted galleon alone in space."

"Could we be less graphic?" she asked.

"And could we also be a bit less touchy?" Slight impatience tightened his voice. "I need your help here."

"Sorry. But you're setting the distance between us and the derelict at the same separation Jayne did. That's a little disturbing."

"No big surprise. Standard procedure." He lied. But to admit the coincidence would have made it more scary.

He walked to the airlock, nervously backed into an open spacesuit hanging on a rack.

Ranglen hated spacesuits. He wasn't claustrophobic but he had a morbid fear of suddenly *becoming* claustrophobic, which could be as bad. His head enclosed, his face just centimeters from a transparent barrier too crowded with read-out and displays—this bothered him. He worried about the minor things, like sneezing, a runny nose, tears, flatulence, or an itch he couldn't scratch. And imagine if a fly got in there with him. Or a cockroach, or a scorpion.

And spacesuits reminded him too much of coffins. He could die inside one and—how convenient—already be enclosed in a casket. He didn't feel the way he pictured old spacemen saying, "Oh, if I die just leave me in my suit and shoot me off into space." No, he wanted to be dissolved in the biomass of a planet, absorbed into the next generation of life. But out here you just rotted alone, decayed progressively, got drenched in a sleet of over-killing radiation—encountered death to yet higher degrees.

Mileen noticed his discomfort as she helped him fasten clamps. "Now who's being irrational?"

"You want to go instead?"

"No."

"Then shut up."

She slapped his butt but he hardly felt her through the layers of insulation, pressurized fabric and air-conditioned undersuit.

He lumbered awkwardly into the airlock, taking along lights, hook-ups for computer "ferrets," cleaning materials, an information-recording cellpad, an extra communicator, extra lights, extra oxygen, extra food and water—those last were extravagant, he admitted, but you never knew. That Mileen hadn't laughed at all this showed how nervous they both had become.

The hatchway from the corridor shut behind him. He stood in the airlock alone. "You read me okay?" he said into the comm as the atmosphere cycled out.

"Five by five," she replied from the bridge. *"What does 'five by five' mean, anyway?"*

"I have no idea." But he knew it referred to signal strength and clarity. He hoped she could keep up this playfulness because it made him feel a little more alive.

The accelero-gravity weakened as the air pumped out. He felt himself rising from the deck, becoming weightless. But, as always, he had grabbed an anchoring handhold as soon as the pumps started.

The lights turned green beside the outer hatch. He flipped the switch. The hatch slid by, noiselessly in the vacuum. He saw a field of bright stars, a few wisps of nebula, and, not far away, the perfect spaceship.

He pulled himself out of the opening and on cautious thrusters glided over toward the ship. The experience was horrible. To be isolated in space, padded all over like a specimen in cotton and unable to move quickly, with his eyesight limited by the helmet frame and the cheek-and-chin instrumentation that provided data but blocked his vision—all this disturbed him. He felt no solace, no communion with the universe, no stellar sublime. He seemed trapped, removed from his senses and too cocooned in a hardened pillow.

Mileen's voice shocked him when it filled the helmet. *"I think you might go a little faster,"* she said.

Maybe he didn't want her joking after all.

He neared the hull of the other ship. Up close he finally could discern detail, but it was smoothed out, almost hidden. He saw the recessed crank for the airlock portal, just as Mileen described it, and the frame for the entranceway made to blend in as much as possible.

More slowly—Mileen must be growling—he settled his boots onto the hull and activated the grips. They would adapt for the quality of the material, smooth or coarse.

He bent down and turned the crank.

The door opened.

Mileen had said when they explored the ship earlier they changed nothing, which didn't surprise Ranglen. They could have sealed the hatch, blocked the airlock, scorched the interior, even partially broken up the craft. But once they got the coordinates for the Clip world, they didn't care about anything else. They smashed the console on which the figures and the Clip symbol had been found, but then they flew away, to treasure-hunt.

They left the bodies just as they were. Ranglen didn't look forward to those.

"How're you doing?" asked Mileen.

"Okay so far. The hatch is open now."

"You're not saying much. Omar talked on his way over."

"Should I recite a poem?"

"That wouldn't help."

"I always recited poems to myself when I went to the dentist, as they probed and cut. I never felt pain but just knowing that I might—that I was on the verge of it—made me want to keep occupied. I'd think through every poem I memorized."

"Could we talk about something else besides dentists?"

"I've got ancient mysteries here—ghosts, secrets, dark empty airlocks. You want that?"

"All right, do the poem."

Ranglen grinned.

The humor went away as he entered the airlock. His head-lamp glowed but he ignited the floods on his shoulders too. Since he was alone he didn't have to worry about blinding companions—a constant problem with people in spacesuits. Normally you shifted between low-beams and high-beams, just like on groundcars. He had a more powerful torch to carry but he wanted to keep his hands free.

The airlock appeared more functional than the outside of the ship—Mileen had mentioned this. But here too he encountered stylization, a smoothening and curving of edges. Switches and controls were bigger than necessary. Again, he felt a sense of archetyping, or stereotyping, of striving for an imaginary essence—the *idea* of an airlock and not the reality. It wasn't drastic, but if he took the time to look, he felt it.

Or maybe he was just delaying going inside.

The controls could be read for the cycling of the lock, easily so. They were in English, the buttons large. It all looked almost pre-spaceflight, like a movie set for an early science-fiction film, or even an old submarine interior.

He noticed no EVA suits hanging in the airlock. He wondered about that. And he would have liked to see what they resembled. Maybe they had transparent fishbowl helmets, rings of pads around the arm and knee joints, and came in different colors. Or, worse, they were like old deep-sea diving suits, with round metal domes and small grated windows—Jules Verne gothic.

He curbed his pesky imagination and opened the inner hatch.

Pure darkness beyond.

"Will you please talk to me?" Again, Mileen's voice scared the hell out of him.

"I'm at the goddamned door to the goddamned interior. You happy now?"

"Are you *happy?"*

"No. I apologize. I'll try to keep talking."

He leaned into the passageway, letting his lights shine about. A wall, almost bare, with pipes running across it amid bulky control consoles, colored in pastel shades, primary tones—as in an old comic strip.

"This is so unreal," he said. "I feel I'm in someone's toy."

"What do you mean?"

"It's like a future predicted in the past. Retro-modern."

"I know what you're getting at. I had the same feeling."

But he wasn't sure if she really understood. She agreed so quickly that maybe she was just trying to be helpful.

He glided down the hallway arm over arm, as if swimming, grabbing handholds and passing them on to invisible followers. "I'm maneuvering the passage toward the nose, the bridge."

Ranglen felt conflicted as he spoke.

He wanted to talk just to maintain contact with Mileen, to fill up empty space and soften the tension. But another part of him wanted only to look, to stay focused and not have to describe anything. This part of him actually enjoyed the experience, the primal contact with mystery. He almost wished he were totally alone, severed from humanity, Earth, the comm-link, even Mileen—for only then could he be open to the new.

The square screens were large and raised, the numbers on the gauges bigger than necessary, the swing needles long, the joy sticks and switches more prominent and elegant than what was essential. Yet all was still designed for human hands and human reach—just formed by an imagination that seemed archaic.

"You're clamming up again."

"I'm just looking. Not ready yet for words."

He was surprised she didn't complain. Maybe she did understand.

He reached the entrance to the bridge. "Okay. I'm there. Going inside now."

She didn't ask him what *there* meant.

He looked in, and at first couldn't orient himself. The glare of his lights flattened everything, or made black shadows that jagged out from every raised edge and prong.

These shadows swooped around him as he drifted in and turned his head. The view teased, deceived and taunted, had little sympathy.

Then he saw the four acceleration couches.

They struck him as old-fashioned, not even needed with accelero-gravity—again like something out of a past. They were huge, sumptuous, gracefully curved with big cushions. He saw just their backs and arms, and the instrument panel beyond, as he came up behind them.

Slowly, he glided alongside the couches, slid between the front of them and the control board to get the best view of the bodies. He was reluctant to examine them, but he knew he couldn't stop himself.

The three figures sat there undisturbed, a man, a woman, and a young boy maybe eight-years-old or so, though it was amazing they still could be identified. They looked more like mummies than skeletons, though the bone structure was dominant, down to the large sockets for eyes and the protruding chin and bared teeth. The faces retained more features than expected—the man's blondish hair, the woman's dark locks now unnaturally long—preserved because of the dryness and coldness in the spaceship.

But the bodies had lost all muscle tone. They looked emaciated, atrophied, the initial swelling in vacuum from interior air pressure now long gone. Any bulk mass seemed sucked out of them. The fallen skin was desiccated, like shredded cloth, parchment or leather, and had lost all color of life, now a mottled bluish-white and gray. And the extremities—the ears, the lips, and especially the fingertips which had suffered the most from loss of oxygen—were a pure darkish blue in color.

Finally he noticed the puncture wounds in the faded spacer jumpsuits that hung like deflated sacks. Five wounds each, in pentagons. And the bodies were strapped down in safety braces. Otherwise they'd be floating about the room.

He was glad they weren't.

Ranglen turned away, having seen enough and not wanting to know too much about them. Once this whole escapade was over and he came back to Annulus—if he were still alive—he would tell the authorities about this ship so these bodies could be studied and disposed of. He'd be curious then, but not now.

With relief, having passed what he believed was the worst moment, he focused on the instrument panel.

And realized he hadn't said anything to Mileen. "Mileen, are you there?"

"Finally! I think I've been incredibly patient, Mykol."

"You have been. I'm sorry—again. I was...looking at the bodies."

"I guessed that." A pause. *"Are you okay?"*

"The expectation was worse than the view. But I won't look much more at them. I'll work with the instruments and then...I'm leaving."

"Don't forget to examine the lifeboat cradle."

"I'll do that. Don't worry."

At one time the control panel must have been a model of simplicity and style, easy to operate. But now several of the screens lay broken, one console smashed and others damaged—the result of Jayne and Omar and Rashmi. But, even with so much destroyed, the internal drives had hardly been touched.

The panel was not dead—which surprised him. Jayne or Lonni would know the ship's records could still be accessed. Maybe one of them wanted to make sure that if the people in the group failed—or killed each other—the location of the Clip could still be obtained. Ranglen was confident he could find it. He had brought his own power unit and he knew several tricks learned from Hatch.

He took from the storage pouches on his suit the computer ferrets, programs in portable drives that accessed buried files. Luckily the ship, even if so idiosyncratic, was standardized enough for its files to be read—computers ever since the Confederation used compatible languages. Even the ones aboard this ship fit the template.

Indeed, the more Ranglen thought about it, he saw that the ship's internal systems weren't as different as the overlays—again, the emphasis seemed more on appearance. The ship had an exhaust tube, but the control instrumentation was for standard accelero-gravity propulsion and Clip drive components. If any "exhaust" actually worked, it had to be for show, all sparks and fireworks.

The access ports accepted the prongs of the ferret attached to Ranglen's cellpad. He initiated the protocols and the programs ran, infiltrating whatever systems were still operational. Depending on the size of the drives they could access, this would take a minute or two.

"The programs are running. I'm just waiting now."

"So am I," she said.

He wondered if she were as lost in thought and as nervous as he was. Her playful banter had long ceased.

As he waited, he glanced at the bodies again. Damn, he couldn't help it. He wondered if blood had seeped out of the wounds and formed arcs in the zero-g, as Lonni had thought, whether these had frozen into tiny whips or reddish snakes and eventually broke off and wandered about the cabin. Lonni had described the room in that way, but now any grit or dustlike debris—frozen blood traces—had glided into the corners from the recent passages of people.

The ferrets finished their tasks. Ranglen scrolled through banks of information. He accessed navigational records, and, after a not-very-difficult search, found a chart with a Clip symbol, the one apparently on the screen when the group from Mileen's ship came on board. He recorded all this on his portable databank and personal cellpad.

But, selfishly, he didn't send the information to his ship. You just don't do that when dealing with Clips. He didn't believe that Mileen, once obtaining the data, would take off and leave him there. But such behavior wasn't unknown and he felt it best to obey his paranoia.

"Okay," he said to her. "I've got what we came for." He didn't say anything more specific. Of course he believed they were the only people for light-years around—but he wanted to be careful.

"Great! Don't forget about the lifeboat."

He hid his irritation over her reminders. When you're alone with someone far out in space you always try to get along. "Moving there now."

He gathered his equipment and drifted aft, along the opposite side of the couches. And this time, because he saw the bodies from their right sides, he noticed something he hadn't seen before, something that neither Lonni nor Mileen had mentioned.

A small chunk of the side of the head behind the right ear of each of the three corpses was missing, as if calipers had yanked out a piece of flesh. The holes weren't large, the size of a chestnut, but each body had one and in the same place. The grizzled wire-like hair covered much of each wound, and the bodies had become so wasted the holes were easy to miss. A basic reluctance to examine the corpses might well have prevented their discovery.

Ranglen filed it away for later. For some reason—for the sake of privacy or propriety—he didn't mention the grisly find over the comm to Mileen. Also, he wanted to avoid delay. He had been there long enough.

He drifted into the chamber that once held the lifeboat.

The cradle indicated that the RLV had been large enough for only one person. He was sure other emergency rescue equipment remained on board, like the inflatable balloon-pods that could hold a person for days. But they didn't help much in deep space where signals took years to reach assistance.

An RLV was equipped with a Clip drive, but, in order to save everyone, it would have to be almost as large as the parent ship itself. Any powered vehicle was thus a compromise. The one on board Ranglen's own ship could hold two people, thanks to Hatch's retooling of the cradle, but not comfortably, and life-support would be cut in half.

Maybe the one on this ship could in a pinch also hold two, especially if they were kids.

Ranglen didn't speculate on what happened and why. He read the instruments on the cradle and the coordinates highlighted there, the targets of likely planet-bearing stars. As always, a lifeboat was a one-way trip. If the world didn't support life, the craft couldn't lift away again.

He recorded the data into his cellpad, then attached a lead and downloaded the information into the portable databank, to be sure he had a back-up.

This took only minutes, and he soon turned to make his way back.

"I've got the lifeboat information, Mileen. I'm returning now."

"I look forward to seeing you."

"Heat up a pot of coffee."

"I'll heat up the whole ship."

Ranglen smiled.

As far as he knew, the chamber for the lifeboat was not attached to the passageway that led from the airlock where he entered, so he had to go back through the control room to return to his ship.

Later, he'd realize he might have opened the hatch that allowed the lifeboat to egress, and he could have left that way. But he didn't think of that then.

This later would haunt him.

As he passed through the control room, he of course turned to look at the bodies one more time.

But something was different. It took him several seconds to realize what it was.

Four bodies lay there now. The fourth couch was occupied—with a new corpse.

The corpse was Lonni.

Ranglen had to force himself to accept what he saw.

She wore the same clothes she had worn when he visited her. Her head rocked slightly back and forth, maybe leftover motion from having been placed there. She looked too relaxed—past the rigor mortis stage—with her skin still fresh if swollen from the lack of outside air pressure. The breakdown of her cells wasn't advanced yet but Ranglen knew—perversely—that even now bacteria in her intestines were eating away her internal organs. She was strapped in so she wouldn't float away, but her tongue, like a half-swallowed fish, lulled out of her open mouth. And her eyes, slightly open, exposed a darkness he would not look into.

A hole sat in the middle of her forehead, like a black multi-pointed star. Puncture wounds formed a pentagon on her chest.

Ranglen couldn't move, his stomach gripped in a fist and being torn out of him. Lonni's body had to have been placed there while he examined the lifeboat cradle—just *minutes* ago.

He was not alone on the derelict!

And whoever hid there with him *knew* he had visited Lonni, knew he was coming to the ship, knew to wait in the shadows and to put her body here where he'd see it—to get maximum effect with her. Ranglen was *meant* to be terrified.

"Mykol, we have a problem!"

He almost screamed at Mileen's voice. What other problem could there be than this?

"There's a ship out there, right at the edge of sensor range. It popped onto the screen and isn't moving, as if it wants us to know it's there."

Ranglen looked around him before he could answer. He expected someone hiding and ready to kill him—to fill his chest with darts. A jumpy tangle of brights and darks drifted by, every shadow a threat.

"Mykol! Are you there?"

"Don't talk. I'm on my way."

Ranglen flew out of the control room and tossed himself down the passageway. He banged into a pipe at the airlock hatch, grabbed a handhold to stop and only then looked back. He saw nothing in the flash-lit darkness. But he didn't stare long—he was too afraid of what he might see, of what suddenly might emerge from around a corner.

He flew through the airlock and out the side of the ship.

Using the thrusters to guide himself wasn't graceful, and he approached his craft much too fast.

He plopped into the hull and missed the entrance. Then he pulled himself frantically across his ship and into the airlock, punched the controls to close the hatch behind him.

The air pumps took forever.

When the cycling stopped he threw off his helmet and rushed to the control room, thankful for the return of weight.

He jumped into the pilot's seat. "Strap in! We're leaving."

Mileen had already tied herself down. "It hasn't moved," she said, referring to the new ship. "Are you that frightened of it too?"

"I'm frightened of more than that."

Concern and shock filled Mileen's face as she looked at him.

Ranglen tried to be calm, asked, "Did the inner airlock door open while I was gone?"

"What? Of course not."

He opened the outer hatch to purge the lock of air—forcing anyone out who might have snuck in. This caused the ship to move in the opposite direction—Newton's second law, the air acting like an exhaust jet. The accelero-gravity quickly compensated.

"Why did you do that?" she asked.

"In case anyone was hiding in the airlock."

"But why—?"

"Someone's on board the derelict!"

Mileen froze.

"I didn't see who it was. But they knew I was coming. They left something…for me."

"What?"

"It was Lonni."

Mileen kept quiet as she stared back at him.

"Someone placed her, *dead*, in the last acceleration couch after I left the control room. When I came back from the lifeboat, the seat was filled. They killed her earlier and then left her there—while I was on board!"

Something changed in Mileen. The threat seemed to bring out her survival instinct and she clamped down any wayward fears. She turned to the sensor screens with tight concentration and repeated, "That other ship still hasn't moved."

"Doesn't matter. We're leaving." He kicked in the thrusters to push them from the derelict, his thoughts scurrying to find more ways to protect themselves. Should he purge the entire ship, just in case someone slipped on board? Had anything been attached to the outside hull?

Ranglen worked the accelero-gravity drive and quickly withdrew from the derelicts. He wanted to jump into light-space as soon as possible but he needed to enter the coordinates from the derelict first—and he needed to make sure nothing was riding with them!

He ran a security check of the entire ship. Such automated checks were thorough but they took time. Distribution of mass, air density, changes in life-support, and the very important examination of the hull. He ran all three levels of the search: quick, more thorough, and nothing missed. But he well might be in another universe before the second and third were done.

The silver ship fell behind as they gained speed.

Mileen said, "The ship on radar—it's not following."

"Good. Good."

The first security sweep finished with a chime and an "all clear" indicator. "Also good," he said, but he wanted to get through the second one too.

He pulled out his databank and hooked the leads to the onboard computers. By downloading data, he searched for the coordinates of the lifeboat world.

"Wait a minute," said Mileen.

Ranglen didn't like that tone at all—uncomprehending, on the verge of fear.

She whispered, "The other derelict...."

Ranglen stared at the screens, read the data that came up beside the blip representing the second derelict—the ugly one, the sinister one.

He couldn't believe what he saw.

The driftwood object, unlike the silver ship, was not getting smaller.

Instead, it grew steadily bigger—

It followed them! And it was gaining speed.

"Let's get out of here," Mileen said.

Ranglen worked frantically, his fingers flying over the keys, seeking what he needed. "What about that other ship, the one on radar?"

"Uh...it's gone. It must not have moved and now it's beyond our range."

"Good," he said, though the information seemed minor while the spiked mace of the driftwood derelict now rolled down at them.

And it *was* rolling, tumbling over itself. They could see it better now as it drew closer, matching their acceleration and gaining more speed. A jagged tangle of lumps and peaks somersaulting down at them—like a wire cage stuffed with wreckage and flung over a cliff with their ship in its path.

The second security search concluded. No anomalies. "Good," he said, but he felt foolish repeating that word.

The databank fell off Ranglen's lap, crashed on the floor and pulled out a lead. The screen flickered and then steadied. Luckily the program wasn't interrupted

The object filled the screen now, prongs and archways and sticks and pipes bearing down on them like a solid wave—cresting, jagged.

"Can't we jump into light-space?" Mileen asked.

"Not until we enter the exit coordinates. Otherwise we'll never come back out."

"But if that thing gets too close—"

"I know, I know!—the transition will stop automatically with a proximity alert. But I almost have it."

He found the numbers and entered them. Too late, he realized he could have typed in an already logged location, like Annulus. But he would have needed to close out the program, which would take time—and he didn't want to pull any part of the object back to Annulus, which would happen if it got any closer.

"Mykol!"

The outer spikes swung too near. A few already passed by them, their ends beyond the ship's location.

A big arch flung down to pass *ahead* of them, in the direction of their velocity. The inner wall of the object avalanched not far behind.

He hit the switch for light-space transition.

An alarm sounded! Proximity alert—an automatic reject.

The drive didn't start. The arch swept by too close, putting too much mass both in front and behind them.

An instant later the arch fell away.

Ranglen kicked the switch again, prayed they were clear.

The ship exited time-space.

The object, Ranglen assumed, kept on rolling—right through the spot where they had been.

Chapter Eleven: Rift Valley

After their escape Ranglen felt no euphoria. He was too worried.

The outside of the hull could not be examined while in light-space so he had no way to see if they dragged in anything with them, like a torn piece of the pursuing object. A probability wave extended beyond any ship during the transfer, and though its value fell exponentially, debris from outside could be sucked into the jumps.

Mileen peered at the instruments. "Did we make it away all right?"

"As far as I know. If it wanted to catch and hold us, it failed."

That troubled Ranglen. The whole chase, leading up to this last-minute escape, struck him as too coincidental. He believed it was meant more to scare than apprehend.

Like Lonni's corpse.

Which meant that getting away held little advantage. Indeed, if they were *supposed* to escape then the reason might be to plant a tracer on them.

Yet that could have been done easily without them suspecting it. Why throw a tumbling mountain at them?

He had not completed his third search of the ship but it was too late to run it now. The hull was compromised by the light-space probability functions.

"Mykol, you said Lonni was on board the derelict.

"That ship you detected probably dropped off whoever was on board, with Lonni, and then moved out of detection range. Maybe it returned just to disturb us."

"What about the other derelict? Was it controlled, or did it act on its own?"

Ranglen didn't know and he didn't want to speculate.

Mileen eyed Ranglen, and he felt her look. He sensed she was suspicious of his unwillingness to talk, probably believing he held something back or else was now uncertain he could trust her. But he was just too deep in thought. Too much had happened, and he was not one to think out loud.

A distancing silence grew between them.

Ranglen downloaded all the data the ferrets retrieved from the computers on the derelict. But just as he was about to decode the star charts and get a location for the world with a Clip, a command-line appeared requiring a clearance code. He didn't have it. And when he entered queries, an icon for a lifeboat flashed on the screen.

They needed further information, and maybe, the icon suggested, it was on board the RLV.

No one had mentioned this, not Jayne, Rashmi, or Lonni. Had they misread the chart? Or maybe the star coordinates they took were those of the lifeboat world and not the one with a Clip? Did Jayne and the others know this? Or did the files they accessed, and then destroyed, give only the coordinates of the Clip world and not the other?

Ranglen applied himself to finding an answer. For the next two days, he researched everything he could about Clips, but many of the articles had been written by himself. Mileen helped him but she soon grew tired of it. She lolled about the ship, did no drawing or painting. The closeness they had felt on the asteroid seemed on hold, contaminated by the recent events. Ranglen was too busy to try to resolve it.

The ship emerged into normal space.

Dust and broken metallic pieces formed around them. Ranglen quickly ran checks. The fragments didn't fit known devices. No communication signals were intercepted, no power sources recognized. No wreckage jumped back into light-space to deliver a message. Displays showed only shredded metal, apparently pieces of the staves that formed the object.

"We must have ripped out a small area," Ranglen said. "But if the stakes served any function, they don't seem to have retained it."

He gunned thrusters and accelero-gravity, raced away from the cloud of fragments. It didn't follow them.

He ran programs similar to those on board all lifeboats, designed to seek the nearest main-sequence star similar to Sol and then, on reaching it, to approach any terrestrial planet in its system, which of course were rare.

But Ranglen found a likely world and flew towards it.

"If the lifeboat landed there," he told Mileen, "I should be able to pinpoint its location. They're meant to be found, so if it still has any power at all—the signal-generator has long-life batteries—I can find it. We'll land, check it out, download its computer files if it still runs. If we get the information I need to reach the Clip world, we'll leave as soon as we can."

"We'll do a search for a survivor, right?"

"If anyone survived and they're not near the lifeboat, or they're not making an active effort to be found, then our chances of detecting anyone are small."

Her face hardened.

"Mileen, we can't stay here long. I'm sorry, but what happened back at the derelicts changes everything. That object *moved* on us. Maybe there's more to this Clip than what I thought. And if that's the case, the sooner we find it and get it to the authorities—to *all* the authorities—the better off we'll be."

She still said nothing. She didn't look at him.

He focused on his instruments.

The world grew nearer, a bright shield patterned in strange violet and gold. It reversed the normal contrasts of a planet. Clouds usually shone brighter than the surface, but here the yellow background glowed more strongly than the dull lavender vapors of the air. At first Ranglen wondered if the cloud tint was a result of the eye's imposition of an opposite color after staring at the gold, the way early astronomers believed that the darker areas on red Mars were actually green. But he dismissed that theory as they drew closer. The colors became more pronounced. Even the bow of atmosphere at the edge of the planet formed a vivid golden arc, which Ranglen couldn't understand. The star was K3, redder than Sol but not enough to make such a difference—it had plenty of the narrower wavelengths for Rayleigh scattering to produce a blue sky.

As they went into orbit and studied the surface, Ranglen said, "Plate tectonics. The continents look like puzzle pieces that fit together." Between the purplish banks of cloud and against the bright gold oceans the continents seemed like huge fragments, stained with a suggestive olive of growth, creased with mountains like rippled copper. "See those peaks running along the shores? Trenches must lie right off the coast."

"You're saying a Clip might be here?"

"It's possible."

The Airafane dropped their precious Clips into deep sea trenches where continents, riding on stone plates, collided and squeezed beneath one another, to be picked up by the mantle's currents which, in a hundred million years or so, would spew them back to the surface in mid-ocean ridges, where the floor of the sea spread apart and molten rock seeped up from below.

"Is that a rift valley?" Mileen pointed to what appeared to be a trench that emerged from an ocean and ran across a continent, where the spreading of the plates came up to the air. The depression would widen until someday it formed an arm of the sea.

"Yes, and it's odd you should point to that." Ranglen had just caught a signal on a frequency reserved for lifeboats. "That's where the RLV is located, though the signal coming from it is weak. In fact…" He applied magnification to a visual sensor, enhanced the image. "I can just make out the lifeboat, but…another ship has landed there also. I don't think it's a relic but something new." He glanced at Mileen. "We're not alone here."

"Jayne and Rashmi?"

"I don't know."

"Maybe they encountered the same location trouble that you did. They had to come here to find the Clip world. Or…maybe this *is* the Clip world."

"The Clip symbol on the charts was not for here."

"Then…"

"Let's not speculate. I want to get out of their line-of-sight before they detect us."

He changed orbit, ran recordings of the sensor input to check the data more closely. His passive instruments detected no searching from the ship below but he wanted to be safe. That ship would also have passive sensors but it needed to know where to look in the sky.

"Whoever they are, they found the lifeboat. They're parked right beside it. That means we're too late for an aerial approach. We'll have to go on foot."

"Won't that be dangerous?"

"I think we can handle it." He sounded self-assured.

The rift valley withdrew behind them, and Ranglen's sensors established it was filled with jungle. Both the lifeboat and the other ship had landed on a rise that emerged from the growth. "This second ship complicates things, but we'll sneak in under cover."

"Maybe they're meeting someone here, using the lifeboat as a beacon. That would explain why they're so close to it."

Ranglen didn't answer, again not wanting to speculate.

He dumped speed and brought them down near ground level, flew over savannas and thin forests, beneath the reach of radar and scanning. He wondered if the other ship had established any satellite surveillance. Ranglen had sent out a satellite of his own and set it into geosynchronous orbit above the valley and the lifeboat, to be used for location-finding on the surface—standard procedure when coming to a new world, though usually at least three were used. He ordered his satellite to check if other objects floated in its neighborhood but the results were negative.

He landed on a grassy plain above the rift valley, several kilometers from both the lifeboat and the visitors.

"You think they know we're here?" Mileen asked.

"I don't think so. I was careful coming in, and they shouldn't see us if we approach on the ground."

"It'll be a long walk."

"The air's breathable. That's why the lifeboat came here. The planet's rotation is 32 hours so we'll have plenty of daylight. Temperature's warm, but it's early in the day and it'll get hot. If that's jungle in the valley it could be uncomfortable. We'll need different clothes."

The ship was well-stocked with wilderness gear. Ranglen chose for both of them loose-fitting and quick-drying outfits, light waterproof boots, "leech guard" ankle sleeves, brimmed hats to counter both the sun and the local equivalents of insects, detoxin filters for safe breathing, hunting and utility pocket-knives, canteens with purifier tablets (the tablets designed for human-based biologies but those not human were probably too incompatible to pose a threat), waterproof tracking equipment that linked to the satellite in orbit, generic anti-louse body powder (lots of that), and several pairs of socks.

Mileen accused him of over-preparing. He countered by suggesting, "Don't wear underclothes."

"Excuse me?"

"If the humidity's high they chafe the skin."

She looked unconvinced. "I'll wear loose ones."

He was trying to lighten the mood. He could see she wasn't happy about the walk and he suspected it was because of delay, not danger.

He debated whether to take hunting rifles but he decided on pistols instead. The guns shot lasers with ion-beam cores. Better for interpersonal work.

The ship had landed beside a copse of trees in wide grassland soon after dawn. Ranglen energized the expensive chameleon defense shield, giving the ship the coloration of the environment. It imitated and reflected the readings of local compositions too—metals, gases, humidity, temperature. Though the program should fool most sensory probes, Ranglen didn't trust such technology in general.

They emerged from the hatch into morning light and cool moving airs.

Tall blond and ochre grass scraped against the bottom of the ship. Dazzle ran through the dew-laced savanna. Tints of red and burnt-sienna streaked the meadow. The wind carried scents of basil and almond. The grass made soft cracking sounds, like static electricity. The trees rose in supple hands, held nets of narrow olive leaves that shaped the boughs into aerodynamic pods, pointing away from the wind. Above everything spread an unbelievable sky, serene, immaculate, more vivid yellow here than seen from space, tinged apricot in the east where the sun glowed and a lean lavender cloud stretched.

Ranglen loved alien landscapes.

He watched Mileen turn her head, red hair glinting gold in the recurring sunrise light of this world. In her khaki outfit she looked part of the landscape. Woman of the plains.

She said impatiently, "Are you ready?"

"We used to live for moments like this."

"I'm not an artist right now, Mykol, and you don't have time to be a writer. We're here to find that lifeboat."

He chose not to argue and set off toward the valley.

He looked back at the ship to see if the camouflage had blended it correctly into the trees. It seemed to be working.

The grass rose above their heads. These lower areas held cloaks of mist, not as dark as the few clouds in the sky but the grayness had the same purplish cast. All else was soaked in gold light—the green shrubs, the tawny-yellow and rusted grass, their clothes, their skin, Mileen's hair.

He wondered, did the sky's contrasting colors come from two types of airborne bacteria? Ranglen had seen such effects on other worlds. But the gold here seemed almost luminous, and the violet vapors were dull in contrast.

"Mykol, there's smoke."

To the north a cloud, darker and brown, lazily stained part of the sky.

"Probably from a volcano. I saw many of them at the head of the rift. Fumaroles and soda lakes fill the south, closer to the sea. It's what you'd expect. The crust is new and still thin."

He didn't state the obvious, that an active rift valley might not be safe. If the lifeboat had landed here twenty years ago the chances of it, and any survivor, encountering an earthquake or eruption were strong.

He used his satellite to run a topographic program on the northern volcano with the plume. The results were sketchy since he had no comparative timeline, but they suggested the dome might be swelling from internal pressure. This made him anxious.

A herd of four-legged creatures ran past them out in the plains, resembling bronze antelope with green sails along their backs waving as they ran. Though they seemed agitated it wasn't the stampede preceding an eruption or an earthquake. They looked dangerous since they were as big as horses with nests of sharp horns on their heads—the antlers almost resembling the derelict that had chased them.

Ranglen never trusted coincidence.

They encountered more pockets of mist. The vapors moved along beside them.

And then they reached the edge of the rift.

"How do we get down there?"

Ranglen didn't answer as he looked into the valley. At least 500 meters below lay the graben or depression of the rift, the opposite cliff about 50 kilometers away. And, as Ranglen saw from orbit, vegetation filled the valley. This surprised him because the land there had to be recent, formed by volcanic upwellings. So the jungle had to have grown fast. And why was humidity—so necessary for a rainforest—present in the middle of a praire where the rain seemed too scarce to support more than grass and scattered trees?

The jungle looked sinister, thick, black-green, congested with the violet mist—like vegetable mounds in frothy milk or a lumpy and unappetizing cream soup. And the place was too quiet, in a shadowy "lost world" mood, secret, in hiding. Flying creatures hovered in black clouds and looked primeval.

Ranglen turned to Mileen, and found her engrossed with the cliff-face to their left. The mists that accompanied them fell over the precipice like a graceful slow-motion waterfall. Clumps slid down, whole sheets of lilac blankets dispersing in the air as they drifted lower.

"I've seen this before," said Mileen.

"It's a common phenomenon. When the mist reaches the rim, it's caught in a downdraft, then dissipates when it enters the warmer air of the valley."

She quickly lost interest. "How close are we now?"

He took a reading of the lifeboat's beacon, pinpointed its location five kilometers away, though he couldn't see it in the forest.

The cliff face looked treacherous. Columns of basalt had solidified from lava into hexagonal pedestals, gray and black and splotched with red. Some columns had fallen. Descending through them could cause ankle sprains or broken legs. Ranglen warned Mileen to test all holds, to always secure three points of contact.

She nodded curtly.

They crawled down the cliff, the igneous rock savage on exposed skin. Ranglen wished he had brought gloves. Their packs added to their awkwardness and the brimmed hats pooled sweat on their heads.

The sun rose higher, the light now fiery instead of mellow.

They heard noises—like something attacking!

Black-winged creatures swept from above. Each squealed a piercing "creech!" as they dived and snapped claws at their heads, like insectile bats or praying mantises with bent fore-claws and leathery wings.

Ranglen and Mileen retreated between the columns.

The creatures swooped by, each one at least two meters in wingspan, sounding like burlap torn in a storm. As he crouched between the vertical rocks, Ranglen saw their black hides had purple bars across their bellies and purple circles around the eyes. A long sword with a tiny red sail protruded from the back of each head and swung like a whip—a rudder or a blade-weapon. The claws hung dark and deadly.

The flyers rose, swung back and dived again, creeching sharply. Needle beaks snapped at the humans. But they stayed wedged between the blocks.

The creatures rose and landed on the columns at the top of the cliff, staring at the intruders. A few glided above the rim where cries mingled with raucous wings.

Mileen said, "Will we ever get out of here?"

Ranglen shrugged, not knowing what to do.

Then the creatures—in a pack—took to the air. They hurled beyond the cliff and disappeared.

Ranglen and Mileen glanced at each other, kept still. Then they quickly moved further downhill.

The flyers thundered across the edge of the cliff. They screamed at something running below.

One of the deer-like animals they saw earlier was being chased. It tumbled off the cliff and fell into the basalt columns, hitting like a filled sack on the rocks.

In a horrible cloud of snapping beaks, the creatures dived onto the animal. Their wings opened to cushion their landing and they swarmed over the carcass. They ripped into its sides, yanked out haunches, flung them in the air. Their tongues doubled as long knives, lilac blades that sliced methodically. The sails at the ends of the whips tossed strips of meat like fat snakes, to be splattered on stones or caught by other beaks and claws. The creatures made no shrieks now. They were too busy—chomping, devouring.

The humans felt sick. They moved lower as the slaughter continued.

"They make good use of the environment," Ranglen said.

Mileen didn't answer. She looked drained and bleak.

Ranglen didn't say that the chances for a survivor from the lifeboat were now smaller.

They left the rocks as the slope became gradual with grass and shrubs. They entered the mist that lay in the valley. The gold light of the heights weakened and a cloying gloom crept over them, but they felt more hidden from the predators above.

Between the trunks the ground felt resilient. The limbs formed layers throughout the trees, like floors in buildings without walls. This close to the forest-edge a thin light still entered but further within the haze thickened.

A figure—suddenly—stood in their path. A humanoid staring back at them.

The "person," though tall, seemed insectile, with narrow legs bent at the knees, curved feet and a forward-tilting stance. On its thin body the head looked too broad, but the plume of purplish-black hair surrounding it—like a lion's mane—made it seem bigger. The rodent face had a long nose slanting down to small nostrils, a ski-jump slope of bright yellow fading into purple. The eyes gleamed golden bright—intent, pensive. Blue crescents framed the eyes, and the rest of the face had purple hatch-marks similar to those on the black-winged flyers. The arms hung gaunt with big hands and claw-like fingers. Skin crescents rose from the shoulders that once might have been wings but now connected into a sail similar to that on the deer-like creatures, apparently more decorative than functional.

The body shone porcelain-gray, dark with almost the same sheen as the bat-creatures, but the purple hints were more pronounced and the sleek covering was of fur instead of leather. The eyes caught the most attention, like amber sap or gold gems in their pools of blue astride that striking yellow-purple muzzle. They looked curious, grave, penetrating.

Intelligent.

Then Ranglen saw—

The creature vanished into the woods.

Mileen said, "It wore something around its neck."

Ranglen had seen it. A cord made of woven plant fiber. It stood out because it was lighter than the neutral skin. And hanging on that necklace…

"It looked like…"

A crystal of fluorite. Octahedral, a few centimeters in width. Exactly like the carrier-lock Ranglen had found on his asteroid, and in the same colors of purple and yellow.

Like the colors of the planet itself, he realized.

Did that crystal hold a Clip?

Chapter Twelve: Volcano

The air grew humid under the trees, the odors dank and cellar-like, rotten. Ranglen and Mileen sweated heavily, felt claustrophobic. The mist was like soft violet fungus, the vines like arteries and fat veins, the leaves like cells of green blood, the blue-white trunks like dried bones that reminded Ranglen of the corpses on the derelict.He felt they had been swallowed and were inside a body. Even the ground felt supple, like stretched canvas or tightened skin.

Ranglen suddenly realized—they weren't standing on the ground. They walked in the trees.

"We're in a tier of the forest," he said, "walking on leaves that are built into thick mats on the branches."

"How do we get to the ground?"

"I don't think we do. It would be too dark down there anyway, and maybe too wet. Traveling up here should be easier."

The pads lay firm, the limbs bridging one vegetable floor to the next. Ranglen wondered what lurked beneath them. He knew that in typical jungles the animals were smaller than the big herd creatures in tropical savannas, and they came out more at night.

The liveliest creatures, sadly, were the insects, or what resembled them. Huge green dragonfly-creatures trailed whips, large butterflies resembled kites with hanging ribbons, the patterns on their wings like stained glass. Most life-forms had a membraned tail dangling behind them or a sail that rose above their heads. Ranglen wondered if these once had been weapons, built-in evolutionary knives.

He feared the local equivalents of beetles and ants creeping into their shirts, boots, ears. If they stopped for a rest, they'd need to shake out their clothes. Snakes too might stalk about. And plants were known to have poisonous thorns.

"I don't understand," he said. "This jungle shouldn't have enough time to develop such complexity."

"Maybe if that humanoid controlled…"

A Clip. The miracle worker, the stuff that corrupts.

A tremor shook the drum-like "ground."

They looked around. Another quake followed.

Ranglen checked his satellite link and downloaded updates on the volcano to the north. The baseline still wasn't detailed enough but his first reaction was not good. "We'd better hurry."

"Are we in danger?"

"More from the bugs." They shook their loose clothing and proceeded on.

Emerald beetle-things scurried up from beneath the mats, and Ranglen looked through the openings to catch, or maybe imagine, a network of pale lights down there. He pictured night-filled depths where bioluminescence made fireworks, fancied jaws with glowing teeth, cavernous mouths made of light-dripping daggers.

He tried to curb his surging imagination.

Mileen grabbed his arm, pointed.

To their left on a lower mat lay the body of a small animal, almost covered by the butterfly-birds that, from the sounds, seemed to be sucking its blood. The dangling whips jabbed at the corpse and made crude slurping noises.

A paw of the fallen creature moved, maybe still alive.

The two hurried on.

The ground rose before them. They had reached the rise in the middle of the valley and walked on actual ground now. The jungle provided good cover as they crept upward, though soon the trees were replaced with shrub that, luckily, grew dense enough to hide behind. The light was stronger, yellowish again under a hazy sky, the grass beige and the shrubs olive, just like on the plains.

They moved up beside a thicket where Ranglen checked his positioner. He whispered, "We should be almost there."

A few of the dark bat-like flyers glided overhead.

They could see nothing from where they hid so they moved on cautiously, pushed their way around the line of shrub.

Through a screen of leaves they saw the lifeboat.

Apparently it either had broken on impact or was pummeled by a falling tree. Though vines nearly buried it, the nose and tail poked up at different angles and lay farther apart than the craft's length would have allowed.

Ranglen said, "It doesn't look too good for survivors."

"It's still sending a beacon. Something's intact."

But Ranglen believed the lifeboat's systems had to be long corrupted. The craft never should have landed in the middle of a jungle near active volcanoes, though at least it found the rise and didn't plunge into the trees.

Had it followed another signal? Been controlled somehow?

He turned to Mileen. "Wait a minute, before we get closer—"

He held her gaze for a moment. Then his hand reached behind her head and he pulled her face to his. He kissed her.

She didn't resist. But she asked, "What brought that on?"

"The lust before danger. Have to grab it while you can. We don't know what we're getting into."

She looked curious, but she didn't deny him.

They moved to a position where they could see further into the clearing and observe the second ship he detected from orbit. Ranglen doubted if it had the expensive camouflage programs his own ship used.

Mileen followed.

The other ship lay on its belly, a flattened lozenge with a rounded front and a narrow tail. It was larger than Ranglen's own ship, able to hold five or six passengers comfortably, probably the size of the vessel that went to Ventroni. It was not camouflaged, which meant they didn't expect company—or else they did and they *wanted* to be found, which also would be a reason for parking so close to the lifeboat's signal.

Two people, inspecting the aft engines, stepped from behind the ship. Jayne Fowler and Rashmi Verlock.

Ranglen was not surprised, but the craft looked expensive for just the two of them. Too large for anything that might have belonged to Jayne. They probably rented the ship, then left Annulus right after they talked to him.

Perhaps they ran into the same problem that he encountered—the coordinates indicating that the location of the Clip world was in the lifeboat. But if they had the information already, why were they still on this planet? From all Ranglen knew this was not the world with the Clip as indicated by the derelict.

He wondered if Jayne and Rashmi knew about the bat-like humanoid, that it possibly wore a carrier-lock around its neck.

Another person came from behind the ship.

Hatch Banner.

Mileen and Ranglen both stared in astonishment.

This didn't make sense. Hatch hated Clips, and what could he provide that would allow him to participate? Jayne certainly could have gotten a ship on her own—not one so large, perhaps, but it wouldn't be needed anyway.

Hatch and Jayne worked on the stern of the craft. Rashmi watched.

Ranglen and Mileen looked at each other. He indicated they should return to thicker cover.

"But it's just Hatch," she said. "Why do we have to avoid them at all? Even Jayne and Rashmi—they won't hurt us."

"They're after the Clip. You don't know how they'll behave. Remember Henry."

"But I *know* Hatch. He'd never hurt me. He was like a father."

"I don't trust them," Ranglen said. "We don't know why they're here."

"Mykol, I'm sure we don't have to—"

"Let me sneak over and get the coordinates for the Clip world from the lifeboat. Once we have that, then we can decide what to do. We have to get that first or we might wind up with nothing."

She looked disturbed. "All right," she said tartly. "Get the data."

"You have to keep watch for me. I'll look inside the lifeboat and work on the controls. If I can't get the coordinates—Hatch might have purged the system—then we'll come back here and decide our next move."

She nodded, looked away.

Ranglen waited for more.

"I'm disappointed," she said finally, defensively. "I thought we'd find evidence of a survivor."

"We haven't looked close enough yet."

"The boat's broken in half! And this planet is dangerous."

"I'll see what's there. We can still get back to my ship before dark."

"All right," she said. "Go."

The two of them removed their backpacks and hats and left them hidden beneath a bush. They crept on through the shrubs, staying under cover. They were lucky that the lifeboat sat between them and the other ship.

Another tremor rippled the ground, swayed the branches and shook the leaves. Black flyers took to wing, creeching loudly.

"Let's move," Ranglen said.

They approached the broken halves of the lifeboat. "You stay here. Can you see all the others through that shrub?"

"Yes."

"Good. I'll be busy so I won't pay attention to them. If you see anyone approaching, come get me. We should be able to sneak out before they see us." Ranglen wasn't convinced of that but he didn't want to sound uncertain.

Though she didn't look confident either, she nodded and agreed.

He crept to the lifeboat.

The ship was torn apart so he had excellent access to the small control panel, which leaned toward him for a better reach. He could work on it while out of sight of the other ship.

He glanced at Mileen. Her khaki outfit blended in perfectly with the grass.

Another shudder ran through the ground.

Ranglen hurried, while thinking that the quakes might help him, diverting the attention of Hatch, Jayne, and Rashmi.

The instruments inside the lifeboat had been recently smashed, like those on the derelict. But a new power source was attached to the circuits to keep the signal-beacon going. Ranglen wondered why. Maybe it was used as a homing device. The data-ports through which he could access the onboard files were the same as on the derelict, so he hooked up his information bank with his portable ferret and started downloading. Since this would be his only chance to get the data he didn't take time reviewing it—he just hoped for the best. He gathered all navigation material.

And he glanced at Mileen several times. She hadn't moved. She looked back-and-forth between him and the other ship.

While the downloads ran he examined the wrecked lifeboat. He saw no indication that the ship had been lived in, no trace of a makeshift shelter. Only fallen trunks and thick brambles occupied the ruin. A path had been worn leading off toward the other ship but apparently it was recent.

He finished his download, unplugged the connection. He turned to signal thumbs-up to Mileen.

She wasn't there.

What the hell? He moved away from the lifeboat to where she had lay hidden in the shrub. No sign of her. He looked toward the other ship.

Shock hit him. He saw Mileen walking openly toward it.

Hatch came forward to meet her—with a smile of satisfaction. They ran together and hugged each other. Jayne and Rashmi came up too, expressionless, not as eager.

Ranglen felt discarded—she had deserted him! *Why?*

A paranoid anger burned inside him. He debated if he should try to get her back. She had left on her own, made her choice. Did she expect him to follow? Or was all this planned—just so he could bring her here to meet with them! Was the tie between Hatch and Mileen that strong?

He fought a selfish bitterness that wanted to leave all of them and go after the Clip himself.

But the people around the ship started an argument. Jayne and Rashmi swung their arms, their voices rising.

And another tremor swept the field. Ranglen felt certain an eruption was imminent—but did they have hours, days, or minutes before it occurred?

The uncertainty and danger decided things for him. They had to work together.

He left the protection of the shrub and walked toward them—joining the party, he thought to himself.

An argument *had* started. Hatch and Jayne stood in front of Mileen as if protecting her while Rashmi faced them separate and alone. They glared at each other, their hands clenched. If they noticed Ranglen they gave little sign.

He walked up toward them and openly listened. They saw him, but were more concerned with their disagreement.

Hatch snapped at Rashmi, "We're leaving with her." He indicated Mileen.

Rashmi shot back, "We need to meet Balrak."

Ranglen moved backward a pace.

Hatch insisted, "We're not meeting anyone—"

"That was the deal," Rashmi said. "Balrak will kill us if we don't do what we agreed."

"You stay if you want," Hatch said, "but the three of us are leaving. I got what I wanted." He and Jayne headed for the spaceship. Mileen followed them, obviously willing—as if she had already made her choice. She looked back at Ranglen and yelled to him, "Mykol, you come too."

But stubbornness silenced him, made him withdraw. If Mileen wanted to leave with them he wouldn't stop her.

Rashmi yelled, "Jayne, we were partners."

Jayne looked guilty as she started up the ramp, but didn't respond.

Rashmi pulled an Arms-Watch dart gun from his jacket and aimed it at Hatch. "You're not taking her. We made a deal with Balrak."

Hatch walked faster.

Rashmi shouted, "*He* gets Mileen. And Ranglen, too. I'm keeping that deal. You and Jayne can leave, but *she* stays."

Hatch pushed Mileen and Jayne before him.

Ranglen pulled out his own pistol and moved quickly behind Rashmi.

But a dart whisked from the rear of the ship and planted itself in Rashmi's hand, the one holding his gun.

Rashmi stared at it in disbelief. The gun slipped from his grip as if his fingers had gone numb. He looked up and muttered.

Omar Mirik stepped out of hiding in the trees, holding his own dart-gun. He shouted, with an affected arrogance, "Balrak's here already so no one's leaving. He wants Mileen and—"

He saw Mykol and waved his free hand. "Hello there, Ranglen! He wants you too. Don't be surprised that he knows you're here. We had sensors on board the lifeboat so we knew when you made your download. We've been waiting for you. And you can put that gun back into your pocket."

Ranglen didn't.

The earth shook—violently. Omar and Ranglen fell to the ground.

A flight of the stained-glass butterflies swept from the trees, rushed by them and disappeared into the woods, followed by a quick-march of green beetles scuttling through the grass on furious legs.

Ranglen understood. They fled the volcano before it erupted.

Hatch shoved Mileen and Jayne inside the ship. Rashmi, after hesitating, chased after them up the ramp.

Omar shot at him from the ground.

A dart hit Rashmi in the leg. He staggered forward, managed to pull himself through the entryway. Omar pummeled the opening with darts. The door closed.

Omar jumped to his feet and rushed to the ramp. Ranglen also stood and fired his pistol at him. The laser-and-ion beam slashed against Omar's upper arm, the one holding the gun.

Omar looked down at the steaming burn with the same disbelief Rashmi had shown.

The volcano exploded.

What must have been a vast buried chamber of compressed steam broke forth and tore apart the mountain. Cauliflower clouds of ash and debris rushed skyward, dark plumes boiling into heaven—like mad fists thrust up through the earth or continuous blasts from hidden artillery, a landslide in reverse. It looked alive, a self-spawning detonation that rushed outward to invade the world.

Omar froze, paralyzed.

Ranglen waved his arms at the spaceship, yelled—hoping they could hear him—"Take off! Get out of here!"

He knew that the ash, abrasive as glass, would clog all intakes, sandpaper the viewports. They'd first be blinded and then the thrusters and even the accelero-gravity would fail—if the gust of hot air didn't overturn and smash the whole craft.

Ranglen was struck in the back. He fell. Animals ran past him, just missing his head as he lay on the ground. A pack of lizards two meters tall roared by. Ranglen tried to stand—again was knocked down, by a small elephant with a yellow anemone for a head. Helpless, he watched the feet and hooves stampeding past.

The sky turned black, churning like a battlefield. He knew that a second cloud of the same hot ash would be tearing like a freight train toward him now, flattening every tree in its path. The roar of its destruction rocked the earth. A blast of hot air would kill him first, then the needle-filled ash would slice away his skin and face—like sand shot at him from the exhaust of a jet.

He didn't care about Omar now, who too must have been flattened by the stampeding wildlife.

He thought he heard the ship flying away. He prayed it was true. Wisely, Hatch wasn't trying to save Ranglen and Omar.

Then, inconceivably, out of the swelling death-cloud in the sky emerged an equally ugly object.

The driftwood derelict.

Ranglen watched in horrid fascination.

It punched through the ash like an emerging planet, the gritty fumes lacing its arches and falling through its sides. It looked like a solidified part of the cloud, an evil offspring.

And from it little pieces flew. Spikes plunged down to the earth, struck and stabbed at it.

Ranglen couldn't understand what was happening.

And he had one last impossible sight.

Looming above him, careless, nonchalant, ignoring the catastrophe surging forward and about to destroy them, stood the purple-gray humanoid with the necklace of fluorite. It stared at Ranglen, weirdly pensive, oblivious to the oncoming disaster, even to the spikes shooting down from the sky.

Then the superheated air hit.

Chapter Thirteen: The Underworld

He lay in a drowned cathedral. Or a cave.

Have you been here before?

"No," he replied.

You're not the first.

"I think I guessed that."

It was like the dark interior of a temple, with windows and colored sunbeams in the ceiling, with rafters or branches thick before it. A labyrinth of small lights, glittering green and blue and violet. All else was dark.

Columns lifted toward the roof, spreading at their tops and bases. This might be a cave, Ranglen thought, a purple cave though most of it was black. And inside it the soft lights drifted. He couldn't tell if they were insects or birds or some other kind of creature. Pixies? Fairies? Each in its little glowing globe. Or maybe they were plants, flowers in flight.

Sometimes a shaft of light came down amid all the barriers and networks above. It was no javelin from a horrifying cloud. Ranglen shuddered at the memory, if that's what it was.

"Who's talking to me?" he asked.

Unintelligible.

"Are you the creature Mileen and I saw on the edge of the forest, the one leaning over me during the eruption?"

Close enough.

"What do you mean?"

Everything we say is an approximation. You don't see or know enough.

"You have...."

You're interested in what I'm wearing.

"No."

Yes. You don't need to hide it.

"Was that what saved us?"

It helped. But everything around us helps.

The ground steamed, felt warm. Water made lakes that in some places boiled. But it still seemed cool here in the depths. Damp, saturated. Coils of roots spread like tentacles. The steam created a purple talcum that floated in wisps. The place had an epic narrative feel, but it was no dark night of the soul. It was lovely, really. He wanted to stay.

For a time he couldn't remember who he was. He felt disembodied and yet part of a whole, lost in aromas of basil and almond. Maybe he hallucinated. For now he couldn't tell and didn't want to know. He was comfortable with losing himself.

"How can you speak to me?"

By the thing I am wearing.

"A translating device?"

Unintelligible.

"Telepathy?"

Unintelligible.

"I won't ask anymore."

Good. You understand now. The communion is not perfect.

"Why?"

Probability functions surround us, like localized fog, or a cloud of insects.

"I don't understand."

It's an accident and won't last. It's not very pleasant.

"I don't mind."

I think you will.

He felt in a recurring episodic dream, the end linked back to the start. He felt lost in too much—or too little—significance. He fell into himself and got pulled out again. Maybe what happened wasn't so good, like approaching a shore but never reaching it. He felt sick and giddy, serene yet blank. Inhaling too much powder, he thought. He was seeing purple.

"Who's been here before?"

Someone you know.

An image of a tall man with short white hair.

"Balrak?"

You're surprised?

"What did he do?"

He brought others like you.

"You mean other people?"

Everyone is people.

"I mean humans."

Yes, he brought humans.

"Colonists? Indentured servants?"

What's an indentured servant?

"Laborers under contract to work for a specific length of time. They probably were promised parcels of land here."

Then he brought many indentured servants. He killed them.

"But—"

He brought them and then they died. So...he killed them.

"From what? Disease?"

From hard labor, maltreatment, neglect. Also disease. Then he killed us.

"You? But why?"

We were making up for the deaths of the servants.

"You mean...you fought him for neglecting the laborers?"

For killing his people, yes. We hated him.

Beings gathered around Ranglen. Protoplasmic creatures crawled across him... he lay on something but it wasn't a bed. They glowed in his face, gelatin depths full of lights. Small elephants came with squid-like heads. The antlered "deer" from the plains too, with green sails. They stood on their hind legs and made messages with their horns. At least he believed so.

And the attack lizards that knocked him down during the eruption came too—he remembered the eruption now. They had yellow-green bodies and purple-green sails, bright, like gems. And finally the humanoid he had seen up above, the one he believed was speaking with him, with colored face-markings and lion mane and something hanging around his neck. This creature carried an object and placed it in his lap. His databank.

Ranglen asked, "Do you know what a Moyock is?"

We understand them, but we don't understand wanting to be them.

"What about the Airafane?"

We don't understand them, but we understand wanting to be them.

"You're being cryptic."

It's a survival mechanism.

"Survival against what?"

All those bastards lurking out there. You've met some of them.

"Who? What?"

You have more answers than you think. Your anthropomorphism is not as blanketing as you assume. You haven't grown yet.

"So, I'm a child?"

Isn't it wonderful?

The humanoid talked like Mileen, trading wit and teasing Ranglen. He wondered if he saw the humanoid through the mask of her behavior to make things more understandable for himself.

Humans are so clever.

"I didn't ask."

No, you wouldn't. You accept being adrift, estranged, unplumbed. But maybe you're not even talking to me, just talking to yourself. You move in widening circles, you know, with no straight lines.

"I wish you'd make sense."

Never ask for what you can't receive.

The creatures led him up "stairs," "vines," "limbs"—insufficient substitute words. Steam rose around him as purple ash fell. The trunks rang like rubber when he bumped them. He saw no habitats, no holes in the trees where people lived, no "signs of civilization." He saw many things but he didn't understand them.

An asteroid sat in the distance. Impossible, of course, for it to be down there. Ranglen felt that it was *his* asteroid, the one where he had been with Mileen. He rose through labyrinths, content, unquestioning.

He wondered how they had brought him down there. He should be dead. At times he even thought he was, that all this was just some long dream of suffocation. But he was certain now he was alive. He heard no one "speaking." The voice in his head didn't "speak." What language they had must be different from his. What is language? More than different words.

He said, "The lifeboat had a survivor, didn't it?"

What's a lifeboat?

Ranglen pictured it.

What's a survivor?

"Now you're joking."

What's a "had," an "a," a "didn't," an "it"?

"Stop that!"

Yes, it brought someone here. Gone now.

"Dead?"

Hard to say. You'll have to decide.

"I don't understand."

You will in time. But time is confusing. You don't have the right context yet.

Unintelligible.

Ha! That's good.

"We use humor as a defense."

Most intelligible.

"Why did the lifeboat land here?"

"It" called. It came.

"It?"

You know—you looked at it first.

Ranglen assumed he meant the Clip. But—

You really should laugh more. If you do use humor.

He knew now about the mats in the forest, though he didn't know where he got the information. Volcanic ash. The tree canopy caught the discharge and filled it with new growth. But he still didn't know how the forest survived. The trees should be unstable, blown away in periodic quakes.

"It's only one tree?"

Depends on your definition of "one." It's not a real plant. It has no boundary. It uses the mountain, the air, the world. Think of it as exposed planetary skeleton.

"It grows in spurts after each eruption?"

More like jumps between quantum states. We live inside a lifeform. Remember you once felt like you were being swallowed? Don't call us parasites, though—it would be insulted.

Ranglen tried to ask something simple. "Why is the sky yellow?"

Because that's the way we see it. Same as your blue. It's not blue, you know.

"Then why are the clouds purple?"

Makes good contrast—the universe runs on aesthetics, right? They're made of seeds. Or cells.

"The powder that's in the air down here—seeds too?"

Life! Life!

"I guess it's inside me now."

Congratulations, friend!

Up and up. Walking for hours—at least Ranglen thought they were walking for hours. Time was as relative here as it was constant in light-space. Indeed, he felt in some other universe. The light grew. He approached spectral leaves.

"Did the ship that was near me get away?"

I saw flight. Nothing wrecked.

Ranglen pictured the driftwood derelict. "Do you know what this is?"

We don't talk about such things.

"Is it old? New?"

We live in a rift valley. Everything is new. But that *is older than all of us.*

"Did you ever see it shoot spears before?"

Once, long ago.

"At the colonists?"

No. At us.

"Tell me about it."

We don't talk about such things.

They finally emerged. The light bloomed—brutal, intoxicating. Instead of feeling liberated Ranglen seemed more oppressed, the sky a weight. A mass of gray and violet ash covered everything, abrasive dust you dared not breathe. But he still breathed. He knew he should be dead. How could any culture survive, even if hidden beneath a forest? Eruptions like this surely happened often. The valley looked like a hardened sea. What the hell did their Clip give these creatures—did they even have a Clip?

"How did you get the thing around your neck?"

Found it. Easy.

"Did you ever open it?"

Never had to. It functions well without interference.

He pictured Mileen, Hatch, Jayne, Rashmi, Omar. "Do you know any of these people?"

The last two I saw only once.

"You mean they kept to themselves, didn't disturb you?"

I mean the last two I saw only once.

"The last one, then, Omar, did he get away?"

The arrows came down and surrounded him. He's not here now.

"So Balrak was present when the volcano erupted."

He was untouched. He doesn't die. He's one of the bastards.

"Why did he kill those colonists and your people?"

He was finding himself. Playing, challenging. He wanted to be reborn.

"You mean it was religious?"

Religion for one is profanity for another. He was too human. Human in extreme. It's our nature to despise him.

"You don't like humans?"

We don't like humans in extreme.

"Did Balrak ever notice what you wear on your neck?"

Yes, but he showed less interest than you did.

"Then why did he come here?"

To gather his enemies, to winnow his flock. How should I know?

"We're not a threat to him."

You scare him enough that he wants control of you. You have to ask yourself—why?

"It's his secret."

And that's his nature. But we don't ever want to know it.

They led Ranglen toward the cliff on newly made mats, not yet overgrown with trees. Walking was dangerous. He saw shoots of vegetation plowing up through the fake soil. Life already. Was this a forest, or some new mutant growth that used the planet and a magic Clip to swell in leaps until someday—why not?—it absorbed the world, or the universe, or redefined it, depending on how you defined "absorbed" or defined "universe" or defined "define" or—

"I still have so many questions."

You expect too much from answers. They don't make your sense. I'm getting tired. Doesn't this bother you?

"No. Maybe."

The farther we walk from beneath the trees the less I'm able to "talk."

"It doesn't bother me, but I'm very confused."

Good. You show hope.

They reached the edge of the forest. Ranglen faced the rise and the rock cliff he would have to climb. These slopes were also mantled in gray with the obligatory violet tint. "Life! Life!" he remembered the voice saying. Maybe the marvelous restoration of the valley was contained in the volcanic dust itself, what tinted the clouds.

He turned and faced the humanoid, who had remained expressionless throughout the walk. The creature almost blended into the neutral background. Ranglen tried for contact again.

"So, are you there?"

Silence.

"Is it over?"

Silence.

"I won't be able to speak with you again? The powder's gone? I'm divorced, exiled?"

Silence.

"Well, you take care."

Silence.

"A suggestion: Don't show that necklace to anyone. Especially not to anyone like me. Humans. And certainly not humans in extreme."

Silence.

"I hope you know that."

Silence.

"Oh, well. But one last question. Are you an Airafane?"

The creature said nothing, but he pointed behind his right ear, tapped his scalp and shook his head.

"Meaning *no*?"

Silence.

But Ranglen remembered the bodies on the derelict and the gaps behind their right ears.

The creature then backed into gray growth. Disappeared, just like before.

Ranglen shouted, "You didn't say goodbye!"

Silence.

He recalled what he told Henry long ago. "You don't find a Clip—it finds you." And *this* Clip, if that's what it was, clearly had found its intended owner and intended place. Ranglen felt no need to interfere. This world had its right to its future, whatever it might be.

He turned to the cliff and climbed.

His ascent went quicker than expected. When he reached the rim he looked north to see the volcano spewing a steady and diffuse smoke into the sky. The mountain looked half-blown away.

He gazed behind him across the valley. It lay like thickened dull mist, vague and mysterious—turning green again, almost changing as he looked.

Ranglen headed toward his ship. The savanna lay covered with ash though not as densely as in the valley. The wind already blew some of it away. To his right, one of the elephant beasts lay on its side, hopefully dead since three of the sail-backed lizards devoured it. They used the sails to toss the meat back and forth or to clean the dust away from the kill. More reasons for having them, Ranglen thought. But the creatures hadn't acted like that down below. He wondered why. This return to rational questions indicated how far he had emerged from the "shadows."

When he reached his ship, nothing looked changed. The camouflage programs still ran, though the hull was buried in dust from the eruption.

Ranglen entered, drank fluids, quickly ate food. He transferred the information from his databank into the navigation system—all he had collected from the lifeboat. He found the coordinates of what now was apparently the Clip world. He set these for the jump into light-space so he could make the transition immediately once he left the atmosphere. In case he was attacked.

Before preparing for lift-off he searched the exterior hull. He found, in a recess for the thrusters, a small attached tube about eight centimeters long. It had the coppery color of the staffs on the driftwood ship. The searches conducted earlier hadn't found it.

He pried it off the hull with a knife and tried to smash it with a hammer, but failed to dent it. He buried it in the ground, but then guessed it still could function. So he piled several rocks on top of it, but also realized it could throw those away if it were strong enough. After digging it back up, he radiated it with UV, infrared, microwaves. He applied heavy voltage to it with leads from his power plant. He soaked it with flammable oil and ignited it. He sprayed it with an electrical fixative that could be read on his instruments if it followed him. He locked it into transparent plastic that was solid, unbreakable, and as big as a brick.

He buried it again—deeper this time with more rocks piled on top of it—in a location that would be torched by his thrusters when his ship lifted off.

Ranglen wanted to do more.

Then he walked on board, sealed the hull, planted himself in the acceleration couch. He felt exhausted, in need of medication, but he had plenty of time for that once in light-space.

He lifted away. Not followed by the dart, from what he could tell. At least he hoped.

He said goodbye to the planet behind him. He knew the place would haunt him forever, and he wondered if he might return someday. He had achieved something he always longed for—to lose himself, to drown himself in the fecund uncategorized mass of something beyond his body and mind. Mileen once accused him of using women to do this, idealizing them as the undefined "other," replacing what they were with what he desired—forsaking a foreground in order to reach an intangible background. But, to be honest, and especially with Mileen, he wanted both, the landscape *and* the figure before it. And in terms of dissolving into another world, he felt that maybe here, if only for once, he might have achieved it.

But he didn't know if he felt accomplished, or foolish. What's the point of experience if it can't be defined? The place didn't fit classical deduction—as, alas, defined by humans.

The place did provide him with some answers, though. Ranglen was certain now—Balrak didn't care about the Clip.

What he really wanted was Mileen.

With a sudden and grim determination, Ranglen slapped the button for light-space.

Chapter Fourteen: Fire and Ice

The next world was colder. Ice spread from both polar caps, and though its sun was hot, an F2, the planet orbited further out. The world had plate tectonics, of course. Through scanning devices that searched for heat, magnetism, and tensile stress, Ranglen traced the pattern of the sea-floor ridges where spreading occurred. Most of them lay deep underwater and thus out of reach.

One fault spanned an ocean from almost the southern to the northern pole, disappearing under the ice. But a quarter of the way up the face of the planet rose a pimple above the ridge, an island about three-to-four-hundred kilometers wide.

It made him wonder.

Ranglen then did something *very* secret. He even looked over his shoulder before doing it, though no one rode with him.

He pulled from a sealed pocket the shard of "fluorite" he had shaved from the carrier lock now nestled in his safe—still nestled, he hoped—back on his asteroid. He polished it on his cuff. Then he held it close in front of his eye so that he looked through it to the image of the world. The material did not make a good window. But by moving the shard back and forth, covering and uncovering the planet, he could line up landmarks with the murky image in the sliver.

Seen through the shard, the world had a new pinpoint gleam, barely noticeable.

It came from the island.

"Damn, I'm good."

The one anomaly that stood out to him was this raised piece of seafloor ridge, high enough to emerge from the ocean but sitting on a spreading fault. Such a formation was rare. And that's where the Clip, he had guessed, would be found.

Ranglen pocketed the shard again, buried it away, sealed the cover. Again he looked over his shoulder.

This was his most well-kept secret. He had told of it to *no one*, not Mileen, not the Federal Investigators. And if he had his way, he never would—the secret was too big, too world-changing.

When Ranglen reached a planet he knew possessed a Clip, he had his own private means of finding it.

He discovered the method by accident. After he found the third Clip and turned it over to the authorities, they—at that time, the Commonwealth—insisted on keeping the carrier-lock too. But Ranglen had pealed a slice from it, just for devilment, as a souvenir of his luck. He kept it and said nothing about it. Then one time in his spaceship when Annulus was being built, he playfully pulled it out and looked through it to the stars beyond. If he had gazed at any other part of the sky, nothing would have registered. But he happened to select the one spot where a gleam appeared. When he moved the shard, the gleam vanished.

He later calculated the odds of picking that spot at three million to one. But stranger things happened in the search for Clips. He believed the governments analyzed the carrier-locks as much as they obviously did the Clips, but with odds like that he doubted if they ever made the same discovery.

As always, the Airafane had a way, even from deep in their own past, to control how people interacted with their creations.

Knowing this also made Ranglen more paranoid.

Tracking that gleam, moving further into space as he looked through the shaving, he was led to finding his asteroid with its labyrinth of tunnels inside. And the fourth Clip.

Now, as he neared this new planet, he avoided the shard and followed his instincts. The island was the spot he would have picked anyway. It *was* a geologic anomaly, though not impossible. It provided access to the hot depths below the crust, a window normally confined to the smoking confusion of underwater vents with their hot-water ooze and laborious emergence of pillow lava, like bodies squeezed through hoops of fire. Good places to look for Clips, but not easy to access.

Yet on this island you didn't need to go underwater to see the spreading of the planet. It would stretch in a long surgical incision there on the surface, always seeping, never completely cauterized or healed.

Ranglen smiled.

The planet grew big in the viewscreen, not as brightly colored as the previous world but still dramatic—the clouds white, the oceans indigo, the landmasses raw with metallic grays and sleek blues.

Ranglen sent off the same kind of positioning satellite he had used on the other planet. Then he entered atmosphere, braking on the growing densities beneath him.

The sky, lightening, didn't lose its stratospheric purplish-blue tint all the way down to the surface. The sun, though white, appeared bluish to terrestrial eyes. Cloud cover spread thinly, much water vapor frozen from the air. The land masses looked bleak, the mountains starkly chiseled by ice, the tundra wide and pale but empty. Any dense vegetation looked darkly brooding, struggling to survive, lining the lower slopes of mountains like bad insulation. Everything seemed forlorn, neglected, abandoned.

Ranglen flew toward the island, its presence indicated by a large plume of black smoke.

He groaned. More volcanoes.

The smoke emerged less from the island itself—a bank of mist in the distance—than from a spot about ten kilometers north of the island along the mid-ocean fault. There a volcano erupted beneath the water and a small ridge of hard cinder had formed above the surface. It had to be only a few weeks or even just a few days old. On the black hump, lava sputtered. The sea waves cooled the newly formed rock, sent bursts of steam into the sky to follow the smoke from the vent itself.

As Ranglen flew on and passed the shoreline of the big island, he saw craters filled with red lava and fountains of fire. Columns of smoke smudged the horizon like traces of a distant war. He guessed that a good third of the island was still active. The newest rock lay black and rough, tinted red by iron-oxide or yellow by sulphur. But while the island still grew, creation was only half the story. He saw signs of erosion from melting snow, shallow streams netting the flatlands. And the heavier snowfalls in the heights made glaciers that carved the original shield volcanoes into knife-edged ridges and peaks. Fire and ice thus warred with each other. If an aboriginal race existed here, its mythology would be savage, a saga of conflict between primal forces with little left for the gentle or weak.

And he could see the gulley of the fault itself, a trench dipping through active lava or rising into a hardened ridge. He followed this running continental wound.

A proximity alert sounded.

A ship flew overhead. It moved on his same southern heading—following him.

He ran identification checks. The craft's Type 3 engine was larger than Ranglen's, larger than Jayne's and Hatch's ship—and thus similar to the one Mileen detected back at the derelicts. Maybe it was the same.

That was enough for Ranglen to assume it was hostile.

He had intended to search the island but he didn't change course or speed now. Maybe he could fool the craft into believing he didn't mean to land.

Ranglen approached the southern shore. His radar told him the other spaceship now descended to a lower height with a speed approaching his. It soon caught up and matched velocity, stayed a few kilometers behind.

It knows I'm here, he thought. Was it waiting for me?

Ranglen tried to remember all he knew about aerial combat, everything that Hatch once had taught him. He knew you should always get *behind* your adversary—exactly where this ship was located now in relation to him.

Assuming the other craft didn't want him dead yet (it could have killed him in several ways already), he brought online his combat instruments for atmosphere and gravity: a "head-up display" in a forward screen, a threat indicator, a flight-path maker geared for intercept, a lock-on particle-beam projector and a multi-barrel machine gun—whose bullets could pierce armor but had no "smart" tracking ability. Hatch had charged him a fortune to install them. Now Ranglen was grateful.

The other ship—the "bandit"—approached. An alarm said its weapons had gone on line.

Ranglen accelerated.

The pursuing craft also accelerated and drew closer, toying with him. Ranglen could make out its flattened outline, like the forward view of a shark. He saw pods for scanning equipment, ports for multi-barrelled cannon, carriage assemblies with missiles attached.

It had to be Balrak.

He tightened his restraining harness and transferred power from interior inertia-control to thrust. He reduced ship controls to manual as he brought his craft to its corner velocity, the speed at which it could turn most effectively—

He banked hard, "pulled Gs" since he no longer had gravity control in his cabin.

By turning fast he hoped to get the other ship outside the curve of his path, making it lose its advantage, and if it turned too soon it might overshoot. Then Ranglen could wind up on *its* tail. He assumed his own craft was more maneuverable but with weapons that had less range, and he carried no missiles.

His instruments showed the other ship—bigger and heavier—not following the turn close enough.

Ranglen charged forward over the ocean, wanting to escape. To gain acceleration he dived, trading altitude for speed. But he remembered in such encounters the craft with more height had the advantage.

The threat-indicator sounded a warning. The pursuer had returned. It closed the angle between its heading and Ranglen's. The range between them narrowed too.

Ranglen maneuvered another tight circle. This time, with the other ship again outside his curve, he didn't run but gained enough room to come back on it. He now forced a head-on confrontation, like old jousting knights galloping at each other.

He fixed the ship in the display grid of his forward screen. He locked on with both particle ray and machine gun. He fired—a "snapshot."

The ship roared by him. Bullets grazed the side of his hull.

His craft's flying ability was not weakened—the damage must be slight. But the other ship scored a hit while his own instruments said he did not.

They flew away from each other. What next? Run and leave?

Ranglen saw the pursuer coming behind him in another tail-on six-o'clock chase.

Expecting a torrent of 2,000-shells-per-second, Ranglen savagely pulled up his craft.

A klaxon filled the cabin. An air-to-air missile had locked on him and fired.

He threw out chaff and heat-producing decoys, more of Hatch's expensive add-ons. He turned his craft as tight as he could—to confuse the weapon seeking him. But he knew the missile would detonate even if it missed and overshot its target, and still cause damage.

The chaff and infrared-jamming didn't work. The ship counted down to impact.

Nothing happened. The missile overshot.

It exploded anyway and shoved his craft almost vertical. Ranglen slammed against the acceleration couch. Alarms blared.

Another blast rocked the hull. The ship raced forward with its nose 30-degrees above the horizon. Ranglen tried to work the controls. He was over the island again, crossing a plain. The altimeter spiraled but he still had airspeed. He flipped switches for his landing-gear but they didn't deploy. He hit thrusters—not all of them worked.

The ship's tail hit first. In a wrenching scream and rip of metal it dragged across the earth. The deck lurched. The lights went out and the screens blanked. Ranglen bounced but was held by his restraining harness. Loose objects shot past him and smashed into the control panel. The nose of the ship fell downward, struck the rocks, made a crash.

Everything stopped.

Ranglen realized he never had thought of emergency ejection.

A hiss, a crackling, sudden smoke.

He stared at the shambles of his control room. Escaping steam, dancing sparks. The cabin grew hot. He smelled burning fabric and wiring—his ship was on fire.

Ranglen disengaged his harness and hobbled from his chair. He felt pains but he assumed no bones were broken—the harness should have protected him. Batteries kicked on and the screens came up, showing the field outside but no read-out displays. He couldn't see the other craft.

Emergency diagnostics showed fires burning, life-support fading, propulsion dead, energy production critical—the ship wouldn't fly.

He was marooned.

Instruments said the atmosphere was breathable though oxygen was thin.

He blew open hatches to access supplies and staggered toward the airlock through debris. Though the seal to the inner door was broken, the airlock's instruments—on back-up power—would warn him of any problems with atmosphere, radiation, or toxic materials. They said the ultraviolet was strong.

He emerged onto a crusty plain of solidified lava, with patches of snow, pockets of grass and low shrubs. Snowy hills rose in the distance. The sky's deep blue had a purplish zenith. The sun glared—a fierce little fireball. Ranglen would need a hat and sunscreen. The air was chill but not bitterly so, dry in his nostrils, free of smells except for the sharp burning of his ship.

He heard the other craft approaching.

It swooped over him at low height—he felt the wind from its passing. He could see its missile-rack, ex-military.

Ranglen felt horribly vulnerable.

The ship banked, made a wide loop—returning.

He hurriedly unloaded emergency supplies, getting a second ionic pistol to replace the one lost on the lifeboat world. He dragged all this quickly away from the wreck.

The other ship came, a big ugly condor of prey.

Its cannon lay a stream of high-caliber bullets across the plain—toward his ship. Pieces of rock, dirt, and branches festooned up from the impact trace.

He sprinted and dived into the bushes.

The high-impact shells plowed through his craft. Debris tumbled down around him.

The killer flew on, banked again for another turn.

Ranglen ran back, got more supplies, pulled his load further into the brush and then flattened to the ground.

He saw a fast thread of steam—an incoming missile! He covered his head and tried to squeeze further into the earth.

A thunderclap slammed. Smoke rushed by, dust choked him, metal splinters pummeled his back.

He raised his head and glanced behind him. A globe of flame rushed into the sky, turned black. Even less of his ship remained now, scattered in fragments across the ground. The blackened area sputtered with flame and sent oily banners after the fireball.

It was overkill. His ship had been wrecked already from the landing.

Ranglen looked toward the other craft. It flew on, headed for the low bank of hills, and when it crossed the first ridge another white stream fell from it. A second missile.

A flash of light from behind the ridge, smoke followed. A muffled crack, then a long boom rolled across the plain.

It felt as though he had been forced to wreck just so he could witness this second destruction. Was he left alive to be a recorder?

The ship didn't return.

The sun lowered. Soon night would fall. Though days should be long in these latitudes—the world had axial tilt and the season was summer—the planet's revolution was only nineteen hours.

He organized his traveling supplies into a pack, wondering if he already had sunburn. He was pleased to see he had grabbed necessities for a cold environment: insulated parka, padded trousers, winter blanket and small tent, heavy sleeping bag, heater, boots, an already stuffed backpack of rations, a winter emergency kit with sunscreen and dark glasses.

He decided to walk east to the hills to see what had exploded.

Ranglen had a bad feeling he already knew.

With his shadow pointing 45 degrees from his forward direction, sharp and indigo where it crossed snow, he moved steadily toward the slopes, burdened under the supplies on his back. He left the smells of combustion behind, replaced by aromas sagey and dry. The pale bluish-beige grass formed a soft background for dark blue-green shrubs. The growth made the volcanic pavement easier on his feet.

The sun touched the horizon when he reached the hills. He trekked up to the ridge-line through sparse ground cover.

Before him stretched another plain like the one he just crossed, and at the bottom of the slope lay the recent wreck of a spaceship, its flames almost burnt out by now and smoke curling up and dissipating.

He recognized the craft. He last saw it on the lifeboat world carrying Jayne, Rashmi, Hatch...and Mileen.

They too were marooned. Or killed.

He hurried down the hill in the fading light. He negotiated rocks and puddles of snowmelt as he approached the wreckage.

Had Balrak left another calling card for him, like the body of one more Anne or Lonni? But when he reached the wreck, and after a search through the twisted metal and surrounding landscape, he found no trace of life *or* death. If Balrak left him something to find, it would be obvious.

He breathed slightly easier, remembering how, when Balrak had kidnapped him, Ranglen could have been killed but wasn't. Apparently Balrak intended them to live...at least for the moment. Maybe he was waiting till the Clip was found and *then* he'd kill them.

Ranglen didn't know how long he remained in the under-forest on the other planet, but he assumed Jayne's ship came straight here and they had at least a one or two-day start on him. He also assumed all four of the crew had gone searching together. No one would have been trusting enough to stay back on the ship.

In the last rays of light Ranglen found four different sets of tracks leading away from the ship toward the southeast, paralleling the tectonic gap running across the island—the best place to look for Clips. Tracks didn't show well on the hardened lava but the snow and clay by the streams still held them, plus signs of a small wheeled vehicle probably used to carry supplies.

He walked far from the wreck to set up his tiny tunnel-hoop tent. He found a clearing in a shrub thicket and erected it quickly. He was cold now.

Night fell and he crawled inside, ate cold rations.

The stars came out. There'd be no snow tonight. Later he'd set up his portable heater. He didn't care if the infrared signature could be spotted. He assumed Balrak would leave him alone.

He thought of bringing out his shard of carrier-lock to see if he could catch any indicator of the Clip, but he needed greater altitude for that, and the paranoid in him wouldn't expose it. Who knew how much he was being monitored?

He stepped from his tent and stood in the cold air beneath the sky. Three small moons rode above him tangled in the Milky Way, hardly more than stars. The air was clear enough to show traces of a nebula. The serene sky lightened his fears.

But then he saw distant riding lights of a cruising spaceship that didn't bother to hide itself. Red and white as they moved to his left, then green as it prowled to the right. Balrak on patrol.

What was he preparing for?

Chapter Fifteen: The Trench

He awoke to chill air, a dry taste, a slight coppery sagey smell, a sluggish breeze, and the rasp and crackle of long grass. He opened his tent flap.

Dawn came green in the east, the spectrum of the parent star too slanted toward blue to allow much warmth in its tones. Into the brightening indigo sky ascended trails of dark smoke—not from wreckage but distant volcanoes. When the light of the sun burst in a glare from the horizon, it ignited frost on the scattered shrubs.

He packed his things, ate quickly and soon headed out.

The pavement looked spongelike but it struck back, sharp and hard. He was grateful for strong boots. The plant life, the clumps of blue-beige grass and tan moss, broke down the hardened lava and allowed darker shrubs to take hold. Streams meandered about the flatland, half-frozen.

Mud helped him in following the tracks. Mileen's tread was like that on the lifeboat world. She wore the same boots, and he knew they weren't best for winter conditions.

For all the fierce sunlight the day was dark. The sun made a harsh little spot in the sky. It seemed distant and not overly illuminating. Ranglen felt he was in a cavern with a single floodlight high in the ceiling.

A bank of clouds grew in the west, threatening storm.

He approached hills bulking before him. Snow lay in finger-like patterns on their slopes. He followed a pathway carved by snowmelt but avoided the rapid stream itself. He hoped to reach high enough ground from which he could see the people he followed.

The dark blue-green shrub of the plains disappeared while pale moss grew in mats, dense and squishy. Hardy trees rose arrow-sharp with black-green needles, but they vanished too as the land grew rougher. Basalt rose in tumbled and eroded columns, brutal and stark. The landscape was too new. It resembled an abandoned construction site.

He topped the ridge.

Flatland spread into the distance before him. Braided threads of snowmelt shown cobalt from sky reflection, or fierce blue-white where they caught the sun, arteries in a yellow-blue carpet. Far in the distance lay a shimmer of sea.

To his right, in the direction of the wrecked ships, a banner of dark cloud arose. Ranglen assumed it came from the sputtering new island he had seen yesterday, though it sat beyond the horizon now. To his left, southeast, mountains spread in both directions, the peaks feathered with volcanic plumes and the flanks shingled with white glaciers.

A strange feeling came over Ranglen, one felt before in his past explorations. Most people can be intimate with only other people, but he sensed the deep strain of this landscape, its destruction and birth, the creation here that was never quite done. He felt his alienation justified, his established role to give voice to these great material forces. He was lost, and found, in this primal sublime.

And he wanted to stay alone, just to absorb the site's power. But people called to him. *His* people. He couldn't escape his own humanity. And—for once—he didn't want to.

He saw no sign of those people.

He checked his cellpad for his location. He knew what the walkers sought. He furtively pulled out his shard and quickly glanced at the landscape.

No glimmer showed. The Clip was not in his line-of-sight.

Ranglen hid the shard again. The cruel little sun drew behind darkening clouds, which had swelled in size. The landscape seemed sinister with this late afternoon twilight ambivalence.

Not far ahead stretched the land version of the mid-ocean ridge, the seam where new crust formed. Heady stuff to anyone who thinks in deep time and knows how a planet works. And to anyone searching Clips.

He continued upward. The volcanic plumes rising in the distance mixed with the storm-clouds and shut in the world. In the hills columns of steam danced. The groundwater bubbled in hot springs and geysers. Beneath him, the oven of the world still cooked.

He finally topped the ridge, a saw-toothed line of hard debris, and looked down into a gulley. The gap was not wide, nothing like the rift valley on the previous world, only a hundred meters across with an equally igneous wall of rock on the opposite side. In between lay a grassy enclosure, lined with a stream. The two crests with their little swale wandered off in either direction.

The trench where the planet gave birth to itself. Surely the walkers came here, the ideal place to seek Clips.

He saw movement.

Inside the gulley and to his right, something quickly disappeared.

He scurried along the ridge, difficult since the ground was so rough. He dropped down into a snowy area then ran up and peered into the trench.

A lone figure moved beside the stream, his face almost lost in the gloom but his spiky hair easily identified.

Omar Mirik.

Ranglen stayed out of sight.

He could use his pistol to capture and overpower Omar. Or stay away and search for the others. Maybe Omar too was looking for them.

The sky clouded over. A bitter wind blew from the west. The storm was coming faster than Ranglen expected, some factor of the world's speedier rotation or high-energy input from the sun.

He scrambled over rocks, tried to keep Omar in sight as the man marched between the two walls and splashed through puddles. The trench rose and fell. The stream, made of runoff from the two ridges, would run for a while and then pool. Sometimes it flowed in the opposite direction.

The sky darkened more.

Ranglen looked ahead and saw that the trench descended in a staircase to a recent field of lava flows where little vegetation grew.

Snow fell. It flew horizontally because of the wind and struck Ranglen's face. He'd have to erect his shelter soon. Night wasn't far away. And, though he assumed the four walkers had followed the trench to the lava area, if this new snow fell heavily it would bury any trace of their trail.

He found a spot where the wall had tumbled, making descent into the trench easy. He waited for Omar to walk past him.

Mirik strode briskly but peered around him and up into the clouds. He too must be nervous about the change in weather and it made him hurry. He lacked a hat and looked sunburned. His short coat didn't have a hood. He walked with hands stuffed in his pockets as if he had no gloves.

Ranglen waited for Omar to get ahead of him, then he lowered himself into the trench. Down there, the wind and snow lightened.

He found a depression in the rock-wall and set up his shelter, not easy to do in a growing storm but the equipment was made for rough handling. He pegged the tent carefully to keep it stable.

After moving inside he set up his heater and made a hot rehydrated meal, but he stayed in his parka and boots, kept his backpack handy where he could grab it. He didn't care if the stove's exhaust left an obvious heat signature. Omar, without a tent, would be thinking now of only survival.

Ranglen's pistol lay ready beside him but hidden from view.

The wind sang, and darkness fell with the thickening snow. He was glad to be here in the trench and not up along the rim. Hail struck the tent like buckshot, making the fabric rattle and whine.

He unzipped the door and reached out for snow to melt into water. An alien world demanded purifiers but he wanted to appear careless and unguarded. A chaos of wind and billowing flakes muscled back at him through the opening.

An arm thrust in, pushed Ranglen back.

Omar jumped into the low-hanging shelter with a dart-gun in his hand. Stooped over, he aimed it at Ranglen, quickly reached back and closed the flap behind him.

"I...I need your shelter." His teeth chattered. His face glowed red and his hands shook.

Ranglen stared at him, seemed more curious than threatened. He sat down casually—beside his hidden pistol. "I thought you were ahead of me."

"This trail...flattens out....There wasn't any shelter." Omar's lips quivered as vapors rose from his shoulders in the heat. "The wind...I came back, thought I could find an opening in the wall...saw your tent."

"Without shelter you could die out there."

"I *know*, dammit. That's why I came in....I..." He looked around. "This tent is too small."

"It's big enough for me."

"I was thinking it's big enough for *me*." He waved his gun.

Ranglen laughed. "So you're kicking me out? You don't need me now? When everyone else has wanted me so badly?"

"You decided not to come, remember?" Omar said this with surprising bitterness. "And we got here all right without you."

"You were about to get lost in the snow, and die."

Omar bristled, not as self-confident as the last time Ranglen saw him. The man still trembled from the cold.

Ranglen thought his best chance was now.

He kicked the near edge of the tent, knocked out the stake he had left loose.

The tent flew up. Wind and snow struck at both of them—and immediately buried Ranglen's pistol. He reached for it but it was gone.

He jumped onto Omar and slammed the man's gun-hand against the heater. The gun fell, along with the stove. Omar scrambled for it but Ranglen kicked it into the snow. This scrambling pulled another stake loose.

The wind separated the tent from its moorings, blew it away—like a paper kite in front of exhaust fans. Everything not heavy or tied down rolled into the dark.

Omar ran after the tent but he lost direction in the snow-filled wind. Ranglen let him become more scared. When Omar almost vanished in the murk, Ranglen leapt on him. He grabbed Omar's right wrist, yanked it across his back and rammed it in his spine, shoved him against the stone wall with his knee in his back. The side of Omar's head slapped into the rock—forced his mouth open, drove snow into his eyes and down his throat.

Ranglen yelled into his ear, "If you want to survive the night, do what I tell you!"

Omar didn't move. He probably debated whether to fight Ranglen off, since Ranglen knew Omar could do it and that only the weather gave Ranglen the advantage. Ranglen also remembered that the arm he held was the one Omar had burned on the lifeboat world. He twisted it harder.

The rock against Omar's sternum made him gasp for air. He tongued, "Okay"—but it sounded more like clearing his throat.

"Grab my jacket and hold tight. Follow me exactly. If you let go you'll never find me."

Omar mouthed a gulping assent. The wind blew more snow into his face, forced his eyes shut. Where it struck Ranglen it cut like sand.

Ranglen bluffed—Omar looked robust enough to survive the night, though he might lose fingertips or part of his nose from frostbite. But Ranglen assumed Omar was fed up with walking alone and that this latest incident would be enough to persuade him.

Omar clutched Ranglen's coat and followed him. Ranglen retrieved his small heater, the sleeping bag, its insulation mat, the emergency blanket and his backpack, which he purposely left only half unloaded. But the tent was gone, and his gun and Omar's must have fallen deep into the snow.

Ranglen pulled a hat with earflaps and mittens from his pack and gave them to Mirik, who covered himself quickly. Then Ranglen crept downward toward the lava plain, using his left arm to maintain a distance away from the wall. Omar clung to him.

The wall fell into tumbled blocks and the walking grew more difficult. They must have moved out of the trench and the wind struck harder. Ranglen looked to his feet. He could barely see as they crossed the cobble which disappeared under piles of snow. He pulled out a flashlight but it didn't help—the beam just reflected off the blowing flakes.

Ranglen followed a zigzag path, trying to cover as much of the rocky terrain as possible. They fell often. The snow and wind pounded them, deadened their senses. Omar complained at one point and Ranglen yelled back, "You want to lead?"

Omar shut up.

The snow built on both of them, their legs weakening, their backs in agony from leaning forward. Ranglen now regretted his trick with the tent. It got him the upper hand—and flung Omar's weapon out of reach—but that warm little space was lost now.

He believed he found what he was looking for. A rocky slope tilted sharply downward. He could see—sense—a hole in the ground he assumed stretched away from him.

He pulled Mirik closer, yelled in his ear. "It's a steep drop and very rocky. It'll be dangerous." He didn't wait for a response before starting down.

They both fell. Omar slid brutally on the slope but the snow helped to soften his impacts. Ranglen crept down beside him to a relatively level spot, where the rocks were the size of melons instead of barrels.

"You all right?" he asked.

"I hurt."

"Glad to hear it. Get up and follow me."

"My back feels broken," Omar said.

"Then you'd be screaming and couldn't move at all. Get up or be buried."

Ranglen swung his beam and moved in the direction where the wall seemed darkest. The ground descended. "Watch your head." The overhang almost slammed both of them. But as they moved downward they cleared the roof.

Ranglen crept forward. The wind lost its strength but they still could hear its raging brawl. Less snow struck their faces.

"What is this?" Omar asked. "A cave?"

"An old lava tube. It should run far enough for us to manage some shelter inside. Watch your step."

The flashlight helped now, and as the wind weakened, Ranglen stopped and looked around. This rock cavity would not be comfortable but it should provide protection from the weather. He still had the sleeping bag, the insulation mat and a blanket. He laid these down so the two of them could sit on them, though he was concerned that the sharp rocks beneath might tear the fabric.

"Rest," he said.

Ranglen set up the heater, and though the place was too large to trap much heat, this spot of warmth between them helped.

"I'll bet you don't have many provisions," he said.

Omar shook his head.

Ranglen pulled a vitamin-bar from his knapsack and handed it to Mirik, plus a container of water for both of them and a bar for himself. They ate in silence.

Omar asked, "How did you know this cave would be here?"

"It's part of a lava field I saw from up above. It had pits in it. When the lava flows, it cools and hardens on top first, while the rest of the liquid keeps running beneath. When the flow stops, the roof stays, leaving an open tube under it. The roofs sometimes collapse. I assumed that's what the pits were. We climbed down one."

"I *fell* down one."

"Yeah, well...."

"Could this ceiling still collapse?" Omar asked.

"Only in heavy snowfalls like this."

For a moment Omar believed him. "Look, just so you know, I have another gun on me. I'm not helpless."

Ranglen didn't trust him. "I have one too." He lied.

They stared at each other's hands then, made sure the fingers weren't close to any pockets. They both felt the stalemate of equality.

The wind blared as they ate. They didn't talk at first. Then Ranglen said, "What the hell were you doing up there all alone?"

Omar's expression looked almost sheepish. Then he took a long breath and said slowly, "Well...to be honest...I was defecting."

Ranglen gave no reaction at all.

"Yeah," Omar added. "I want to be on your side now."

Chapter Sixteen: Omar

Outside the cave, the wind howled in a whirlpool dance, kicking shrouds of snow before it like ghosts imprisoned in a large well. Sometimes the wind blew strong enough to reach the two men where they sat, stinging their eyes, drowning their voices, but usually it left them alone. It sneaked in just to remind them that they were not wholly safe.

"Defecting?" Ranglen said. "That could be dangerous."

"I know. I like to feel I made the decision, but, hell, maybe *he* made it for me."

"Balrak?"

"Who else?"

"So, what happened?"

"After I shot down your spaceship—"

"So that *was* you."

"Yeah," Omar said. "Good piloting, right?"

"I thought you were just a steward."

"I did chauffeuring too once, including spaceships. Did you think he would dirty *his* hands by driving? He just sat behind me and watched."

"He does whatever he wants, eh?"

Omar nodded. "But I wasn't supposed to hurt you. Just force you to the ground. He was emphatic about that."

"Why destroy the other ship?"

"He wanted Jayne's group grounded too. He wants all of you stranded here together. 'Let's have a big party,' he said. But only he gets to be host."

"We're meant to meet over the Clip?" Ranglen asked.

"That's his plan."

"No one's found it yet, right?"

"He figured Jayne and the others would just wander until you showed up, and then you'd find it for them. Or, as he intends, for *him*."

172

Ranglen didn't say anything for a moment. "But why were you walking by yourself?"

"He dropped me off near the base of the hills, away from the wreckage. He said I needed to set up some tracking equipment for him. 'Carry it outside,' he said. So I walked out the spaceship—and he takes off! Just left me there! That's why I don't have any food. Or a hat."

"You didn't have your cellpad?"

"I didn't think I'd need it. I should have known he had something planned when he said, 'Put on your coat. It's cold out there.' He never was thoughtful like that toward me."

"So he deserted you."

"I waited for him to come back. But he never did. I wasn't far from the trail the group took, so I followed it."

"You had no idea where they were going?"

"I assumed they followed the trench. We had taken some surveys and knew the best places for the Clip."

"But why did he leave you?"

Omar looked annoyed. "You don't understand what he's like. He has fits of…anger's not the right word. He's never angry. It's more a self-indulgence in irrationality—if you know what I mean. He doesn't feel he has to follow rules and sometimes he needs to prove that to himself. He wants to be unpredictable."

This didn't tally with Ranglen's earlier impression of Balrak, when he seemed to emulate rationality, a "cold equations" cosmic view. "Was he always like that?"

"I only knew him by reputation before. He had a big name on Ventroni as a tough businessman—an octopus, unemotional, everything planned. Yet this…I don't know. I guess it's the Clip. Everyone says you get crazy around them. He's not acting like I expected him to."

Ranglen said nothing about people acting in unexpected ways. "You met him while working for Hatch, right?"

Omar stared back at him. "How did you know that?"

"Hatch said you got in trouble with a client a while ago."

"Yeah, so?"

"So…was it Balrak?"

After a moment of suspicious silence Omar explained, "I was steward on a flight that Balrak commissioned. I got into a disagreement with the men on board—they were scum. Balrak defended me, persuaded Hatch not to fire me. I was grateful."

"So he got you into a position where you owed him something."

Omar snapped, "He didn't *buy* me, if that's what you mean. He learned he could trust me. It turned out these men were trying to cheat him, steal his own goods. Through my interference he found out about it. He was glad I helped."

"So Balrak vouched for you directly with Hatch."

"Yeah, and it was nice of him."

Ranglen's head tilted. "Doesn't that strike you as odd? He's someone who stays behind the scenes, right?"

"That's why I was impressed. I felt he believed in me."

Ranglen kept quiet for a bit, let the uncertainty stew in Mirik. "So then you smuggled for him, right? Through Hatch's spaceport, where you already knew the inspection procedures."

Omar looked insulted. But then he must have realized Ranglen's conclusion was logical. "I didn't handle the stuff directly. Balrak wanted to keep me clean. I let him know Hatch's methods so he could fool the security scans on his own flights."

"And during all this, in order to keep everything quiet, you apologized to Hatch and stayed on his good side."

"I tried. But he never liked me anyway. I think afterward he despised me."

Ranglen silently agreed, remembering Hatch's attitude toward Mirik. But he also recalled that Hatch hadn't said anything about meeting with Balrak over the incident with Omar, stating only that Omar had caused trouble and then apologized.

Ranglen stared at Mirik with what he hoped looked like pity. "I hate to tell you this but I think you've been used. The arrangements might have been more complicated."

"What the hell do you mean?"

"Come on, Omar! Don't be naïve. It was a classic set-up. The disagreement between you and Balrak's men was probably planned."

Omar looked scorned.

"Think. This was Balrak's way to get directly to Hatch. Why else would he compromise his anonymity? Just to save your hide? Someone he hardly knew? He and Hatch probably made an agreement on how to manage the smuggling. You worked for Hatch—you must have noticed that nothing could get past him unless he allowed it."

"That's crazy." But Omar looked disturbed. He asked, "Why are you assuming Hatch was smuggling?"

"Because Hatch can't help having business on the side. I've known him for years and he was always like that, though he tried not to be. Or maybe he just made it more secret. He saw you when you arrived on the ship from Ventroni—when you came in with Balrak's car, remember? I was there. He recognized you and clammed up immediately, though I didn't know who you were then. That made me suspicious. And besides, Balrak was big on Ventroni and Hatch ran the biggest spaceport on Annulus. Their paths had to cross. Didn't you meet Balrak because he was Hatch's client?"

Omar's eyes glazed over.

"And from then on you and Balrak were 'bonded,' in touch. Right?"

"Only briefly, and nothing too formal."

"Which, obviously, was just to keep you 'clean.'"

Omar paled.

"I'll bet that Balrak was doing just the opposite, laying a trail that led solely to you. If the smuggling was discovered, you'd get the blame."

"God*dam*mit!"

Ranglen waved his hand in dismissal. "Never mind. It's all in the past. Let's talk about other things, like you getting onto Henry's business trip from Ventroni, turning up conveniently in search of a ride back to Annulus. That was a set-up too, right?"

Omar looked threatened again.

"Didn't Balrak know about the derelicts before you ever saw them? Wasn't Jayne's ship stopping there planned by him?"

Omar's eyes hardened, grew stubborn.

"It's not tough to deduce," Ranglen added. "You used equipment from the InQuest consignment in the cargo—I saw what was included in the shipment. Those programs interface with Airafane machines, so you used them to change the exit point of the light-space jump so you'd emerge *there* and not at Annulus. It's the only way to explain how you stopped 'accidentally.' Balrak told you to do that, right?"

Omar hesitated, then admitted, "Yes, but he didn't tell me why. He never said anything about the derelicts. He just showed me how to change the settings. The whole InQuest consignment was *his* cargo—why he got it onboard. But he just said, 'Be ready for something interesting. You'll see what I mean.' I felt he was playing with me."

"He's played with all of us. He's 'finding himself.'"

"What? What do you mean?"

"Never mind. Something someone told me." He wouldn't describe to Omar the bat-like humanoid on the lifeboat world.

"But if Balrak knew about the derelicts," Omar said, "then why would he need us to arrive there—accidentally or otherwise? He could have taken the information and gone after the Clip himself, before any of us got involved. Why the big plan?"

That Balrak wasn't interested in the Clip seemed inconceivable to Omar, as it would be to anyone obsessed with them, and everyone was. So Ranglen let Omar keep thinking that way. "Let's go with what you said, that knowing about a Clip has made him act crazy."

"But he's not that crazy. In fact…" Omar now theorized. "If he did find the derelicts before we did, then maybe *he* murdered the three on board."

Ranglen didn't want him speculating too much. "Maybe, or maybe he found them more recently. Why would he wait twenty years or so to make any move?"

Omar kept thinking.

Ranglen said, "When you told Hatch you were quitting, how did he react?"

"Do you mean…wait a minute, maybe Hatch knew about what we found. Maybe he and Balrak worked together."

Ranglen stayed neutral. "You knew Hatch. What do you think?"

Omar pondered. "I don't believe they did. Hatch wasn't happy about Jayne, Lonni, and me quitting, and he was certainly curious. He looked too angry at being left out."

Ranglen remembered Hatch's expression when he saw Omar get off the ship from Ventroni—like someone excluded. He silently agreed with Omar. But he asked, "Those on board the business trip, what did they think about the derelicts themselves?" He knew the reactions from Lonni and Mileen but now he wanted Omar's.

"We all had different opinions. Some thought the bigger ship was responsible for the murders—we assumed it was alien—but we couldn't see how. Where were the killers? Some thought the human ship had awoken some kind of defense system on the other derelict and the crew was then killed. Maybe the deaths were just the aliens' way of saying, 'Get out! Scram!' Hell, maybe they dragged the little ship with them just as a symbol. 'This means stay away!'"

Ranglen let Omar ramble on.

"But the idea I wondered about most was that there had been a fight among the crew of the little ship, that once they discovered the location of the Clip, someone in their crew decided to go off on his own, get it for himself, so he killed the rest and took off in the lifeboat. Hell, maybe the alien derelict was the ship's own security system, or guardian, and not something they discovered. Maybe they brought it with them to ward off intruders and they weren't victims of it at all. That's why I didn't want to track down the lifeboat. I didn't know what the hell we'd find."

"What about Mileen's theory that a child was in it?"

"I didn't believe her. Nobody did."

"Nobody wanted to search for it?"

"Only Mileen. I felt she was trying to be our 'conscience.' We only cared about the Clip. Hell, the killings happened twenty years ago—no one could have survived that long. And a child? Ridiculous."

Ranglen threw in suddenly, "Did you kill Henry?"

"What? *No!* Balrak did."

"Why?"

"Now you *are* kidding. I was supposed to ask him? Gosh, I forgot!"

"Stop it! You know he wouldn't kill without reason."

"Well, he didn't tell *me* about it. Besides, Henry brought it on himself. No one believed him after he came to see you. We all thought he kept your information, or that you and he, and Mileen, planned to leave on your own and find the Clip. If I hadn't been working for Balrak I might have killed him myself. Or Rashmi would have done it. Even Jayne. They all went nuts, you know."

Ranglen kept a straight expression. "What about Anne Montgomery? Did you kill her?"

Omar looked away. "No, but I helped him set up the explosion after she was dead. I got the components for the bomb. But I didn't agree with that, Ranglen. You saw me when we got you in the car. I hated him that day."

Ranglen remembered Omar seething then. "I did wonder."

"I never understood why he had to kill her—and then to add the bomb on top of it. It wasn't necessary. He does things like that."

"Did Balrak know her?"

"He had dealings with her. He didn't tell me what they were. On the day of her murder, he sent me to her to see if she'd accept some business agreement he set up. I didn't know the details. I just went to ask what her answer was."

"This was after you shot at me when I visited Lonni?"

Omar looked almost apologetic. "Yeah. Right after. Balrak had me do that. I wasn't supposed to hurt you."

Ranglen felt an urge to strike him. "What was Anne's answer?"

"She said no."

"Then you silenced her and brought her to Balrak?"

"I waited till she left the building. Then I cornered her and pulled her into the car. He said he would talk to her while I drove them to the station where you found her. We got there and when I opened the door she was already dead. I was shocked. Then he had me set up that stupid explosion."

"What reason did he give you?"

"For the murder? I assumed her not agreeing to his deal. For the explosion—he said he wanted to scare you."

"You questioned that, didn't you?"

"You don't understand. You don't question him. You—"

"But you did! And he reacted, right? You looked scared that day, and angry. He took you down."

Omar's face turned redder. "You don't know what he's like."

"Then how did he react?'

"I won't talk about it!" He looked ashamed.

Ranglen was shaken that Omar's line was similar to that used by the humanoid on the lifeboat world, "We don't talk about such things." Apparently more than one person believed certain matters were best left untouched.

They listened to the wind sing and howl.

Ranglen said, "Both of you must have been surprised that her death didn't persuade me to go along with him. I'll bet that bothered you. He screwed up."

"I never saw him miscalculate. What he did was stupid."

"Did you question him again?"

Omar said nothing.

Ranglen finished for him. "You *did* question him—and that's why he abandoned you here. You're kicking yourself for not seeing it coming."

"He's a bastard! I tell you—"

"You must have felt proud for standing up to him. But then he dumped you, left you here to die."

"I hated him!"

Ranglen ignored that, asked instead, "Did either Henry or Rashmi meet with Balrak when they were on Ventroni?"

"I don't know. I doubt it."

"He never mentioned them before you found the derelicts?"

"Just that he knew the business trip he wanted me to get onto was Montgomery's. He said this when he told me about the InQuest cargo."

"And what about Lonni? Who the hell was *she* hurting that she had to be killed?"

Omar paled. "That was…unnecessary too."

"Especially that trick you pulled when I was on board the derelict, sneaking in her corpse and putting it into the one empty couch."

Omar raised his hands, palms out. "Balrak told me to do that."

"I'm sure! He murders someone more innocent than all of us, who wouldn't have said a word—just to give me a fright—and you helped him. I'm certain *he* wouldn't wait on board an abandoned derelict with a dead body."

Omar said with spite, "He stayed in his ship after dropping me off."

"And he piloted it in and out of radar range just to distract us. He gave you all the dirty work."

Omar nodded, looked tired of defending himself.

"What would you have done if I hadn't checked the cradle for the lifeboat?"

"Balrak was certain you *would* check. And you did."

Ranglen waited. In the silence the faraway wind grew louder.

Omar suddenly squealed, "It wasn't my idea! You have to believe me!"

"Is there *anything* you did that you decided yourself?"

Omar looked down, then away.

"Did you make a pass at Mileen?"

That tripped him. "What?"

Ranglen shook his head. "Never mind. What happened after you put Lonni's body in the chair?"

"What did you mean about—"

"*Never mind!* What did you do after?"

He stared at Ranglen with guarded apprehension. "I went back into hiding. You flew out of there and then Balrak picked me up. We left for the lifeboat world, where we were supposed to meet Jayne and Rashmi."

"Nothing else happened while you were on the derelict?"

"No.... What are you getting at?"

Ranglen pondered. Omar didn't know about the driftwood derelict chasing after him and Mileen. Apparently he hadn't seen it and Balrak hadn't told him about it. Ranglen chose not to enlighten him. "So you were supposed to meet Jayne and Rashmi on the lifeboat world. Had you spoken with them?"

"Right before leaving Annulus. I came to them after they talked to you, after we dropped you off at the station with Anne. I offered Balrak's services, said I had gone to him for help, that he had resources and probably could beat all of them to the Clip. I came across as friendly—'You deserve part of this too,' I said."

"So you were the sweet and helpful 'old friend.'"

"Hey, I said if we could work together we could share the results. I apologized for walking out on them. They hated to give in to me but they were too desperate, and very unhappy you hadn't gone with them. You put them in the perfect frame of mind for me—I persuaded them easily."

Though he knew Omar was trying to bait him, Ranglen still felt regret. "Why did Balrak plan to meet them there?"

"We knew Mileen wanted to find the lifeboat and Balrak figured she'd persuade you to do that. He wanted all of us together, just like here, everyone who knew about the Clip—you, and particularly Mileen."

"So he could kill us all?"

"He just said he wanted everyone together. He didn't say why. But if he intended to kill us it would have been easier to do it one by one. He's had every chance to do so."

"He killed Lonni. Didn't he want her there too?"

"He preferred using her to scare you. Lonni was an idiot. She brought it on herself. From the time we got back to Annulus, nobody trusted her."

Again Ranglen felt the desire to strike him. "How did Hatch Banner turn up on that planet?"

"Good question. We weren't prepared for that."

"And what happened after the volcano erupted?"

"I don't know. The animals knocked me over. That's all I remember."

"Nothing else?"

"I woke up on Balrak's ship. We already were in light-space. He said he had rescued me. He didn't say how. I thought quite a lot of him then. He said that Jayne and Rashmi's ship got away, but that you must have been buried in the eruption."

"Guess I wasn't."

Omar looked sly. "You know, it's strange, but Balrak predicted that. He said you'd turn up here somehow. He waited for you to arrive so we could destroy your ship. How did you make it out?"

"That's *my* business." He moved on quickly before he got more questions. "And you saw nothing else on the lifeboat world?"

"No. Should I have?"

Omar didn't know that the second derelict was functional, that it shot stakes into the ground in order to protect him during the eruption, probably lifted him away. Why hadn't Balrak told him? And, for that matter, if Balrak wanted Ranglen to survive, why hadn't he tried to save him too?

"You said you were defecting. What was that all about?"

"I'm tired of Balrak. He doesn't make sense. It's just random and sadistic violence."

"It's not that random. He seems to know exactly what he's doing."

"You haven't seen him. When I first met him he was great. You knew you'd get ahead with him. But now he's just a manipulating monster, playing a game he doesn't tell you about. He changes the rules as he goes along. It's the damned Clip."

"There are no rules."

"There's no reason either."

Ranglen shrugged. "So now you're having moral qualms?"

Omar missed the sarcasm. "I got scared. I assumed he'd kill all of you eventually. But I felt I was his partner. Yet he began…tormenting me. He played jokes on me, nasty things. He once burned me." He showed Ranglen an angry welt on the back of his hand. "He spilled hot cooking oil on me—an accident, I thought. He apologized over and over, to the point where I didn't believe him anymore. And then every time when he held something hot, he said, 'Come over here, Omar, I want to burn you again,' laughing as he said it. Then he actually *did* shove a hot-plate against me. He just laughed. 'Oh, the expressions you make!' I knew then he'd kill me when he got the rest of you."

Again, this didn't tally with Ranglen's earlier impression of him, the stoic machine driven by what he called "faith." "You didn't know the risk before?"

"Of course I knew. But before, on Ventroni, he had been fair to his people, fair to me. Not now. He's ready to find a Clip—so he says, screw you! Screw everyone!"

"Why doesn't he just get it himself, like you said?"

"I think he's enjoying our degradation," Omar said. "He enjoyed mine. Killing isn't enough for him. He has to experiment with us too."

"And so he deserted you."

"Yeah, just left me there. So what else could I do but change sides?"

"So this defection is as much his decision as yours."

"Well, it's not—"

"He's dumping you, Omar! You're on your own!"

Omar reached in his pocket and showed a bulge that was supposedly a pistol. "But I've got *you* now."

Ranglen sneered. "Kill me and you won't last a day out here. You'd probably be dead now if I hadn't shown up."

Omar lost his arrogance. "Okay. I need you, I admit it. But I want my part of the Clip too."

"How will we get it with Balrak out there?"

"He'll wait till we find it. He doesn't know where it is either. With you here we have a better chance. He won't bother us till then, and that's when we'll grab him."

"That's your plan, eh?"

"You got anything better? We're stranded here. He has the only spaceship."

"Thanks to you."

Again he looked offended. "Ranglen, even you can't say no to him. He has plans for you too. He wants you as his partner."

"You're kidding. Why?"

"He thinks you've got all the answers."

Ranglen growled, but he kept any questions about this to himself. "What about Mileen?"

"He...doesn't talk about her."

"He says nothing? Come on! Why?"

"Oh, he wants her," Omar said. "He asks more about her than anyone else. He just doesn't comment on her. He was furious when he lost her after Henry got killed. On the planet with the lifeboat, her arrival was the signal for when I was supposed to move in on the rest of you. 'The minute you see Oltrepi, go get them all'—that's what he told me."

"You said he asks about her?"

"He wants to know where she is, whether she's all right. I think he feels she'll find the Clip, that she's the one with 'the touch,' that it'll open for her. He wants you too but more he wants her. He never says why."

Ranglen remembered her taking a shard from the carrier-lock on his asteroid. Had she learned how to use it in the way he did?

If so, she was in even more danger now.

Ranglen sat back—for the first time during the talk. He leaned against the jagged wall of the lava tube, his muscles strained. He took a long breath of cold air. He opened the emergency blanket and wrapped it around him, shared it with Omar.

Mirik asked, "Well, what's next?"

"I'm in charge now? You're asking me?"

"Let's call it mutual benefit. I still have a gun."

"I don't need you, Omar. If I left you here, I'd lose nothing."

"You'll need me when you confront Balrak."

"*If* you're really against him now."

"You think I'm not?" Omar asked.

"You're a leaf in a big wind. I think you'll go wherever you get blown."

"Screw you!"

"You're the one who's screwed."

Omar snarled.

"Go to sleep," said Ranglen. "We've got a long walk tomorrow."

"Where do I sleep?"

"You're sitting on your mattress."

Omar looked down at the small corner of the sleeping bag.

"If you don't want it," Ranglen said, "move away. I'll slip inside it and stay cozy. Otherwise we both have to sleep under this blanket."

Omar scrunched himself together, pulled his flimsy coat around him. The wind still managed to sneak its way through. "It's going to be cold," he said sadly, glancing with envy at Ranglen's parka.

"Next time you enter wilderness, come prepared."

Omar snorted.

Ranglen wanted to kick him. He told himself he'd try to be more polite tomorrow. Maybe.

Chapter Seventeen: Fist of Thorns

Before dawn the wind died.

After a back-breaking night of half sleep, Omar and Ranglen tried to stretch, felt sore, ate a slightly warmed breakfast of trail rations—which Ranglen always hated after just a few days.

As the light strengthened they moved from the cave to the collapsed opening. Snow padded the downfall. They crept up the hole, into a starkly changed world.

Gray clouds hunkered down and covered the field like woolen packing. In rippled waves the snow eddied against black reefs, the drifts not abundant enough to hide the outcrops that broke through. Molten rock welled up under columns of steam. A line of fire fountains squirted lava into the air, orange, then red as the droplets fell. They seemed almost gentle, like flame creatures preening themselves, splashes of color in a black-and-white world.

Ranglen spied with his field-glasses for a trace of people. Did they mean to approach those sputtering fissures to look for crystals holding Clips? A good place to look, but they'd need self-contained thermal suits to avoid fumes laden with sulfur. They'd have to walk through 2000-degree lava streams, and in places the crust would be treacherously thin. They could fall into a flow of melted rock, find themselves boiled, then encased in stone.

Ranglen couldn't see anyone.

He turned left and gazed southeast to the mountains, to slopes newly covered in snow. Sweeping down between two of the peaks was a vast ice sheet with a plume of smoke rising from its middle. No volcano could be seen there.

Ranglen wondered. Maybe a volcano sat under the ice, its heat squeezed up through fissures. Another rarity. Maybe Jayne and the others thought the Clip was there.

He would have unpocketed his shard but he didn't dare with Omar around. He surveyed the area at the base of the hills—and saw what he thought were moving figures, on the opposite side of the field and heading south. "I think I see them."

He handed over the glasses. Omar said, "They're approaching the slope beneath that big ice sheet. What are they hauling?"

"A container for a shelter. It would have its own motor to cross the terrain."

"You think they know where they're going or just walking till they find something?"

Ranglen shrugged, took the glasses and stared again. "They seem to be moving with purpose, not stopping to search." Ranglen didn't tell him his theory of the volcano under the ice—because of standard Clip reticence, and more.

He mapped a path across the lava field, curving it southward to avoid the fire fountains. It was a less reliable but faster route than what the other party had taken, which had followed the hills to his left. But by taking this other route, Ranglen and Mirik, if they hurried and encountered no obstacles, might reach the smoking glacier not long after the first group.

But the road was dangerous.

He described his plan to Omar, who automatically agreed with it. "What choice do I have?"

"Defectors can't be choosers?"

Omar grunted.

They moved across the tortured land, the snow melting from the warmth of the ground. Soot from lava sprayed into the air, fell over them and darkened everything. They avoided the fire fountains that danced, swayed, and spat cinders.

Omar griped about hunger and tiredness. He infuriated Ranglen, who preferred geology to bad company.

The ocean drew near, indicated by banks of billowing steam. Hardened lava in black heaps formed the shore. Liquid rock ran beneath the surface and spilled red-orange billows down to the waves—sporadic, heavy, or in fast flurries of pounding rain. When the hot lava hit the water, a furious hiss screamed back and steam exploded into the sky. The beach looked like a metallurgy works, a factory with huge cauldrons of pouring rock. The land plodded forward to lay down weight, then the sea crashed back in conflict. Ranglen's face grew wet with spray and the sulfur fumes came bitter in his throat.

Omar said, "Are we there yet?"

"You don't understand any of this, do you?"

"This place isn't yours, Ranglen. It doesn't exist for your personal enjoyment."

"I don't want to own it. I just want to experience it."

"Same thing," Omar said.

Ranglen had no rejoinder, which bothered him.

Since the shore was undermined, the crust could buckle and fall with no warning. Ranglen said, "You're in danger of your life. Just wanted you to know."

"Huh?"

"Never mind."

They swung back toward the mountains, their path more northerly now. The talus slopes that spread out from the hills on their right formed an older and more stable landscape than the treacherous one by the sea.

Then Ranglen saw something more disturbing.

They passed slow arms of creeping glaciers, slabs of grindstone wearing down the mountains, and he noticed that the talus aprons formed wide lobes, like hardened mudflows. Signs of catastrophic flooding. If a dammed glacier partially melted, the water could burst and inundate the flatland, picking up dirt and stones along the way and becoming a near solid wall ironing out everything in its path. If the smoke from the large glacial sheet *was* caused by a volcano under the ice, then another such flood might occur. The heat could melt a huge pocket of water which could break forth in unpredictable and perilous ways.

Omar complained. "Surely we're almost there."

"Shut up," Ranglen muttered, but he stopped to search ahead for the group.

He found them not at the base of the hills but climbing to the bottom of the ice sheet, in which the steaming volcano sat.

Ranglen worried. He had hoped to reach the group before they scaled the crags leading to the icefall at the end of the glacier, which dipped down like a serrated loaf of cracking bread. Any glacier was dangerous, especially now with new snow filling unseen crevasses. But this one with its buried volcano was especially so.

Omar had to race to catch up with him now. They traveled faster on more even ground, over snow drifts that brightened the day—the sky remained gray and cloudy.

Ranglen stopped to check ahead with his binoculars. The climbers hadn't reached the glacier yet. At this close distance he could identify them. Hatch led, Jayne and Rashmi brought up the rear with Mileen in front of them.

He felt joy and anger at seeing her again—glad she was alive but remembering her abandoning him and making him suspicious.

The hot little spotlight of the sun broke the clouds, brought glints of metallic blue to everything. The mountains sharpened painfully and the glaciers looked crusted with glass. It was the visual equivalent of a high-pitched squeal.

Ranglen flung a pair of dark glasses to Omar and donned his own. He hoped their sunscreen still held.

Omar grew eager and pulled ahead. Ranglen took a chance and did something foolish, but he needed to do it while the buried volcano still appeared in his line of sight. He pulled out his shard and looked quickly at the ice field.

No gleam shown. The Clip wasn't there.

He pocketed it before he was tempted to scan the whole landscape.

The ground grew rough as they moved downhill nearer the tongue of the glacier. But as they drew near, the people on the slopes saw them. They even waved. Omar waved back.

Ranglen hurried.

The climbers scrambled down the cliffs to meet them, Rashmi, Jayne and then Mileen. Hatch for several minutes stayed where he was.

Omar walked up to their erected shelter, like an old-fashioned hexagon-shaped military tent with stove-pipe exhaust and ventilation screens, a heap of backpacks dumped by the door. Apparently the four treasure-hunters didn't expect to stay long on the glacier, maybe just reconnoitering.

Omar stopped by the shelter, perhaps feeling ambivalent or guilty. Ranglen came up behind him but kept apart, not wanting to be too associated with him. He dumped his own pack with the others.

Jayne and Rashmi reached them first. They looked weathered—cheeks like crags, sunburns peeling, eyes nestled in ugly wrinkles, the anguish of wilderness hard in their gait and weary expressions. They approached Omar and seemed more bewildered than threatened by him. Jayne, gasping in the thin air, said, "What are you doing here? You want to shoot at us again?"

Omar tried to look humbled but he didn't succeed. "No, I'm done with that. Besides," he added cavalierly, "you and Rashmi weren't getting along well when I last saw you."

Jayne shrugged. "Hatch and I weren't dealing with you or Balrak. Rashmi agrees now."

Rashmi's nod was tight but emphatic.

"Look," Omar said, "I'm sorry I shot at you. They were just warning shots anyway. The one that went into your hand," he pointed to Rashmi, "that wasn't lethal. You're fine, right? I was working for Balrak then. I'm not now."

Jayne remained firm. "You expect us to welcome you?"

"I don't expect anything. I just want you to know I'm on my own now. Balrak's abandoned me."

Jayne looked disgusted but also uncertain. She faced Ranglen instead, not happy with him either. "So *now* you make it."

"Well," he drawled, "I know I'm late, but…"

"Never mind. You still can help." Her not taunting him suggested how desperate—or tired—they had become.

Mileen arrived.

She and Ranglen stared at each other.

Wary smiles broke between them. They hugged, awkwardly, with just enough hesitation that he felt unsure of their feelings. She looked regretful. He felt disappointment.

They pulled slightly away from the others. He knew that both of them didn't like to be reproachful or defensive, so he regretted his first question. "Why did you leave me?"

"I didn't," she insisted. "I needed to see Hatch."

"You could have waited and told me instead. We then could have walked into the camp together."

"I didn't think they were a threat to us, especially Hatch, and I wasn't sure if you'd agree. I just wanted to talk to him. I didn't know what I was walking into—that they'd *fight* over me."

Ranglen believed her but couldn't help resisting. He was so accustomed to keeping to himself that since he *had* opened to Mileen, he felt compromised, used, hurt. His typical aloneness rose to protect him.

He said, off the subject, and maybe in response to how fatigued she looked, "You got away all right when the volcano erupted?"

"Thanks to you. We saw you waving for us to leave. We didn't mean to take off but we saw the cloud was coming. Hatch insisted. We hoped Balrak would grab both of you."

Had they not seen the driftwood derelict then? As Omar didn't see it? Ranglen wanted to ask but not with Omar so close by. "Balrak didn't get me," was all he said.

Mileen looked sad at his reticence, which made him retreat into more silence. "Then, how...?"

He turned away.

Hatch, now down from the glacier, walked over and joined them. He made a surly and grave appearance. "Hello, Mykol," he said flatly.

Ranglen nodded with a brusque coolness.

The clouds broke again, but the glaring light gave no sanctioned aura to the group. It was more like an interrogator's lamp, unforgiving.

"So..." Omar said, regaining his sarcasm, "here we are again, like when we found the derelicts, only now we have newcomers. You can't stay alone when you have Clips, can you?"

"Shut up, Omar." Jayne was still captain.

Omar continued. "So what kind of choices have we got now? The Clip? Balrak? You've all become like me, you know—thieves on the run. How are we getting out of here?"

"Shut up!" Jayne repeated.

Hatch moved toward Omar, threatening. "You better—"

"Better *what?*"

"Control your—"

"Oh, *stop* it! Your ship's destroyed. Did you even know that?"

"Of course we knew," Hatch said. "We heard the blast and then lost communication. Our satellite sent back an image of the wreck."

"And you never returned to save anything, did you? You kept on searching for the Clip, getting further from help. You haven't found anything yet though, right?"

Painful silence.

"You're all pathetic!"

Hatch and Jayne looked ready to beat him.

Ranglen watched with clinical objectivity.

"You're just like Balrak now," Omar said. "Obsessed. Mad. You're marooned here and you don't even think about it. You feel the Clip will work a miracle and take you home. You're crazy…and you think *I'm* the bad one."

Rashmi yelled, "We're not *murderers!*"

"Give yourselves time! It still can happen!"

Hatch reached for Omar but the shorter man slid away, laughing.

Then Ranglen realized—they all were gathered together here now. Exactly what Balrak said he wanted.

Rashmi shouted, pointed at the sky.

A dark shape glided upward past the edge of the glacier—a mass of spines and complex towers turning with grim menace in the air, racks and pylons and javelins of metal glittering in the hard bluish light.

The driftwood ship. The second derelict.

With an agonizing slowness it ascended over them, an object too extreme to be understood—like a mountain torn apart in battle, a junkyard squeezed into a jagged ball—threatening to plummet and bury them.

Nobody moved.

They then learned the secret of its function.

Portions of its skin disconnected and spread, broke into a thousand component stakes. These quickly dispersed and turned their pointed ends to the ground, working in perfect concert together, an entity cloud. Then the spikes plunged, stabbed into the earth like aimed harpoons. More volleys followed. They pierced deep into the ground and formed precise lines of stakes—

Making a barrier around the six people, a wide ring that included the shelter.

More spikes fell, filled gaps, made the fence impenetrable. The spears thrust so hard into the earth they didn't shake once implanted. Ranglen doubted if anyone could pull them out—and if any were removed, others surely would take their place.

The people clustered together in fear. They faced outward while nudging against their companions for protection. The enclosure was solid.

The derelict didn't seem smaller for all the lances tossed at them. It resumed its slow revolution, changing shape, rearranging itself after the discharge. Clearly now it was only a vast collection of spikes that could modify its aggregate form. This made it more ominous. It now had teeth.

A small flyer glided across the lava field. A sleek shell of metal that was half transparent, it passed over the stake-rim and landed beside the group.

Balrak stepped out.

His thin cap of gray hair seemed brighter now, maybe from the sunlight. His face was still chiseled and lean. He wore a beige wilderness suit, multi-pocketed and spotted with technological extras. It was much too new, the boots polished and un-broken-in, obviously expensive. He seemed a slightly aged model showing off the latest in all-purpose wear.

The flyer lifted, remote-controlled or on automatic pilot, and came down again outside the enclosure.

"Good afternoon," Balrak said, in the deep tone Ranglen remembered. It countered Mirik's claims about his madness.

Omar yanked out a small laser projector and aimed it at Balrak. Hatch and Rashmi followed with dart-guns.

Spikes fell from the derelict and struck the weapons out of their hands. Larger spikes then smashed the guns into the ground.

Balrak walked toward the group. A hornet cloud of finger-length knives came from the derelict and hovered in two attack formations above his shoulders, pointing at whoever he addressed. "You all should know now what I can do. I fully control that object up there, and you can be killed by its spears in an instant."

Ranglen asked, with a neutral curiosity, "How do you control it?"

"By thought," Balrak said. "A form of quantum tunneling, 'telepathy.' You don't have the context to understand it yet. Think of it as my extra and private *fist*. A fist of thorns."

Ranglen thought the phrase overly appropriate.

Balrak walked closer. "Before we continue, I need to prove to you what you're dealing with. It's not very original but...effective. I need to kill one of you."

No one breathed.

"You're wondering, of course, who I will pick." He smiled now. "Will it be Omar Mirik, once trusted business partner who strayed from me? Or Hatch Banner? Another client, and owner of the largest spaceport on Annulus—*and* he's a smuggler.

Or Jayne Fowler? A good pilot but a bit too independent now. Or Rashmi Verlock? Who, unlike Jayne, says little and keeps to himself, but maybe he just misses his Henry too badly. Or will it be our *star*, Mykol Ranglen? Poet, philosopher, explorer, Romantic. But I have other things planned for him. I don't intend to hurt him...yet. So..."

Balrak faced Ranglen. "*You* know who I'll kill, don't you?"

"I have a guess."

Six of the daggers over Balrak's shoulder shot forth.

They all went for Jayne.

Five punctured her heart and one stabbed her forehead.

Hatch screamed, ran to her as she fell.

The others, stunned, looked at Balrak but also to Ranglen, as if awaiting explanation.

Ranglen spoke only to Balrak. "You chose one of the women."

"You think I dislike women?"

"You're playing to the stereotype. You went after a breeder, a potential mother. 'Wipe out the queens'—isn't that what the stock villainous aliens always say when they fight each other?"

Balrak looked serious. "You've got all the answers, don't you?"

Ranglen's expression didn't change.

"And answers frighten you the most, Mr. Ranglen. Isn't that correct? You're disturbed when you *can* find explanations, because explanations to you are fulfilled predictions, and you hate events too rational and determined. You're distraught even now because I didn't include *Mileen* in my list of possible victims. That's much too planned, you feel. Whereas..."

Balrak looked to Omar. "...with Mirik there, it's just the opposite. *Un*predictability scares him, behavior that seems insane with no purpose. Aren't you scared now, Omar? Aren't you wondering, '*What is he doing?*' Since I have no reason to kill you at all—I don't give a damn that you betrayed me or that you even just now tried to shoot me. I'm sure you're very, *very*, frightened at the moment."

Omar looked terrified.

Six daggers leapt for him. Omar fell.

Rashmi screamed, *"Just what the hell are you?"*

Balrak looked to Ranglen again, awaited clarification.

Ranglen said, with his own dry and barren certainty, "You're a Moyock."

Balrak smiled.

Chapter Eighteen: Out of the Past

The staffs from the derelict flew up from the ground, rearranged themselves and thrust downward again, formed a larger fence around the camp.

More stakes slid onto the bodies of Jayne and Omar, made cylindrical coffins for both of them and lifted them away. To where, no one knew.

Balrak insisted that the four left alive, prisoners now, surrender their hand-guns. The spears hanging over them made this mandatory. Ranglen was appalled as he watched the weapons that went into the pile—ion projectors, pocket lasers, kinetic pistols, revolvers with explosives, and the omnipresent dart-guns. The treasure-hunters could have killed each other ten times over. The flying staffs formed a shovel and took the pile away. Balrak then left the four of them after promising he'd return.

They fixed a meal and ate it slowly. Talk was sporadic and the tension heavy. Both Hatch and Mileen stayed quiet. Rashmi looked disturbed but he didn't speak. Ranglen kept to himself.

Eventually he wandered out to the fence. He stared through its chinks to Balrak's flyer but he saw no movement there. He paced back and forth, watched the derelict's jagged moon hanging above him. It could change so quickly into volleys of missiles. It wasn't one weapon—but a million.

"A fist of thorns."

Balrak's voice. He stood behind Ranglen by an opening in the fence. A length of it hovered several meters in the air, left a gap big enough to let Balrak through. The stakes must have risen very quietly for Ranglen not to notice.

"Is that what you call it?" The derelict gleamed in the last turquoise light of afternoon.

"Depends on the mood. Do you know what the thing is?" Balrak spoke with a calm self-revelatory wonder, like a statue come to life and fascinated with itself.

Ranglen offered, "A weapons cache that doubles as construction equipment."

Balrak sighed. "Not even close. Oh, I use it in that way, but that's not what it *is*.

The best name for it is 'our collected works.' I know that doesn't make sense but I'll explain later."

Ranglen's eyes narrowed.

Balrak said, "How did you know that I was a Moyock?"

"I didn't know, I guessed. I've suspected since the derelict came alive." It had more to do with what the bat-like humanoid said on the lifeboat world—that Balrak had visited the planet before, that he let his indentured colonists die, that he killed inhabitants, that he was "finding himself" through conscious play—as Omar had suggested too—and that, especially, he was "reborn." But Ranglen didn't say any of this. He didn't want Balrak going back to that world and killing anyone.

The man—or the Moyock—replied politely, as if to be helpful, "It's more accurate to say I'm a human who's inherited the essence of being Moyock, like an overlay. Their beliefs live on in me."

"Does that mean you've been 'reborn,' that you're 'finding yourself'?"

Balrak looked appreciative. "That's very good. Yes, exactly that."

"But isn't a Moyock overlay and *being* a Moyock the same thing?"

"Well…"

"It's not a philosophy, after all. It's becoming a member of a different race."

"Yes," he admitted. "But you need to realize that genuine Moyocks, the originals, are extinct—as much as the Airafane."

"So you've taken on a template."

"Something like that."

Ranglen knew nothing for sure. "It's not something you chose, right? You started as a human. And then somehow you were selected, in the same way that the Clips choose their finders."

Balrak gave an acid impression. "Please don't compare me to a so-called Clip. We're very different."

"You don't want to be associated with them, do you? You can't stand being like the Airafane."

"We're *not* like them. That's the whole point."

"Old hatreds never die, eh? They just get passed on—to the innocent."

Balrak said darkly, "I wasn't that innocent." He looked around at the stakes, the cold plain. "It's a little uncomfortable standing here. Come to my flyer." He walked through the section of open wall.

Ranglen followed, knowing he was ordered and not invited. The opening in the fence closed down behind him as Balrak led him to his roomy aircar. Between the front and back seats was an open area with a small table. They sat on opposite ends of the couch there. Two drinks waited on the stand before them. Ranglen avoided his.

He was struck by how artificial this felt, sitting in plush surroundings with a man who intended to kill him—to kill all of them. He asked, as a means of hiding his ire, "Do you mean that all of us have the chance—or the 'privilege'—of becoming a Moyock?"

"Originally you did, but I think only a few of you could do it now. It takes a special person, and the stimulus to bring it about is rare. But at one time…You see, we didn't imitate the Airafane. They imitated us. They got the idea of burying their little information nuggets from what we did."

"But you didn't bury just information, did you?"

Balrak beamed at Ranglen's insight. "No," he said, tilting his head to make the word more significant.

Ranglen finished for him. "You buried your*selves*. And not in the mantles of planets, but in *us*." He remembered the humanoid saying that Ranglen had other "powder" inside him, and that the creature hated when humans became "extreme."

Balrak gloated. "That must really scare you to say that."

"No. You just want it to scare me."

"You realize you'll never understand what we are."

"I'm happy to agree."

"Maybe that's better for you. You'd have a hard time going on if you knew the real truth."

"Which of course you'll tell me anyway."

Balrak's smile grew dry. "We buried ourselves into the genetic codes of as many races we could find. You see them as ancient viruses that no longer affect you but that still are contained in your genes. That code has evolved. *You* have evolved. You weren't yet human when we found you. And much of our code eventually was lost. But I imagine we're still there in a number of you."

"What's the trigger that brings you 'online'? Cues in the environment?"

Balrak nodded.

"Like an ancient derelict that looks like a piece of driftwood? Maybe even both derelicts, but certainly the 'fist,' as you call it."

"That's how it happened for me anyway."

"This is the first time the derelict has become active, right? If it had been used before, people would have noticed."

"It sat there for millennia, doing nothing. After the Moyock in me took over, I tried to find if it had activated before. I discovered no evidence."

"So you found it about twenty years ago?"

He nodded again.

"That's when the murders on the first derelict occurred. Did you commit them?"

"No. I got there soon after they happened. Or at least I assumed it was soon after. The people on the first derelict must have encountered the fist and it responded by killing them. It's programmed to do that. Then it went back into its holding pattern. I shut off the response mechanism that automatically killed intruders."

"What made you go there?"

"When the fist became active it...called to me. Something in me responded. At the time—you might laugh—I thought it was my *business* sense, my nose for profit. So you could say it was my intuition that led me there. But when I arrived, something different emerged in me. The Moyock emerged. It heard the call, but I didn't know that then. Once there, I assumed control of the fist. The Moyock—now me—knew how to do that."

Ranglen realized, happily, he had no embedded Moyock inside him—nothing happened when *he* saw the derelict. Glad about that at least, he said, "On the first ship, did you download the information about the Clip world?"

"Yes. But originally not all the information was there. You had to go to the planet with the lifeboat to get the rest of it. The people on board the ship—the people killed—were clever to require that."

This was the download that Ranglen got, the deeper original and not the one that Jayne and the others must have tapped. "You changed it?"

"Yes. I went to the lifeboat planet afterward, got the coordinates for this world, the Clip world. Then I went back to the derelicts and put the information in, deleting the need to go to the lifeboat world. I also shut off all the computers, so if anyone found the derelict, nothing could be read."

"But the computers were functioning when Omar and Jayne and the rest of them got there."

"I went there again, right before I had Omar set up the arrival. I turned them on, with the new information that didn't require going to the first world."

"So it would all look accidental."

"I wanted everyone together here for when we find the Clip." He sounded proud.

"Well, let's be accurate, you wanted me, Mileen, Hatch, and Rashmi. Others are missing—or killed—by you."

His grin showed a subtle appreciation. "Hatch was a surprise. And Rashmi I don't care about. I'll kill him next. But I did want you and Mileen there. I think you can appreciate it. You're both artists, after all."

Ranglen stifled his sarcasm. He needed questions answered. "If you found the derelicts twenty years ago, why didn't you search for the Clip then?"

"Because I don't care about the Clip. I hate Clips. I just don't want anyone else to find them."

"But you want us to find this one."

"I didn't say you'd get to *keep* it. Think of the irony—you'll watch me destroy it. And then, maybe, I'll let you live to write about it."

"And Mileen?"

"We'll see. Maybe she can paint a picture."

Ranglen moved away from who would survive and who wouldn't. "When you visited the lifeboat years ago, on that other planet, did you find a survivor?"

"No. I think the people on the derelict sent the lifeboat away not to save anyone. I found only three spacesuits on the ship (which I dumped overboard, and then I drained the ship of air just in case anyone *did* survive). I feel they did it to preserve the information about the Clip world. Finding the fist must have unnerved them... before it killed them."

"But you changed the information on the derelict to prevent people from going to the lifeboat."

"I didn't want anyone visiting that planet. I had a colony there once."

Ranglen raised an eyebrow. "The police said you supply work-groups for such colonies."

"Yes. Good profit."

"But something happened to this group that you didn't want people to know about." Ranglen said this speculatively.

"That's true. But I realized it wasn't important. There's no evidence left of the colony anyway, or of what happened."

"No evidence that, maybe, they all died, and that, maybe, you were responsible."

Balrak said coolly, "What else did the natives on that planet tell you?"

Ranglen stared back at him and added no more.

"You don't need to hide your adventure there," Balrak said. "I saw that creature watching you as the volcano erupted. I meant to rescue you but it pulled you 'underground.' I'm sure your talk with it was quite informative."

Ranglen said, in truth, "They don't talk."

"Well, they don't *speak*. But they 'say' an awful lot."

Ranglen left the subject of the natives. "My question is, would you have let that colony die before you became a Moyock?"

"I doubt it, but...you never know."

"So you were testing yourself. Steeling yourself. Experimenting with your new Moyock ways."

"I wanted to learn what I was capable of doing."

Ranglen sat back and crossed his arms. "Sometimes you talk as if you *are* the Moyock, but at other times as if it speaks *to* you and you're still human. Which is it?"

"We're a hybrid. A new 'I.' Let's say I was reborn, as you put it. I challenged myself to see how far I could go. I don't know if I'm the only active Moyock or not, since I'm certain the implants exist out there. I know what most Moyocks knew, but I assume it's watered down, at a level where I can comprehend it. Since the takeover occurred, or the inheritance, I haven't aged much, so who knows how long we survive. I've done a lot to cover my trail so I assume any others would have done the same. But I wonder about the history of humanity. The dictators, the gangsters, the wealthy and powerful, even the great benefactors—I wonder if any of them were really us. We'll probably never know."

"You must feel isolated, alone."

The nod was slight but genuine.

Ranglen added, but not sympathetically, "How sad for you."

"If you want to blame the miseries of human history on us, feel free to do so. But it's a dangerous move. It's better to accept responsibility for each action you make. I always hated when human achievements were assigned to 'others,'—like aliens building the pyramids. It shows a horrible lack of pride. Your race, at the core, is like that...weak."

"We're talking about you, remember?"

"All right, then, let's talk about me."

Ranglen swallowed. "Why did you kill Omar?"

"I had no further use for him."

"Strictly logic, eh?"

"That scares you, doesn't it? Like I said before, it's the predictable you don't like."

"What did you mean when you said that?"

"I try to understand the people I deal with. As I said, Mirik's great fear was irrationality, people behaving for no understandable reason. So I played that part for him—a random destructiveness. Did he tell you about my burning him? How pointless that was and how it unsettled him? But you're not bothered by illogic. You feel it's already a part of the universe. Your great scare is the opposite, *too* much logic, or too strong a belief in correctness, too much near religious certainty. I created both roles, just for the two of you."

"I'm not grateful."

"It wasn't a gift....Don't underestimate us, Mr. Ranglen."

"There is no 'us.' There's only you."

"So *far* there's only me. Or I'm the only one I know of. But who can guess what this incident might do. It could send a ripple across space, wake up battalions—legions, armies. Your future might be terrifying, Mr. Ranglen, dark for the human race indeed. That's why I might let you live—to tell others, to spread the word. You're my chosen voice perhaps...my prophet, my publicist."

"I won't play that role for you."

"You think you have a choice?"

Ranglen didn't answer. "Why did you kill Anne Montgomery?"

"She was moving into my territory. She wanted part of my business on Ventroni. She first asked to become my partner. I said no. Then she sent feelers and agents. The trip with Henry Ciat and Rashmi was part of that."

"Did Henry and Rashmi know what they were doing?"

"Rashmi knew. He spoke with me on Ventroni. But I don't think he and Anne trusted Henry. Anne was smart....Hey, maybe she was a Moyock too."

"If she was, then you killed your own kind."

He shrugged. "So be it."

Ranglen shifted uncomfortably on the couch. "You raided her company's computer files, didn't you?"

"Of course. Standard procedure. If she wanted to do business with me, I checked her out first."

"But you raided her *twice*. And the second time, you went after personnel records, not financial."

Balrak's eyes probed. "Why did she tell you that? Why didn't she go to the police?"

"She wouldn't want the police to know she was dealing with you. And, maybe in a roundabout way, she was trying to warn me."

"If she was, she deserved everything I did to her."

Ranglen controlled his reaction. "Omar told me he came to speak with her on the day you murdered her, that she said 'no' to a business deal from you."

"And for telling you that, Omar deserved what he got too."

Ranglen clenched his teeth. "You learned something during the second security raid—that she had something you wanted."

Balrak looked eager. "That's quite true. Do you have any idea what?"

Ranglen didn't want to reveal it in case he was wrong. "Well, you said you thought Anne was a Moyock."

"I wasn't serious."

"Maybe she was an Airafane instead. If one of your race survived, perhaps one of theirs did too."

"Maybe, but I doubt if Montgomery was Airafane. I would have known."

"Then why did you kill her in the way you did? It seems like, I assume, what a Moyock would do to an Airafane."

"No. If she *had* been Airafane, I would have tortured her first, ripped her heart and soul out of her, made her feel pain. I killed her only to scare you. I knew you'd wonder if there was a plan behind it, and that you'd obsess over finding that plan. And you have to admit I did get to you."

Ranglen admitted nothing but he did change the subject. "Why kill Lonni?"

Balrak suddenly became impatient. "Because I *wanted* to! What the hell does it matter? After they found the location of a Clip everyone in that group was doomed. It was just a matter of time. If I hadn't killed her, they would have done it to each other. And…" He settled. "How about that game on the derelict with her body? I got to you there too, didn't I? Good play, all of it. I've learned so much about myself."

"Why do you want to scare me, 'get to me,' as you say?"

Balrak looked at him with almost admiration. "Because I believe in you, Mr. Ranglen. You're my mirror, my test case. I perform for you. Only you understand me. You have the perception—I see it in your writing. You're my own private audience, my selected observer. If I touch *you* then I can touch anyone."

Ranglen had no comeback to that.

"Are there any other murders you want clarified? Jayne's? You were right. In doubt, always go for the breeders."

Ranglen feared that his own anger was exactly what Balrak wanted out of him.

"Shame on you, Mr. Ranglen. You didn't ask me about Henry Ciat."

Damn it! He made the same mistake he had done with Pia—providing information by the questions he *didn't* ask.

Balrak added, "I'm saying no more about that anyway. Let's get on to more interesting matters. Remember how I described the fist to you?"

"You called it your 'collected works.'"

"Yes, and that's a very appropriate title. Not *my* collected works, not me individually, but the outcome of all the Moyocks together. It's their legacy."

Ranglen waited.

Balrak sat back and took pleasure in his narrative. "The derelict hovering above us is composed of near sentient components that follow my commands. They react instantaneously because, as said before, the bond between them and me is quantum-based. The Airafane were clever. They perfected teleportation of information and had it instilled into their neurological systems. So, when we captured any of them, we ripped that system from their brains and incorporated it into the staffs of the fist. The neurons of one dead Airafane run through each of the stakes.

He added, "Ironic, isn't it? We used their own brain cells, their technology against them. Count the staffs—that's how many Airafane were killed, sacrificed, to build it. I think it's several hundred million or so. The fist is a monument to our genocide of them. Or a rape, if you think of it as 'giving birth.' Not a bad achievement for an oppressed race. And yes, it wasn't us who oppressed them but the other way around."

Ranglen was appalled but not totally surprised. "What could they have done to you to make you treat them that way?"

Balrak tried to sound cavalier. "They made assumptions about their superiority. You see, we believed in *action*, while they believed in meditative stasis. We were engineers while they were philosophers—Romans versus Greeks, to put it in your own historical terms. And while they exploited their environment—an environment that was part ours, understand—we in turn exploited them.

"They used material and sensory objects, things that belonged to us. But we used people. *They* became our resource. They were in decline anyway with too much inbreeding. They had wallowed in their new telepathy and created endless virtual worlds made of futures from their past. They lived in hive-like habitats with all of them looking inward. They became fair game for us—we, the heroic individualists. We put them to better use than they did."

He leaned closer to Ranglen. "Don't look at me so shocked. You should feel wonder instead of revulsion. Humans are more like *us* than the Airafane. That's why I fit in to your race so well, why no one noticed I was different. A gangster is a type of primal human, fully self-reliant.

"You've always struggled for social community, a civilization of equals and mutual help. But it's impossible for you to achieve. It's not in your genes. You create it and then you hate it, unable to live in it. You're all too selfish. Self-interest is your standard. Your intellectuals criticize everyone but themselves, your saints and philanthropists are what you want to be but not what you are. You think you're determined by society and tradition but that's self-evasion—you just want something to blame. The gangster, the 'entrepreneur extreme'…that's the real you."

"This is the Moyock speaking now, right?"

He grinned. "No. It's me, but whatever 'me' I am now, so it's hard to tell. We built more than one fist, by the way, from the corpses of Airafane. Few of those people ever fought back. They were too fatalistic. A radical group inside them tried to rebel but of course they failed. And then they developed what they saw as their master plan, a revenge scheme that would cover hundreds of millions of years—storage devices buried in worlds with plate tectonics. It seemed overly dramatic to us, and a mighty long time to wait for victory. We just laughed.

"But they couldn't help themselves. They had to manipulate. It was part of their nature. They never could let go—not of us then, and not of you now. You'll pay for all you get from them. Hell, we'll liberate you more than they will."

Ranglen felt both anger and fear. He asked, "On board the derelict, in the three people who were killed, a part of the backs of their heads were missing, a spot behind their right ears where the flesh had been torn out. Did you do that?"

"Yes, and I commend you for noticing."

"You were looking for something?"

"I'm not certain, but I think the Airafane took another idea from us. It wasn't just technology they buried away."

"Meaning?"

"Some of *them* are out there too."

A queasy apprehension crept into Ranglen.

"Your universe is much more contaminated—'haunted'—than you think. I know you use a shaving of the carrier-lock to find Clips."

Ranglen went numb.

"Yes, but don't worry. It's still your secret. I'm the last person in the galaxy who would share it with anyone. My point is that the shard works because of the Airafane inside it, showing you the way."

"You mean…Airafane are in the carrier-lock, like you're in our genes?"

"Of course. And you can only bring them out by implanting a shard into the human brain, planting it directly behind the right ear."

Ranglen could say nothing for a moment. "Through surgery?"

"No. Just placing it there is enough. The nano-technology inside does the rest. It anesthetizes the area and then grows through the scalp. Soon…presto, the person is an Airafane. They got the idea from us."

Ranglen concentrated. "So the Clips are just 'rewards,' the bait, and the real point of all this is to implant Airafane?"

"Oh no. The Airafane added to the carrier-lock was a late idea. A desperation, really. There weren't many Airafane left by then. Not every lock carries one. They're quite rare, actually. You were just lucky."

"Then the three on the derelict spaceship who were killed. Were they Airafane?"

"Only one. The woman. Not the man or the child. That surprised me. The flesh I pulled out—with a pair of sharp wide-headed pliers, by the way—was empty in two of them."

"Then who were they?"

"I checked the records on the derelict even though they were hard to follow. Someone, the Airafane woman apparently, distorted the programs without deleting them. I learned the man was a spaceship-builder connected to the company that found the first Clip. He was very wealthy, and his wife, soon after they were married, persuaded him to build the sleek spaceship.

"Maybe she got a shard from the original carrier-lock, for the ship *is* an Airafane design. That naïve retro-futuristic look was typical of them. Decadence, really. But making the ship was a bad move for her. It probably activated the fist and brought it down on them. The fist would have recognized the craft as Airafane and automatically kill everyone on board. So her own arrogance and foolishness brought death to her family."

Ranglen kept his thoughts to himself.

"The Airafane were like that. They felt they were placed in the universe to give it form, not to bring it a political order but a balanced aesthetic. Harmony isn't the right word, and certainly not justice. It was more a symmetric composition, everything in its right and approved place. They didn't care about exploitation or gain. They weren't capitalists. They were indulgent sensualists instead. They wanted to *touch* the future, hold it, sculpt it, in order to say, 'We were there—we *are* there!' And…lo, there she was, dead in her faux rocketship to nowhere. Killed by our fist. I thought she looked perfect."

Ranglen tried not to writhe in his seat.

"They did things like that: plans big and small that were ultimately stupid. They didn't scheme in the way that humans do. They were…architects. They wanted a future that would become a monument to their own influence. And, understand, we were grateful for this. They gave us purpose, something we could counter and corrupt. We evolved to take advantage of them while they remade our worlds without our permission. They provided us motivation and even became our gods. It's good to worship one's enemy—it keeps you sharp. And we had plenty of room then for our holy wars, there at the beginning of the galaxy. All was bright and new and rich. We felt no restraints. We had time for amusement, and enough life to make up for all that we did."

Ranglen muttered, "Life. Life."

"What?" Balrak said.

"Never mind." This remembered comment from the bat-like humanoid slipped out. He moved on quickly. "How many Airafane are in a carrier-lock?"

"Just one, but any shard from it can 'download' the personality. Once it happens, the probability functions collapse, and the rest of the pieces don't hold her anymore."

"'Her'?"

"Neither the Moyocks nor the Airafane had sexuality, but I like to think of the Airafane as women and we as men. It seems appropriate somehow, in a mean sort of way. A human thing."

Ranglen felt nauseated. He asked, wildly, "If you didn't have sexuality then what did you have instead?"

"I thought you guessed that. We had religion. But…you'd never understand."

This was too much for Ranglen. He asked, again to change the subject, "Have you encountered any Airafane who aren't dead?"

"I'm not sure. Some people I've met seemed like them but never close enough. I wondered about the inhabitants on the lifeboat world but I decided no. I've kept my eyes open for any Airafane during all those twenty years. Recently, I felt I might have had a lead. No big deal, just a hint."

Ranglen stayed quiet, allowed his nerves to settle. He asked after a moment, "You talk so much about the Airafane, but why did the Moyocks plant themselves in other races? Weren't you just as obsessed as they?"

"Obsession? Hardly! We did it out of pride. We couldn't let them be ahead of us. They made us that way. And we didn't send technology down through time. We sent *us*. We didn't want space. We wanted *time*—in the same way they did."

"But why? To build an empire, to rule over everything?"

"No, no!" he said in disgust. "That's so simple-minded. That's *your* way of thinking. You always impose your own interpretations. Humans pride themselves on being so impartial and yet you can't see beyond aspects of yourself. You assign a label, then you see just the label. Your theories blind you. You develop personal attachments to them. Your psychology is self-therapy, your sociology is politics, even your physics has possessiveness and greed. Those of you who feel you are most objective are the most deluded, most easily fooled. You want truth, but it's not part of your nature. Detachment isn't in you. I'm not sure if you can ever overcome yourselves. I'm very different from you, but you impose on me structures from your horrid past—empires, slavery, holocausts, dictators. I'm not one of your pathetic Roman emperors, or even some latter-day fascist maniac."

"Then...what do you want?"

He stared back at Ranglen from an icy distance. "I want to *haunt* you. I want to be an annoying ghost, a methodical specter from your buried past. I don't want to rule or own you. I just want to play, to lurk in your border spaces, to always stay beyond your meager comprehension, to harass and trouble your thin understanding. I have no agenda, no plan for vengeance like the Airafane had. I do not perform out of habit or inertia. Think of me as a long silence given sudden and spastic voice, a hint of disorder in your complacency, something irreducible, always out of reach."

He leaned forward, "You see, for you, 'the misunderstood' is just 'the understood' with a minus sign in front of it. That's how you make the unknowable part of your system, how you contain it and thus feel like you've conquered it. But I don't want to be part of your knowledge or your lack of knowledge. I want to move at right-angles to every one of your directions, hide in some folded intangible dimension from which I can foray into your smugness. I want to stay radically other. I don't want to be stable enough for you to know me. I want to live at your margins. Like the fist out there—drifting, reassembling, never quite defined. Think of it, Ranglen...I want to be like you. *You*, specifically."

Ranglen shuddered.

"That's why I talk to you and no one else. You understand me. You're already out there in the realms I'm describing. I sometimes feel you're half Moyock yourself. On the edge, alone, paranoid, with your secrets. But your problem is that you still think in terms of linear narrative and individual stories. I've read your writings. They're good for humans but not accurate enough for the universe. You would try to 'understand' our struggle, turn it into clear cause-and-effect. But there's no story behind us. It's just fragments and shards. Our past is in ruins. We're a virus now, not a culture. A dispersal of parasites. A supplement to the mainstream. I'm not part of your history, of anybody's history. I'm beside it. I'm the great unspoken. I'm trauma and guilt and a challenge to logic. I embrace the unthinkable. And...I kill people."

On a whim, Ranglen asked, "Does this make you happy?"

"Happiness is not one of my goals. I confess to a certain boredom, but maybe that's part of the deal, part of the definition of what I am. I feel I've done everything, that I'm very old. And I *am* old. Sometimes I'm weary. I await more memory, more justification for experience. And in the meantime…I lurk. I play. I've had more pleasure in the last few weeks than I've had in decades."

He was silent then. He relaxed and looked vaguely inattentive, even wistful.

Ranglen said, in a long drawn-out breath, "Well…" He leaned forward as if to leave, "This has all been incredibly enlightening."

"I'm sure it has," Balrak said.

Ranglen looked about the flyer's cabin. He felt exhausted—physically, emotionally. "Are we done?" he asked.

"We can be. Or we can talk a little further."

"No, that's enough." Ranglen couldn't endure Balrak any longer. He reached for the door.

And froze.

On the wall beside the exit hung a picture of postcard size, a reproduction of an e-painting ("e" for the use of pigments with embedded circuitry, programmed for special visual effects). It was a painting quite familiar to Ranglen.

A field of wild grass backed by stark hills, the landscape evasive, misty, withdrawn, the sky a roiling tunnel of clouds. Huge rocks stood on end in the middle of the plain, some fallen, the remains of once proud menhirs that now barely survived, forgotten. The e-paint hinted at subtle movement inside them, hidden indications of lurking pasts, layers of civilizations buried in strata. These stand-alone pillars seemed half alive, playing at archetypal memory like darkly toned music. And Ranglen realized it must be a favorite picture of Balrak's for it to be hanging here, if only in small size. It would have rested in his field of vision as he talked to Ranglen even now.

The picture's title was "Deep Time."

The painter was Mileen.

Chapter Nineteen: Mileen

Balrak followed Ranglen from the flyer. The night lay thick around them. A section of the stake-fence lifted away, allowed them to approach the group gathered in the tent. Balrak told them to move apart. He warned everyone to "use the facilities"—the portable toilet they had brought—and to take any food or drink from their supplies. They'd be spending the night outdoors, he said.

While they gathered blankets and sleeping bags (the weather was chill but not bitter), Ranglen caught Hatch's eye and carefully pointed to the digging equipment they had brought. Hatch looked puzzled. Ranglen gestured toward a specific pack. Hatch shrugged but grabbed it and took it with him.

Everyone, outside now, moved away from each other. "Further," ordered Balrak. Ranglen made sure he was next to Hatch.

Then, with his army of spears, Balrak formed straight walls between them, four squares about ten meters on a side. The walls slashed down in lines. A few slim openings shone here and there, wide enough for a pencil to squeeze through, resulting from the different widths of the stakes. Otherwise, each person was sealed off completely.

Out of sight behind the walls now, Balrak shouted, "I'll see all of you tomorrow morning! It'll be a party! We'll gather at the Clip!" Ranglen assumed he then walked back to his flyer.

Ranglen was surprised Balrak didn't bring his bigger ship down, the one that had chased him earlier. The sleeping accommodations in it would be better than in the aircar. Maybe Balrak didn't trust anyone and wanted to make sure he kept control of it. Ranglen couldn't see the flyer over the wall, and if the ship came in later he never noticed it.

He set out his insulated blanket and sleeping bag. To his right sat Rashmi's cell and to the other side Hatch's. Mileen was beyond the corner between them.

He heard a message from Rashmi first, who walked to the wall and peeked through a small opening. The man called his name just loud enough to get Ranglen's attention but not for anyone else to hear.

Mykol walked to the wall.

"He's going to kill us, isn't he?" Rashmi said.

"Seems likely."

Rashmi kept quiet.

Mykol added, "He wants us to find the Clip first. I'm pretty sure he'll wait till afterward. And maybe he has other plans for us."

Rashmi still kept quiet.

"Tell me the truth, Rashmi. After you and Henry quit working for Anne, she called you in alone, didn't she? Tried to make a separate deal with you."

Rashmi made no comment.

"Tell me. I knew Anne. She'd smell your scheme immediately, that you found something. She wouldn't let the two of you just walk away. And anything discovered on her business trip she'd make a claim for. She'd have the legal right to do that, and Anne would never pass up the chance. So she came to you, right?"

Still no comment.

"And, before that, when you still worked for her, she asked you to meet with Balrak on Ventroni, right? Balrak said so. To set up illegal deals with him when Henry was out with Mileen."

Rashmi persisted in saying nothing.

"And she tried to persuade you. She probably said she'd give you money for whatever you planned after the Ventroni trip. In fact, isn't that how you got the ship that you came here in? It's new, and too large to belong to Jayne. You and Henry couldn't come up with the money for it, but Anne could. She wanted a cut, and she bought into your scheme through you."

Rashmi finally admitted, "We needed her backing."

"What did you tell Henry when you bought the ship?"

"Just that I saved more than what I said."

"And he believed you?"

"He *wanted* to believe me."

"Okay, so after you got back from Ventroni and the derelicts, Omar went to Balrak, you went to Anne, and Henry came to me." He couldn't help interjecting, "So much for everyone swearing to stay together and be loyal to each other. And Jayne, did she then go to Hatch?"

"Yes, yes!" His voice sounded filled with frustration.

"Stupid, isn't it? The big secret, and nearly all of you told someone else. Except Lonni—and she got killed."

Rashmi didn't seem to recognize irony. "I thought Mileen had stayed quiet. But she must've told Hatch too. The three of them—Mileen, Hatch, and Jayne—acted like they had worked together."

"Do you mean back on the lifeboat world, when Jayne and Hatch protected Mileen?"

"I assumed they wanted to bring her into their partnership."

"Against you?"

"And against Balrak. But I could understand that. I was glad they stood up to him. I never was happy letting him in."

"You didn't have a choice?"

"Omar made it clear that we had to. He laughed about it."

"So the best-laid plans—"

"I don't want to hear it!" And he walked away.

End of conversation.

Ranglen moved to the other side of the square, to the wall that was part of Hatch's compartment. As he peered through the chinks, he was not surprised to see Hatch pacing nearby, apparently waiting for him.

Ranglen said, "That bag I told you to grab. I noticed earlier you brought rocket charges." Mykol had searched the equipment they brought with them when they sat disconsolate earlier in the shelter.

Hatch sounded amused. "That's what I *thought* you were after. We brought them to break through the ice. We believed the Clip might be embedded there."

"They're shaped for excavation?"

"The blast penetrates a few meters of ice and then spreads and shatters it. But they won't be effective against Balrak's defenses. They're rocket-propelled but the stakes from the derelict move faster, so they'll just get knocked down."

"The charges don't use separate launch tubes, right?"

"They're self-contained. But the shells are supposed to be set in the right direction, and their range is just over a hundred meters."

"I want you to shoot half of what you've got into the smoking part of the icefield, and the rest to where the ice meets the rocks directly above us—but hitting the ice, not the rocks."

"When you say 'half' that's only one charge each. There's only two in the bag you had me bring. And the smoking area can't be reached from here."

"I don't mean now. Can they be launched while we're walking to the glacier?"

Hatch thought a moment. "I don't have the positioning data, and I'd have to encode the destinations into the guidance program beforehand. If I had that I could drop them along the trail with time-delay ignitions. If they fall pointed correctly, they should seek out the targets on their own easily. But—"

"I'll get the coordinates from my satellite. I still have the link."

"But Balrak's stakes will still stop them."

"Balrak might be confused for a second—the charges won't be heading toward him or the flyer, so maybe he'll wait to see what's happening. He's arrogant and won't believe he's endangered until it's proven to him. We might have enough time." Ranglen felt less confident than he sounded.

"What happens when they hit?"

"Maybe nothing. But if we're lucky, all hell will break loose. Be prepared."

"That's damned vague."

"That's all I've got. Let me find the locations." He downloaded coordinates and spoke them to Hatch. They were only approximate, based on what he remembered of the landscape and long-range surveillance from his satellite.

Not wanting to call attention to the two of them talking, Ranglen walked away as soon as he gave the figures. He wandered to the corner where all four of the squares met. Mileen, Rashmi, and then Hatch soon did the same. They didn't speak much. None of them admitted they all believed they would die tomorrow.

He couldn't see Mileen—their squares joined only in the corners—but he caught glimpses of the other two. He wanted to warn all of them to be ready tomorrow when Hatch shot off his charges, but he was afraid of being too open, that Balrak might suspect something. He wondered if Balrak knew already. Maybe the stakes transmitted sounds. But the communication between the stakes and Balrak seemed all one way, coming from the Moyock. Besides, Balrak appeared so certain that he probably didn't bother with anyone's chit-chat.

The companionship there in the corners helped to calm apprehension. They stayed clustered throughout the night, sleeping briefly. Ranglen wanted to talk to Mileen but privacy was impossible.

He stared up at the stars, at the aurora that came and went like ghosts, dancers in long green curtains fringed with delicate violet-red. Ranglen loved the aurora, a proof that the universe still made beauty.

Green dawn.

Above them the fist still hovered. The low sun awoke a sheen on the slivers—they looked like coppery-green needles or bundles of dried hardened grass, pins jabbing the indigo sky.

From the base of the glacier water trickled, tumbling gently down to the plain to form a small rivulet. Ranglen had touched the water yesterday. It was slightly warm.

He thought that a good sign.

All the stakes in the artificial walls rose simultaneously, a majestic crescendo, to join with their companions above. Balrak walked from his flyer to the prisoners, his bigger ship still absent.

"All right, boys and girls," he said, imitating the late Omar. "We're about to make history. Ready yourselves for sudden greatness. And if you're not prepared for it, know that it still will be thrust upon you."

Ranglen, wearied by such rhetoric, followed the others as they grouped together.

Balrak added, "We depart in a few moments. Get what you need from the shelter and grab something to eat for along the way. I'm not waiting."

They took up their packs, pulled out bunches of trail rations and water and walked off in the direction of the glacier. The brooding cloud of wasp-stingers stayed above at a respectable distance.

They approached the rocks that sloped up to the ice. Ranglen tried to picture the huge ice-sheet above them. He was certain a pool of water had formed inside it from the heat of the volcano. The steam alone suggested this, as well as the warmth of the rivulet water. But he didn't know how large the pool might be. He hoped it was held back by just the right thickness of ice to have allowed a huge reservoir to form. If the pool wasn't big enough, any disturbance to it would just make the small stream a little larger, hardly destructive. He wanted a big crash and flood, something that would shock Balrak and tear them free.

He believed Balrak's control of the stakes worked only if Balrak were conscious. Ranglen saw no sign yet of automatic behavior in the shafts—as Balrak said, he had "turned that off." So now, Ranglen assumed, every move of the stakes was controlled by Balrak, and in order to stop them, he had to be knocked unconscious, or killed.

The rest of them might get killed too but they probably were dead anyway.

The path they took, where the rocks were most passable, bore to the left of the ice shingle. They maneuvered up this slope with care.

Hatch, in the rear, yelled, "*Dammit!*" His pack dropped from his shoulder to the ground, spilling its food cartons, water containers, assorted gadgets, and two small cylinders. "Shit, the clamp broke away from the strap." He bent down quickly to retrieve the pack's contents.

Everyone stopped walking and waited for him.

He threw fallen things back into the pouch, those he could reach—stuff had tumbled into deeper gullies. He even kicked objects aside in anger (including, Ranglen hoped, two foot-long yellow-banded tubes with swollen heads that would fall into position between the rocks—Ranglen knew what they looked like but he couldn't see them). Then Hatch flung on his pack and strode off in a huff. Everyone trudged onward.

Well played, Ranglen thought, but he hoped the cylinders were in correct orientation.

Hatch didn't look at him as they continued walking.

Several minutes passed.

From behind them they heard a loud hiss. Two trails of steam flashed from the rocks with narrow cones at their heads. One flew over them and aimed for the ice sheet. The other tightly curved for the shingle to their right.

Balrak's stakes either leapt after both of them or formed two shields between the missiles and him.

The charge aimed for the ice sheet never made it. The staffs pushed it out of the air and forced it to crash on the lava plain below—where its shaped detonation had little effect. It made a small plume of an explosion, a flurry of smoke.

Other stakes tried to maneuver the second charge but not until it reached the edge of the ice. By attempting to ground the missile, the stakes pushed it deeper into the glacier, where its probing blast might have more effect.

A small explosion. Ice flew outward and tinkled onto the stones below, sounded like chimes.

Nothing happened.

Disappointment flowed through Ranglen.

But then a huge slab of ice, a flank of the entire shingle, broke from the glacier and slid downward, crashed onto the rocks below.

Behind it burst a flood of water.

The torrent gushed, flung over the blocks. More chunks of glacier broke free, collapsed and tumbled. Plunging water thrust up breakers against the rocks, like storm-waves on a boulder shore.

Ranglen leapt aside, tried to reach Mileen.

The water hit him.

He was thrust under and carried away, the sudden icy-cold like a blow.

The flood tossed, rolled, crushed him. The massive current and his thick clothes prevented him from swimming.

His strength drained. Exertion quickly used up his air. He kicked, tried to rise, lost his direction. Debris pummeled him and his lungs screamed.

He broke the surface—

And went under again with no chance to take a breath.

He emerged a second time and his mouth gaped wide to breathe. He choked—couldn't swallow! Panic seized him.

Coughing, frantic, he tried to hold his head above the water. Arms flailed to prevent him from sinking.

He swallowed air and managed to breathe—steadily, steadily. His head went under again. He struggled to stay on the surface but his limbs stiffened.

Ground scraped against his feet.

He was deposited on a slope. The water still flowed around him but slower now, the level dropping. He crawled up the hard black stone. The weight of his saturated clothes burdened him. He made a puddle where he stopped.

He felt so cold, the breeze bitter. He coughed again, more strongly each time. The cold scared him more than his breathing. He couldn't have been in the water for more than seconds and his clothes were designed to discard moisture, but total immersion overcame their protection. His teeth shuddered. His whole body shook.

The fear of hypothermia possessed him. He had to get warm, out of his wet clothes.

He tried to think but he felt confused. Where was everybody? His muscles felt stiff and his hands were dead weights.

Then he saw Mileen, struggling to open the door of a flyer. He remembered—Balrak's. It had been hit by the flood and now sat canted. She was trying to get inside it. Smart move!

His shivering stopped—which frightened him more! *Think*, dammit!

He tried to shout to Mileen. His mouth opened but he could barely shape words. He panicked—moved his legs, forced himself to stand. He staggered upward and was surprised he could walk. He stumbled toward Mileen on feet going numb.

She saw him, grabbed at him, pulled at his clothes. "Get out of your coat!"

He did, slowly.

"Stay alert, Mykol! Take your shirt off too, as much as you can!"

He struggled to act faster. "What...how did you..."

"The water knocked me over. I got up and ran out of the way. You fell in and disappeared. I ran after you but I thought you drowned. You came out near the flyer. Dammit, you're like ice!" She reached inside the aircar and turned on the heater. It blasted air that soon grew hot.

She forced him inside. "Get under this blanket." She pulled more coverings from the back seat.

Bare-chested now and wiped dry, he draped himself with the blankets and sat in the stream of heat from the dash. Fumes rose from his wet trousers. His reason and clarity slowly returned. He stamped his feet to get feeling back. The shakes resumed, which he welcomed, telling him his body wasn't shutting down. He hunched over and made a pocket of warmth.

He glanced outside and could see that part of the glacier's front had broken away. The pool under it must have been big—and, thankfully, not *too* ice-cold because of the volcano. The water now spread across the plain, where steam rose from the heated ground, sending curtains of vapor flying.

Ranglen had been caught by the edge of the flow, enough for him to get chilled. He thought if Mileen hadn't yanked off his wet clothing and pulled him into the heat, he might not have been able to do it himself.

He looked about at the drowned landscape. Where was Hatch, Rashmi? And Balrak?

Then he saw the fist above them had resumed its original derelict shape— apparently its default position. This gave him hope. Balrak *had* to be unconscious, or dead, or struggling too much to send out commands.

It brought back his strength. He yelled for Mileen.

She jumped into the driver's side and slipped a programmed delock master-key into the ignition. "Hatch gave this to me yesterday, said he knew the car's make and its overrides." She overstepped initiation-and-flight protocols and roared the engines. She took to the air.

"What about the others?"

"I'm circling, looking."

They peered down and saw that the shelter had been torn apart but not washed away. A line of camping gear trailed downstream. They flew over and spied two figures on the opposite side of the camp. They landed quickly.

Rashmi lay on the ground and looked unconscious, maybe dead. Hatch gingerly walked away from him to the flyer, his face and right hand bleeding. He held his left arm straight down, close to his side, apparently broken. As he approached them, his face showed pain.

"I think Balrak got swept away. I'll stay here with Rashmi. He's breathing but hurt. I have a heater working from the shelter." He winced with each sentence— Ranglen guessed a broken rib. "Get to Balrak's ship. This flyer must have a homing device. Take to the air and go on automatic, enter 'home berth' and you should be taken to the ship. Get on board and try to get it running. But I don't have a key for that, and the security will be tough."

Mileen yelled, "You're both coming with us."

Hatch shook his head. "Balrak might be alive. If he turns up I'll try to kill him. I'll find a way. I don't think Rashmi should be moved. Go! Go!"

"You—"

Hatch reached in, shoved the autopilot lever and slammed the door. They rose away.

"God*damn* him!" Mileen said.

When the autopilot asked for a heading, Mileen shut it off, resumed manual controls. "We're going for the Clip."

"What? Now?" Ranglen still shivered but his thoughts were clear.

"I'm sure Balrak's alive. And I'm not letting that bastard get it."

The fist of stakes hung above them. It didn't move. Mileen jetted away.

The landscape below, with all the steam rising from the new flood, looked broken, the result of a war.

"You're not going for the icefield?"

"The Clip's not there. I lied to them."

Ranglen smiled.

"Still cold?" she asked.

"I'm getting better." His chest warmed under the thermal blankets and his pants shed water. Mileen must be baking in the heat of the cabin but he was feeling more himself each minute.

She steered the flyer along the ocean's shore, northwest, paralleling the rift trench. Ranglen had an idea where she was going.

"I delayed until you got here," she said. "I knew you'd make it. I wanted to lead Balrak astray."

"It worked. You fooled even a Moyock."

"I'm *good*, aren't I?"

She reminded him of the Mileen from long ago, passionate, focused. And he was impressed by how well she handled the flyer—for someone who didn't like to pilot a spaceship. "Where'd you learn to drive?"

"Never mind. Dry off." She said this almost playfully.

Ranglen—sitting in his puddle of water with his boots seeping and tightening in the air-blast—got very serious. "What's happening, Mileen? What's the *real* reason you left me and went to Hatch back on the lifeboat world?"

She stared ahead. "I've changed, Mykol. Are you sure you want to know me now?"

"But I *do* know you. You think you're some bloody Airafane, don't you?"

Her expression didn't change. "You're aware of that, eh?"

"The shard from the carrier-lock in my asteroid. What made you take it?"

"I…" She hesitated only briefly. "I knew I had to have it. It called to me—is that the right phrase? Didn't you use that once?"

"But you lied when you said you didn't go into my asteroid when I wasn't there. You went to my safe and opened it. You pulled out the carrier-lock and examined it. Why didn't you take a piece of it then?"

"It was yours, Mykol. I couldn't overstep that. I waited till you showed it to me, and then I asked you."

"So you're not completely an Airafane then."

"I opened the safe—I couldn't figure that out on my own. And look at how well I steer now." She tried to smile and make light of herself, but it seemed forced.

"God, Mileen! You, Balrak—where do you end and the Airafane begins? Where does it stop?"

"I know what I've become. If you don't believe me—"

"Then you'll show me the little bulge behind your right ear? Where you placed the shard from the carrier-lock?"

She stared at him. "How did you know that?"

"When I kissed you before we approached the lifeboat I felt the back of your head. I saw the corpses on the derelict, where Balrak ripped out that section of their skulls to get at the little piece of Airafane inside them. He knows where they're hidden—in the carrier-locks themselves."

"Then why won't you believe me?"

"I *do* believe you. I'm just…in denial! Hell, Mileen, I loved you once. *You*—not some ghost from the past."

They flew over the shoreline where the lava curtains fell into the waves. Steam fought back in frantic clouds. She banked inland. "Mykol, you have to know—so much of that means little to me now. I'm different. I'm like Balrak…reborn! Someone else lives in me."

"Or is that just some elaborate self-justification?"

"Don't be foolish. You *are* in denial. You sound like some stupid jilted lover."

"My species has been jilted. Yours too. You've abandoned humanity."

"And didn't you sometimes want to do that yourself?"

"Not in this way—not by housing an alien parasite. Not by choosing it and holding it up to my head and allowing it to take root inside me."

"I *didn't* choose. It chose me."

"Everyone says that—about the Clips."

"Why don't you take one of the shards yourself and place it behind *your* ear, see what we're talking about?"

"You already took mine. Balrak said there's only one Airafane to a lock."

"That shouldn't stop you. It might be the best thing for you, Mykol. Something you've really always wanted. Think of what you'd learn. It might be the same personality as mine. We'd be exactly alike—imagine the great love we could make. We'd know precisely what each other wants."

"Shut up! Shut up."

"And *this* is the man who doesn't believe in boundaries? You're as confused as the rest of them."

"Mileen, why are you—why are *we*—doing this?"

"Because—" Hopelessness swept her face. "It's all I have to work with now. I'm *different* now. I can't go back. We're all changing and I'm struggling with it. What more can I do?"

He adjusted the blankets around him. He had stopped shivering—from the cold anyway. The cabin was too warm now. He turned down the heat.

She said, "Sometimes I don't know what I'm doing. It just comes over me."

Ranglen hated her for saying that. He felt she was giving up choice and freedom. "So why did you go to Hatch on the lifeboat world? And this time don't lie to me."

"I had to ask him something."

"About where you came from, right?"

"Mykol, Mykol—"

"Back on that planet you said you had seen the falling mists before, that everything was bothering you. You got more distant from me the further we walked. Memories were coming back, weren't they? And when you saw Hatch, you had to ask him how you were found. Balrak said there was no one in the lifeboat, but the people on that world, the humanoid we saw, he told me there was. And he said he had seen you before, and Hatch. *You* were the child in that lifeboat! *You* came from the derelict!"

Mileen's face glazed over. "Yes, yes. I had to know. Things were coming back to me."

"Hatch encountered the distress signal from the lifeboat, landed there, and took you away—twenty years ago."

"He never told me that before. But I guessed while you and I walked through the jungle. I confronted him with it. I *had* to."

Ranglen sighed—it was more like scorn. "No wonder you went with him when the volcano erupted. You two had so much to talk about! Old times, growing up. Did you tell him you were Airafane?"

"Yes, everything. But it seemed too much for him. I don't think he believed me. He didn't want to talk about it."

"Of *course* he didn't. He *hates* the Airafane. He probably stopped trusting you—and you better get used to that!" He was being too hard on her and he didn't know why. Maybe frustration, maybe having his life in danger for too long, maybe being so devoted to her and now not knowing who "she" really was.

She steered, said nothing.

They flew above the sea. At the bottom of a wayward column of smoke sat the microscopic island that Ranglen had seen when he first approached for a landing—a new landmass, only a few meters wide and made of cinders still steaming and warm. Its breaking the surface of the ocean just now, just when they reached the planet, was too wildly improbable, too coincidental, too anomalous.

The ideal spot to look for a Clip.

Ranglen didn't need to observe through his shard. "I thought the same thing when I came here. I felt all along you were on the wrong track."

"Balrak was after me. I was waiting for you. I needed to delay him." She flew past the island, swung wide for a landing approach.

"When did you realize he was a Moyock?"

"After I discovered that I was Airafane. The way he killed Anne, how Omar described him, it all seemed familiar. But I don't know how he first found out about me."

"He knew of the lifeboat and he suspected there was a survivor. He claimed there wasn't but he would have assumed the worst. I think he waited for twenty years to see if there were any signs out there. He's that patient, that methodical. And then he saw your artwork. Look at the wall." He pointed to the postcard reproduction of her painting.

She almost laughed. "Good God, he's a fan! The filthy little—"

"He must have seen Airafane influences in it."

She thought to herself, as if raiding the files of her new memories. "He's right. I wouldn't have guessed. It's the time thing, the overlap of eras."

"Then he became a business partner with Anne. He raided her files and he either found you mentioned there or else he saw you with Henry on Ventroni, because during the trip he then raided Anne's *personnel* files, where she kept her own journal—she mentioned that to me. And I'm sure you were a subject in it."

She grinned wickedly. "Yes, and I'll bet it was nasty stuff."

"His recognizing you must have started all this. He knew you were on Ventroni with Henry. So he got Omar on board with you as part of the trip, with instructions to change the exit-point for the light-space jump, to take you to the derelict. He probably wanted to see if all this would come back to you. And it *did*, didn't it?"

"Yes. I know that now. I was having feelings the minute I saw the derelicts—it's why I wanted to find the lifeboat. But why did Balrak go to all that trouble?"

"It's not trouble for him. It's play. It's what he likes to do. Torment his ancient enemy from the past—torment you, us, everyone."

Her eyes looked distant. "The Moyocks were like that. But he's not taking me, Mykol. I'm taking him!"

These shifts from one Mileen to another disgusted Ranglen. "Let's get the Clip."

They came down through the steam and smoke to the little black island that sputtered away, that spit red droplets to fall as more cinders.

The flyer hovered. Waves roared around them and steam limited visibility.

"I'll hold here," Mileen said. "You'll have to jump out."

"Where's the Clip?"

"Right there! Can't you see it?"

A purplish glint sat beside the cone. How long ago had it emerged? An hour, a minute? It had arrived here to greet one of its makers, the Airafane from out of the past—of course it would be on time.

Ranglen threw his damp coat over his bare chest. He lifted the door and jumped out, made aware again that his feet in his boots were still damp. He almost laughed—this environment might help to rush the drying. Steam gushed away from his feet as he walked on the hot ground. Alternating waves of heated air and cold spray blew over him.

He pulled on a glove from his pocket—it was still wet. He walked over to the spewing hole. The flying cinders made him duck his head, pull his hood over him.

There it was. Only a gleam of purple crystal, nothing more.

He couldn't help feeling the intensity of discovery. He reached down. His gloved hand wrapped around it. Steam came out from between his fingers. It was still hot. He opened his hand and looked at the octahedron on his palm. Lines and planes of deep purple ran through the murky crystal, more intense here in this sunlight, with sections of yellow that were almost white.

His hand closed again. The future and the past held in a moment.

He hurried back on board. "Got it," he said.

"Give it to me."

He hesitated. But if she truly were an Airafane, she must be the rightful owner. Besides, he was so tired of Clips.

He handed it to her.

She glanced at it as if it were only a curiosity, her expression blank of either awe or fear. She shoved it into her vest pocket. "Balrak's not getting this."

They both saw movement outside the windows.

Meter-long stakes surrounded them. A globe of javelins pointed inward at the flyer. Ranglen said needlessly, "He's alive after all."

The stakes moved so that an opening appeared on only one side of the globe, and the staffs opposite moved inward—to prod at the flyer, coaxing it in this one direction.

Mileen gunned the engine and tried to blast away.

Every window smashed, threw glass over them. A hundred spears thrust into the car, made a forest of spikes.

Mileen and Ranglen dared not move, trapped in a labyrinth of sharp metal. With exquisite precision, not one of the spears had cut them. But the seats, the consoles, the steering controls and almost all other instruments were skewered and smashed. Broken glass lay everywhere.

The globe of spears backed outward, reformed around them, with one direction left open—to the camp. And this time the spikes pushed the flyer so Mileen couldn't steer it herself.

Ranglen said, "We have no choice."

Cold air streamed in as they moved forward. The heaters still worked but they had to run harder to compensate. The batteries and engines functioned too, apparently untouched. Only their means of control had been destroyed.

Any stakes left in the car withdrew, joined the directing sphere outside.

Ranglen grabbed the rest of his clothes. He thought of how carefully the javelins had avoided their bodies. Balrak still wanted them alive. He donned his near-dry jersey and shirt, then his coat again. It wasn't easy with all the broken glass but he wanted to be ready for their return. He still was affected by the earlier immersion but he had no time for misery now.

Mileen said, "We're getting out of this, Mykol. Especially you. I want you surviving."

"Let's just focus on what happens when we get there."

"That was a great idea about the flood, by the way." She seemed to want to distract him. "You told Hatch to set off the missiles, didn't you?"

He nodded, closing the gaps on his parka for protection from the cold. He tried turning up the heat.

She said, "I knew Hatch wouldn't think of that. It's always you, Mykol. I was silly to go to Henry after you. I should have come back after we broke up and pushed you harder. Think of what we could have done together—what we might have been, where we could have gone."

"Stop it! I don't even know who's talking to me. You or the Airafane."

"She and I are the same. I've accommodated her. I assume she's a 'her' but their sexuality's a little unclear. She and I have melded easily. I only touch in her what's needed, and she seldom surprises me now. Sometimes she's there, very strong, especially around Balrak. But usually it's me."

"Do you think Balrak feels the same, more human than Moyock?"

"I think he's just using the Moyock side as self-excuse. I understand that. I also do it. It's too tempting not to."

"It wasn't just the shard's implant that made you like this, right? You had something inside you from the start. Your art wouldn't have shown anything if you hadn't."

"Looking back now I agree. I think maybe that's why I was unhappy with Henry. We got along worse after I saw the Airafane ship and the other derelict."

"According to Balrak the woman on that ship had a shard inside her, which made her Airafane. And if she was your mother, then maybe it added to what you inherited from her, what you were already."

Her eyes seemed to look at things far away. "I don't know. Even 'she' doesn't have an answer to that. If I did have something in me from birth, and if that was why Henry was bad for me, maybe that's what made you so good. Maybe that was the basis of our whole relationship."

He said, with an irony she didn't catch, "Alien love."

"Ha—you'd like that! Can you imagine you and me out there? I could be your guide, your historical source. I'd take you on a galactic tour."

"That's you talking now, not her."

"I'd use her, bring her out when she was needed. I'd want her there when you and I were close, when you made love to me. She'd enjoy that too."

Ranglen grew furious. "Mileen, you're dreaming! We have to stop Balrak before we do anything."

"Yes. Balrak. He ruins it all. But what if he didn't?"

"For God's sakes, Mileen. None of this makes sense."

"I loved you, Mykol."

"And I loved you. I love you now. But things are different. *We're* different."

"You're too negative about change. It's something to ride on—a pleasure, not a threat."

Ranglen heaved a long breath. "None of this will happen. Why are we talking about it?"

She looked at him with her own hard wisdom. "Okay. It's impossible."

"And that's the Airafane talking now, correct?"

Expression drained from her face.

He turned away.

They saw the camp, still washed by the new streams. The fallen shelter was slipping away, more equipment strewn about. Hatch still leaned over Rashmi, who was covered with a blanket and who, conscious now, turned his head toward them. No one else could be seen.

The cloud of harpoons didn't let them land there. It pushed them up toward the glacier itself. As the cloud and the flyer passed over the camp, Hatch down below tried to follow it, hurrying across the tortured land, leaving Rashmi and struggling up the rocks toward the ice, still holding his arm to his side.

The stakes led them over the edge of the glacier where the ice had collapsed, beyond the still smoking spot of the buried volcano.

And there Balrak stood, in the middle of the ice-plain, like some dark statue emerged from the snow, wearing a long coat (which the stakes apparently brought him) that hung open and swayed around him. He waited, content, not moving.

The spears forced the flyer down. The two inside had no choice but to land.

The engine died. The spikes rose from around them, leaving the car filled with glass. The spears drifted over to hang above Balrak, formed an inverted crown in layers, the javelins pointing out at all potential threats.

Mileen and Ranglen sat there for a moment, stared at each other.

She leaned over and kissed him quickly. "You take care, Mykol. Remember that I loved you."

Then she flung up the door and jumped out of the flyer, ran across the glacier away from Balrak. She ignored any crevasses that might be hidden beneath the snow.

Ranglen shouted at her but she raced away from him.

Balrak followed her in a wide-stepped gait, not a run but an implacable walk. It wasn't as rash as her speed but it seemed more relentless, inescapable.

The demonic cloud of spears followed him, not ceasing its protection of him and not yet chasing Mileen. This seemed to make it even more ominous.

Ranglen searched through the flyer for a weapon, found none. He had only his pocket knife. But he took it out and ran after Balrak anyway, intending to do what he could to stop him.

Hatch approached from the edge of the ice sheet, yelled, "Mykol! Get down! I found another charge in Rashmi's kit." With his one good hand and his face twisted in pain, Hatch set the missile-tube onto a lump of ice and aimed it toward Balrak. He thumbed a release and stepped away.

A loud steam-trail leapt for the Moyock.

It never got there. The staffs flew down and formed a wall. The charge exploded harmlessly against it, swallowed up by the brightness of the ice.

Balrak strode on, didn't look back.

Ranglen raced toward him. He pulled closer and ignored possible openings in the smooth-looking ice. He held his knife and moved up behind Balrak until only a short space, and the stakes, separated them. He slowed, breathed hard in the thin air, kept his distance and gauged his chance.

Mileen still hurried up the vast whiteness of the ice-sheet's grade. She would run, stop, look back, continue. Was she taunting Balrak?

The Moyock's pace didn't change, his walk inexorable. He shouted to her, "There's just you and me now. Nothing human is left between us. We meet again, after millions of years. I'll get to kill you once more."

She stopped, looked back, then still ran.

Balrak continued, "I first learned of you twenty years ago. I waited for signs. I was patient. Did you enjoy this little frolic between us? The unfolding of what you are? It must be terrible to inherit such a legacy. So much hate!"

She yelled back, "Only you Moyocks hated! We were just surviving."

"Then you *should* have hated. Evolution gave you the upper hand and you thought you were doing us a favor—being generous, so altruistic. It was an insult."

"You killed us for no reason."

"And we'll do it again. *I'll* do it again. Each one of you I find, I'll rip out your implant and make another stake, add you to our trophy—spreading your shame."

"You've brought our war to people who don't deserve it."

"*You* brought it here. You couldn't be defeated so you had to contaminate the future too. You can't let go. You—"

At that moment Ranglen acted. He ran up behind Balrak with his knife.

The stakes plummeted and formed a wall that stopped him. Spears knocked his weapon away.

Again, Balrak didn't turn around.

Mileen yelled, "Stay out of this, Mykol!" She hurried off backward, tripped in a small crevasse, jumped back up and still raced on.

Her fall made Ranglen look more closely at their path. Snow could cover unseen canyons into bottomless depths.

Balrak yelled at her, "Shall I torture you now?"

The hornet cloud of staffs stretched in a line between him and her, wrapped a fence of daggers around her. It moved in. As she ran they followed her, changed paths when she did.

Ranglen realized she maintained a distance between her and Balrak that never shrank. What was she doing?

Ranglen kept close. Hatch had dropped far behind.

The knives now pricked at Mileen, at her neck and hands, made bloody wounds on exposed skin. She stumbled. Daggers struck at her fingertips and lodged there, gave her long metal spears for nails. She almost fell but kept her hands off the ice— any pressure from the ground would force the knives into her further. She tried to pull out the prongs as she ran. Blood spurted when she yanked at them and threw them to the ice. But the knives flew up and followed her, jabbed at her again.

"I can do this forever," Balrak said.

Ranglen couldn't stand it. He raced for Balrak if just to distract him—to do anything at all to him. But bigger spears fell in his way and made another wall. He struck at this fence in bitter frustration, leapt around it.

A shadow came over him. He looked up.

It wasn't the fist.

It was a mountain falling out of the sky, turning slowly, almost gracefully. It moved down on top of them, like a mythic visitation of some other world, incredibly huge.

It reminded Ranglen of an asteroid.

Hell, he thought, it *was* an asteroid! It was *his* asteroid! From back at Annulus— he recognized its features!

He stopped following Balrak, quickly turned around and ran downhill instead, tried to get out of the growing shadow.

The asteroid swelled, descended like a roof as big as the sky. It overwhelmed with its horrifying weight, a wide blunt fact of inertia sliding ponderously down and down.

Ranglen felt he was being stepped on.

It pushed all of Balrak's spastic little sticks out of its way.

Ranglen staggered as he ran down the slope, his mind shaken in profound disbelief. The energy employed was too incredible. A fury of air should be squeezed out now, a sonic blast knocking him over and flattening the land. The heat from the friction should start everything burning. But he felt little, only disturbed pressure, rising winds and growing heat—but nothing like what should be happening!

A hunk of rock dropped out of the bottom, hurled downward toward the Moyock, like discharge from artillery the size of a moon.

The rock fell on Balrak.

Then the whole asteroid followed.

A horrible wall of grinding ice squeezed out from beneath the mountain, an endless rolling avalanche roar. Gushing clouds and water followed. A hot wave of damp air knocked Ranglen over. He could smell burnt charcoal and dust, melting rock. Needles of ice jabbed his face. His skin burned. The land rocked thunderously beneath him.

He lifted his head to see the catastrophe. The asteroid didn't crash. Its front end had settled slowly onto the icefield, just enough to grind downward, mashing the glacier beneath it—and anything that happened to be standing there.

Nothing could resist so much mass. Even Balrak with all his flying toys had to be dead, crushed out of existence.

The asteroid poised there for one long impossible moment—a monstrous and deformed egg nested in the smoke and steam that fountained upward around it.

Then, slowly, it rose back into the sky, trailing tiny pieces that fell.

Ranglen stood up, grit embedded in his skin and hair, burns on his face, eyes caked with searing grime, clothes tattered and blackened and singed. And yet he still watched. What kind of power could have brought the thing here? For all his exploration of the corridors in his planetoid, he had found no gravity plates, no FTL propulsion, nothing indicating the asteroid could be controlled and moved.

The mountain lifted upward, became small. It hazily withdrew behind thin clouds.

Ranglen, alive if incredulous, stared at the damage caused. A huge crater lay before him, belching columns of steam, roiling with heat and falling cinders, with rain and sour carbon stench, with waves of dust and ash and burning. The ice had evaporated down to the bedrock, a deep cauldron swept clean with no signs of life, no signs of anything.

It was impossible. The whole event—all should have been so extreme he'd be killed, the landscape abolished.

He glanced up and could not see a hint of the asteroid now. *His* asteroid, his island in space…now an unbelievable weapon of destruction.

A few stakes that avoided annihilation sailed up too, supposedly to join anything left of the fist. All those javelins had no master now. Ranglen assumed the object would hover above the planet or go off into some holding pattern in space.

He saw no sign of Mileen.

He didn't expect to.

Hatch limped up behind him, still holding his arm, pain and shock in his bloody face. He fought to breathe. His clothes smoked. "Where's Mileen?"

"I think we've lost her."

Hatch looked forlorn.

Ranglen added, "Balrak survived the flood, but he didn't survive this."

"I don't think he was touched by the flood. He must have seen it coming and allowed it to happen."

"So Mileen would leave and get the Clip. Yeah, I wondered."

It was impossible to comment on what they had just seen. It was too beyond human experience.

They maneuvered down and across the glacier, now heaved up in crested waves. It took a long time to manage the terrain and Ranglen often had to guide Hatch, who looked terrible.

Then, surprising both of them, a spaceship crossed the sky.

With quick thrusters it landed nose-up on the plain below, beside the remains of the camp. The ship looked authoritative with its many blisters, sensors, and ports for weapons. It bore the insignia of Annulus security.

Two ramps emerged and people in uniform ran down the planks. They carried big guns. With practiced precision they established a perimeter around the remains of the shelter. Several hurried over to Rashmi and quickly gave him medical attention.

As Ranglen and Hatch walked further down the slope, they saw Pia Folinari march down the ramp, her pale hair even brighter in this light. She was followed soon after by the recognizable bulk of Hussein Hathaway.

Our man from Federal Investigation, Ranglen thought.

Then another spaceship came down from the sky—bigger, better armed.

"Uh-oh," said Hatch.

Ranglen said dryly, "We better get our stories straight."

Chapter Twenty: The Longing

Ranglen sat in a cabin alone on board the Annulus Security ship. They now traveled in light-space for that usually wretched, but sometimes welcomed, two-day stretch of isolation as they "moved" through an alternate universe—or the alternate universe moved through theirs—with its never changing interval of time.

He had been granted this privilege of privacy. His status with the authorities was still maintained, which surprised him after all that happened. But he felt he was given his own cabin more because people could spend private time with him, away from the formal interrogations that occurred in the common rooms run by the police. Such a non-public place was needed for casual trading of information. And when it wasn't invaded, Ranglen kept it and used it for himself. He checked it for hidden microphones but found nothing. He assumed that anything he said could be heard—but he also felt they didn't care.

There in his cabin, after recovering from both the glacial flood and the fall of the asteroid (all this physical distress caught up with him), he opened his cellpad and simply wrote, securing his files from any wireless interference or surveillance—which, who knows, maybe even worked. After all that ensued, he felt it was the best way to review everything, to ascertain what happened and what it meant to himself—to clean out his mind and make sense of it all. He said nothing "revealing," but he laid forth his emotions as the words took over. He would keep writing until he felt emptied, which would take a while.

Rashmi had brought in Annulus Security—Rashmi, the quiet one. Bless his heart, Mykol thought. Rashmi had gotten too nervous before his group left Annulus, after he and Jayne made their deal to meet Balrak on the lifeboat world. Suddenly scared of the consequences, and struck by a fit of selfless conscience, he ran to the police and spilled everything.

They enlisted him, made him their agent, and told him to continue the treasure-hunt but to contact them immediately after the Clip was found. They gave him a small homing device that could be sent off through light-space and reach Security at Annulus. It followed Jayne's ship and went into orbit at both worlds.

When the Clip was found, Rashmi was supposed to enter his location into a small comm-unit that had been surgically implanted in his side. A message would be sent to the homing missile, which would fly to Annulus, and Security would immediately come and confiscate the Clip, with a promise to Rashmi of a "cut."

After Henry's death and Balrak's involvement, Rashmi accepted this deal with eagerness. But not waiting till the Clip was found, he sent off the message right after the flood, when he was half dead and felt he had done all he could. The doctors promised him a full recovery.

Ranglen had to admit that Annulus Security got there fast, even with the instantaneous interval in time-space.

Hussein, being part of the security group and knowing what Rashmi's message implied, and being a good spy, contacted Earth and the Federal Investigators—who landed right behind the Annulus group. This started the jolly round of political negotiation. The Bureau of Investigation from Homeworld came next, on the heels of security leaks from Annulus and normal command-chain information flow. Then everyone grew vigilant and distrustful of each other—a subdued gathering that Ranglen watched but stayed away from.

His donating the Clip helped much in keeping them occupied and happy. Though Mileen had taken it from him, she apparently placed it in his jacket pocket when she kissed him after landing on the glacier. (And Ranglen—darn!—had thought the kiss to be pure affection.) He didn't notice the crystal in his pocket immediately, and when he did he waited for all the representatives to show up before he conveniently "found" it.

This made them suspicious. But they got what they wanted and thus couldn't complain.

Balrak's ship apparently had a command programmed into it that if it lost a continuous signal from Balrak it would plunge into the local star. From all they could tell, that's what happened. A shudder passed through Ranglen when he realized that without Rashmi's action, Balrak's death would have marooned them on the planet forever.

Ranglen's asteroid also didn't stay, due to whatever orders Mileen gave it. Ranglen assumed she was the force behind its arrival. She was Airafane, after all. No wonder she had baited Balrak on the glacier, keeping her distance, telling Ranglen not to interfere.

No trace of her body was ever found. No one expected to.

There had been little time for private conversation with all the government officials around. The interrogation had been extensive but also half-hearted. Neither Hatch nor Ranglen said anything about Moyocks or Airafane still existing. As far as they were concerned, Balrak was just a gangster from Ventroni who didn't like people talking back to him. And Ranglen said nothing about template personalities contained in the carrier-locks.

Ranglen wasn't certain if keeping these secrets was wise. He also doubted if their stories were believed, and neither he nor Hatch knew what Rashmi had said, or whether his word would be taken or not. But each of the governments got what it wanted, a chip off the old Clip, so to speak, and each was disinclined to be too inquisitive. They didn't want to dig up anyone else claiming possession. The Interstellar Peace Force from the Commonwealth also arrived, surely informed by their own spies in the various levels of administration, so everyone wanted to conclude matters quickly.

No trace of the fist of thorns remained. Not one of the stakes had been left to be examined. Both Ranglen and Hatch said any killing was a result of the dart-guns.

No one seemed to want to learn much more, but Ranglen's own thoughts plunged on. His deepest questions (of the new appearance of Airafane and Moyocks) he kept out of his writing, but he argued the dangers of the Clips, and the advantages too, of what they could do to humanity and the future. He described—if generally—all those who had been killed, Jayne and Omar and Anne and Henry. And especially Lonni. Lonni was his focus, Lonni and her world "under the ring" and why she had gone there. How she represented all who were lost in the mad human rush outward that had started after finding the first Clip. No planetary wonders decorated his writing, no brooding for an interstellar sublime. He wrote only of "friends."

He didn't allow himself to think of Mileen.

The first person to visit him after the formal debriefings—and to interrupt his work—was Hussein. The big policeman closed the door behind him and came right to the point. "The Federal Investigators hate your guts. They're severing all ties with you. No more privileges."

"Is this room bugged?"

Hussein looked disappointed. "On an Earth ship, it would be. But no, I checked. You think I'd say such things if it were?"

Ranglen wondered but for once he didn't care. "I don't need the privileges any longer. And Annulus still likes me."

"The Investigators are angry that Annulus got the message about the Clip first."

"And they're happy you sent the same message to *them* right after you received it, correct? That was a smart move. I bet they love you now. It was also good for 'civilization' in general. You got the word to everyone. That was nice of you."

"There are still questions about what happened."

"I've got a lot myself. But nobody cares much, do they?"

"That's what disturbs me."

Ranglen smiled disparagingly. "Hey, we're lucky we got the Clip. That's the bargaining point. Both Earth and Annulus will be grateful to you. You probably don't need to be a cop anymore."

A far-off look passed over his eyes. "Yeah, I thought of that."

"And you and Pia don't have to be partners. Which means…" He meant that she and Hussein could get back together. But he said nothing more.

"Yeah," Hathaway said, listlessly, as if it didn't matter much. Maybe he was caught up in wealthy dreams and looked forward to a new life without the police, and—sadly—without Pia. Or maybe he was just covering his emotions. He was a spy, after all.

Ranglen thanked him again for letting him escape Annulus. "Earth should be happy about that too. The Clip would have been lost if you hadn't allowed me to find it. Balrak would have taken it."

"I think they know that, but…" he snorted, "they'd never admit it. They were pretty rough about my freeing you. But you read it right. They strutted and fumed and then backed off. It's scary—they're our leaders."

"They still want you to 'spy'?"

"Yeah, but…we'll see."

Hussein left soon after.

Hatch arrived next. He looked humbled—surprising for him. His arm was dressed in a sling, two damaged ribs had been repaired also, and several bandages covered his face. But, like Hussein, he came right to the point. "I have a confession."

Ranglen felt he knew what was coming but he waited anyway.

"I want you to know.…Balrak didn't kill Henry. I did."

Ranglen kept his expression neutral.

"On the day he was killed," Hatch explained, "Mileen came to see me. She wanted her spaceship. I argued with her, wanted to know why. She wouldn't tell me. It was very unlike her. She was struggling with something. Then Henry showed up, with one of those dart-guns from the Ventroni cargo. I think he and the others always carried one. He insisted she not leave Annulus. Mileen got angry. Henry got more angry and went after her, waving that gun at her. I tried to pull him off her and managed to get the pistol. He came after me. So…I shot him."

"You shot him five times?"

"Yes."

"In a tight ritualistic pentagon, right over his heart?"

"I thought he'd kill me."

Ranglen let the silence brew. "It's noble that you're telling me this. Heroic, humane. But it's also a lie."

Hatch stared back at him.

"You never would have shot him like that. You might have fired at him once, maybe twice. But not five times. If he even came after you at all, which I doubt. Someone made the decision to keep shooting even after he was killed. I don't think you'd do that."

Hatch didn't move.

"You and I both know who killed Henry, who pumped five darts into him one after the other. And, now, you're covering for her."

Hatch still kept quiet, but he looked beaten.

"Mileen did it."

Hatch looked down, barely nodded.

Ranglen said, "Even at that time she knew there was something happening inside her, something she didn't understand. The Airafane in her had to come out. Henry, her authority figure then, was stopping it. Not intentionally, but remember what he was like—needy, possessive. He was holding her back. She had to be free to follow the path decided for her.

"It started when she first saw the derelicts—she described what that was like to me. The objects 'called out' to her. And when she went to find the lifeboat, she wasn't tracking down just any victim, she was tracking herself. I believe everything else you said—Mileen coming to you, Henry showing up, the argument, a fight. But Mileen, or, to be accurate, the new Airafane stirring inside her, did the killing. Not you."

"But how did you…?"

"Because Balrak always added one extra bullet—or dart, whatever—through the forehead. That was his own little private addition, his signature on the five-point killing. Henry didn't have that head-wound, but Anne, Lonni, Jayne, Omar—they all did."

Ranglen didn't add that the people on board the derelict didn't have it either, and that Balrak admitted he hadn't killed them. That's why Mileen assumed it had to be done in that way—if it *were* Mileen and not the Airafane herself. But Ranglen didn't say any of this. He didn't want to belabor the realization that Mileen, with or without the Airafane, just might have murdered someone. He still had to deal with that himself.

Hatch finally said, "It was self-defense, Mykol. Henry was crazy."

Ranglen nodded. He assumed she shot him only once, but then decided, or the Airafane did, that it had to resemble the killing on the derelict. So she or Hatch added the rest of the wounds.

Yet he would always wonder how much Mileen, the human Mileen, remembered of the killing, and how much she—or "she"—had told Hatch on their flight together from the lifeboat world. Was it she or the Airafane who talked to him then—or to Ranglen? Who was she really when either man had been with her?

In the end, maybe he didn't want to know.

He said, "You and Jayne, you were close at one time."

Hatch looked wistful. "Yes. It was something I never told Mileen."

"Was Jayne with you when you found Mileen as a child in the lifeboat?"

"How did you know that?"

"I learned it on the lifeboat world. Don't ask me how." He had told Mileen that the humanoid said that she and Hatch had been there before. But he hadn't told her that the creature also said Jayne had been there too.

Hatch said, in a voice tinted with nostalgia. "Yes, Jayne and I were always together. Finding Mileen is what broke us apart. Jayne didn't want to be a parent. Too much of a restraint for her. But maybe it was because she was just unsure of herself. She knew she could run a ship but she had no confidence about raising a child. Or that's what I told myself. I don't really know.

"She soon left both of us. I tried briefly to handle Mileen, but I didn't know how. A lone kid in my life was too difficult. I gave her up to an orphanage. There were a lot at that time—everyone wanted freedom to tear off into the universe. She never remembered me. I wasn't happy about what I did. But I felt that maybe Jayne had been right. When I met Mileen later in life, I felt I had been given a second chance."

Ranglen sympathized with Hatch's regret. "So you loved her like a daughter."

"As far as I was concerned, she *was* my daughter."

Ranglen now felt it was no surprise that Hatch got mad at him when he neglected her. "She turned out fine. The Airafane might have hurt her, but…not you, not Jayne."

And, he wanted to add, not himself.

He said instead, "Anne claimed she knew that Mileen had gone with Henry to Ventroni, yet you said she didn't know. Was that because you felt you were sneaking her on board—in order to have her meet with Jayne, maybe to get them back together?"

He almost smiled. "Yes. I tried, anyway. It was foolish. Neither of them knew each other, but I thought maybe something would happen between them. They'd talk, become friends. And then I could tell both of them the truth. But Jayne barely said a word to her for the entire trip."

"Maybe she didn't want interference in her own relationship with Lonni. I think she was treating her as a daughter too, if a bit roughly."

"Maybe. I don't know."

"Don't beat yourself up, Hatch. I think both of you would have made fine parents."

Hatch looked empty. "She was adorable when we found her in the lifeboat, not crying at all, using the spacesuit as a blanket."

And there it was, thought Ranglen, the fourth spacesuit. It being in the lifeboat would have occupied the room that might have been used to save the other child.

Ranglen believed now that the Airafane mother must have known Mileen had the potential for becoming an Airafane, that maybe she had put something into her already. That's why Mileen was saved and not the brother, since leaving one child on the spaceship might fool the fist into thinking it killed everyone. The mother put the codes for finding the Clip into the lifeboat so the world would be visited and Mileen rescued, but she also threw in the spacesuit so the fist wouldn't recognize that more than three people had been on board, and thus it wouldn't pursue and kill the child too.

Maybe the whole point of building the retro-spaceship was to *attract* the fist, to bring it out of hiding—and to bring any Moyocks out of hiding too. Maybe Mileen had been set up by her own mother to become a tool of retribution. After all, it was Mileen who got Balrak in the end—twenty years later. And the Airafane were known for long-term vengeance.

Ranglen guessed that Hatch's conspiracy obsession would have loved this scenario, but since it involved Mileen, he described none of it. He asked instead, "Why did you wait before looking for her? That *is* why you left Annulus, right? You could have joined me and we both could have searched."

Hatch gave Ranglen a regretful glance. "I didn't trust you, Mykol. Clips, you know. And I felt you were as bad for Mileen as you were good. Besides, at first, I wasn't worried about the police. I felt she could handle them just by staying off Annulus, and she apparently had already left. But Balrak—when I saw Omar getting off the ship from Ventroni, I knew something bigger was going on, that Balrak might be involved. I had to do something. I did try to reach you but you were in the hospital and the police would have known. So I talked to Jayne and Rashmi. They had come to me to purchase a ship and already had negotiated with Balrak through Omar. So I left with them, figuring if Mileen was coming to the jungle world, then that's where I wanted to be."

"They used Anne's money to buy the ship, didn't they?"

"I assumed that."

They sat quietly. Ranglen added, "You left a real prick in charge at your spaceport."

Hatch laughed. "Hey, he's just more organized than me. He follows rules."

Ranglen nodded. Hatch sank into another depression.

"It's been a rough few days, hasn't it?"

"Everything seems darker now," Hatch said.

"Because of losing Mileen?"

"Because of her, yes, but also because of the Airafane and the Moyocks, what we've inherited."

"We'll manage, Hatch. We always do."

They said little more and Hatch soon left. Ranglen felt his getting back to his spaceships would help.

Then, after another burst of typing, Pia came in. Ranglen was glad to see her—glad she visited him before he went to her, which he intended to do but he hadn't found the time yet.

She made herself at home, sitting not on the chair but on his table and folding her legs beneath her. She wore a black turtle-neck pullover with big silver tech-lined bracelets, glossy gray mesh tights and tall black heeled boots. She looked like a high-placed secret-opts agent, or a superhero.

Ranglen loved the games she played.

She pulled out her cellpad. "There's a lot of weird stuff about everything that's happened here."

"More than you think." Ranglen realized immediately he should not have said that—to her, the professional investigator. But maybe he didn't care anymore what people discovered. Or maybe he wanted to know just how much she *would* ask, as a cop, but also as a person.

"Like what happened up on the ice," she said. "Rashmi claims that an 'asteroid' fell on Balrak, killing him, and then it left."

"That's one way of putting it." He was ready to suggest a meteorite instead but that sounded almost as silly. Besides, he could argue, what kind of view did Rashmi have?

"So what do I write in the report under 'mode of death'?"

Ranglen offered, "'Severe landslide'?"

She closed her cellpad. "You haven't changed."

"Neither have you."

"Well, whatever fell on him certainly killed him. They found traces of his DNA—very *few* traces—at the bottom of the crater right in its center. It's hard to believe anything would be left. Maybe it was planted. And you have to agree, that's pinpoint accuracy for a bloody asteroid."

Ranglen tried to look blank and innocent.

"And then there's Oltrepi...your Mileen. No trace of her was found at all. Rather funny that."

Ranglen still kept quiet.

"And I sometimes wonder about Henry Ciat's murder."

Ranglen reminded her, "Balrak did it. You said so yourself."

"That's the official answer. But we always wonder when a loose end's dangling."

"What's the loose end?"

"Where's Mileen?"

Ranglen, in all honesty, had no answer.

Pia said, "You know, I have a feeling that someday you'll get a message from her. It'll be simple, but untraceable. It'll say something like, 'Hi there, Mykol. Just wanted you to know that I'm doing well. Don't look for me. Don't forget me. You have a good life.' Something like that."

"You're saying she jumped a ride on the asteroid?"

"Well, I'm not one for outlandish explanations, but..."

Ranglen kept his thoughts to himself. He intended to see if his asteroid had returned to the Annulus system, but somehow he doubted it. He was fairly certain he'd never see it again, nor all the trinkets and heirlooms he had stashed inside it, like Mileen's paintings, and the carrier lock of the fourth Clip.

He had wondered too if Mileen had survived. In the middle of one of his naps that day, he awoke from a dream in which she appeared. After waking he said to the darkness of his room, as if speaking to a memory or even a ghost, "I found you once, Mileen. I can find you again."

He knew he still wanted her, but he was uncertain what this "her" had really become. He didn't want some new transcendent unity with an alien specter or ancient demon. He wanted to love for one reason only...because humans were alone. And because they—and he—always would be.

"Okay," Pia said, "I promise, no more questions. I just find it annoying that no one cares now since they got their precious Clip. It's enough to make a cop not want to be a cop."

"You thinking of retiring?"

"Not a chance."

"Mmm," he said.

She studied him. "Ranglen, when you come back from your next voyage into the universe, which I'm sure you'll take, and if you're behaving sensibly then, you might look me up. There were times I liked you. You can tell me your stories. You can tell me the *big* story you're fighting to keep to yourself right now. I can see that, you know. I *am* a cop. You're trying hard to keep yourself still now, to not reveal anything. You've got secrets, Mykol. I think you know something that would change worlds—or at least you fear it would. You fear big time. You're scared that the slightest twitch in your control will let it all out, break down your defenses, unleash what you hold."

Indeed, he sat very still.

She waited. But not for long. "Yeah, I know. You won't talk to me. Not you. How many other people have said that to you? How many other women?"

He kept quiet of course.

She stood up. "Well, you take care of yourself. And watch out if you do get a message from Mileen. I think it could be dangerous for you. You won't come away unhurt this time."

"Who says I'm unhurt?"

"You know what I mean."

And she left.

For a long time afterward he thought of what he'd do and where he might go, of planets to discover and wonders to see and haunted landscapes to find and explore.

He thought of Mileen.

And, the longing.

About the Author

An early interest in astronomy, the comic books Strange Adventures and Mystery In Space, and the Sunday comics of Flash Gordon led Albert Wendland to a life-long fascination with science fiction. Science projects, early efforts at art, and "creativity exercises" all had an SF vein, and the first novels he read were by Andre Norton, Poul Anderson, Arthur Clarke and Robert Heinlein. His dream career was to do astronomy in the day and write science fiction at night, but majoring in physics at Carnegie-Mellon (as preparation for graduate work in astronomy) was not satisfying or inspiring enough, so he double-majored by adding English with the intention of eventually teaching literature and writing. In graduate school at the University of Pittsburgh, he wrote one of the first dissertations on science fiction, and his interest in both mainstream literature and popular culture brought him to the attention of Seton Hill University (a College then), which hired him. He taught there happily for many years, pursuing his interests in the contemporary novel, Romanticism, the sublime in art, the graphic novel, popular fiction, and, of course, science fiction, while getting many of his poems accepted in the school's award-winning literary magazine and publishing articles on science fiction. Then a call for graduate programs led him to co-create the MFA in Writing Popular Fiction, which—unique in academic writing programs—focuses solely on the popular genres. This experience in developing and eventually running the program, and the ongoing communal inspiration provided by its students and faculty, encouraged a return to the thrill of writing SF novels, which he excitingly is continuing now. With his current book, he is planning both a prequel and sequel, a collection of poems, and a nonfiction work on Description in Popular Fiction.

CPSIA information can be obtained at www.ICGtesting.com
Printed in the USA
LVOW11s0244031214

416874LV00003B/212/P